The American

A MIDDLE WESTERN LEGEND

By Howard Fast

New York · DUELL, SLOAN AND PEARCE

To the Memory of Sam Sloan.

Where is McKinley, Mark Hanna's McKinley,
His slave, his echo, his suit of clothes?
Gone to join the shadows, with the pomps of that time,
And the flame of that summer's prairie rose.

Where is Cleveland whom the Democratic platform
Read from the party in a glorious hour?
Gone to join the shadows with pitchfork Tillman,
And sledgehammer Altgeld who wrecked his power.

Where is Hanna, bull dog Hanna,
Low-browed Hanna, who said: "Stand pat"?
Gone to his place with old Pierpont Morgan.
Gone somewhere . . . with lean rat Platt.

Where is Roosevelt, the young dude cowboy,
Who hated Bryan, then aped his way?
Gone to join the shadows with mighty Cromwell
And tall King Saul, till the Judgment day.

Where is Altgeld, brave as the truth,
Whose name the few still say with tears?
Gone to join the ironies with Old John Brown,
Whose fame rings loud for a thousand years.

NICHOLAS VACHEL LINDSAY

CONTENTS

The American

Part One

PASTORAL PROLOGUE

THE FATHER WAS A HARD man; he was like flint. If he had ever been anything else, weak or sentimental or loving or kind, there was no trace left now, no trace at all. Between him and the boy, there was fear. And when the boy did wrong, or what the father conceived to be wrong, there was punishment You would have to have a sheet of paper as long as the Ohio River to write down all the hard, bitter things which had left their mark on the father, and a little of each of those things went into the punishment. The father didn't drink —except beer—but anger let things out of him and relieved him, the way drink lets things out of some men. And anger went into the punishment.

On the wall in the kitchen, there was a piece of an old harness, and when the father got angry, he would walk toward it, and the expression on his lined brown face would tell the boy all the boy had to know. There was a special expression for the boy, a singularity of rage that would indicate his guilt as separate from that of his two brothers and his three sisters.

"Come," the father would say. "Come!"

And the boy would understand. If it were the turn of one or another of the others, they might flee or whimper or plead; not the boy. For the others, sometimes, the mother would plead, although she knew that pleading only increased her husband's anger; but she didn't plead for the boy, at least not until he cried aloud.

And that point came. The boy, on his short, solid legs, was hard too, and ugly and mean, as the neighbors would point out, but the harness strap was heavy, and the father's arm could lift a hundred-pound sack of meal at stiff length.

The father would take down the strap, and the boy would walk ahead of him out to the barn, and there was something in the boy's walk, each step he took, that added fuel to the father's rage. The father would beat him with even, merciless strokes, and the boy would grind his pain under his teeth. The flesh would seam, welt, and then raise up, and then the blood would drive through in pin-points. And through the father's brain, down his blood-stream, into the nerves and muscles and tendons of his arm would come the pain he had suffered, the wrongs he had bent to, the injustices of life which had made him what he was—and all of them would pour into the harness strap.

Until it snapped, until the father realized what he was doing to his son. Then it was over. Then the punishment was through and finished, and the half-naked boy could stumble away, and the father could walk stolidly back to his house, purged.

II

IT WAS not long before the great War Between the States, and at that time much of the State of Ohio was still forest land, the tall virgin forest which climbs up to the sky, making a house where the pillars are eight and twelve feet through, where inside there is no underbrush, no saplings, nothing but the dead leaves, the wet sod, the moss, and the silence. The forest meant something to the boy, who was eleven years old, whose name was John Peter Altgeld. He was a good worker, but when there was no work for him to do, he ran to the forest. People said, "What else could you expect, when he looks like a thing from the forest?"

And that was so. He was nothing at all to look at. His hair was black and stiff, and it stood up from his head like a bird's nest. His legs were too short. His body was not misshapen, nor was it shaped right; looking at it was like looking into one of those cheap mirrors which place objects just a little out of focus, but so little that you can never put your finger on the fault. He had a very slight harelip, but it was enough to make speech harder for him than for the average child. His jaw was too big; first, you thought, this is a child who has never been young, but after a while you saw that it was only because his jaw was too big, giving him an older and more melancholy look than he was entitled to. His blue eyes were pleasant, but with the rest of him the way it was, who went so far as to examine his eyes? The more so since he hardly ever looked straight at you.

It was no wonder that he went into the forest.

But what he found in the forest was his business, and he didn't have to talk about it. The farm was work and hate, from before the sun rose until the sun set; maybe there were farms where it was different, he didn't know; maybe there were poorer people than his family, he didn't know that either. His thoughts were simple, uncomplicated. The forest was in opposition to the farm; it was peaceful, and whatever was there left him alone. There were toads and small, scampering animals in the forest;

they did him no harm. There was a brook in the forest, and he walked up and down in the bed of the brook.

The road went away into the forest, straight as an arrow down the side of the section. In the summertime, when they let him go to school, he went down that road to the district schoolhouse. He didn't go eagerly; they only let him go in the summertime, and that was all right with him. Those who were educated were natural enemies of his father, but they were not friends of his. For one thing, they spoke a different tongue; they spoke the Yankee tongue, which they made him learn, laughing at his guttural German speech. The schoolmaster whipped him with a birch rod, and the lessons made his head ache. But going to the school gave him a concept of the road, which took its deep-rutted course through the forest to the log lesson house, and then beyond that point over hill and dale into the blue dream of anywhere. So when he was in the forest, he had the road within easy reach, and he knew a time would come when he would go down that road with no coming back.

When he followed the brook through the forest, stepping catlike among the slippery rocks, he eventually came to the place where it emerged and ran across the cleared lands of Ichabod Morrison, the Yankee farmer who was a neighbor of theirs. Morrison had a swarm of children who were all towheaded, and although the boy, John Peter, didn't play with them, he liked to watch them from the edge of the forest and create a life for them that was fine and gentle, although in actuality it was none so different from his own. There was one little girl called Lulubelle, who he thought was the most beautiful creature on earth, and after he learned to read a little, he identified her with the princess in his reader. His imagination, struggling through the sterility of the few concepts open to him, found a place for her in the wonderful life he would have some day. But his concepts were few, and his idea of a wonderful life was mostly negative—not to be beaten, not to be laughed at, not to be hungry.

In the winter, however, the refuge of the forest was denied to him. Cold and snow made it a forbidding place —and the days were very short. Also, there was work for him; there was always work for him.

III

THE family moved to a bigger farm, a hundred and forty acres, and the father starved, scraped, haggled, pawned, and somehow bought the place and bought with it an enormous mortgage. There was one whole night when the father was a human being, smiling, even singing a little, and remembering what it meant to have a place like this in the old country, for a peasant and the son of a peasant and the grandson of a peasant. Mulled beer and a pudding made an occasion of it, and the mother wept with pride. The boy, John Peter, had been an infant of only a few months when they came to this new country from the old one, but he had a link of language, legend, and custom with the old country, and from what the father said, he surmised that it was a place one was glad to leave yet also glad to remember, puzzling as that contradiction might be. Yet the separation of old country from new country was never really clear, for always around them were German families, Norwegian families, Bohemian and Lithuanian families, as well as those stranger folk called Yankees. And as for coming to this particular place, Ohio, well, the Yankees were not long here either; only the

5

Indians, the mysterious red folk, who were sometimes dirty and homeless bums in towns and sometimes romantic bands passing out of the forest and into it, were native to this region, old to it, accepting it, and not having to struggle against it and break their hearts, as the Yankees and the others did.

But on this night of celebration, which went with the acquiring of the new farm, there was no talk of heartbreak. The father told stories about the old country, and John Peter, who had never heard him tell stories before, listened with open eyes and open mouth. There was a broad world, and as each piece of it became a little more apparent, he tried to fit it into place in his head, and that way dreams came, imagination and longing and hunger for the half formless; a mental change that went along with the physical change in him, the change which brought the budding hair, the swelling glands, the blood coursing, the nervous, wonderful restlessness that made despair and hope play on him like a bow on the chords of a fiddle.

Change was the new theme motif; the ugly became beautiful, as so many of the tales he read told him. The impossible became possible, as this new farm proved, in spite of the broken siding house they inherited, the stump-filled fields, the rotten log barns. His old life where he ran to the forest for refuge was no more; refuge was in the new possibilities; his wirelike hair would be soft and curly; his body would become slim and long and graceful. Even the father, whose anger was so terrible, was not angry, not even granite-like this one night.

So he listened to the father's tales of what was and what would be.

IV

IT WAS not many weeks before the boy realized that the father had exchanged an old master for a new one, and that the rapaciousness of this new master, one hundred and forty acres of land, could not and would not be satisfied. If they had worked before, they worked twice as hard now, and "mortgage" became a personalized monster in the boy's mind. Instead of a pig being killed for food, it went to the market; mortgage explained that. Mortgage took the potatoes away, and they ate turnips. Mortgage made the father harder and more bitter than he had ever been. When the harness strap came down on the boy's back, it was mortgage that made it quiver with additional force.

In the old place, the boy worked only for the father, and since there was not enough work to fill all his time, and certain days when there was almost no work, he had a little time to himself always, and sometimes hours and hours to play, to wander alone, to go to school. But now he was thirteen years old, and the father said that was too old for school and too old for idleness. What the boy had done, his brothers and sisters would do; the father worked twice as hard, if such a thing were possible—to a degree where the neighbors said, "The devil has him." And the boy was hired out to work. First on this place and then on the other. "Strong as a man," the father said. "He can do a man's work." So the boy went one day to the Bjornsons', and the next to the Schwabs', and the next to Joneses' place, and then maybe back to Bjornsons', or three days at one place and five at another, or half a day's work in the forenoon with three miles to walk, and then a five-mile walk to the next place in the same day, to get more work in.

He became a work-weary, dulled, and senseless animal. He fell into bed at night and woke in the morning with all his bones aching. "Growing pains," his mother said. "He should rest a little." But the father was like a man insane when the thought of sickness was suggested. Everything could be fought but this. Suppose he himself were to fall sick, or to break an arm or a leg, or crush a hand, the sort of accident which is never far away in heavy manual work, just suppose, just realize that would be the end of everything; the farm would go, mortgage and taxes would smash down, the wife and children would starve— then don't speak of it. "The boy has growing pains, the boy is lazy. You spare the rod and spoil the child. The boy brings home three dollars a week."

John Peter worked. He pitched hay. He churned butter. He shoveled manure. For a thousand years, his ancestors had done such work, and those who were weak or prey to disease died; he was strong. He walked twenty miles in one day, and if it rained, he had growing pains. And inside of him, the glands matured, the heavy juices ran through his body, and there came a day when he raised a hand to stop the harness strap, a hand that held his father's wrist with power and determination, while the hate sparked out of him.

"Devil!"

"Then don't beat me," the boy said. "Then don't beat me again. I been beat enough, I tell you." In English this.

In German, his father said, "Speak my tongue!"

"This is mine. Don't beat me."

"Speak my tongue!"

"This is mine!"

The wrist tore loose; the father was still stronger. Though he fought back, the father beat him. "A devil," the father said. "A devil from hell."

After that, the boy knew he would go away. What bonds there were had worn thin. He would go away and never come back. The world outside was a fearful place, but nothing it held could be more fearful than the wild, inhuman struggle that the father had to make for this brood to live.

V

Now he faced his father differently, and that was a part of the difference in him, of his own subjective realization of that difference. He thought of himself now as "Pete." Pete was an American word. I am Pete, I am going away, he would think to himself, and then tell his father so.

"Where will you go?"

"I'll go, I'll go, you'll see."

"You'll go? Well, you'll go out and starve. So you think you're a man now. Go ahead then."

Time went by without his going, because the threat of the world was so great a threat, because the unknown was so tremendous, stretching away from the farm on every hand, with a thousand facets of suggestion and only one or two facets of actuality. But his dreams were more complex, more stirring, richer as he reached the age of thirteen, fourteen, fifteen. A ferment was in the nation, and it stirred every corner, even the remotest rural corner of Ohio. The ferment was war, and the catalyst was old Abe Lincoln who had come from somewhere in these very parts. News which came to the backwash farm where Pete Altgeld lived was none too clear; no newspapers reached the farm, except, very occasionally, a German language paper, and by word of mouth the war appeared as confusing as wars have always appeared to such earthbound folk. A villain's name was Jeff Davis, and already there was a song about him, about hanging him high on a sour apple tree, and down along the river were strange people called "Abolitionists," and they were on the side of the black men, the slaves, and that also was somehow bound into the war. On the farms where he worked Pete heard sung, "Old Union of glory, Let's die for her, boys"; and he sang the words to the fine, lilting tune, and even felt something curiously blood-stirring as he sang it; yet he had only the haziest notion of what the *Union* was, and the word *glory* meant absolutely nothing to him, so primitive and simple was his knowledge of English, a work-knowledge, a field-and-barn knowledge.

For the most part, those people for whom he worked were against the war; they had come from one place or another in the old country, and they had an ancient folk-knowledge of war, which Pete somehow shared. It was a visitation, like the plague or the pox, and though they were used in it, it never concerned them. Once, however, when Pete drove to town with Bjornson, there was a patriotic rally on the main street of Little Washington. A unit of the 33rd Ohio National Guard was preparing to march off to the war. They stood in the dusty street, fourteen of them lined up very straight, blue uniforms, red sashes, while old Meyerburg, who kept the feed store, addressed the crowd in German. Then Stacy, the justice of the peace, spoke in English, and then old Fritz Anderson, veteran of the Revolution, white-bearded and just a little drunk, told about the Battle of Bunker Hill. As the number of Revolutionary veterans narrowed, the number of battles in which the remaining had participated increased, and by now Anderson's lexicon included just about every engagement, large or small.

Peter asked Bjornson what was the Revolution, and Bjornson, on not too certain ground, said it was a war like this one, but a long time ago. A drum began to play, a long roll, a short roll, and then a rat-a-tat-tat, over and over. The National Guard began to march, and some of them picked up a tune, "Susybell was from Kentucky, a loose-limbed gal an' durn unlucky." Pete leaped from the wagon and ran after them, Bjornson shouting, "Hey, Pete, hey, where you going?"

Asking the soldiers, "How old you got to be? How old you got to be?" Pete kept pace with them, until Bjornson grabbed him by the shirt and said, "This I'll tell your father."

"How old you got to be?"

The soldiers, most of them freckled farm boys, well under twenty, grinned at Pete and advised him, "To hell with the old Dutchman. Come along, kid."

And though he drove back to the farm with Bjornson, the words echoed and reechoed, "Come along, kid, come along, kid, come along, kid"; the quality of warmth which had accompanied the offhand phrase magnifying itself more and more, developing a richness like old wine, "Come along, kid," one comrade to another, "Come along." Nothing like that had ever been said to him before; nothing like that had ever happened before.

VI

"I'M GOING to war," he told the father.

He was not given to many words; sometimes, in a week,

he spoke to the father only once or twice, to the mother no more, and only a little more to his brothers and sisters.

"Yes," the father said. "You stay here. The work—"

"I'm going to war," Pete said. "To war. That's all. I made up my mind—I'm going."

And seeing that he meant it, that in his words there was neither doubt nor hesitation nor indecision, the father measured his son, as for the first time and very likely the first time, measured him up and down and sidewise too, the short legs, the hard muscles, the ugly face, the brush hair, and the split lip; and the son's eyes met the father's in return appraisal, telling him—No more beatings. I am a man, you hear me, a man. Then the father said:

"When you go, you go. All right. Until you go, you do your work. You work, you hear me?"

"I hear you," Pete said.

So for another year, he bided his time and worked; it did not occur to him that the war might be over, for by now war was a natural condition of the land, just as rain was and snow was. Inside his head, a dream developed, and for the first time he knew a curiosity for his country. The war was in the south, and he would ask questions concerning the south, or sing *Dixie* to himself, "Look away, look away, look away down south in Dixie," where there was no summer, no winter, only balm and blue skies and pink pelicans. There were beautiful women, and who knew what might not happen to a soldier? The rhythm of his body was different now, and the things he had wanted once were nothing to the fires that began to consume him. It affected his work; he would pause in the middle of a job, slow down, do things wrong until complaints came back to the father:

"That boy of yours, his head is empty."

But the father didn't beat him; it was understood that a beating would mean a struggle, and the struggle would have only one outcome. Instead, the father warned him:

"The neighbors call you a fool."

"Then I'm a fool."

"A halfwit, you hear me, a person with only part of his senses."

"All right."

"The shame is mine," the father reminded him. "But you do your work, do you hear me?"

In English, Pete answered, "I hear you, sure."

For a whole year Pete waited, bided his time, asked questions, gleaned information, became crafty and sly about the ways of warfare. To just go out and become a soldier was not so simple; it could be done, but it was a complicated procedure, and Pete learned that those who did it were fools. A smart man sold himself into the National Guard. Group by group, the militia were being called up as volunteers, and for every volunteer, the county paid a bonus of one hundred dollars. In this anti-war region, there was an active business done in substitutions, for a hundred dollars might be a fortune to one man, and yet to another nothing as compared with the hardships of war. Thus, when talk became current that the 48th Regiment of the National Guard was being formed, Pete hunted up a militiaman whose name had been given him. A little talk, a signature on a piece of paper, and the deal was concluded whereby the boy became a soldier of the Republic and a hundred dollars richer all in one moment. Pete returned to his home, frightened, freed and bound at the same time, breathless with the wonder of what he had accomplished by his own will, his own forethought, his own planning, and wealthy by the hundred dollars he clutched in his hand. He returned home and told the father, "Well, I done it, I became a soldier," and then found the old fear returning as anger flowed into his father's face, mottling it, purpling it, making the muscles bulge and the veins stand out. Fear made him thrust out his clenched hand, and the greenbacks unbent themselves like a flower blooming, blossomed and fell to the floor, like a contrived scene in a bad play. And both he and his father stared at the money until the old man said:

"Where? How?"

They were the bereaved, father and son, the world moving and changing, positions reversing, for here was more money in actual dollars than either of them had known, turning, curiously, their anger and resentment and fear into the blocked and tired emotions of the wholly frustrated. The father knew that his son would go away, and the son knew it too, although now, this moment, the father was no longer an enemy, no longer a dreadful foe, but only a work-tired, life-tired, aging peasant in a dirty shirt and dirty jeans. And the barefooted, sunburnt boy, shock-haired and ugly, was suddenly the father's son, the first-born, the lifeblood, and the only realization of immortality a man has or can hope for. The boy bent, gathered the money, and said simply:

"Bounty."

Then he gave it to his father, who took it, held it a moment, and counted it, counted it twice. One hundred dollars. He called the mother, who came, and then the brothers and sisters came.

"A hundred dollars," the father said.

"A hundred dollars," the others said.

The mother sobbed, and the father muttered, knowing

that his words sold his son into bondage, "You will need money to be a soldier."

"I need nothing," Pete answered, speaking in his father's tongue, taking victory and admitting defeat.

"A hundred dollars," the mother said, for her thoughts were so tumultuous that no other phrase could even approach them.

"You need a little money."

"Nothing." He was free; didn't they understand that?

"But ten dollars," the father said, offering it, a gesture, the first such gesture in the boy's life. What matter how the money came? It was the father's now, and he was giving his son ten dollars. The boy took it.

VII

AT A quartermaster's depot they were given uniforms, blankets, messkits, canteens, guns, and ammunition. Pete would see war, some day, become a different thing from this haphazard, hit-or-miss method. He would see other things too. When the blue uniforms fell to pieces after a few months' wear, he would have something to remember that eventually would work itself into a part of a great pattern, as when a gun blew up in a soldier's face, or a canteen poisoned the water, or leather shoes turned into paper and woolen blankets into shoddy. But now it was all wonderful, and by virtue of the sovereign State of Ohio, he was garbed as never before. It was true that the uniform was several sizes too large, and it was also true that on the first day the guns were issued, one of them went off and blew a tall, slow-spoken, and good-natured young volunteer out of this world, but those were minor incidents in the first romance he had ever known. How could it compare with the major fact that for once in his life he was treated as a man among men, sharing their doubts and uncertainties, sharing their surprises and excitements, not so ugly as he had been considered once; for in this amazing variety of the short, the tall, the thin, the fat, the gainly, and the ungainly, his own ugliness was a smaller factor than it had ever been before. He rode on a train for the first time in his life, but so did half the regiment for the first time in their lives. For the first time in his memory he was out of the State of Ohio, but that was also the case with most of the regiment, excepting the few hard-bitten veterans, non-commissioned officers mostly, contemptuous of these green recruits, warning them this was not war, this frolic from the supply depot to the training center; but what use was it for a veteran to describe a rebel when they knew so well that Johnny Reb was a dirty, yellow, slinking coward who would run away the first time a shot was fired? Anyway, the war was almost over; they would add the finishing touch and they would do it gloriously. No one could tell them different. So they swaggered on the train and boasted and chewed tobacco, many of them for the first time, and got sick, and threw out their chests proudly at local stations where crowds turned out to receive them, until the veterans could only say, "Hayseeds, hayseeds, Jesus God Almighty, what stinking lousy hayseeds." But they only grew more proud of themselves, roaring, "We are coming, Father Abraham—" and Pete added his voice to theirs.

But a hundred miles from Washington, the situation changed. They were turned out of the cars into a pouring rain at a little wayside station, and now the non-coms had their revenge, driving them into line, snapping and snarling at them, and there in the rain they stood for two full hours, waiting for the colonel.

The colonel was a small, dry, bearded man, who drove up in a chaise, chewed an unlit cigar, and stared at his regiment long and coldly, stared at the home-guard officers who grinned at him and then suddenly stopped grinning. The colonel had been wounded three times, the last time when his battered line of Ohio Abolition Volunteers had been wiped out at Shell Mound. Now he called for Captain Frank, who came on the double and saluted smartly.

"We have twenty-two miles to march before we make camp," the colonel said.

"But it's getting on to night, sir, and it's raining."

"I saw that it was raining."

"But—" Then the captain nodded and turned away. Then he remembered, halted, turned once more, and saluted.

VIII

THEY marched through Washington, but they were not proud any more. Their uniforms were faded and dusty, and their shoes crunched ankle-deep in the June mud. Two weeks of training had convinced both them and their colonel that they would not be soldiers, yet they had learned how to load their rifles, how to fire in unison in the same general direction, and not to sneer at that legendary figure, Johnny Reb. They had learned too to make camp and break camp, and they were beginning to learn how to march. In Washington, they were just another regiment passing through, and there was an endless stream of such regiments, and in the end they all came back, limping, decimated, on litters and in wagons—or sometimes they did not come back at all and they would be canceled, as it was termed, since you can't reconstitute a regiment out of two or three survivors, not when you're in a hurry, not when the situation is as desperate as it was then, in the summer of 1864, so desperate that this bedraggled line of Ohio farm boys was ordered to the front, as the colonel said, "To murder?"

"To murder, if you think of it that way," the general answered.

"With two weeks of training? They're not troops, they're nothing."

"They're men, aren't they?"

"Then it's murder."

"If you want to call it murder, call it murder," the general agreed.

Of this, only rumors came to Pete; he knew that they were marching south, and already he had seen more of the world than he had ever dreamed existed. He had seen great cities, and he had seen the nation's capital. And the edge had gone; fear came into his heart and mind, and into his legs too, the whole fabric of him, fear that hung like a pall over the nation, so great was the slaughter, so constant, so fruitless. Yet he was harder than he had any right to be at the age of sixteen, harder than the ten or twelve who had run away already out of homesickness and terror, harder than the one who was caught, brought back, and hanged before parade ranks. Sergeant Jerry O'Day said he had the makings of a soldier, and some of the men shared chewing tobacco and liquor with him, and he was strong as a young horse, used to going barefoot, so that when the paper soles of his shoes wore through, his feet did not bleed, but only became tougher than before. If not for the fear, if not for the sense of disaster which increased constantly as they moved south, translating itself into confusion, hesitation, marching and countermarching, he would have been reasonably happy. He had enough to eat, and marching was not as hard as work. They no longer sang, it was true, but at night, in bivouac under the summer stars, he had men around him who were his comrades; he had never known that before. There was talk, and he loved talk, loved to listen to it, to the sound of words, to the soft, lazy American accents, and to the wonderful commonplace of:

"God, I'm tired."

"Sonovabitch, I ain't going to have no feet left, just wear them down to the ankles and polish the bones."

"Tell you something, Jed, you wear them down to the ankles and sure enough they'll send you home."

"You ain't going home a long time, soldier."

"Going to write a letter to Johnny Reb."

"How?"

"Going to pacify us both—just meet and shake hands."

"Just shake, stranger, huh?"

"That's right."

"And he puts a lead in your belly, huh?"

"That's right."

Every night there was such talk, so much of it. Pete didn't want to be shot—he heard terrible tales of men who were shot; but he didn't want to give up this life either.

He was not a demanding person; he complained far less than the average soldier, and he was so grateful for small favors that the men in his company came to have a real affection for him; if they wanted something done, the kid would do it. If they put turtle eggs or live frogs into his pack, the kid grinned as if he really enjoyed it. One day, bivouacked outside of a little town, four or five went to see a prostitute, taking Pete with them, he who had never even

kissed a girl or spoken to one outside of necessary do or
don't words, outside of his own sisters, and then they
laughed at his fright and shame. But the shame passed, and
his dreams turned more and more into the three dimen-
sions of life. The force inside of him throbbed so hard and
so wildly sometimes that once, when asked what he was
going to do after the war, he answered:

"Everything. Everything."

Speech, which had been such a halting, difficult thing
for him, came more readily, and he gained a sense of confidence and power from the black fuzz that began to cover
his cheeks, thinking that some day this would be a full fine
beard, covering his split lip, covering his large chin. Change
fermented in him, and he groped for ideas that would
have never started in him only a few months ago. A soldier
from Cleveland, who had been a parson before the war,
gave him a novel to read, *The Redemption of Blackfist
Megee,* and as he struggled through it, only half understanding it yet losing himself in its incredible vulgarity,
still another horizon opened. And he sat one night by the
fire, listening to a furious argument between an Abolitionist and a blackbaiter, taking from the talk, for the first
time, a whole impression of the war in which he was involved as one minute and unimportant unit. Yet from this
came the beginnings of consciousness concerning many
things, four million black slaves, a Union that had grown
from the blood and suffering of men, abstract principles of
right and wrong, natural rights, and many other half-
formed ideas which set his head to spinning and aching,
and made him partly crazy at the thought of how full and
large and incredible the world was.

IX

YET fear and confusion predominated, and he could make no real pattern either from the war or his concern with it. A great battle was going on across the James River, and although they approached it for crossing four times, each time they turned back. He heard that an argument was going on between their own officers and headquarters, as to whether they were ready for battle; certainly, the lines of wounded coming back across the river told of the need for them, raw as they were, and the fact that their own officers held them in such contempt didn't add to morale. As a reaction, they took to boasting, and once, when a report came through that they would be sent west into Kentucky to work on a railroad as service troops, the mood of the men turned black and savage, and they spoke of a strike. It was the first time Pete had ever heard the word mentioned, and it was more puzzling to him than the desire of his comrades to see action, for he too felt something of the growing drive that impelled them to fulfill themselves or die.

The nearest they came to battle was when a detachment of Rebel cavalry forded the river one dark night and struck a savage, slashing blow at the reserve's flank. If the blow had been followed in force, the whole of the Ohio and Illinois reserve might have been routed, and temporarily at least the course of the war changed; but the Rebels sent over only a few companies and the raid burned up and died away like a quick brush fire. But the time it lasted was the wildest, strangest few hours in Pete's life—turned out of bed half naked into the night by shots and trumpet call, men fumbling for guns, bayonets, and outside in the moonless camp woeful confusion, random shots, shouting, and then finally panic. It surprised Pete that he was not wholly a part of the panic, that when several hundred men ran helplessly in whatever direction they thought least dangerous, he stayed outside his tent until a bugle called him into ranks, then marched under directions of his sergeant down to the river and kept his station there all night long.

He might have taken great pride in the fact that he was not a worse soldier than most, but the next day he came down with fever, and both pride and confidence disappeared in a malarial oven. For two days he lay in his damp tent, shivering, pleading for blankets to keep himself warm, while his brief glory died away, while his brief manhood changed itself into the adolescent whimpering of a half-grown boy. During much of that time, the tall parson who had given him the book sat beside him and begged him to prepare himself to leave this world and enter the next; but Pete's good nature had gone, and he snarled back like a cornered animal. The sergeant tried to find a doctor for him, but when two days had passed with no hope of getting a medical man, they gave it up and carried him by litter to the nearest field hospital.

Afterward, there were two reasons for his not remembering the days in the field hospital any too well; for one thing, much of the time he had a raging fever; for another, the things he saw at the field hospital, in between his spells of delirium, were not good to remember. When he was conscious and clearheaded, he saw them bringing in the battle cases from the south, men in blood-soaked bandages, men without hands and without feet, men who screamed with pain, and men who wept. The doctors, in their filthy, bloodstained aprons, reminded him of the farmers at home when hog-killing time came, and once, when the man next to him died of a hemorrhage, blood spilling from his lips all over the sheet and bed, and lay all night beside him, a corpse, the hard thing inside of Pete broke, shattered entirely, and let him weep the way he had never wept before.

His delirium was to be preferred, for then he went back to the forest where all was still, and the boughs overhead a high roof, and the soft south wind humming way up above, and there was not one girl with golden hair but a thousand, and all the mingled images of his dreams came together into splendid structures.

After two weeks, he was pronounced cured and told to go and join his regiment again.

X

FOR Pete, the war was as permanent a condition of life as any he could imagine. It seemed to him sometimes that there was never a time when there had not been a war, nor did he speculate a great deal on what would become of him when the war was done. He had not written home because there was no one there he desired to hear from, and he had never received a letter from home. Thus, when it came to an end so suddenly, his regiment demobilized and sent home, he could not react the way most of the men did, whooping, shouting, paying fantastic sums for bad liquor. What a war, what a war! No real battles, none of the stuff like Gettysburg or The Wilderness, none of that, but still they were soldiers, and that was something for a man to look back on. It was not something for Pete to look back on. Marching north to Washington, he was silent in the ranks of singing, happy men—"Farewell, mother, you may never press me to your heart again; But oh, you'll not forget me mother, if I'm numbered with the slain"—derisive and contemptuous; but he was silent, facing not the inverted joy of his comrades, but the inverted tragedy of his own rejection from the only good life he had known.

XI

THE farm was different, the people different. He had come home, not out of deep desire, but like an animal who knows only one burrow. He had come home in a uniform, and he stood among his family as a stranger, looking at his brothers and sisters as if he had not seen them before, looking at the worn woman who was his mother, at the father. The very phrase and threat and anger of fatherhood was gone; old Altgeld was a man no taller than Pete, no stronger. He watched his son almost with apprehension, and the mother showed plainly how much she wanted to please. She smiled and kissed him; she even cried a little. This son was not to be beaten with a harness strap; he had seen the world and the enemy, and he had made his compact with the mysterious warlords. As peasants, with the peasant tradition of father and grandfather and twenty generations before that, they accepted the separation; actually, they had not expected the son to come back, but he was back now and he was a stranger to them and so was to be suspected and feared, even though tears had flowed. Tears must flow; he was blood of their blood and flesh of their flesh.

To his brothers and sisters, he was also a hero, a man who had been to the great and bloody war and seen the terrible face of Johnny Reb. They were prepared to admire him, to grant him leadership, to listen to his tales of glory, and even to like him—but he threw them off. They remembered that he was sullen once, and he was not too different now. He told no tales. When pressed:

"Did you fight?"

"No."

"Kill anyone?"

"No."

"Seen Jeff Davis?"

"No."

Just that way, and he lost them; having almost had them, he found himself cut off, and after a week or two of farm work, work never so hard as he had done once, he knew that he must go away, and told his father that.

"Where do you go?" the father asked him.

He had worked out a plan. He knew something now; if they thought he was a piece of driftwood only a war could claim, he would show them different. He could read and write English, and he could do sums, simple sums, it is true, but a beginning. He was going to be educated, and some day he would come back here, not as a soldier from the wars, but as a lord and master. He told his father that he was going to the school at Mansfield.

"School," the father said, not as he would have said it once, but trying to grasp the word, feel it, relate it. "School is for the rich, for the Duke's son or the son of the merchant—" In his own tongue, he fell into references from the old country, and his German took on a whining, bitter accent. "School is not for a worker, not for a farmer, not for us. Were you born with silk stockings, or did you get these damned notions from your companions at war? Are you a worthless loafer now that the army has sent you back to take the bread from the ground once more, the way our kind should?"

"Maybe I am, I don't know," Pete said.

"Then go back to work."

He knew there was no use talking about it, no use arguing it. Pick up and go off, yet he was old enough to know that the world isn't a mother to men. He had strength to sell for food and drink, yet he had never sold it as a free agent, without even a burrow to crawl back to. When he left the farm this time, there would be no returning. His mother begged him, "We are old folks, your father means no harm. So stay here." When they pressed him, he felt an anger that was unlike anything else; he burst out. He left without even saying goodby.

XII

THOUGH the school was free, it took away his working time. Hours he could have sold at wages had to be put into study, and still he had to have a place to sleep and something to eat. With two other boys, he found a miserable little room over the Mansfield tannery. It stank like a chemical vat; it was hot in the summer, cold in the winter. There were no beds; they slept on the floor, sharing a few old horse blankets.

They ate what they could get when they could get it, scraps from the butcher, cooked meal, stale bread. If Pete earned three dollars a week, he could live, but three dollars was a goal, not a regular achievement. School was work too; he didn't learn quickly; it took him ten hours a day to keep up with the normal progress of a boy three years younger than he. He was big and ungainly and a dolt, a man back from war sitting in a schoolhouse, and not bright; he heard that expression used about him many times, not bright. A sense of himself returned; here was not the struggle of an army in the field; they looked at him, and again he realized fully his ugliness, his harelip, robbing himself of any assurance he might have had. Even the two boys he lived with didn't trust him; they would talk in whispers, apart from him, and sometimes they would stare at him as if they had never seen him before. He had to hack his way through the basic mysteries of multiplication, subtraction, division, and if he dared to ask a question, he would find the whole class laughing at him. The teacher asked him once:

"Are you sure this is the place for you, John?"

Inwardly, he cursed and fumed at the sleepy, smug Ohio town. "Get out again," he told himself. There was something wrong, something woefully wrong about the inside and the outside of himself; he put it to himself that way. Inside him, nothing was impossible; he was sure few people dreamed his dreams; inside, he was glib, assured; he made speeches mentally and talked fluently and intelligently. He read a story about Thomas Jefferson and thereafter devoured everything that he could lay hands on which in any way concerned the man, but when he tried to translate his wonderful discovery of democracy into speech in the classroom, the words came forth distorted and wrongly accented, and his thoughts crumpled in a maze of laughter.

And with that, he had to keep himself alive. He had to earn at least three dollars a week. He loaded carts, ran errands, cleaned outhouses, forced himself awake in the middle of the night to help clean out the tannery. But that made for only a few pennies here and there. "Bad times," they told him, and paid him five cents for an hour's work. Once, when he hadn't eaten for three days, his mother came in from the farm with a basket of food, and though he ate it and would eat it again, he resented her, offered her no word of thanks.

He came to understand what he wanted. He wanted to be a teacher. He wanted to stop being a work-beast and live in that other life he saw all around him, where people wore decent clothes and ate enough and seemed so happy, where small children had more learning than he did. A teacher was paid over twenty dollars a month, and a teacher didn't have to work the way he did. A teacher walked down the street and he had the respect of the community. Well, it was better to know what he wanted to do; the weariness had a purpose, and there was a certain insanity now in his driving toward an end. In a fashion, he became happier than he had ever been; he was creating for himself a code and a philosophy of opportunity and advancement by hard work. He would show them that he could work harder than the next man.

A year passed, and he was still alive; he had lost some weight and been sick twice, but he was alive, and he had schooling. He walked to Lexington and called on a Mr. Gailey, who ran a school for the instruction of the teaching profession. He was not a desirable contact for Mr. Gailey; he was not well dressed; but he talked for three hours about why he must be a teacher, why Mr. Gailey must give him a chance, and how he would pay back every penny of it afterward, even if it took him all his life. He sat crouched over, talking and pleading and even threatening, a fire in his eyes that suggested to the instructor that this farm boy was not quite sane; but there was a real need for teachers, and an even greater need for some who could speak both German and English. Gailey agreed to give him a chance.

XIII

So THERE are no gates closed to a man with talent; he had always known what was inside of him, and at nineteen he was a teacher at a salary of thirty-five dollars a month. The people round and about said, "You wouldn't have thought it about Altgeld's boy, but it just goes to show that you can't judge a man by how he looks." He bought a black broadcloth suit out of his first month's pay, he cut his hair short, and a mustache was beginning to cover his split lip. He affected a thin cane, the hallmark of a teacher, and when he performed his first thrashing, he kept telling himself, "Hard work and guts. What did I come from— nothing. So a beating doesn't hurt." When he walked down the streets of Woodville, people said hello to him, and whenever he entered the Woodville School, his first appointment, he had a fine, proud feeling of identification. The students disliked him, but that was a matter of course with every teacher, and if he had any doubts about the rigid mechanics of what he taught, he never allowed them to trouble him greatly. Education was like a god; he read many books, and each time he finished one, he felt like a man who has come from profound worship. He was invited to tea by the Misses Carteret, the maiden sisters who were one of the town's best families and the bulwark of culture in Woodville, and though for a while he was made speechless by the sumptuous beauty of their home, the overstuffed pieces, the ornate horsehair sofa, the lifelike pheasant under a wonderfully wrought glass bell which had a china figure of a hunter perched on top of it, the delicate lace antimacassars, the Oriental carpet, the crystal closet, and the many painted lamps, he was nevertheless able to relax after a while and even agree with them that Whitman was a rude barbarian, although he had actually never heard of Whitman, and hardly knew whether he was a general or a local politician. But he had read Lamb's *Tales from Shakespeare* and was able to make a credible pretense at knowing the plays, and agreed that the theatre, while ungodly, could make a contribution to a select few; and he found, in telling some of his experiences from the great war, that he could also be amusing, for both the sisters and the Methodist minister laughed with real appreciation. But the fires inside him were not quenched by warm tea; as much as he had, still he wanted and lusted. He, who had once regarded a girl as the unobtainable, now played suit to a pretty little teacher at the school, and, rebuffed, thought that he could only die. He couldn't put out the fire inside himself; the daughter of Charles Adams, who ran the wagon works, was still unobtainable; he dreamed of her and set himself new lands to conquer.

The father and the mother came to him again, now. They plucked at umbilical cords, and when he attempted to be superior and disdainful, the mother broke down and wept, and the father stared embarrassedly at the ground. They were peasant folk and their son was a gentleman of quality, but they were going to lose the farm unless they could lay hands on a little money; they were still in the jungle where a man attempts to crawl uphill on hands and knees, and he was making thirty-five dollars a month. "All right, all right," he said. "Whatever you want, I will give it to you." They kissed his hand; they had never dreamed that they would father and mother such a son, and it was not their fault. "All right, all right," he said.

Everyone said that now Pete Altgeld would settle down, because the boy had quality and drive and perseverance, as you could see. If one girl had rebuffed him, another went walking with him one evening, down to the edge of town, past the lumber yard, and along the winding cow-path, talking quickly and vapidly, and it was all so easy; but fear followed on that, and like a caged animal his mind lurched from side to side, and when he was once again invited to the sisters Carteret, there was a musty smell of decay he had not noticed before. Anton Schwab, the town drunkard and atheist, cornered him one day as he returned from the schoolhouse and said, "How is the paragon of virtue?"

He wanted to get away; it did no one any good to be seen talking to Schwab, and certainly not a schoolmaster, but the atheist held onto both his lapels, "Now listen to me, Altgeld, because in a little while your blood's going to stop running, like the blood of everyone else in this place. You got a soul, you understand me? I can say that because I don't believe in their Methodist-Baptist-Lutheran God, and anyway in a place where there are only two or three souls, stretching a point, you can spot them, believe me. But you won't have a soul soon; soon you'll have just a little hard rock under your shirt and, believe me, I know the signs. I used to say, Pete Altgeld, he's a man—tell them all to go dirty their own damned outhouses. No—you're changing. Maybe you ain't got a soul. Bigots, dirty, lousy bigots. What do you teach in that school of yours? I'll tell you—lies, lies. Two and two make four, the ultimate truth? Lies. And you're becoming a lie yourself, a dirty little leering lie. Get away, get away before it's too late. I know. I know how quick it's too late."

He was afraid afterward that someone had seen the drunkard talking to him. It gave him new confidence to see the moral wreck that Schwab was, unshaven, unclean, reeking of liquor. And Schwab was an educated man, a man who had had every possible opportunity. What did Schwab mean—give up a job for thirty-five dollars a month? No, he had worked too hard for this, too hard. Others had childhoods; he had none; it was used up and thrown away, but at least now he had something. He tried to make a refrain of that, now he had something, now he had something. But as days passed, weeks and months, the props fell away, so gradually that he never noticed, but fell away and left him as he had been before, bound in, bound tight, hand, foot, and breast. The bonds were different, he began to see. This wasn't the castle he had planned for himself; he was going to conquer the world, and he had conquered the Ladies' Poetry Society. Even the workingmen, standing each noon in front of Meyer's saloon with their big cans of suds, seemed to be laughing at him. And he was expected to marry. He was twenty years old, and there were three available girls in town whom it was right and proper for him to marry. For all his pay, he had not enough money left, with what the farm took now, to support a wife, so he would take her back to the father and the farm.

Again and again, he asked himself, why am I different? Am I sick, rotten, cast out? He saw holes where others saw things solid. These fine and upright citizens, why didn't he worship them properly? What did he want?

When he left, he knew that he was running away. He left without cause or reason, and a hundred different explanations were brought forth by his family and the townsfolk. They talked about him for a time, and then they forgot him. In any case, even at his best, he had troubled them in some fashion they could not comprehend, nor did the town drunkard help by voicing around the opinion that Pete Altgeld had gone off to save his soul.

XIV

But he wasn't troubled with his soul; he was like a man on a spree, and he stopped thinking. Enough of thinking, he told himself. For five years he had studied and thought. He had arrayed himself in a black suit and a cane. He broke the cane into little pieces now. As he walked along the road to Cincinnati, he carried his black coat over his arm, but it was hot and the coat was heavy, and finally he threw it into the roadside ditch. His black string tie followed the coat. He rolled up his sleeves and bared his veined, muscular arms. A teacher! He knew nothing, he knew less than nothing! It was a trap, everything a trap, back to the farm, the father. Three girls eligible, take your choice. He spat in the dust, shouted, leaped up and down, and slapped his thighs.

You had to know how, and if you were wise, you learned. He, Pete Altgeld, was wise. Look how nearly he was trapped; well, he would never be trapped again. Squeeze fortune, he thought; put its neck between your hands and squeeze until it screamed mercy. But give no mercy, give no edge. The town drunkard was a fool too. Who in hell was he to preach sermons? And that was all he did, preach sermons, even if he had no God to tie his sermons onto. Pete Altgeld had more sense than that, more sense.

He vaulted a fence and collected ripe apples. He bathed his hot feet in a placid brook. At night, he curled up in a haystack, and watched the shooting stars. You had to watch sharp for them, sharp and quick, and then they arched like a rocket. He listened to the night-sounds, the call of the owl, the croaking of frogs, the bassoon grunt of cows. If he was a tramp, all right then, he was a tramp; he wasn't the only one. The roads were full of old soldiers. Sometimes he walked with them; sometimes he sat around a fire with them, toasting a can of stew, and listening to them swap tales. And then Cincinnati. In Cincinnati he found work, a week in a corncob factory, and then—telling them to go to the devil and be damned—another week on the loading platforms by the railroad; but no bonds, no chains, no shackles. He was a free agent, and when he put his teeth into something it would be the right thing. He thought, if there was a war again, he'd enlist; but there was no war. Then the road. He saw the men in the factories, and for him, that was as certain as any slavery. He saw an abortive strike in Cincinnati; they were fools if they thought it would get them anywhere, he told himself. Stay away from chains in the beginning. Keep to the road, that's the way. Work when you have to eat. And reading—well, he had read only one thing since he left Woodville, a thin volume of Thoreau which another tramp had given him. That was good, but he had a deep-seated suspicion of books. Stay on the road, with the sun in the daytime and the stars at night. That was the way.

XV

HE DRIFTED through Indiana and Illinois. He wasn't afraid of work, and in that season there was a meal or a dollar to be gotten at almost any farm. Actually, he enjoyed work; it was the state of his life; he had worked since he could remember, but now it had to be work without chains and without bonds. Sometimes, at a farm, he would be invited to dinner with the family and the hired man; he was farm-wise, so he got along, and he was a veteran, which was a bond with men he met everywhere, that being before public sentiment turned against veterans of the war who were out of jobs and labeled them loafers and bums. Sometimes, for a few hours, he could be near a round-cheeked, smiling girl, and knowing that she was his now, for the moment, not before and not after, be more at ease than with any other of the women he had once known. He got a feel of the country too, realizing that the only way to know the land is to let it seep into your bones and flesh and blood, moving slowly through it, becoming a part of the fields and hills and woods. This was the rich, ripe heart of America, this black-loam land of the middle states.

Nor could he escape the intense surge of the country, even if he had desired to. He moved west on an almost visible tide, and along with him moved thousands and hundreds of thousands. Along with him moved the railroads, the farms, the factories, and families and tribes and whole provinces. Sometimes he spoke German, sometimes English; his tongue had loosened; movement gave him the flavor of speech, and although he didn't know it and would have denied it, all the books he had packed into his head so mechanically were reasserting themselves, breaking apart and coming together, as he needed them, as he wanted them.

Talking to the people, he found something of himself; under their surface slowness they were a fierce people, with many of the qualities he had known in his father, and their reticence was a part of the drive westward, for freedom and bread, which had obsessed them and their fathers.

But then winter took them into their clapboard shells; the fields were gleaned, and the homeless moved to the cities. He moved with them, and now, the road turned cold, the fruitfulness of the fields a thing of the past, the dwellers of the road were demarcated. They were the homeless, the disinherited, the men without family or land, unemployed workers, veterans, field hands, and those others who scavenged, who had never worked and never would, and in this latter category were those who had turned against life and who preyed on both the farmers and the drifting workers.

It was with them that Pete had to make his break; what they were drove him to St. Louis to join the lines of unemployed. Otherwise, you stole, whored, and went down lower and lower. That wasn't for him; he was going to win out and stand on top, but even to begin that you had to have a place to sleep and food to eat. Only, for each job, there were four men, and you had to fight, cut, scramble, climb onto the shoulders of a man who was weaker. And then, if there was nothing and you had spent your last nickel on some beer and free lunch, you cut the price, sold yourself cheaper and cheaper as the crying will to live became louder. That was how he came to work over the stinking sulphur vats for seventy-five cents a day.

And now there were no songs to sing, no dances to dance, just keep alive, keep alive, and on Sunday go to a beer garden with twenty-five cents for the only kind of a good time you can afford, make eyes at the girls, eat and drink slowly, and listen to the steins being stamped in unison as the voices chanted out the waltz. But life can't cherish and foster itself and grow rosy and bloom on four-fifty a week. He was starving by inches. He sank back down and became beastlike, and beastlike he watched the milling crowds of those who had no jobs and listened to their voice, feeling something he had never felt before.

But then, when it was at its worst, the railroad agents came into town, recruiting with torchlight processions and bands for anyone who would take up a pick and shovel at from three to four dollars a day. Ride to heaven on the M.K.&T.! America was going west, and it was a free ride for any Yank or Mick or Hunky who had a strong back and a weak head. So they proclaimed, with free beer flowing golden from the broached kegs, and Pete Altgeld climbed on the bandwagon to glory.

XVI

You worked for three dollars a day. The gangs were shipped west and south, to where the yellow prairies rolled on and on, over the horizon and apparently forever. The iron horse chewed forward, with, as the men told Pete, sonovabitch Jay Gould riding that boiler up there, his —— looking like a smokestack, and he rode the backs of more Irishmen than had ever lived in County Mayo. Pete took his place in a line of hammer, pick, and shovel men, and the line stretched on for miles. The song of iron on iron and spike in wood ushered in a new age, and the men roared, "Lay it in, lay it in, with that hammerhead, That iron's so heavy that you'll soon be dead!" The tracks pushed forward like a thing alive, ten thousand men, three hundred chow wagons, a traveling brothel, and a canvas hospital where they took those who had lain down to die. The camps sprang up every few miles, and they were wild and sinful places, run by the same companies who put through the roadbed, taking every Saturday night what the men had worked six days from dawn to dusk to earn, liquor at a dollar a shot and women at twenty times more, and three-card faro, roulette, the shell game, and blackjack to pick up what was left.

In this, Pete worked. The first day on the job, he learned why they had held torchlight processions in St. Louis, why beer flowed like water, and why they were paying three and four dollars a day against seventy-five cents in St. Louis. For one thing, in the summer, heat casualties were greater than on a battlefield; men dropped like tenpins from the heat. There had to be replacements. Men wore out. At the spot of dawn, you picked up your pick, hammer, shovel, or spike-brace; when it became too dark to work, you dropped it. The railroads were pacing across the continent, and men had to walk fast.

Pete Altgeld was young and strong; he prided himself on his strength. When the Irishmen on either hand warned him, "Take it easy, youngster, or they'll lay you out under this dirty Kansas sod," he laughed and showed them what he could do. As everyone knew, the Irishmen were shipped over like cattle, sent by the carload to work the roads, and they didn't have the fire inside them that he did, the certainty of sitting on the top. And he could work! The muscles were laced over his broad back like piled-up leather, and his lean hands had clasped some tool for as long as he could remember. And, anyway, it was only natural that when a man became old and couldn't keep up, he should be thrown aside. If you had imagination, you saw the iron rails going through, hell-bound for glory; it needed a man to put them down. These Irishmen were skinny and underfed, and after twelve hours' work, they'd take out what was left with drink. If a man held onto his three dollars a day, he'd soon be rich! Pete Altgeld would hold onto it; day after day, under the broiling sun, he told himself that.

And then, one day, he began to burn, and his legs turned into rubber. They carried him into a tool shack, and by then he was trembling with cold. The Irishmen shook their heads over the damfool kid, and he lay there under a load of sacking until a harried doctor came and suggested that he be admitted to the hospital at three dollars a day.

Pete refused. He said he would die first.

"You'll die all right," the doctor agreed. "There's nobody going to bring you grub here. You'll die sure as hell."

"Three dollars a day! For three dollars I work all day."

"That's right," the doctor agreed.

The fever loosened his tongue, and Pete Altgeld raved about the money. He needed the money; it was going to ride him right up to the top of the world. He was going to study law; he wasn't going to swing a pick and shovel for the rest of his life. Hadn't he put his money away, dollar by dollar, and now they wanted it back, three dollars a day. He'd die first.

"All right," the doctor agreed. "But you can't die here. This is company property."

He struggled to his feet, and then collapsed. The doctor called the two litter-bearers, who were waiting outside. They took him to the hospital, a long clapboard and canvas lean-to, where they undressed him. The money was in a belt around his belly. The company stood for no nonsense when it came to diggers' savings, and all the money was delivered over to the staff accountant. There were sixty dollars in all, and this was entered against twenty days of service. But when, on the fifth day, it seemed that Pete Altgeld was dying, seventeen dollars was allocated for a pine coffin and a grave, certified to be at least three feet deep. However, he took a turn for the better and lasted the full time. By then he was able to walk, if uncertainly; he had lost twenty pounds, and he had severe and chronic headaches, and he was penniless. Since his gang had moved twenty miles along the line, he asked the hospital superintendent for a pass to ride free.

"Ride where?" the superintendent wanted to know.

"To the job."

"You got no job," he was told. "You're not fit to work, and we're not paying three dollars a day to corpses."

He pleaded. He reminded the superintendent that he had outworked the Irishmen. Hadn't the foreman said that he was one of the best men on the job?

"I can't give you a pass," the superintendent said stolidly. "You want to join your gang—then walk it."

Pete set out along the line to walk it. It was a hundred degrees in the shade, but there was no shade. After a while, it seemed to Pete that the prairies were rising and falling like a sea of ochre sulphur. He crawled into a toolshed and lay there until dark, sleeping a little. At nightfall, he came out and began to walk again. At a chow house, he talked the sleepy cook into giving him half a loaf of bread and a piece of sausage, and by morning he staggered into his old camp. The Irishmen, just coming onto the job, rubbed their eyes and stared at him. "The strong man," they nodded, but without hatred; if Pete could have seen himself, he would have known why. When he found the foreman and asked for his old job back, he was ready for the swift reaction.

"No good, Pete."

"What's no good?"

"You. You're no goddam good. Why don't you get out of here and push up north? This is fever country."

"I got no money," he said. "Please, please, mister, give me the job."

"Get some rest and then we'll talk about it."

"I'm all right. I tell you I'm all right now. Put me on the job. Put me on the job and see."

The foreman shrugged and nodded for him to join his

gang. But now the Irishmen set the pace. For two hours, Pete kept up with them; then his legs buckled and he rolled over on the ground. They carried him into the shade, and that night the foreman gave him a pass to ride back along the line. The foreman gave him some good advice, too:

"Clear out, or you'll be dead inside of a month."

XVII

DURING the war he had felt fear, but it was not the kind of fear that gripped him now. Turned twenty-two, in the prime of his young manhood, his power to work was gone, and he was thrown out like a used-up tool. In the whole world, no one gave two damns about Pete Altgeld. Whether he lived or died simply did not matter. Society had laid down a demand, and when he couldn't meet it, it turned its back. Now he was a bum, a tramp, a creature of the roads. He walked north, and his clothes became ragged, shabby; his beard grew. He had no strength, none at all, and when he tried to take a job at a farm, the fever returned. He begged for food; that he had never done before, nor had he ever considered that he would do it, but his body cried out to keep alive, and he answered its demands. He slept in barns or in the open field, and in the morning he rose, stiff, aching, and hopeless. Sometimes as he shuffled along the roads which led north, straight as arrows, binding the sections, his old dreams would return, and out of the impossibility of reality would come the confidence in his own power, but his dreams were drugs now, not plans. He had only one plan, to remain alive.

Some of the people he met were kind, and others were cruel, and others were just indifferent. Some met him with a shotgun, for he was, by appearance and definition, one of a ravenous pack, cast out by society, and preying on those who had turned them into beasts. But others met him with kindness, and one Kansas family nursed him through an illness, giving him food and shelter for a while at least, remembering that not so long ago they were the dispossessed and the disinherited, searching westward with nothing but their own strength; yet even they recognized the law and bowed to it and sent him on his way.

He took his path across Kansas, into Missouri; if it had been winter, he would have died; but in this gentle weather he was able to stay alive, to move on—to retain a small hope concerning what lay over the next hill. Yet as the days passed, even that hope waned. His young strength had ebbed away, all of it, and presently both past and future merged into a confused pattern, senseless and purposeless. He went on only because the will to live was a strong, demanding call, prodding him when all other prods were bent.

Part Two

THE STATEMENT

THE ACT OF AWAKENING IS, IN a small way, a rebirth; as, for example, the way primitive people speak of sleep as the little death, and of death as the long sleep. At night, the brain relaxes; all the thousand currents of thought, which tugged with such remorseless contention, loosen; somewhere, there is a washing and a cleansing. Even the dreams which come with morning belong to another world, and this morning, when the Judge awakened, his dreams flurried for only an instant and then sank back into the pits of memory. For just a short while he clung to remnants, as people do, a face out of the past, a long road he had walked, a terrible thing happening; but the wonder of dreams is to prove to people that nothing is changeless; horror is washed away in an instant, and sunlight is a testimony to the goodness of life. And there are other testimonies upon waking, the softness of a warm bed, embracing, the way a mother folds a child into her gentle bosom, clean white sheets, a feather pillow, and downy blankets to keep out the nip of the autumn air. It is true that same may wake differently, on the hard, cold earth, on the wooden board of a prison cell, on a crunching cornshuck bag, on a vermin-ridden floor—and some into a horror of life from which sleep is the only surcease—yet the Judge was not prone to dwell on the copybook maxim: "There, but for the grace of God, go I." He could too clearly trace back the steps by which he had gone, and although occasionally one or another had lent a helping hand, it was, to his way of thinking, his own strong hands which had pulled on the bootstraps hardest, and credit should be given where credit was due.

So to him, in the moments after awakening, this was the little rebirth after the little death, and the broad slab of sunshine intersecting the window and the room was the new compact life made with him. Unhurriedly, for it was still very early in the morning, he returned to the business of living, turned first from side to side, opened his eyes and then closed them, stretched with the warm and comfortable ease of an animal, sighed, sensually relaxed with the enfolding grasp of the bed, and experienced that wonderful sensation we know only upon awakening or in times of great weakness—that drift in and out of consciousness which enables the ego to float like a disembodied spirit. Starting to live again, he was not wholly in either the present or the past, and in quick succession he became many things, Pete Altgeld the farm boy, Pete Altgeld the soldier, Pete Altgeld the tramp, Pete Altgeld the wanderer who sought hope where there was no hope, Pete Altgeld dying, living, defeated, triumphant—he remembered the beginning of the change, when at the lowest point of sickness and despair, he found people who were good to him, helping him, feeding him; that was a nice point to come to life, to full consciousness, wondering only what there was back of his mind that disturbed him.

II

He heard voices through the door:

"Be quiet! You'll wake the Judge!"

"Who's shouting—you're shouting, yelling all the time, yelling be quiet."

"Quiet."

"Quiet yourself."

"I don't want none of your lip."

"Well, I should say! I don't want none of yours."

"I never seen a parlormaid who wasn't a hussy. You're a hussy."

"I'm not. You don't call me that, lording it high and mighty. You think you own this house?"

"I'll turn you out."

"Will you? I could tell a thing or two."

"Just remember I'm housekeeper here. Now go down to the kitchen. You hear me? Down to the kitchen."

Then the Judge heard the door of his wife's dressing room open, and she stepped outside and said, "Both of you go downstairs and stop this horrible racket."

The Judge sat up in bed. Life was complex and even the servant problem was not simple. He knew what was disturbing him now. Today was November eleventh, in the year eighteen hundred and eighty-seven.

III

The Judge turned back the covers, let his feet dangle over the side of the bed for a moment, then wriggled his feet into the slippers. He went to the window and looked out into the sunny Chicago morning. November in Chicago is a good month, cold and fine and clean. Most of the leaves are gone from the trees, and those of the tree birds who haven't gone south are alive and brisk. Already, at this hour, still somewhat before seven, people were on their way to work. A policeman stood not far away, and a brewery wagon clattered by. All was right in the world. The Judge shivered a moment, found a bathrobe, and wrapped it around him.

This morning, the Judge was uncommonly alive to sounds, smells, to heat and cold, to the compass of the four walls of his room, to all the sensations which usually the body accepts so readily and unconcernedly. Irritation was ready and waiting, and many things contributed to it, a picture of Daniel Webster on the wall—What a stupid, ridiculous decoration for a bedroom wall! Why don't I throw it out! Black Daniel, black as his own ignorance!— an ugly carved curl in the back of a chair, the wallpaper, the rug on the floor. But he knew that he was consciously irritating himself, and he fought the feeling. He paced the room, back and forth, several times, stretched his arms, revolved them once or twice, opened the window, and breathed deeply of the cold morning air. But the chill was depressing rather than exciting, and he closed the window hurriedly, seating himself on the bed and rubbing his beard. He was not yet fully awake, and a drowsy reminiscence of sleep still lingered, expressing itself as a thoughtfulness, a slowly revolving wonder and meditation which could be shattered in a basin of cold water and soap, but which the Judge did not choose to shatter yet. Rather was he concerned with his irritation, his state of mind on this special day; and letting his thoughts drift, he sought to recover himself.

He took refuge in an old and reliable counterpoint; he

was a judge and he despised judges, more so now than ever, and with that idea he smiled for the first time this morning. A case he had tried outlined itself, and for at least the fifth time he considered the sardonic and clever remark he might have and should have made at a certain point, a remark which would have been repeated for weeks all over Chicago—Judge Altgeld said that the other day—but which he did not make simply because he did not think of it until a good deal too late. And then, annoyed at himself for returning to this egotism so readily, he wrenched his thoughts away and dropped back into a vague trend of recollection.

Some things always stood out, leaped into silhouette effect, presented themselves as a matter of habit. A miserable and unhappy rainy day during his army service always recalled itself, although there was nothing so very special about it; it was just a lasting and well-remembered discomfort, and it stood out more sharply than anything else. Also, there was a consideration of chance and purposefulness which presented itself whenever he was in such a mood as this; he was a great believer in purposefulness: didn't the thread of his own proud ego run back into the mistiest memories of childhood, so that when he was the miserable, ugly child, standing before the father, he nevertheless felt within him his destiny, and knew so surely that it could not elude him? But in his recollection of his fever-blurred walk northward from the railroad, there was not so much certainty of destiny. He was a tramp, a dirty, ill-smelling, sick tramp, when he came to a farm and pleaded for shelter and work.

"But a sick man can't work," Cam Williams, the farmer, protested.

How well he remembered Cam Williams! No, a sick

man can't work; so craftily, exalted by his fever, grinning as over a well-hidden joke, he bargained with the farmer. If he got well, he would work it off; he was a mighty worker in his health, and he boasted of what he had done on the railroad. "And if you die?" the farmer said. But the farmer wasn't taken in, not even a little bit. There are men who are kind and who love other men; and though the Judge did not fully understand this broad, encompassing love of a species that is so basic in some, he recognized that it existed. Otherwise, why had the farmer made the poor bargain, sheltered him, fed him, and given him work? Hadn't that been the beginning, there outside the little town of Savannah in Iowa? But his refuge lay in the fact that if it hadn't been this farmer, mightn't it have been another? The primer of success said that man was strong and mighty, and the clue to destiny lay in his head and his own two hands; and revolting against the broad, soft, species-loving man, the unreasonable humanitarian, the Judge sought for a train of events to bear out the primer. Memory paraded and collected and sorted, spurred on by the very fact that this was November 11, 1887. Had anyone been worse equipped, so ugly, so little gifted, so poorly raised, so miserably educated; all this was against him at the start, was it not? And he had gone down, deep down, before he came up. Was Cam Williams to receive the credit? Yet he, Pete Altgeld, John Peter Altgeld, Judge Altgeld, might have remained at the farm all his life, a laborer and then perhaps a farmer himself. Wasn't that to be weighed in the balance? Ambition is dissatisfaction, and on that thread the world spins. From farm laborer, he had gone to a job in Savannah, teaching, but that was not the end; he read law, worked on farms to swell his small earnings. It was not just that he came to know people; rather, he developed in himself those qualities which made people admire him, and thereby, not by chance, came his appointment as city attorney.

Sitting on his bed now, the Judge looked at his own two hands, strong, square, purposeful. "My doing," he reflected. "And I could do it again—and again."

No one gave him anything. He practiced law from the bottom; the smallest cases were not too mean for him. He fought his own campaigns; he stood on his own two feet, hammering his way into the job of prosecuting attorney of Andrew County, Iowa. Did they say he climbed on the Granger bandwagon without ideal or principle?—if a man walked there were mice enough nibbling at his feet. What would they say if he told them that he had known this same dominating purpose in himself when he was twelve years old? Was he jealous of his ambition? Did he hoard it? He could have remained there as prosecuting attorney; no one forced him to walk out on the job and go to Chicago. It was his doing; step by step, he saw his way and he took it.

And now he was Judge Altgeld of Chicago. Not Cam Williams! Not one of these damned species-lovers. Yet he could not hide from himself that this whole train of thought, this whole protest against the kindness of a simple farmer so long ago, came from the disturbing fact that to-day Albert Parsons and the others would die, that in not too many hours they would be hanging by their necks, with the life gone out of them.

IV

HE DRESSED methodically. Though his friend, Joe Martin the gambler, had once remarked to him, "Pete, you're the damnedest Yankee, inside and outside, I've ever known," he retained certain habits which might be called German. In some things, he was extraordinarily methodical; he had a sense of place for things and for people. Now, as he dressed, the routine of doing a simple thing he had done so often relaxed him, and when his wife put her head in the door and asked, "You'll be ready soon, dear?" he answered, "In a few minutes. And I'm hungry, too." "Do you want eggs or hotcakes?" "I want hotcakes," he nodded firmly. "Well, I just don't know if we have honey." "Then butter. Butter is just as good. My goodness, does having hotcakes depend on honey? I remember hotcakes when honey was a dream. Believe me, a dream." "All right," she said. "Butter. I got some fresh butter yesterday."

He took his little silver scissors and went to the mirror, to see whether his mustache or beard needed trimming today. A hair here or a hair there made all the difference in the world. Looking at his reflection, he was pleased, for on top of the train of memory, it was nice to see this dignified and not uncomely jurist of forty years. The close-clipped beard and mustache gave his face dignity, lessened the prow of his chin, yet did not age him as beards age some men. The mustache was carefully groomed to cover his harelip, and it was surprising what a difference that made in the whole aspect of his face. As a matter of fact, men who knew him long and fairly intimately were completely unaware of his defect, and of late he had even ceased to allow it to be a weight on his own mind. His face had become leaner, and that too helped. A good barber trained his unruly shock of hair to fold back over his fine brow, and he had a habit of so carrying his head as to give that clean, well-shaped brow its fullest effect. All in all, his appearance was not anything he would have to resist, anything to hold him back; it is true that he was not as tall as he would have preferred, but he had long ago formed a theory that small men fight better.

Trimming his mustache and beard, observing himself, half detachedly, the way men do in their morning mirror, he decided that he had made the best of a poor face, very much the best of it, even to the extent of winning the girl he wanted. That thought pushed away the last unpleasant connotations of the day, and he nodded agreement at his reflection. He had a penchant for storytelling, and some day he would write down the tale of his love and courtship. Actually, it was as good as those romances people are paid to write.

It was another ugly-duckling tale. Long, long ago, when he had held his first teaching job in Ohio, he fell in love with a girl named Emma Ford. Just to think of what he was then could explain why the girl's family would have nothing of him; but he always felt the girl cared for him, and his boyhood love was something he sought along with the more solid values men put store in. The girl was a dream that walked with him; she was part of loneliness; she was part of the indescribable ache when he lay on his back on the hard ground and looked at the stars. This was not to say that he had loved only one woman; women, to him, were beautiful, to be wanted, to be desired; but there were many women and only one who inhabited that time when he had nothing and wanted all. So it was not surprising that at the age of thirty, with a future, some property, and certainly some standing in the world, he had returned and asked for her hand again.

And she took him. This tall, beautiful, well-educated girl took him, Pete Altgeld, the disinherited, the self-made. Some might be cynical about this, but he couldn't be; he knew her better than any of them. He had her, in the morning, in the daytime, at night. This was the romance that life gives to only a few, and life had given it to him.

It was no wonder that looking at his face in the mirror, snipping a hair here, a hair there, he was able to forget that today was sure to be profoundly disturbing, and take comfort from the man who had married the woman, Emma Ford. He had a fine wife, and it was a boyhood love, the best love, the most lasting. When other men looked at her, casually at first, and then more intently, he felt the fierce pride of possession. Shouldn't a man stand on the firm foundation of his own things? Here he was in his own house, in this fine graystone mansion that was his; he had been only twelve years in Chicago, and the achievement was no small one. Actually, he had grown with the city, grown with the brutal, creative vigor of it.

How well he recalled what kind of a place Chicago had been in 1875! There, already, America's peculiar triumph, the railroads, converged. From the west and southwest the cattle came, by the millions, to be gutted, blooded, and rendered; a crazy-quilt of a city grew around the process of slaughter. Coal came from the south, iron from the north. Lumber drifted in through the lakes. Five hundred miles of Godforsaken street alternated between ice and mud, and an endless vista of shacks and sprawling factories spread like fast-multiplying mold. Here, a whole creed of power, success, wealth, and brute energy came into being. Alongside the horsecars came cattle riders from the vast prairie lands westward, and alongside the sooty trains were magnificent carriages. From the east, the south, the west, from the across the seas, workingmen poured in by the hundreds of thousands—Yankees, Rebels, Germans, Irish,

Bohemians, Jews, Slavs, Poles, Russians—hard, desperate men who fought to put enough in their bellies to maintain life, and always it seemed that for every job there were two men; and even as these men fought, others fought them, a new kind of giant, emperor, king, the man of the million dollars and the hundred million dollars. So there was blood let, and violence, and such a ferment as existed nowhere else in all the known world, and still into every corner of the earth Chicago sent forth her hungry cry for men, and more men.

This was it, his city, making him and made out of him. A man should stand on what is his own.

V

HE WENT down to breakfast, and when he was at the foot of the stairs, his wife said to him, "Isn't it a fine morning, dear?" "A fine morning—yes, a fine morning," he answered. She was wearing a gray skirt and a white blouse, crisp, clean, and bright; a person whom mornings agreed with, she smiled confidently. It might be said about her, if you were to say one thing to define her, that she was poised, and it was poise the Judge needed and appreciated. If it came to him that other people were speaking about her childlessness, and what a shame it was that a man like the Judge had no children, his reaction was furious anger; what did they know, and what did they understand of marriage and of what a man wanted of a wife?

As they sat down at the table, he looked at her again, nodded, and returned her smile. As usual, his paper was folded alongside his plate. As he unfolded it, he was already spooning into the heavy applesauce. "Cream?" his wife asked him. He nodded. He read, in the large black head, ANARCHISTS TO DIE TODAY. Then he took his second spoonful of sauce. ANARCHISTS TO DIE TODAY.

Emma, his wife, poured heavy, yellow-tinted cream onto his fruit as he read, "At long last, after a year and a half, finis will be written to the Case of the Anarchists, and honest citizens can draw a deep breath and sleep soundly in their beds once more. We express our approval that in spite of so much malignant pressure put to bear, the verdict—"

His wife interrupted him by asking what it was.

"What?"

"I don't think," she said, "that it's good for you to read at meals. I don't think it's good for your digestion, and it certainly isn't polite."

"Polite?"

"It's simply bad manners, Pete."

He always bowed to his wife when it came to manners. He had been congratulated many times, by those of his friends who knew about such things, on his wife's impeccable taste. Of taste, he had a small and carefully and painfully acquired stock, and while he trusted it, he did not stretch it. As long as he lived, he would not forget his first formal dinner, in the not so distant past, where the array of silver baffled, challenged, and angered him all at once, and with what pain and forbearance he got through, always managing to be a little behind the others.

"I'm sorry," he nodded. "Only—"

"I wonder if the newspaper isn't a curse rather than a benefit. After all, what pleasure is there in knowing the misery of the world scarcely an hour after you awaken?"

"Very little, I suppose," he admitted, folding the paper and returning to the fruit.

"Is it the anarchists?" she asked him.

"Yes." And added after a moment, "They're going to die today. They're going to be hanged."

She watched him as he ate. Actually, she knew more of him than he thought, than most of his friends thought. She knew about things inside of him, and when they came up, over the improving surface of the jurist, she took her stand—not entirely with selfishness, but with a fondness which recognized, as so few did, that there was fire inside that had never been allowed to burn.

"It's so long since they've been sentenced—over a year."

"About sixteen months."

"And they've had every chance," she said carefully. "I think people are just tired of hearing about the anarchists. I think people are tired of talking about them."

"Are they?"

"I think they are," she said, still carefully. "With all you've said, Peter, I think they've had a fair trial."

"I don't," he said.

"You change your opinion," she smiled. "I've heard you say that it was a very fair trial, an exceptionally fair trial. Are those your words?"

"Yes."

"And every chance for appeal?"

"Yes."

"But you change your opinion?"

The maid came in with the hotcakes. "Draw the blinds, please," Mrs. Altgeld said, "and let in the sun." When she had gone, the Judge said:

"Yes, I change my opinion, Emma. I don't think that's anything to be ashamed of. Too many people never change. I admit I change hard, but sometimes I change."

"But they're anarchists."

"Or socialists, or communists. I'm not sure I know what they are. I don't see that it matters a lot."

"No. And at least we'll be able to sleep without worrying about bombs—"

"Emma!"

She knew signs of anger in him. She helped him to honey, and he began to eat the hotcakes. "They're good?" she asked.

"Very good. I'm going to get fat, too. Emma, look here. In this damned paper—"

"I don't like you to swear," she said.

"I know. I shouldn't swear. Especially at breakfast, I shouldn't swear. I know and I'm sorry. But look here, in the paper it says: '. . . honest citizens can draw a deep breath and sleep soundly in their beds . . .' The same words. I don't like it when people begin to talk like sheep. Some of us should think."

"Are you calling me a sheep?"

"No, no, no. But what were they tried for—for being anarchists, or communists, or socialists? No! For throwing the bomb. For over a year we've been crazy on this subject of bombs. But there's no evidence to convict them."

At that moment, she brought it up. She was not going to bring it up, not going to mention it. It was ammunition that lay in her lap, ready to fire both ways; he knew it, yet she brought it up. An appeal for clemency for these men who were going to die had been signed by sixty thousand citizens of Chicago, some of them very prominent men. Yet John Peter Altgeld's name was missing. She said, casually, "Then why didn't you sign the petition? Goudy signed it. Brown signed it. But you didn't."

"I didn't," he admitted.

"Would you sign it now?"

"I don't know," he said.

"Then where is the principle in your belief in their innocence?"

"I don't know. Am I supposed to have principles? You knew me the way I used to be, Emma, a long time ago. Should that produce principles?"

What he wanted to say after that eluded him, and he felt ashamed of bringing up the past in so childish a manner. He stabbed at his food and found that he no longer desired it, and he was almost grateful to Emma when she poured him a cup of coffee. "Thank you," he said, contritely, and then became angry again when he realized that she was feeling sorry for him, sorry she had ever brought up the matter of the petition. He didn't want sympathy; he did what was right: suddenly, he told himself that, and then in the saying it collapsed like a pricked balloon. His friend, Joe Martin the gambler, always said that you played the game to win and didn't count the stakes; but that was as childish as anything else, and even his friend Martin worshipped sincerely at the foot of a sort of perverted honesty, not holding his life much higher than a so-called debt of honor, whatever his honor was. Was there a pattern in his life concerning men who were good—in the accepted sense of the word—and did he despise such men? Of course he hadn't put his name to the petition; what good would it have done, in his own terms? He was a judge. He sat on the bench, enforcing the law, whether it was good law or bad law, just law or unjust law —and how well he knew that law and justice were things apart—and yet when he rendered a decision, did he stand on principle or the letter of the law? It was not a good world he inhabited; he had only to look around Chicago to see that, he had only to look back in his own memory to see what the world did to the weak, the small, and even to the strong who were not strong enough; yet hadn't he long ago decided that it was the best of all possible worlds? Hadn't he fought on that belief, up and up, step by step, proving the legend of America and making himself almost a caricature of that legend, a judge in a graystone house? Not, it is true, one of those like Field, or Armour, or Mc-Cormick—he had a different memory from theirs and he couldn't elude it entirely, and to prove that he had written a book, *Our Penal Machinery and its Victims*. Even if his desire to understand what makes criminal men was no more virtuous than Armour's desire to understand what makes sick cattle, as some of his enemies said, he was nevertheless interested in men and believed that crime could be cured as well as punished. But was that principle, or was the only principle that of the advancement of Judge Altgeld within the only frame he knew?

His wife said that she was sorry. "Now I'm sorry," she said. "Why did I mention that? Why don't we forget about the anarchists? Finish your breakfast, please."

He pushed his plate away. He knew the gesture displeased her; it was not right, it was an old, bad habit of his. And his wife said, more hotly:

"It's become like a sickness here in Chicago, this whole business of the anarchists. It's in our blood now, it seems."

"Maybe it is a sickness."

"Sometimes I would want to live anywhere, anywhere but here."

The Judge said, "Here? This is what I am. I came here with nothing. I think a man who had nothing once, he tries to forget it, but he can't. Maybe Chicago is like a mother for me, so I could excuse this or that, and say, it's Chicago."

VI

THEY said of Chicago then, in one of those pat phrases which have as little truth as substance, that it killed pigs and made men; but not long after Pete Altgeld came, he saw the men killed along with the pigs, and if there was a repugnance toward eating the flesh of one, that about limited the ethic. Pete Altgeld could have been king-pin in Savannah; Joe Martin had sketched that out once, saying: "I would have stayed. County attorney, state legislature, congress, senate. The place for a big frog, if he's smart, is a small puddle." "And you?" Pete Altgeld asked. "Well," his friend answered, "some big frogs want to be bigger." But that was not entirely the case with Pete Altgeld when he threw over a good job, a job he had sweated for, fought for, suffered for too, to come to Chicago with one hundred dollars or so in his pockets and not a friend in the world, just a small-town, small-time lawyer, such as were a dime a dozen in the queen of western cities. It was more than that, for Chicago was sending out a call that could be heard a long way, a sound in which the clink of silver dollars mingled with the meshing gears of machines, the squealing of stuck pigs, the cry of many thousand voices, and somewhere, lost in it almost yet not entirely, an echo of the old western warwhoop. Chicago asked for men like Pete Altgeld. When he called it his mother, he was not far from wrong, for it was as much a mother as anything he had known, and sometimes it was not unkind to men who could hold on and suck at those swelling teats. How many days had he spent in his first small office standing at the window and watching the wonder that America had made and which only America could have made. The few cases he got in those days were not enough to keep him busy; he lived in his office, worked there when there was work, and uncertainly at first, but soon more confidently, reached out his fingers to take the pulse of the city.

It was not a very clean game he was playing; honesty and perseverance had a place, but they were strictly limited; of more importance were the people you knew, the way you used them, and the way you allowed them to use you. Nor were most of the cases that came his way fine struggles of jurisprudence; more often they were miserable pieces of the whole wretched melodrama the city presented. Divorce, or petty thievery, or for example the case which brought him the friendship of Joe Martin. Martin ran a high-class gambling parlor. A client came to Altgeld complaining of a good-sized loss at Martin's house, and asking Altgeld to recover for him, as was then possible within the law. Altgeld sent his demands to Martin, and when Martin came to see him, he called Altgeld's client a liar, labeled Altgeld's action as a part of a big blackmail racket, and stated that the client had never lost a dime at his place. Altgeld liked Martin's looks, a small, ruddy-faced, loudly dressed, and well-groomed man. So while he took the money, he questioned the client until he had determined that this time Martin was in the right; he threw out his client, returned the money to Martin, and made one of the best friends he had, better than the friends he made when he learned the method of political deals, when he learned that no lawyer has to starve if he climbs onto one or another of the political bandwagons. And he had climbed on. He had grown with Chicago.

As he sat back now, wiping his lips after the coffee and a crisp little kaiser roll, warm and full of melted butter, he took refuge in the thought that, for better or worse, he was Chicago, this fine house he lived in, jurisprudence, the legal bench, a handsome wife, and many other solid and substantial things. Yet for all of that, he wanted to put his justification into words, talk to someone who would understand all of his position and agree with it. So he said to his wife, "Emma, you'll call on Joe Martin and ask him to drop around." And as an afterthought and defense, added, "About that North Side property."

"But Schilling is coming," she said.

"Schilling? This morning?"

"He called and said he would be here a little before nine. I'm sorry, I forgot to tell you."

"Why did you forget to tell me? Of all people I don't want to see today, Schilling is first. Schilling! Do you know what he's coming here to do?—to put needles into me."

"What do you mean?"

"Nothing, nothing," the Judge said. "I can't see him."

"You can't see Schilling? Pete, what are you talking about? He's coming here. I invited him." In one way, she knew more about politics than he did, more about whom he could or could not afford to offend.

"All right," the Judge whispered, "all right." He stood up, and the security of substance was gone from him. "I'll be in my study. Send him up there when he comes."

VII

EMMA watched the Judge as he climbed up the stairs. She had known that he would be disturbed today; certainly, anyone who lived in or about Chicago and who was at all civilized could not regard with equanimity the prospect of four men hanging by their necks until they were dead; even if these men were cutthroats, ordinary murderers, it was still not a comfortable process to contemplate their last few hours on the earth. But she had not suspected that he would be so violently moved. As with everyone else in Chicago, they had both followed the Haymarket tragedy, from the time the bomb was thrown, a year and a half ago, to the arrests, the trial, the appeals, the petitions, and finally the great, nationwide, desperate effort to save the lives of the condemned men. Yet through it all—so much of it confusing, contradictory—Emma had leaned on the Judge's judicial aloofness. And, when you listened to him and his friends discussing the evidence in highly legal terms, the face of the matter changed from a life-and-death struggle to an intricate and fascinating puzzle.

Her sympathies, and most of the Judge's too, for that matter, were in the limbo of undecided public opinion. Perhaps because she knew less about it, and perhaps because she was less worldly, Emma was more repelled than the Judge by such words as *communism, socialism,* and *anarchy.* Actually, these words reacted upon her with physical force, painting independent images, derived originally from a thousand sources, casual conversation, newspaper stories, cartoons, little leaflets shown about as curiosities, and others too numerous to name. She was a woman who feared violence, who was horrified by pain, who in a curious way admired weakness more than strength, yet was attracted beyond her ability to resist by both strength and violence. Though she knew how much the Judge wanted children, childbirth was a horrible miasma to her, partaking of all those matters of violence she tried so carefully to avoid. Still, in the person of her own husband, violence drew her; do what he might, she would never forget him as he had been when young, and perversely that drew her toward him. The Haymarket affair had all the implications of the unknown, the terrible, and the violent. An anarchist was a wild, bearded devil, a bomb in each dirty hand; a communist was someone unalterably opposed to her, though for reasons she could not define, an unbeliever, an enemy of God and man, and in that a socialist stood beside him. Once, on a tour of the slaughterhouses, a tour she shouldn't have taken and which remained impressed on her consciousness like a bad dream, she saw the men pouring out of the yard gates at noon, and someone remarked, "Those are the workers." Of course, it was nonsense; she had known workingmen before, in her home town, in her childhood, in Chicago too; but this was different, big, bearded, shuffling men, bloody from fingertip to elbow, wearing leather aprons, black-streaked with blood, walking in shoes that were blood from sole to ankle, stone-visaged, tired, sullen. Always afterward, when someone spoke of the workers or labor, this picture came to mind, and seen in conjunction with all her concepts of anarchists and socialists, it was more than terrible.

Her first meeting with Schilling had modified that impression; but it was not difficult for her to tell herself that Schilling was different, the exception which proved the rule. She truly liked Schilling, he seemed to be so simple, gentle, and, at times, wise.

Emma suspected that, at first, Schilling's attraction toward her husband, and her husband's toward him, was purely political. Each suspected that he could use the other. But later, when she saw how they would sit and talk until late into the evening, in German, which her husband spoke so little now, drinking beer, smiling with pleasure, she realized that the men really complemented each other. Schilling was the closest thing to a real friend

her husband had, and that pleased her too; for his loneliness was a formidable thing, so formidable that sometimes she thought it would drive him away from her and
from the world. So she seized on Schilling, and then she
too came to like him.

It was hard not to like Schilling. He was a small, dry
man, a carpenter who built boxes and barrels for the packing house of Libby, McNeill and Libby. For years he had
been in the labor movement, a violent radical socialist
once, though a lot cooler now, but still a left-wing leader
in the great struggle for the eight-hour day. Listening to
Schilling talk, Emma got a colorful impression of what this
turbulent, nationwide struggle for the eight-hour day was,
of the position of the Knights of Labor, of the terrible life-
and-death battles of the Molly Maguires, of the private
armies of the Pinkertons. It was hardly possible for her to
relate this to the quiet and orderly life she lived, and her
first-hand relations with household workers, plumbers,
carpenters, and delivery men hardly gave substance to
Schilling's words. Yet she lent a willing ear when he said:

"And what is labor, my dear Mrs. Altgeld? I will tell
you. Labor is a sleeping giant, a giant who has been a long
time asleep and is only now beginning to stretch himself
and awaken. He isn't one, he is millions, and when he
wakes up, then, believe me, you will see some things happen."

The phrase "he is millions" stuck in her mind; votes,
too, were counted in millions, and she had dreams for her
husband he himself never expected. The whole eight-hour
movement had become political, to a degree, and when
Schilling hinted once that her husband would do well to
make his political alliances where the votes were, she
nodded agreement. But actually, those votes were, for her,

imprisoned vaguely in little Schilling; she could never conceive of any sort of alliance with the awful specter which came forth from the slaughterhouse gates that day. And when she thought of the Haymarket defendants, she thought of them not in the light of Schilling, but in the light of those blood-stained, semi-human things who killed the flesh men ate.

Therefore, she took refuge in her husband's legal aloofness, and she readily became convinced, along with thousands of others, of the guilt of the four men who were to be hanged. As her husband and his friends said, the trial was a test of democracy, and democracy had not failed. Such talk relieved her. Why did people have to do terrible things? Why did they have to take it upon themselves to stir up trouble? Why could they not be pleasant and nice and decent? Naturally, they could not all have everything; there was just not enough of everything to go around, and thereby more went to those who worked hardest. Wasn't her husband living proof of that? Hadn't he started with nothing and worked himself up to where he was now? Hadn't she heard it said, a thousand times if once, that any man who wasn't lazy could find work and advance his position? Wasn't that an obvious truth, here in the United States? And wasn't most of the trouble started by foreigners? She didn't dislike foreigners; some of the most prominent men in the country had come as immigrants, and even her own husband was not born in America, though he had come here as a tiny infant; but wasn't there an obligation upon foreigners not to start trouble simply because for the first time they were in a free land?

So out of this came first a hope and then a belief that when the Haymarket case was finally decided and finished, things would be quiet and peaceful, and though she never put it in just those terms she really believed that the death of these men would lay the ogre in his grave, once and for all. To hear, on top of this, an opinion from her husband that the trial was not a fair one, that the men who were going to die were possibly not guilty, was more than disturbing. As she had said, the case was becoming a sickness in Chicago, and was not the surliness of her husband's actions this morning proof of that?

VIII

BUT as he went into his study, the Judge's frame of mind was not too different from his wife's, and he too took a brief refuge in the fact that death was the final judgment, the unchangeable and the immutable, the end, the finish and the seal on all decisions. This was not to say that he took any pleasure in the fact that four men were to die; quite to the contrary, their impending deaths enraged him; yet he was more enraged by an awareness of his own position. Why had he lost his temper with Emma, and why had he allowed himself to hand down a decision on justice or injustice in that fashion? It opened up too broad a field of examination of all he stood for and all his bench stood for, his achievement, his success and prominence. Actually, he did not feel any great sorrow for the four men; death was an accompaniment to life, and anyone who did not realize that the two were instantly interchangeable was a dolt or an idiot, and aside from that, he had never known these men, nor was he in sympathy with the things they stood for. He knew somewhat better than his wife what socialism was, having discussed it at great length with Schilling, but he took it for the visionary aims of zealots;

and though he had not the hatred and fear of socialists that Field and Armour indulged in, he nevertheless ranged himself against the socialists. As for anarchists, he had no sympathy for them whatsoever; they were a menace to society, and society was correct in removing them. If they wanted to improve things, they could work with their two hands, as he had done, and everything within him revolted from the violence of their talk, the violence that could be wrought with a bomb. Therefore, he joined with his wife in the feeling that, once they were dead, the trouble would be over—or at least he sought for that assurance.

Yet his statement remained, and the more he examined it, the more convinced he became that long and deep-seated reflection had driven him to the conclusion that no one of the four defendants was guilty of throwing the bomb which had exploded a year and a half before in Haymarket Square. But if that was the case, when had he come to the decision, now or a week ago or a month ago—and if he had come to the decision, why had he taken no action? And what would he tell Schilling? Could he say to Schilling, "I don't know whether they were innocent or guilty and, furthermore, I don't give a damn whether they were or not; the fact is that they had a rotten, cheap, biased trial, and even what we call justice was turned into a mockery." Could he tell Schilling that?

On the other hand, why see Schilling at all? Literally, it would soon be the eleventh hour, and at that time they were going to die. Then it would be over, and tomorrow, he, John Peter Altgeld, could sit on his bench once more, arrayed in the long and grand and legal robes of justice.

The Judge sank into a large and comfortable chair, and at this point he was able to smile at himself. Let Schilling come and go; in the last analysis, he, Pete Altgeld, was one individual, and the responsibilities of the world were not his.

He looked around the room, a nice room, the kind of a room he had wanted all his life; not precisely, of course, for a man's life is divided into many stages, and along with a change in taste there is a change in outlook and personality. Still it was the development of the room he had wanted. The walls were lined with books, books he had read, books he wanted to read, legal books, and books he simply wanted to own, although he knew well enough he would never get around to reading them. There was a fireplace, with a fine hickory log burning inside it, and on the mantel there was a bust of Minerva and another bust of Augustus. A definition of the way a man regarded life, and a direction too. He had a carved desk, which he looked at now admiringly.

Possessions were not a drug with him, as with some, but certain things were nice to have, and the pleasure of owning them did not pall easily. They made small monuments, as the desk did, with its book-ends, books between them, its neatly piled papers, its fine and shining brass lamp, topped with two green-glass globes, and its pens and pencils and ornate paperweights. It was surprising what pleasure he could get and what an equable frame of mind he could manage simply by looking at the desk, examining it anew, and placing it properly in the room and the house, as, for example, he himself was placed in Chicago society.

So a man adjusts to the world, whether in large or small things, and sitting in his room, his kingdom, the morning paper spread on his knees, the Judge waited for George Schilling to arrive.

IX

AND when Schilling came in, the Judge smiled and said, "Good morning, George."

"Good morning."

"Take off your coat. Sit down and make yourself comfortable. Do you want a cigar?"

Schilling shook his head as he struggled out of his coat. "On a chair. Anywhere. Cold outside?"

"Not too cold."

"November is a fine month," the Judge said. "The blood runs easy in the veins. It thins out just enough. Of course, here in the city we live like animals in a cage. I remember how November was when I was a boy. All the black pigs turned out into the cornfields to glean. The pumpkins piled up on the roadside. The cornstalks sheaved and standing like soldiers waiting for orders. My goodness, you could go wherever you wanted in the State of Ohio, and you'd find those same sheaves ready and waiting. And the trees were going bare. The wind blew and the sky would rain dead and shrunken leaves."

"Those are good things to remember," Schilling said.

"Well, why don't you sit down? Of course, we remember the good things. What then?"

As Schilling seated himself, he said, "Sometimes we remember other things."

"That's your mood today. I'm trying to cheer you up on this fine fall morning. You come in looking like a funeral."

"I don't feel very happy today, Judge."

"No?" He was making it hard for Schilling; deliberately and carefully, he was making it very hard for him. "What do you expect to do?" he asked abruptly.

The little carpenter stared at him, started to speak, swallowed back the words, and then let both his hands drop on his knees. Altgeld realized that he had lost a day's work by coming here, and he fought down the sympathy this small but sincere sacrifice provoked. Yet he could not help realizing that in a very real sense the room they were in, the house too, was isolated from a somber fermentation which covered all of the city, perhaps all of the country too. And that prompted him to ask:

"Is there any hope?" his voice kinder than it had been before.

"Maybe—but I don't believe that either. Three men went to talk with the governor. What good will it do?"

"Not much good now."

"I think so too."

"Then what can I do for you, George? Why do you come to me?"

Schilling shrugged his shoulders. "Maybe I had to come somewhere. I'm nervous. I'm afraid and I'm frightened. And I'm desperate too. You're the only man in the city with power and reputation whom I really trust. So I said to myself, I will waste a little of the Judge's time on this black Friday morning."

The Judge was forced into denying that. "You don't waste my time, George." It was curious how easily Schilling could get the upper hand.

"No—but I always have that feeling. Perhaps I shouldn't. This morning, I want to talk to you."

"All right."

"You think it won't do any good. I suppose not. But give me an hour, even a half hour. Let me tell you about Parsons. All the way over here, I was thinking, what should I tell you? Then I decided I would just talk about Parsons."

"Why? For a year now, every time I opened my paper, there was something about Parsons. Isn't that enough?"

"I suppose so," Schilling nodded. "If you don't want me to, all right. Only the newspapers don't always tell the truth—you know that, Judge. There are some things I wanted to tell you, even if it don't make any difference."

"Did you have breakfast?"

"I had it, Judge. You don't want me to talk?"

"Damn it, go ahead and talk, instead of sitting there and arguing the point with me."

Nervously, at first, Schilling began to speak. He began in English, haltingly, groping for words; then, as he went on, he lapsed more and more into German, until presently he was speaking entirely in that language.

X

"I WANT to say it right," Schilling began. "I want to say it so that Pete Altgeld will know what I mean—forgive me, Judge, I'm thinking almost out loud, and walking over here, I turned over in my mind the question, what is it here I must tell him? But to make it understood I must put everything in its place. Like a good German—he puts everything in its place. Also, I will think like a German, that is something I cannot help, and maybe that is why I decide to talk about Parsons, not about Spies, not about Fischer and Engel. About them, what more can I tell you— they came from that one land in the world where freedom is held in such contempt, in such contempt, Judge. Didn't you tell me about your father, how with the bullwhip he taught you obedience? I'm sorry again, I mean to make only one thing, to explain why I talk about Parsons, not those three who were Germans and who went somewhere else to look for liberty—"

"Then talk about Parsons," the Judge said coldly.

"Yes, but you will remember that all four of them are going to die in a little while." The Judge said nothing; his eyes strayed to the clock on the mantel, and Schilling continued:

—I know a good deal about Parsons, but I want to put each thing into place. Some would begin by speaking about Albert Parsons' lineage; whether that is a good or bad thing, I don't know, I have so little of it myself. And in this country it is so peculiarly mixed: on the one hand, there is the lineage of wealth; for example, if your father was a millionaire, you are entitled to a place among the great; but on the other hand, there is the lineage of freedom, and that, I think, is the greatest contradiction in all this strange and wonderful country. The lineage of freedom—and it is only here, nowhere else, in no other land, no other place—the lineage of freedom says that if your father's father, or your grandfather's father, fought in the Revolution for freedom, then America has a debt to you which she can never repay. Why do I speak of this?—not only because Parsons stands high in that lineage, very high, for on his mother's side there was an aide to General George Washington, and on his father's side, there were two in the direct line, Major-General Samuel Parsons, who led the Massachusetts troops, and Captain Parsons, I don't know his other name, who was wounded at Bunker Hill; but not only because of these facts, but because how else can one understand America? They haven't our memories here in America; they never had the lord, the duke, the junker, the incarnation of evil to take away their souls as well as destroy their bodies. They never had that, and so they don't know what it means; but a nobility of freedom, that incredible contradiction, that they had, and that we must remember when we speak of Parsons.

- And maybe that's not the least important thing in making Parsons what he is. And we must understand some of the things which went into the making of Parsons; all of them we can't understand, for there is no man whose life isn't a secret book, so much of it in a code which only God himself will ever decipher. But some of the things, yes; the fact that Parsons fought in the war. He fought on the other side, it is true, but that was because he lived in Texas, worked there, and how does a boy of sixteen or seventeen turn against his comrades? And he fought well; no one ever accused him of being a coward. Afterward, however, he could not stomach what happened, the way the black men were driven back to slavery, and he took the side of the Reconstruction government, worked in it, and became a part of it. But how much more there is which I don't know; how does a boy of twenty think the way Parsons thought, against all odds, clearly, lucidly? Well, he made his own pattern for his life; he became the champion of the Negro, of the downtrodden white man, of the Indian who was being driven westward and wiped out, the way the Germans of old wiped out the Slavs because they wanted their land.

—There is so much to tell about Parsons, and such a short time, only enough time to select a piece here and a piece there. For instance, his wife Lucy, who was half Indian and half Spanish, wild and dark and beautiful, like those roses one finds growing in the woods, alone and splendid. Their love for each other is like something out of an old-fashioned romance, but good love. What else

73

should I draw in here? He was a printer, an editor, a news-paper writer, but firstly a workingman who set type. But he had knowing hands; he was a good carpenter, and also, now and then, he rode herd in the cattle country. Do you know the kind of man who is gentle as a woman yet hard as a piece of steel? You must have met that kind in the army; well, that was the kind of a man Parsons was. There is much more I could tell you, I suppose, but I am not trying to make a case for Parsons; in too many things we disagree. I only want to tell you one or two things pertaining to this Haymarket affair, which perhaps you don't know.

—But I must tell you of the first time I met him. You know the old saying, the heart sees only once, and after that the eyes see. So I call to mind the first time I laid eyes on him. It was in 1877, during the great railroad strike. That was like a waking up for the labor movement, like a birth. The very nature of the strike was like a birth, no real organization in the beginning, the workingmen on one railroad laying down their tools, then another, then another, until the land was faced with the greatest strike it had ever known—and a labor movement too. But there were no leaders to speak of; leaders had to come the same way, spontaneously, out of the movement. Albert Parsons came that way. Sure, he had been an organizer before, a good union man, spoken to meetings; but in July of 1877, we had a meeting here that was like no other working-class meeting ever held. The workers were called to Market Street, and they assembled near the junction of Madison. How many were there God only knows; some say twenty thousand, some say thirty thousand. I can tell you this, that they poured in for hours, and then there was such a sea of faces as I had never seen before in all my life, just a swelling carpet of upturned faces wherever men could stand, and over it torchlight and banners; and it made me afraid, and it made me feel like crying too. And then Albert Parsons stood up and spoke to them. That was when I first saw him.

—You've never seen him, have you? But you've seen the pictures, and some of them are good, the high brow, the fine dark eyes, the nose and chin cut like a cameo, the black, silky mustache; I am foolish-looking enough myself to appreciate good looks and also to mistrust them; but it was different with Parsons, believe me; you forgot, right away, that he was good-looking; you accepted him and you listened to him. I listened to him; I tried to write down what he was saying—but only the beginning, and after that I stopped writing and listened. But do you know how he began? He said, "Fellow Americans, whose bread is freedom and whose milk is liberty, I want to talk to you about justice and injustice. Not about the rights of man but about the hopes of man, for we have little enough of rights, yet much of hope." That much I remember, and after that I stopped writing. But later on I asked myself, how much of him is real? How much is the truth? How much is a play actor? He looked like Booth, like Edwin Booth, and he was a strange man for us then.

—I met him the next day at the office of our paper. We shook hands; we talked a little. And while we were talking, the police came for him. You know how, two of them with their guns in his belly. They marched him over to City Hall and up to Hickey's office. He was chief of police then. They filled the room with officers. They asked him questions, and when he tried to answer, they gave it to him, back and forth, across the face. They asked him, what in hell did he mean, a dirty Texas rebel bastard, coming up to Chicago and making trouble? When he tried to say that he had spoken at a meeting of the Workingman's Party, telling workers what was their right with the ballot, the police shut him up and beat him again. Then they let him go. But they warned him; they told him how simple it would be for him to be found dead on some street corner; they told him a mob might string him to a lamppost, if he continued to agitate. All this he repeated to us when he returned. We waited for him.

—It was after that the Albert Parsons I speak about emerged. You don't threaten a man like Parsons; you don't beat him up; you don't tell him to go back where he came from. That is all right with some men, with the kind who shout and bluster and boast; but with Parsons' kind, the Texas kind, the soft, gentle, quiet-spoken kind, with them it's no good.

—You have to see what Parsons became in the years which followed, and you will understand that there was only one other like him, and that was Sylvis; Sylvis died, but Parsons they have to kill. And I don't agree with Parsons, still I must tell you these things. I want you to look at the man, and I want you to see what happened to him. Then, during the last of the seventies, we worked together. He still had faith in the ballot, and the labor party in Chicago was growing with leaps and bounds. What kind of a man was he? He was tireless; a setback made him stronger; if all of our faces were a mile long, he still could smile. He would speak four times in one evening, and you know that nothing else can take the life out of you so quickly as public speaking. He worked in the Knights of Labor. He wrote; he did twenty things at once, and always he had enough time for his wife. He would walk in the streets with her as if there was nothing in the world more important, each with an arm around the other's waist, and looking at each other as if they had only discovered themselves that very day and moment.

—Nothing, as I said, was too much for him. We put him up for office in the next few years, alderman, county clerk, congress, and he spoke, not only for himself, but for every candidate on the slate. And with all that, he found time to organize the first Trades Assembly in Chicago, became its first president, organized in his own trade the Typographical Union, and was free consultant and partner to anyone who wanted advice or strength in building a union. At one time, we wanted him to be the first labor candidate for President of the United States; and, do you know, he was too young. Can you imagine, he was only thirty-five! He's only forty-three today.

—But I'm getting away from my story, and I must make it quick and short, and not lose all your patience. In 1880, he broke from the labor party. Why? You and I are practical men, but Parsons saw what was happening, the graft, the buying and selling of votes, the corruption. Once, he said to me, "You work a man twelve hours a day, and give him half what he needs to live on, and you want him to vote carefully and honestly. Well, I tell you, if his children starve, don't be surprised that he sells his vote."

—I asked him what he intended to do, and he said, work for the eight-hour day, that and organize. We were just gaining our strength in the eight-hour movement then. The trade unions got together and sent Parsons all through the middle west. He spoke everywhere; I don't know if there's one man in the country who gave to the workers what Parsons did. He was sent as delegate from Chicago to the big eight-hour convention in Washington, and the convention made him one of a committee to stay in Washington, coordinate the movements of organized labor, and study the whole question of the eight-hour day.

—What happened to Parsons in Washington, what he saw there, I don't know; you must remember, always, the kind of a man he was; if I believed in saints, I would call him that; but he was so human, so full of life, so enchanted with just the everyday process of living. That isn't a part of sainthood, is it? And he was always so madly in love with this wife of his—not what they call a pure love, but the love of two whose bodies understand each other, and if you ever saw them together you realized that right away. But in Washington, something happened; he changed; he looked at a country governing itself, and after that he talked differently.

—After that, he split with us wholly, and he joined the International Working People's Association. He became a revolutionary socialist. An anarchist? That's a name, a tag; I know what he was; I would be against him in any case— but he was that, a revolutionary socialist, not this crazy cartoon they make of him, a bearded lunatic with a bomb in each hand and the label of anarchist under him. That is not Parsons; even if I regard him as a man who has gone the wrong way, I must still say that is not Parsons.

—Yet when I think of what he did after that, how much can I condemn him? He went to the people. He traveled through the coal fields, the hell-towns of Pennsylvania and Illinois, speaking to the miners, living with them, always, always pleading the cause of socialism. Still, there was no labor struggle within five hundred miles of here in which he didn't participate. He founded and edited the *Alarm*, the first English weekly of their international; that you know. When the great strikes came, a few years ago, he stood with the strikers. Don't think they never tried to kill him before. The Pinkerton armies had secret orders, which I myself saw, to get Parsons. Also to get others, but first on the list was Parsons. The police were instructed to club him to death, first chance they got. And they tried, they certainly tried.

—And what else is there to tell, before I speak of Haymarket? You want to know how he lived? He lived on nothing. Lucy was clever. I've watched her weave his suits back together when they fell to pieces from wear. She could make meals of scraps. There were years when he couldn't work, when he was on the blacklist of every newspaper and every printshop in the west. Then his own people fed him from the little they had. He never took until it was forced on him; he never asked; he never complained. Once, when I met him, he had not eaten for two full days; but I was with him more than an hour before I realized he was faint from hunger.

—I know I will have to bore you by repeating what we both know, the facts of the meeting; I keep saying to myself, thank you for hearing me. But first I want to finish with the man; he isn't going to die if they kill him today; some men don't die. Maybe both of us will have to deal with him, and that's why I want to understand him, for myself as well as for you. They talk of socialism as a foreign importation, but what is foreign about Parsons? Once I met a United States marshal from Texas; he was like Parsons, quiet, gentle, polite, he never raised his voice and most often seemed to apologize, but he had a reputation for being a very brave man, and he too, in his own way, took the side where there was least strength and least hope. But don't think Parsons is a dolt; his reasoning is cold and logical; he's read everything on labor and socialism he could lay hands on. When he talks, there are ideas.

I disagree bitterly with those ideas; I say he is wrong, dangerously wrong, and isn't what happened proof that he was wrong? For him, there is only one solution, for the workers to rise up and take over the land, the means of production, the factories and the schools and the halls of justice—and to me, that is insanity. So you see, I too am against him, and against Spies and the others. But are men to die, to be murdered simply because I do not agree with them?

—You could ask why, believing this, Parsons should fight so hard for the eight-hour day, for every advance and demand of labor. That is very interesting. I myself asked Parsons that; but to him there is no contradiction; every gain for labor is a gain for his own and their own cause—like that. I say that to show that the man lived what he preached; there is only one Parsons, not two.

—I could tell more; I could spend most of the day telling this and that about Parsons, but there isn't most of today. There is only another hour and a half. So let us start with such a man and see what happened.

—You remember how a year and a half ago we decided that there should be a day for American labor, one day which was ours, which would mark our unity and our determination in the struggle for eight hours. We picked May the first. My word, you would have thought that we destroyed the foundations of the country by asking a day for ourselves, our own holiday. As it approached, you remember what happened. A whole army of Pinkertons poured into Chicago; the police armed themselves to the teeth, deputized every no-good bum who could be found on the streets. The National Guard was alerted; even units of the regular army were demanded, to come to Chicago and preserve the peace. Had we threatened the peace? All we proposed was to select a day when we could demonstrate our solidarity for the eight-hour movement. Of course, that Saturday came and went without any trouble; trouble was our enemy. We knew what we were after; we were organized throughout the nation—what good would violence do us?

—But on Monday, the third of May, a bad thing happened. You know about it, but I want to put all things in their place. The demonstration outside the McCormick plant was not held only by the Lumber Shovers' Union; there were over a thousand McCormick strikers there too, and though August Spies spoke there, he did not call for trouble; he called for unity. Is that a crime? The trouble came when the scabs began to leave the plant. The strikers saw them and cursed them, and called them names not fit to repeat. Just picture the scene, some six thousand striking members of two unions holding an outdoor mass meeting, and within sight of them, scabs leaving a plant. I saw what happened. The McCormick strikers began to move toward the plant. No one urged them; no one harangued them; they stopped listening and moved away toward the gates. Maybe they picked up some rocks; maybe they said things not nice to hear—but before they did anything, the plant police started to fire. My god, it was like a war! The strikers were unarmed, and the police stood like men on a range, pistols at arm's length, rifles too, potting, potting away.

—They say the plant called for reinforcements—that would take a little time, wouldn't it? But, within minutes, a patrol wagon filled with police dashed up, and behind them, on the double, came a detail of two hundred armed men.

—Well, it was the kind of a sight one would see in the

old country, not here. The workers dropped like men on a battlefield. When they tried to stand fast, the police rushed them and clubbed them apart; when they broke and ran, the police followed them, clubbing them from the rear. It wasn't nice to see; it wasn't kind; it was a brute thing that made you want to go away and vomit. That's what it made me do, but it made Spies rush back to the office of the *Arbeiter-Zeitung* and send out a wild call for a meeting at Haymarket Square to protest this thing. That's how it began; it began because we were quiet and orderly on our day, May Day, and because it didn't satisfy them to have us that way. Better with guns—with guns they could make real trouble, and people would scream revolution.

—But the point is that Parsons was not there, just as Parsons was not at Haymarket when the bomb was thrown. It wasn't only McCormick and the lumber shovers on strike; Pullman was on strike too, and Brunswick and the packing houses, and not only Chicago, but St. Louis, Cincinnati, New York, San Francisco. Parsons was everywhere he could be, but not here; Parsons was tired and sick; he would come home and collapse into bed. A labor organizer isn't a life to grow old with; first the stomach goes, then the legs, then, when you've been beaten and clubbed enough, the head, the mind.

—So they got up the meeting at Haymarket for the next day. They picked Haymarket because of its size; you see, Spies was like a man gone crazy when he came back from the McCormick plant, his head full of the wounded, the dying. He thought that the workers would come out by the tens of thousands to protest; but McCormick was only a small part of a giant struggle, and already the workers were being defeated. Everywhere, they were being smashed and broken, and what would one more meeting change? But don't underestimate Spies—a brilliant man and honest, too; with the foreign-born workingmen, he was like Parsons with the Americans. He saw this as a chance not to be missed; if twenty thousand workers packed Haymarket Square, the whole trend of the eight-hour struggle might be reversed. Perhaps—I don't know; as I said, I don't agree with these men. To talk revolution is not to promote my fight, but to hinder it; that is the way I feel.

—But twenty thousand men did not appear in Haymarket the next night. When Spies arrived, as you know, there were very few, and as the evening went on, the greatest size of the crowd was less than three thousand. And because the crowd was so small, they moved the meeting from Haymarket to Desplaines, between Lake and Randolph. But I am telling you about Parsons; that is my only reason for wasting your time this morning. I am telling you how Parsons was not there, how he didn't even know about the meeting. As a matter of fact, Sam Fielden didn't know about the Haymarket meeting either.

—But to get back to Parsons. He had left Chicago on the second of May and had gone to Cincinnati to speak. All day on the third of May, when the terrible thing happened at McCormick's, Parsons was away. He got home on the morning of the fourth. He had gone without sleep all night; he was tired and haggard as he listened to Lucy's story of what had happened. It was not too different from what he had seen himself in Cincinnati. All over the same thing. The barons were angry; this dirty monster who had stood up to challenge them must be crushed, and they were busy crushing it, and all over it was breaking into pieces. A hungry, tired, unarmed man isn't any match for a Gatling gun.

—Parsons listened to his wife's story. He played with his

two children. He drank the coffee she gave him and ate a piece of bread. He said to her, "We have to do something." But what was there to do? "You're too tired for a meeting tonight," she said. She was not speaking about the Haymarket meeting; she didn't know about that meeting. "There has to be a meeting," Parsons said. You see, we called the men Parsons led the American group, because most of them were native-born workingmen. He decided there had to be a meeting and, tired as he was, went out to put an announcement in the *Daily News*. Then he came home and played with the children some more. Then he went to sleep. When he woke up, he was much better; he was his old self, laughing it away. Lucy says he spoke about victory instead of defeat; he talked about his children growing up into an America that would lead the world toward justice and freedom.

—In the evening, he and Lucy and the two children went out to the meeting. Like always, he and Lucy walked together, looking at each other as if they were lovers.

—Meanwhile, the Haymarket meeting, small as it was, had lingered past starting time. What a bad night that was, threatening, with every minute looking like rain! It was the instant threat of rain that had kept people away, and those who were there wanted it to start and finish. But, you see, they all depended on Parsons, and each discovered that he had left it to someone else to get Parsons to the meeting. Spies didn't want to start until Parsons came, and when someone mentioned the announcement in the *Daily News,* Spies said he would go get Parsons himself. But that would have probably taken all the life out of the meeting, and they persuaded Spies to start talking while someone else looked for Parsons. So Spies began. I don't have to repeat what Spies said; there's been enough of that in the papers. But it's worth recalling that he spoke in the main about the eight-hour movement. Because workers were shot and clubbed, he didn't say that everything must go; he said we have to pull together and fight harder. And he described what had happened at McCormick the day before. Meanwhile, someone had gotten to Parsons at the other meeting. Fielden was there too; he would be, you see; even though he's English, he can talk to Americans better than I can. Parsons was dog-tired, but he said, all right, he'd come back and talk again. Fielden came with him. Fielden is a big man, slow to anger, as they say Yorkshiremen are, but what was happening everywhere was fermenting in him, and he was bitter. And his bitterness came out when he talked.

—Well, Parsons, with his wife and the two children went to Desplaines Street, where Spies' meeting was. The children were very tired by then. Lucy carried one, Parsons the other. Yes, I'm telling you this to win your sympathy; there's no more time after today, and I'm not ashamed to try to win your sympathy.

—Maybe there were still two thousand people left, standing there under the black sky and waiting for Parsons. You don't know how that is, but there were times when I stood two hours and more, waiting for Parsons to speak. There were two wagons there; the speakers used one for a platform; men sat on the other, but they made room for Lucy Parsons and the children. Spies was relieved to see Parsons; you know how you feel when you think you have an occasion of such great importance, and the crowd begins to slip away.

—Spies was feeling that way. You've been in politics long enough to know that the best man will go to pieces when the audience goes, not one by one, but in clumps. Well, it was nine o'clock when Parsons stood up to speak, and he held them. Think of what the man had been through, almost no sleep in about thirty hours, straight from another meeting to this one, seeing everything he fought for being smashed, knocked out. Still, he spoke—he spoke well too. He started in with the eight-hour movement, then he told about the workers. I don't think anybody in America knows as much about the working people as Parsons. He spoke about the growth of monopoly—all right. You've read his statement; you know what he spoke about. But those transcripts of his speech, lies! He had no written speech; he said the things that came to mind, and no one took down his words. Yes, the next day they invented a speech for him, but that was not Parsons'.

—And then he finished, and then he introduced Sam Fielden. It's interesting, in the way of my sitting here and talking to you, to recall what Fielden said, just to mention that Fielden spoke about law. The rich man's law, but not the poor man's; the rich man's courts but not the poor man's. All right, I'll tell about Parsons. You sit and listen to me, or maybe you don't listen to me, and think, this fool carpenter is wasting your time, but he has political influence in the labor party, and you should listen to him, not hurt his feelings. Very well. Then let me tell it my own way, all of it.

—Parsons walked over to the wagon as Fielden began to speak and picked up the little one. Then it began to rain. One of the children began to cry. Now mark this—in the light of what happened. With the child in his arms, Parsons walked over to the other platform, where Fielden spoke, and said, with the rain coming down, shouldn't they go to the hall, Zepf's Hall, where they hold a lot of their meetings? He thought that way because he had the baby in his arm, because he was so tired. But how can you move two thousand people through the streets, then get them orderly into a hall? "I'll be through in a few minutes," Fielden said. Parsons nodded, but he couldn't stand there in the rain with the children. Also, the crowd was breaking up. By this time there were maybe six, seven hundred people, still standing in the rain 'and listening.

—So Parsons, Lucy, the two children, and a friend walked away from the meeting to Zepf's Hall. They went to the hall only for a moment, to see a few people, and after that they were to go home. But it was there they heard the explosion.

—And the explosion, the bomb—you know how that happened, or maybe not. It is so long ago that maybe my good friend has forgotten. It was while Fielden spoke that almost two hundred police, led by Ward and Bonfield, came storming into the street. Why? How? What for, with this very quiet, peaceful meeting, that was already breaking up of its own accord, maybe five hundred people left by now? And Ward, at the head of his police ranks, screaming out that they should disperse, immediately. What was there for Fielden to do? He broke off his speech and began to climb down from the wagon. The crowd began to move toward the other end of the street. And then the bomb came, thrown from God knows where, falling in front of the police, killing one of them and wounding so many others. Who threw the bomb? For a year and a half, we have heard nothing in this city of sorrow but who threw the bomb? I swear to you, Judge, by whatever God or force or destiny there is, that no one of our people threw the bomb. Yes, that is my opinion, and I am prejudiced; I am a working-man, of course I am prejudiced. But now, a few hours before Parsons is going to die, I swear that. I hate violence;

I hate men of violence; that you know. So I swear what I believe. They—our enemies—they threw the bomb. Look at all that has happened since, and see if it could have been any other way. Think of what happened a moment after the bomb was thrown, how the police drew their guns and began to shoot; it made what happened at McCormick's the day before seem like nothing! They shot like men gone mad. They shot down workingmen and their wives and children. We weren't armed; no shots came from our side. But the police kept on shooting, and the crowd broke up and ran screaming in all directions.

"That is the truth," the little carpenter said. "From a hundred people who were there, I heard the story. That is the truth."

XI

To HIMSELF, Judge Altgeld, staring at the window of his study and the morning sunshine outside, said, "That is the truth, and this is the truth, and were there ever two men who were agreed on what is and what is not the truth?" For he had recalled the very ancient legend of the four blind men who were taken to an elephant, so that they might know this very unusual and wonderful manifestation of nature. These four blind men circled the elephant warily, attracted yet repelled by its strange scent, by its grumbling noises, and by its hoarse breathing. Urged on by their friends, they presently approached closer and closer, until each had laid hands upon the elephant in one fashion or another. Then they came away, wiser men, more experienced and learned in the things nature does. However, when they began to discuss their great experience, no agreement could be reached; for the first blind man

declared, most confidently, This elephant is very like unto
a rope. Which was not strange, since he had felt only the
elephant's tail. The second blind man indignantly declared, How can you speak of the elephant as a rope, when
it is most certainly like a tree-trunk! Which was also understandable, for the second blind man had felt the elephant's
leg. The third blind man only sneered, for, having felt the
trunk, he knew that this whole business of an elephant
was a hoax, and that they had merely been shown a snake.
The fourth blind man, however, refrained from argument,
muttering and puzzling over the wonder of an animal
being like a wall, for he had felt the elephant's side.

This legend came into the Judge's mind as he listened
to Schilling speak of Parsons, and other things came into
his mind too; for already he was overdue at court. The
accusers and the accused waited, and the great body of
man's rationalization, the law, waited with them. The law
would be a tool given into his hand, and he would use
the tool, not as he saw fit, but as those before him had used
it. Considering now the prospect of his lateness, the fact
that he should already be on his way, he was overcome by
a wave of depression; and he turned to Schilling a face that
was tired and bleak and gray. For now, as if only now coming
out of sleep, he realized that Parsons and the others would
surely die; nothing Schilling said could change that;
nothing he, the Judge, did could change that: yet when
Schilling looked at him, hesitantly now, Altgeld said:

"Go ahead. You haven't told me all you want to tell me.
You told me what I know. Go ahead then, and if you
believe something to be the truth, you're entitled to such
a belief; but don't give me oaths. Yours are no better than
mine, and God knows I have sworn to this and that enough
times."

XII

SCHILLING said:

—I told you how Parsons, his wife, and the two children were in Zepf's Hall when they heard the noise the bomb made, exploding. A good many people were there in the hall. The meeting had just broken up. But when the explosion came, it was the same with all of us, tight and silent, and afraid, too. A black thing hung over the city. War had already been declared. We had talked too much about organized labor; we had asked for the right to work no more than eight hours each day. We were organizing those whom no one had ever dreamed of organizing, and men were saying aloud that it was right for them to live and not starve to death; so for that we had to be broken; we had to be taught a lesson; we had to be whipped back into the sewers from which we had crawled. Yes—that was our reaction when we heard the explosion. And so, for a little while, we were silent and afraid, and nobody dared to go outside.

—And then the first of them came running from Desplaines to tell what had happened. Do you want truth? No one could tell a clear story then; some were wounded, some beaten and bleeding, some hysterical. A nine-year-old boy had his scalp laid open. A big stout woman, Mrs. Crane, had a bullet hole in her neck, and yet she had run all the way. And more than that—no, it was not nice.

—But even if no one knew exactly what had happened, we knew it meant sorrow; we knew it meant a witch hunt and a pig hunt all together, and that they would be after us. Hadn't there been enough wild talk of dynamite? Hadn't Gould said that hand grenades were the right medicine for us? Hadn't the City of Chicago been presented with a beautiful, shiny new Gatling gun which, as the *Tribune* informed us, could chew up workers faster than a dog chews sausage? A bomb had exploded; no one knew who threw it, even now no one knows; but it was enough that a bomb had exploded.

—I think Lucy realized first that Parsons had to get away. Then others found themselves looking at Parsons. Whatever it was, large or small, they would go after Parsons first. He knew it; his wife knew it. It did not matter that he wasn't there, that he had not even known that such a meeting had been scheduled; Parsons was marked. You sit in a court of law—you wait for a jury's decision; yet I tell you that five years ago this man Albert Parsons had been condemned to death, and they were only waiting to execute sentence upon him.

—I tell you this, that even as he realized that he must go away, get out of Chicago, hide somewhere, he remembered that he had no money. I speak of the literal, Judge Peter Altgeld. We would sit sometimes with a glass of beer and talk of the old days, when we were boys on the road; then you know what it is to be without money. I mean without money. Without five cents, without ten cents, without even two pennies. Yes, a man, a wife, two children. How did they live? I told you that before. You are a rich man in a graystone house, but I ask for understanding even while I insult you. They had no money. Parsons whispered with his wife for a few minutes, then with some of his friends, and then he had to borrow. He wouldn't have borrowed to eat, but he borrowed to save his life. Don't you think that the man was afraid; I told you enough about him before for you to know differently, and I will tell you more later. He had to live because he felt he had work to do. So he borrowed five dollars, the price of freedom, and he went home with his wife and children, and then he disappeared.

—What will you say?—that Parsons shouldn't have gone? Then I say that everyone who spoke at that meeting or showed his face there should have gone. Or perhaps you've forgotten what happened in Chicago during the next few days. I wasn't at the meeting—I was no anarchist, as you know well enough, yet within a week they were screaming for my blood too. Schilling should die; Schilling should be strung to the highest lamppost! Of course, we all knew that they would be after Parsons first; whatever happened in those few days after the first of May, it would have been an excuse to get Parsons. But in our wildest dreams and fears, we never thought it would be such a witch hunt. Yes, we knew they were organized better than we were, but we thought that truth was a force. Well, we know better now; truth is no force; the force is in men. You read the stories they printed, the crazy distortion of fact, how they accused the few hundred citizens left around the speaker's stand that night of being a bloodthirsty, armed mob.

—But did you read what they did to the workers in their homes? The police went mad, but it was a planned madness. This was what they wanted. They held meetings with the businessmen, and demanded money, money—and they got it, by the thousands. Then they went through Chicago like a whirlwind, beating, murdering, torturing, dragging people out of their homes in the middle of the night, arresting anyone and everyone whom they called suspicious. A workingman's shirt was all you needed. They filled their jails. My God, it was like nothing ever seen in this land, and maybe like nothing ever seen in any other land either.

—And you ask why Parsons fled. At least Parsons was tried; if he had stayed in Chicago, they would have shot him down on the streets like a dog.

—But to get back to Parsons. He and Lucy left Zepf's Hall and went home, still carrying the children, who had finally cried themselves to sleep. It might be noted that most of the men at Zepf's Hall that night were not anarchists, not socialists, but members of the Furniture Workers' Union, and they thought it was right for Parsons to go, they covered him. Mrs. Holmes went with them, and that was a good thing, because by now Lucy was going to pieces. Parsons himself was half dead from weariness, lack of sleep. And when he saw how Lucy was, he changed his mind and said he would stay. Then, after they put the children to bed, the women pleaded with him. Well, they convinced him that he should go. Lucy stayed with the kids, and Lizzie Holmes walked with him to the depot, and bought him a ticket for Turner Junction. She lived there, and her husband was at home. I know this isn't important. I just want to tell you, in the best way I can, about people who loved Parsons enough to risk their lives for him.

—You know what happened in the next few days. Every Pinkerton in the middle west was thrown into Chicago. They arrested maybe a thousand, but it was Parsons they wanted, and a Pinkerton who turned him up could have had ten thousand dollars from the businessmen's association alone. And when the charge against Parsons became murder, then anyone who sheltered him became an accessory. But just look at the whole thing again, just briefly, just with a little more patience, my friend, before I go on to finish my story of Parsons. First, they indict thirty-one men for this bomb-throwing from which one policeman died and God knows how many workers. Then a dozen are

selected to be charged with wilful murder. But one of them
has escaped and never returns. Three become witnesses for
the state. Eight are left, Parsons, August Spies, Michael
Schwab, Sam Fielden, who learned from me, remember
that, my friend, Sam Fielden whom I taught to fight for
his people, Adolph Fischer, George Engel, Oscar Neebe,
Louis Lingg—those eight are charged with murder.

—I don't have to go over the trial with you. Better, my
friend, that some day you will go over that trial, step by
step, word by word, line by line, and see whether ever
before such a mockery was made of justice, or what goes
for justice. No, we'll argue afterward. Now I don't have
to go into the incredible selection of jurors, the false testimony, the way Lingg was murdered in his cell, the way
these men were convicted, and the way their conviction
was upheld from the lowest to the highest court. Now,
only, I want to finish my story of Parsons. Only a few
minutes more.

—He went to the Holmes' house, where Mr. Holmes
gave him shelter. There he remained for a few days, and
then, because it was so close to Chicago, because Mrs.
Holmes had been arrested, he moved on. He shaved off
his mustache, became an itinerant worker, and moved on
to Wisconsin. He stayed with the Hoans, at Waukesha,
doing odd jobs, turning back to his old trade of carpenter.
You see, he was sheltered; in eight states, there were men
who would die for Parsons, and gladly. Am I sentimental?
How many had told me that when he came into a room,
it was like Christ entering! Then, because those who had
trusted him were on trial for their lives, because for him
there was no life underground, no life apart from the
working people, no life apart from his wife and children,
he came back to Chicago and gave himself up.

—The rest you know, how he appeared in court, how he went on trial, and how he was condemned, with the others, to be hanged by the neck today until he is dead. Then why am I bothering to speak about Parsons at all, and why should I bore you with this Haymarket affair, you who listen so patiently, when for a year and a half now, you have heard so much of it? Only this: when they die, something inside of me will die, and I do not want that something inside of me to be destroyed. Because you are Judge Pete Altgeld, and because I believe you are a different kind from the men I see in power.

—So I put in my pocket a statement from Captain Black, their lawyer. Last Tuesday, just before Lingg was found dead in his cell, Black went to see Parsons and begged him to plead for executive clemency. Because now people are being troubled that something like a saint should die. They are remembering that Christ was also accursed to those who ruled. So they say, if only Parsons pleaded for mercy, the governor would have pardoned him. Black went to Parsons and begged him to plead for mercy. Because if Parsons dies, something will die inside of Black too. But Parsons refused. It's a terrible thing to die, so how can I say it so simply? Parsons refused; he would not plead for his life. He explained why, and afterwards Black wrote down what he said. I just want to read that to you, and then I am through.

XIII

ON THE Judge's mantel, the clock, cradled between the expressionless busts of Minerva and Augustus, began to strike ten. The two men listened to the strokes. Schilling was drawing the paper from his pocket, and the Judge, as if loath to confront him, kept staring at the fireplace, where already only embers remained from the fine log.

"Shall I read it?" Schilling asked.

"I've missed court already."

"Maybe I've talked too much."

"Go ahead and read it," the Judge said coldly.

"All right," Schilling nodded. "Here is Parsons' statement. He said to Black: 'Captain, I know that you are right. I know that if I should sign this application for pardon, my sentence would be commuted. No longer ago than last Sunday night Melville E. Stone, the editor of the *Daily News*, spent nearly two hours in my cell, urging me to sign a petition, and assuring me that if I would do so I should have his influence and the influence of his paper in favor of the commutation of my sentence; and I know that means that my sentence would be commuted. But I will not do it. My mind is firmly and irrevocably made up, and I beg you to urge me no further upon the subject. I am an innocent man—innocent of this offense of which I have been found guilty by the jury, and the world knows my innocence. If I am to be executed at all, it is because I am an anarchist, not because I am a murderer; it is because of what I have taught and spoken and written in the past, and not because of the throwing of the Haymarket bomb. I can afford to be hung for the sake of the ideas I hold and the cause I have espoused if the people of the State of Illinois can afford to hang an innocent man who voluntarily placed himself in their power.

" 'And I will tell you, Captain, what is the real secret of my position, but in confidence. I do not want anything said about it until after the 11th. I have a hope—mark you, it is a very faint hope—but yet I do hope my attitude may result in the saving of those other boys—Lingg, Engel and

Fischer. Spies, Fielden and Schwab have already signed a petition for clemency. And if I should now separate myself from Lingg, Engel and Fischer, and sign a petition upon which the Governor could commute my sentence, I know that it would mean absolute doom to the others—that Lingg, Engel and Fischer would inevitably be hung. So I have determined to make their cause and their fate my own. I know the chances are 999 in 1,000 that I will swing with them; that there isn't one chance in a thousand of my saving them; but if they can be saved at all it is by my standing with them, so that whatever action is taken in my case may with equal propriety be taken in theirs. I will not, therefore, do anything that will separate me from them. I expect that the result will be that I shall hang with them, but I am ready.' "

Schilling finished, folded the paper, and said, "That is all." But the Judge was staring intently at the fire, and the ticking of the clock seemed to fill the entire room.

"That is all," Schilling said. "In a little while, Parsons will be hanged. In another hour, I think."

"Yes—"

"Five days ago, they murdered Louis Lingg, who was to die with the men today. That was not clever; that was stupid. When such things happen, even a judge in a stone house isn't safe."

"Now you're out of your head!" Altgeld said angrily, glad at last to have something to strike back with. "Lingg committed suicide, and when he did it, he killed whatever chance Parsons and the others had."

"Suicide! Has a man ever in this world committed suicide by putting a dynamite fuse in his mouth and igniting it, so that with half his face torn away he suffered the tortures of the damned before he died? And for effect,

there were little dynamite bombs found all over his cell.
My God, Pete, will you listen to me? They saw that maybe
it would be a terrible thing if Parsons and the others died;
they saw sympathy was changing. So they went into Lingg's
cell, beat him unconscious, planted those ridiculous little
bombs all around the cell, placed a fuse in his mouth, and
killed him. You live in a land where this happens. How
will you sleep at night?"

"You're excited," the Judge said. "Calm down."

"I'm excited—yes, I'm excited. I look at that clock over
there and count the minutes before they kill four men.
I'm excited! I came to you because I believe in you,
because I said to myself Pete Altgeld can pull down the
walls of that jail, even now."

"I can't."

"You could go to your phone. You could call the governor. You could fight! They might listen to you. No one
in this city is happy today."

"It would do no good."

Watching the Judge's face, anxiously, keenly, Schilling
accepted a verdict, appeared to grow old and tired at once,
and at the same time rose to go.

"Wait a minute," the Judge said.

"For what?"

"Let me say one word for myself, George! What kind of
a son of a bitch do you think I am?"

"It doesn't matter."

"You got a fire inside you, and you think anything you
touch will burn. My God, man, be sane! What good would
it do if I called the governor? Don't you understand there's
nothing I can do now? Nothing! It's too late. If you want
to blame me for before, then blame me. Ask me why I

didn't sign the petition. Ask me why I didn't let my voice be heard."

Schilling shook his head.

"Now it's too late for me to do anything, George."

"I got to go," Schilling said.

"Why don't you stay here? Let me give you a drink."

"I got to go," Schilling repeated.

"Sit down."

"It's all right," Schilling said, smiling slightly. "I'll see you tomorrow, the next day. I'm not angry at you. But I got to go."

"I could explain more fully—"

"You don't have to explain."

"Only the world doesn't end because Parsons dies. Pull yourself together. Even if these men are saints, the thing they represent is our enemy—"

"And that justifies their death?"

"Maybe it does. Justice isn't an abstraction, it's a function of—"

"Go on," Schilling said.

"George, go home and get some rest."

Emma came into the room. She stood at the doorway, watching them for a moment, and then she said, "George, will you have something to eat?"

He shook his head. "Thank you, Emma."

"Peters is on the phone—from court."

"Tell him to adjourn for the day."

"A reporter from the *Inter-Ocean* called," she said quietly. "He wanted to know if you have any statement on the execution." She hesitated a moment, and then added, "I told him, no."

"Thank you, Emma," the Judge said.

Schilling began to go. It was half past ten. The Judge asked, "Where are you going, George?" and the little carpenter answered, "I don't know." "I'm sorry, George." "It doesn't matter now," Schilling said. "I think I'll go out and walk for a while. It's a nice day." And then he left. Emma went to the door with him. When she came back, the Judge was still sitting as she had left him.

"Has it happened yet?" she asked.

"No—in a little while, I suppose."

"Schilling wanted you to do something, didn't he?"

"Yes."

"Can you do anything?"

The Judge shook his head.

"I don't think Schilling is angry with you," she said. "He has very high regard for you."

"Yes, I suppose so."

"Anyway, this horrible thing will be over."

"It will be over," the Judge said.

"I called Joe Martin's office, but he had left. I didn't want to say where he was in front of Schilling. He went to witness the hanging. I think that's disgusting. His secretary was very much excited. She said she'd get a message to him, and he'd come here later. Peters was pleased with having a holiday. Will you have lunch at home?"

"If you don't mind," the Judge said.

XIV

NOT long before this day, Judge Altgeld and his friend, Judge Lambert Tree, had lunched with Phil Armour, the great pork and beef king. Though both Altgeld and Tree were persons of note in Chicago, Armour maintained an attitude of amused condescension all during the meal. Altgeld, with all his innate dignity, found himself cringing under Armour's patronage, and when he tried to hit back, with wit, with sarcasm, with knowledge, he found Armour's bulk impervious to attack of that sort. In this fashion, Armour spoke of Altgeld's book, *Our Penal Machinery and its Victims:*

"I hear you been writing, Altgeld. Got a book out."

"That's so," Altgeld said.

"No harm in writing. I suppose you've done some writing too, Tree."

"Very little," Judge Tree said.

"I don't mind you boys writing," Armour said. "As a matter of fact, the ladies are kind of impressed by your book, Altgeld. We like a judge to show some brains—after the kind King Mike McDonald dropped on us. A judge isn't just a cheap ward politician; you boys got to get up there and show your faces each day."

"I see," Altgeld said. He was incapable of saying anything more.

"But there's a time and a place," Armour continued. "We have some very bad elements here in Chicago."

"Yes, I guess we have."

"Nothing else to do but to make a decent, law-abiding city out of it. A place where a workingman can do a fair day's work for a fair day's wages, without worrying about having his throat cut."

Altgeld could only nod.

"And for that, we need a police force," Armour went on. "Pretty fine fellers on the force. They're not helped by psalm-singing for the poor, abused criminal. Jesus God, Altgeld, there's no point in attacking jails. It won't help your career to become a damned reformer. Charity is one thing; you could live five years on what I give charity in one; but when you attack the very foundation of society, then you sound damn like a communist."

"And you consider jails to be the foundation of society?" Altgeld asked lamely.

"Law and order. That's what I refer to, law and order. When we make a judge, we expect him to stand for law and order. When we break him, it's because he doesn't stand for those things. There's a lot of talk about you being a radical. We don't like that kind of talk."

"Whom do you mean by 'we'?" Altgeld asked.

Armour spread his hands and smiled. "You know what I say—I say, no hard feelings. Have your secretary send me a bill; I'll buy a few hundred copies of the book myself. Maybe your next book will be about honest, hard-working citizens. I don't want to discourage you, young man. Now how about a brandy?"

And Altgeld, raging inside, sat there, impotent; now he recalled that luncheon and mixed thoughts of it with thoughts of the four men who were about to die. Schilling had come and spoken and gone, and now Altgeld wondered how much truth there was in Schilling's contention that he, one man, at this eleventh hour, could reverse the course of the law, or even halt it. Much of what Schilling had said he agreed with. Judge Gary, who tried the case of the Haymarket defendants, had been flagrantly partisan. The question of who threw the bomb had been crudely moved aside, and eight men were condemned to death, not because they were murderers, but because they were militant leaders of labor and therefore enemies of one part of society; so it was put up to him, Pete Altgeld, whether they were his enemies too. Even if he could truthfully tell himself that anything he might have attempted would have been futile—as futile as the attempts of his friend, Judge

Tree, to gain mercy for the condemned men—he still faced the question of how he would have acted had he been in another position, as for example in the position of Governor Oglesby. That was the question which stirred a hundred doubts inside of him, mixing so curiously with his recollection of Phil Armour, and what Armour had said, and the matter-of-fact disposal of democracy, which contends that servants of the people are elected by the people, not made by a handful of men. And while cynicism was easy in the normal course of things, and taken for granted in the normal course of things, so that one never raised one's voice against the pattern in which one lived, the pattern of adultery mixed with respectability, of graft mixed with the time-worn democratic slogans, of vice supporting charity and religion, and religion by inaction condoning vice, of filth and suffering and death turned into profits and men turned into beasts; while these matters and a hundred more like them were accepted easily and naturally day in and day out, today they became symbols of four men close to death: and thereby they stuck in a man's craw rather than sliding easily down his throat. They stuck in Judge Altgeld's craw, and what had been only a few hours ago a lovely fall day now turned sour and uncomfortable.

He could not deny that he was a success, nor could he tell himself that he did not enjoy the very practical fruits of success. All of his life, until now, he had fought for these things; born with nothing, raised with a lash, he had broken through; he was here. He was in his stone house, secure and comfortable. There were beautiful things in his house; there was food, many kinds of food, all of it very good to eat, and if he should want other food, he had only to say so. There was warmth in the house; there was comfort too. There was his wife, so very good-looking and well bred, and there were the many friends she had made for him, also well bred, people of substance if in some cases tedious, and they accepted him and did not remind him of his origins, and played cards with him and gave him their legal business. Nor did his wife resent his having friends of another kind, like Joe Martin, the gambler, or Schilling, the labor leader, or Bro Kelly, the ward-heeler who was a political genius; and all of his friends, even Schilling, paid tribute to his success and position. What if he had memories! All men had memories, and memories were as impractical as abstract justice. Why did he resent Armour's bluntly pointing out that these things he had were retained by the grace of certain individuals, and that his compact with those same individuals must be a real one, not an illusory one?

Yet, in the essence of it, he hated not so much Armour as what Armour stood for; and now this hatred burned through all his thoughts. Reason he might—but in the end what came out? He was a dirty, cheap political climber. He had to tell himself, "Accept that, Altgeld, accept it!" He stood up and paced back and forth, watching the clock. Then he sat down in his chair, still watching the clock. The minutes ticked off, and during one of those minutes, four men died.

His wife called him to lunch, but he ate only a few mouthfuls. Then he went back to his study.

XV

JOE MARTIN stretched out his feet to the fire and lit a cigar. As he took the first few puffs, he watched Altgeld shrewdly. Then it was a little after two o'clock.

"What time did they die?" Altgeld asked.

"About noon."

"Was it bad?"

"The first time I saw an execution. The last too."

"It was that bad?"

"Well, that's a peculiar way to put it. I don't like executions. I can see men die, but not after they've known about it for months, and also know just when the trap's going to be sprung."

"What about Parsons?"

"He died game. They all did."

"Did he say anything?"

"Last words? I don't know. There were about two hundred people in there, watching. I was in back with Kelly. Just about that time, Kelly was asking me if I thought any of them was Catholic; I didn't know. Afterward someone said that Parsons demanded that they let him speak, and then they sprung the trap. But I heard Spies. He sounded off right across the yard. Do you know what he said?"

"What?"

"He said, there will come a time when our silence will be more powerful than the voices you strangle today. You know, funny thing about those damn reds, they got a kind of guts I never seen. Take Parsons; I went into his cell this morning with Wertzer of the *Tribune*. Wertzer said he was going to sketch him today, come hell or high water. I felt funny about it, but Wertzer said, you want to see this character, don't you, you want to be able to tell your grandchildren you seen him. There was also the little matter that Wertzer couldn't get in without me pulling the strings. So we come in there, and this Parsons—he could go on the stage with that face of his—is sitting there at a little table, dressed, shaved, wearing slippers, and writing.

Al, the guard says, Al, there's a guy here from the *Tribune* to draw you. Meanwhile, the guard nudges me. Pete, I felt mad, so damn mad I could have laid out him and Wertzer, right there. I never liked Wertzer; he's a little snotnose, and I felt like a damn fool for being pulled into this. But Parsons isn't disturbed. He puts down his pen, turns to face us, smiles a little, and begins to roll a cigarette. I feel you can tell a lot from the way a man rolls; Parsons does it carefully and slowly; doesn't lose any tobacco, seals it with one swipe, and lights it on one match. I want to sketch you, Mr. Parsons, Wertzer says. This is the last chance to break the news—the little son of a bitch! But Parsons takes it calmly. I have some work to do, he says, and not much time. Wertzer says, It's a living, Mr. Parsons. I got to come in with my assignment, or I'll be out of a job too. So Parsons nods and says, all right. I know what it is to have to take an assignment. And all the time Wertzer sketches him, I'm standing there—my God, Pete, I never felt like that before. Once Parsons looks at me kind of peculiar and says, You're Joe Martin? I say, Right. I met you once, he says, but I guess you don't remember. But I swear to God, Pete, he was not afraid. Look, I don't like a communist any better than the next man, but I wouldn't have the guts to sit there and know that I was going to die in a few hours, and then carry it off the way he did."

"You're a gambler—"

"Sure, but you're not playing for a break when you got a rope around your neck."

Altgeld rose, went to the fire, and poked it alive. Then, still crouched, he faced Martin, as if the thought had just occurred to him. "Joe, I want you to tell me the truth. You know it, if any man does. Did the police murder Lingg?"

Martin leaned back and puffed on his cigar. Altgeld straightened up and stood there, one arm on the mantel, looking at the sheeplike features of Augustus.

"Well?"

"That's a hell of a question, Pete. What do you think?"

"I know what I think. I know what anyone with any brains in this city thinks. I know what happened too. But when you've sat on a bench for even a month, you know what circumstantial evidence is worth. There were eight so-called anarchists tried and condemned to death to begin with. Then public opinion began to be felt; it's as amusing as hell that we still have something left in this country which is called public opinion and which can be felt, but we have. So the sentences of three of these men, Fielden, Schwab, and Neebe are commuted. They can rot in jail, but jail is one thing and legal murder is another, and public opinion is appeased—just a little. And no harm is done, since the two they want to get, Parsons and Spies, are still on their way to the gallows. But then, there's more of this public opinion, mass meetings, petitions, pleas, messages from other countries. And then, very suddenly, Louis Lingg is found dying in his cell, half his face blown off by a dynamite fuse, and little bombs are cached all over his cell. So public opinion is diverted, and it is proved that once a bomb-thrower always a bomb-thrower, even if he throws them into his own mouth and closes it forever. Don't smile. I'm a judge; and I say this man committed suicide until it is proved otherwise."

"What do you want, a signed statement?" Martin asked softly.

"I asked you a question."

"It's still one hell of a question. Suppose I knew. Suppose I even knew who threw the bomb. Would I tell you,

Pete? I like you; I've said it and I'll say it to your face—there's only one politician in Illinois I trust, and that's Pete Altgeld; but I don't trust you that much. I play my cards, you see, but I hold them close. My big stake is down there in City Hall; I never ratted on anyone, Pete."

"That's all?"

"No. I'll tell you what I think; I think that before a man killed himself by putting a dynamite charge in his mouth, you'd have to club him quiet and pry his jaws open. All right. These four gents are dead. I watched them die. And in the past year, I heard a lot of loose talk about them. But I don't talk loose; I found it pays off to keep your mouth shut. A lot of big operators will sleep sound tonight. I may hate their guts, but I got no quarrel with them. I'm just a gambler—a tinhorn gambler."

"And I'm a tinhorn politician."

"Some might say that," Martin agreed softly.

For a while, Martin smoked placidly and quietly, Altgeld watching him from his place by the mantel. Then the Judge walked to a chair, sat down, and said, very precisely:

"Joe, what kind of a stake would you play me for?"

"A damn big one."

"How far do you think I'll go?"

"If you keep your head and play it level, a long way."

"How far?"

"How far do you want to go? If you were born in this country, I'd say maybe to the White House. As it is, the Senate, if you want that, or the governor's mansion."

"How do I play it?"

"You play it for all it's worth, that's all. Or you play it safe. Sometimes they play it safe, and the big operators like that better."

"But either way, it's the big operators?"

"What do you think?" Joe Martin said.

XVI

THIS took place on Friday; the next day, newspapers, in addition to detailed accounts of the execution and many editorials on the men who had died, law and order, democracy, the Constitution and its many amendments—some of which are called the Bill of Rights—the Revolution, the Founding Fathers, and the War Between the States, carried notices of the funeral. The city authorities had allowed relatives and friends to reclaim the bodies of the five dead men, Lingg, who had died in his cell, Parsons, Spies, Engel, and Fischer. The city permitted these same friends and relatives to hold a public funeral, if they so pleased. Mayor Roche named a series of streets along which the funeral procession might proceed on its way to Waldheim Cemetery. The hours were from twelve to two o'clock. No music except funeral dirges might be played; no arms were to be borne; no signs or banners were to be displayed. It was to be expected, the newspapers said, that even though these men were the proven enemies of society, criminals, murderers, a few hundred people might well turn out to witness the last rites. And in accordance with that part of the Constitution which guarantees freedom of religion, it was only just to allow those rites to take place.

On Sunday, the Judge told his wife that he was going out for a stroll; and though Emma suspected where the stroll would take him, she said nothing, nor did she remark that it was curious, his wanting to go out alone on a Sunday morning. As a matter of fact, it was not so curious; making for the line of march, he realized that he was only one of many, many thousands of Chicago citizens; and presently it seemed that nearly half the city would be lined up along the drab, dirty streets, waiting for the procession.

It was a cold morning; that and the fact that he had little desire to be seen made him turn up the collar of his coat and pull his hat down. He jammed his hands into his pockets, shifted from one chilled foot to another, and waited.

Presently, the funeral procession came into sight. It was not what he might have expected; certainly not what the city authorities expected when they granted permission for the funeral to be held. There was no music, no sound other than the slow tread of feet and the soft sobbing of women. And with that, all other sounds, all other noises appeared to die away, as if a great and woeful pall of silence overhung the whole city.

First, there came a man with a flag, the only flag in the whole procession, a worn and faded Stars and Stripes that had marched proudly at the head of a regiment in the Civil War; and the man who carried it was a veteran, a middle-aged man with a face like gray stone.

Then came the hearses and the caskets; then the carriages in which the families rode. They were old, open carriages. In one of them Altgeld saw Lucy Parsons, sitting with her two children, staring straight ahead of her.

Then came the close friends, the comrades of those who had died. They walked four abreast, and their faces too were gray, like the face of the Civil War veteran.

Then came a group of well-dressed men and women, many of whom Altgeld knew and recognized. They were lawyers, judges, doctors, teachers, small businessmen, and many others who had come into the fight to save the five dead men.

Then came the workers, and to them, apparently, there was no end. They were from the packing houses, the lumber yards, the McCormick plant, and the Pullman plant; they were from the mills, the fertilizer pits, the railyards, and the canneries; they were from the flophouses of the unemployed, from the road, from the wheatfields, from the streets of Chicago and a dozen other cities. Many were in their best, the one good suit, the black suit in which they were married; many had their wives with them; children walked with them too, and some carried children in their arms. But there were enough who had no other clothes than the clothes they worked in, and they wore their overalls, their blue jeans, and their flannel shirts. There were cowhands who had ridden five hundred miles and more to Chicago, thinking that where men believed and willed, this thing could be stopped; and when it had not been stopped, they stayed to walk in the procession in their awkward, high-heeled boots. There were red-faced farmers from the prairies about the city, there were locomotive engineers, and there were sailors from the Great Lakes.

There were also hundreds and hundreds of policemen and Pinkerton operatives along the line of march, but when they saw this they stood quietly, put away the guns they had in their hands, and stared at the ground.

For the workers were quiet. You could hear their breathing and you could hear the crunching tread of their feet, but there was no word you could hear. No one spoke; not the men, not the women, not even the children. Nor did any of the people who lined the streets break the silence.

And still the workers came on. For an hour Altgeld

stood there, and still they came, shoulder to shoulder, their faces like stone, the tears running slowly and unwiped. Another hour, yet there was no end to them; how many thousands had passed, he could not guess, nor could he guess how many thousands more were to come; but he knew one thing: that never before in the history of the land, not even when the most beloved of all leaders, Abe Lincoln, had died, was there such a funeral as this.

Part Three

THE FIRST VARIATION

ON A CLEAR, WINDY DAY, IN
the first part of March of 1893, a lawyer, Clarence Darrow
by name, walked across the lawn in front of the Statehouse
at Springfield, mounted the steps, entered, and in a firm
and crisp tone announced that he desired to see the Governor. His manner was so preconceived and so intent that
the Governor's secretary, who knew Darrow, grinned and
asked, as one well might, "Is something burning?"

"That's right."

"Does he expect you?"

"He expects me," Darrow said. "I phoned and told him
I was coming. Won't he see me?"

"Sure he'll see you. Catch your breath. Sit down."

Darrow seated himself in the reception room, and repeated over and over, in his mind, just what he intended
to say. Lest his heat cool and his courage vanish, he en-
larged upon what he had originally intended, and, still in
his mind, he directed the conversation, phrase by phrase,
to the conclusion he intended. All of this served to anger
him, and when he was finally ushered into the Governor's
office, he felt more like a judge than a pleader at the bar.
But the Governor, who had not long ago been a judge,
smiled and extended his hand:

"Good to see you, Clarence."

"Good to see you, sir," he nodded, thinking that for one who had recently been ill, as the result of the most dynamic gubernatorial campaign the State of Illinois had ever known, Governor John Peter Altgeld looked surprisingly well, surprisingly fit, his blue eyes as alert as ever, his handshake as firm and as warm. As some said, he showed signs of age, signs of the recurrent bouts of malaria he constantly faced, and there were streaks of gray in his beard; but there was no doubting the fact that he was one of those men whom age improved, at least in physical appearance, and Darrow could well understand the pleasure so many got from simply looking at that face of his; but, perversely, this too increased the lawyer's annoyance, and though Darrow was less than ten years younger than the Governor, who was forty-five, he felt like an indignant boy before a very mature man—the more so when Altgeld said:

"I thought this might be a social call, but it isn't, is it, Clarence?"

"No, it isn't."

"Business?"

"You might call it that."

"Well, sit down then. You want a cigar?"

"No. I'd rather stand."

"All right."

The Governor sat behind his desk. Staring at the edge of the desk, not at the Governor, Darrow said, "It's about the Haymarket people, about Fielden and Schwab and Neebe."

"Is it? What about them?" Just the trace of an edge had come into the Governor's voice, not too much; he liked Darrow; he liked him immensely, though not entirely as a friend; those who knew the Governor well also knew that he had very few friends in the real sense of the word.

"They're still in jail," Darrow said.

"I know they're in jail."

"This isn't pleasant for me," Darrow said, still avoiding the Governor's eyes. "It's no more pleasant for me than it is for you. But maybe someone has to remind you."

"Remind me of what?" the Governor asked.

"Of the fact," Darrow rushed on, "that thousands of us voted for you for governor because it was understood that you would pardon these three men. It's three months since you took office—"

"How was it understood?" Altgeld asked. "I don't seem to have understood it."

Darrow reacted quickly and antagonistically; his face and eyes told the Governor as much as words.

"Wait a minute, wait a minute," Altgeld said. He was keeping his own temper in leash. "Before you write me off as a Judas, recall what I said. I said I'll look into this. I said I'll examine the case of the anarchists. Don't pull a knight in armor on me; I know how you feel about this. You're in a good spot to feel that way."

"What do you mean?"

"I mean that if and when I pardon those three men, the world will fall down around my ears."

"I don't agree with that," Darrow said.

"No? You come storming in here to tell me what you do and don't agree with. I made no promises! What you thought—my God, I sit and listen, and I ought to throw you to hell out!"

"All right," Darrow said. "All right. Throw me out."

"Don't be an idiot. Sit down. Talk sense."

Darrow said, "Sit down and talk sense, yes. Sit down and

be made to feel like a damn fool for coming in here and walking where the angels fear to tread. Why don't you remind me what an ungrateful swine I am? Who started me in politics—Altgeld. Who put me where I am now—Altgeld."

"I wasn't going to remind you. Only of the fact that I never promised to pardon the anarchists. That's all. I never promised. I'll look into the case. Then I'll do what I think should be done."

"That's all?"

"Yes, that's all. Damn it all, Clarence, don't be an idiot. Don't talk to me about justice. Those men are in jail for the same reason Parsons and the others died, because it suits the best interests of a lot of very powerful gentlemen. I knew that five years ago; should I be more ignorant of it now that I'm Governor? Should I throw away everything I've fought for, hoped for, dreamed of because you have a sentimental ax to grind?"

"Everyone would support you—"

"Don't be a fool! No one will support me."

"The people elected you."

"What kind of drivel are you talking? If there's one thing on God's earth that I know by now, it's politics. So don't extend your homilies to me. When Cregier was elected mayor, and you as a result of that election got your job with the city, it was not the people of Chicago who elected him, but me—on my own. Do I have to repeat the lesson for you? I made the Anti-Machine Ticket; I created it; I paid for it, five thousand dollars and cheap at the price; and I did it because I hate Roche's guts. So don't give me lessons in politics or in political morality. Parsons believed in morality, and he is dead as a doornail."

"I see," Darrow nodded.

"You don't see a devil of a lot," Altgeld said.

II

YET he smarted after Clarence Darrow had gone. The young fool, to come in like that, to presume! To do it like a knight crusader, and to walk out with righteous indignation cloaking him! Childish as it was, Altgeld counted score against Darrow; by what right did he presume? He, Darrow, was a corporation lawyer; his interest in the three Haymarket survivors was romantic and idealistic, while the very people he served had originally led the blood hunt; yet he dared to speak of understandings. There was no understanding, the Governor repeated to himself; my hands are clean; they knew what they were getting: they were getting a politician who could bring the party into Springfield.

Sitting at his desk now, in the Governor's office, he put the label of politician on himself unashamedly. He had learned a trade, and he had learned it well, and he had no illusions, and he had a measure of contempt for those who lived by illusions. It often took a long time for a man to see things clearly, but when at last he saw them clearly, if his stomach was strong enough, he could go a long way, a remarkably long way.

As long as the road John Peter Altgeld had traveled; and where that road ended he still did not know, whether in the United States Senate, or in the cabinet, or in some other place equally high and equally hollow; for after a point, it ceased to be a process of selling out. The ethic and the morality were laid aside; you played the game within its framework, and within that framework it could even be pleasant and life could present a good many compensations. It could have the tense excitement of his triumph over Mayor Roche of Chicago, where, single-handed, he had split the regular ticket, set up a completely opportunist liberal ticket, handpicked his lesser candidates, second-rate reformers who had no chance of election, and then headed his ticket with the regular party candidate he supported. Twelve thousand of the liberal Chicago votes fell for his "anti-machine" bait, and voted for the machine candidate he supported. And when it was over, only a dozen men in Chicago knew that Pete Altgeld had pulled the strings; but the dozen men were important, and the tribute they paid him, over their cigars, in their clubs, and in the back rooms where whisky mingled with rewards, was worth more than a million dollars in cold cash. As to the price of his revenge on Mayor Roche, that could not be estimated; for Roche had committed the worst kind of betrayal that a man in Altgeld's circle could commit—he had fought and exposed Altgeld on a small piece of the mountain of spoils each and every politician concerned with Chicago squeezed out of its citizens.

III

LEANING back in his leather seat after Clarence Darrow had left, Altgeld turned over in his mind the case of these three men, Neebe, Fielden, and Schwab, three men in prison who remained as a gnawing echo of the famous, or perhaps infamous, Haymarket bombing. Do as he would, Darrow's attack had an effect on him; and what Darrow had said was in the thoughts of many others.

A long time ago, his wife had said that this Haymarket thing was like a sickness pervading all of Chicago, yet when the men died the sickness was not, as so many thought, cured. Not only did three living reminders remain in prison, but the presence of Parsons, dead though he was, would not leave Chicago. Parsons lived in the stonegray faces of the men who had marched in his funeral; he lived in the badly printed circulars; he lived in the picket lines, becoming more and more common in Chicago; he lived in his wife too. It would have been romantic to say that Altgeld dwelled overheavily on Parsons, once Parsons was dead; the Judge was a busy man, a successful man, a rich man; as he was fond of telling his friends, he lived a very full life. But now and again, that dark, handsome face intruded, and since no words were spoken, no accusations made, Judge Altgeld could not beat it down as he had beaten down those others who opposed him.

Three times, too, in the six years gone by, he had met Lucy Parsons. That was not strange, since Lucy Parsons, after her husband's death, became as much a part of Chicago as the dirty streets, the unspeakable slums, and the packing houses. Her dark face, aged considerably, became more Indian-like than ever; and she hid her sorrow under a tight, pain-drawn mask.

The first time Altgeld met her, he did not know who she was, but stopped on the street, his attention arrested by the intense face of the woman as well as by what she was saying. She wore an old and ragged man's coat which was fastened at the throat with a large blanket-pin. Her hair was wrapped in a kerchief, and the sole of one shoe was held on by a piece of string. Next to her was a small wooden stand, piled high with books. It was a cold winter's day, with twilight hard by, and the few people on the streets were hurrying to the warmth of their homes and families. But the title on the books caught Altgeld's eye, and that, in conjunction with the woman's words, "Justice shall not perish from the earth while a spark of courage remains—" made him pause and pick one up. The title of the book was *Life of Albert R. Parsons.*

"How much is it?" he asked.

"A dollar. But take more than one. Take more than one and strike a blow for freedom. Give it away."

He got a dollar out of his wallet, but when the woman saw the rich leather, the gold corners, the fat stack of bills inside, her face changed. She gave him the book and said no more, except to answer him, when he asked wasn't she Mrs. Parsons, with:

"Yes, I'm his wife."

He tried to give her five dollars; and when she refused it, he found himself walking away very quickly. At home, he glanced through the book. Published by Lucy Parsons— how, with what funds, he could not imagine—it was a compilation of Parsons' writings, newspaper articles, letters, and speeches, along with some comments and poems certain friends had sent her. He read only fragments of it, yet two parts remained in his mind. The first was the dedication of the book, to Parsons by his wife: "This book is lovingly dedicated to the sacred memory of one whose only crime was that he lived in advance of his time, my beloved husband, companion and comrade, Albert R. Parsons." The other part that Altgeld remembered so vividly was the facsimile reproduction of Parsons' last letter to his children, both what it said and the amazing gentleness of the handwriting; for, as he remarked almost shamefacedly to Emma, in the very manner in which the letters were formed was something close to a benediction apart from these words:

Dungeon No. 7
Cook County Jail
Chicago, Ill. Nov. 9th. 1887

To my Darling, Precious Children:
        Albert R. Parsons Jr. and his sister,
        Lulu Eda Parsons:

As I write this word I blot your names with a tear. We never meet again. Oh, my children, how deeply, dearly your Papa loves you. We show our love by living for our loved ones, we also prove our love by dying, when necessary, for them. Of my life and the cause of my unnatural and cruel death, you will learn from others. *Your Father is a self-offered Sacrifice upon the Altar of Liberty and Happiness.* To you, I leave the legacy of an honest name and duty done. Preserve it, emulate it. Be true to yourselves, you cannot then be false to others. Be industrious, sober and cheerful. Your mother! Ah, she is the grandest, noblest of women. Love, honor and obey her.

My children, my precious ones, I request you to read this parting message on each recurring anniversary of my Death in remembrance of him who dies not alone for you, but for the children yet unborn. Bless you, my Darlings. Farewell.

                Your Father, Albert R. Parsons.

Emma, however, was not impressed by this letter, and Altgeld, though he read it to himself a dozen times over, did not press his feelings on his wife. Out of his childlessness, children became a mystery; he stopped to look at them in the streets, and he was very good with his friends' children; but sometimes, when he thought too much about them, they gave him a sensation of woeful emptiness, and he half suspected that emptiness was present in a far more cutting way in Emma.

His second meeting with Lucy Parsons came shortly after the first. In the early spring of that year, 1889, he was asked to address the Economic Conference Forum on the subject of Prison Reform. That was fitting, for who was better informed than the author of *Our Penal Machinery and its Victims?* It was in such a mood that Altgeld came to the meeting, in a mood of liberal determination, his mind made up that he would speak forthrightly and plainly, saying what he thought, the newspapers be damned. He half expected to be the scapegoat of the affair, to emerge through a welter of bitter editorials the following day; and he had learned that such editorials on such a subject generally did more good than harm; but it turned out quite differently, and instead of being the scapegoat he became the hero of the next day's press. A group of labor people were in the audience, and when the discussion began, Lucy Parsons got the floor and demanded:

"Judge Altgeld!"

"Yes?"

"Judge Altgeld, will you deny that your jails are filled with the children of the poor, not the children of the rich? Will you deny that men steal because their bellies are empty? Will you dare to state that any of these lost sisters you speak of enjoy going to bed with ten and twenty miserable men in one night and having their insides burn like they were branded?"

A storm of protest broke out; cries of "Disgraceful!" and "Disgusting!" came from all over the hall. A parson rose, waving his umbrella wildly and calling for the floor.

Others hissed. But Judge Altgeld, as the papers pointed out the following day, acted admirably. He spread his arms and quelled the tumult. He demanded order and imposed it. He said, "A lady has the floor. Can we condemn courtesy by showing ourselves so discourteous?" And then, turning to Mrs. Parsons, he said, "Please finish your statement, Mrs. Parsons, and then, if you wish, I will answer you."

So it was the notorious Lucy Parsons! The hall hushed, and Mrs. Parsons, who had remained on her feet, went on:

"What is the approach of you who talk reform, preach reform, and make a sleigh of reform upon which you will ride into heaven? How do you solve things? Judge Altgeld advocates gray suits for the prisoners instead of striped suits. He advocates constructive work, good books, and large, clean cells. Rightly enough, he says that the hardened criminal should be kept apart from the first offender. Being a judge himself, I am not surprised that he talks so much of justice, for even if a thing is nowhere present, it is good that it should be discussed. No, I am not attacking Judge Altgeld. I am with him when he talks of the horror of clubbing. I know. I was clubbed, not once but many times. I bear the scars. But I will not rise to your reform bait. This is your society, Judge Altgeld; you helped to build and create it, and it is this society that makes the criminal. A woman becomes a prostitute because it's a little better than dying of hunger. A man becomes a thief because your system turns him into an outlaw. He sees your ethics, which are the ethics of wild beasts, and yet you jail him because he uses those ethics. And if the workers unite to fight for food, for a better way of life, you jail them too. And the sop to your conscience is reform, always reform. No, so long as you preserve this system and its ethics, **your jails will be full of men and women who** choose life to death, and who take life as you force them to take it, through crime."

She sat down and a quiet audience waited. When Judge Altgeld answered, his voice was admirably controlled; he acted as befitted a judge of the commonwealth. "My dear Mrs. Parsons," he said, "arguments on a certain level demand an answer on the same level. Since you deprecate the decent workingman who holds down a job and brings home comfort and sustenance to his wife and children, I must rise in his defense. Hard work, industry, and thrift do not promote crime; quite the reverse. The honest workingman shuns crime, as does the honest employer; although I do not deny that specimens of both classes now walking about belong in jail. You say the system promotes criminals—perhaps, but I answer that it is the best system man has been able to devise, and it is only by sincere and intelligent reform that the evils within it will be lessened and finally done away with. I don't deny the evils; but I face them practically, and I recommend the same practical course to those utopians who would prefer that everything be cast in the waste basket."

As the papers said, a rousing chorus of applause greeted this, and although certain elements at the meeting continued to heckle the Judge, they had little effect on the mass of the audience.

That was the second time he saw Lucy Parsons. The third time, nearly a year later, he was driving with Judge Tree through the packing-house district and he saw her walking on a picket line, only a dozen yards from the road. Altgeld pulled in his horse and said to Tree:

"See that woman there?"

"Which?"

"The one with the dark face and the gray coat. She has a yellow handkerchief around her neck."

"Yes?"

"That's Lucy Parsons," Altgeld said.

At that moment she looked at them, but if she recognized Altgeld she gave no sign of it. As they drove away, Tree remarked:

"She's trying to clear her husband's name, isn't she?"

"I imagine so. They seem to have been very devoted."

Tree said, "She won't help things by being mixed up in strikes."

Those were the three times, but they ran through a period of half a dozen years, and it could hardly be said that the Governor was troubled greatly, either by those meetings, or by the memory of Parsons as Schilling had described him. Yet now, after the scene with Darrow, his thoughts ranged over the many matters concerning the Haymarket affair, that most curious case which would not rest, either by virtue of a hangman's scaffold or a prison cell.

He smiled wryly at the thought that he, who almost alone of liberal Chicago citizens had held back from signing the clemency petition, should be dogged and needled by this wretched case. The details of it were vague in his memory by now, and sometimes he wondered why it bulked so large with such different men as George Schilling and Clarence Darrow, why there should be in existence now a new petition signed by thousands of names ready to be presented to him. It was true that at the time, although he had not followed the case too closely in the newspapers, it had struck him as a miscarriage of justice, but in the essence justice was a stout, blind lady, and the man who had a dollar for each miscarriage she had suffered would be unnaturally wealthy, even here in Chicago.

He was annoyed by the way the matter followed him; he had a large and complex job ahead of him, and didn't he have the right to work as other men did, with a direct relation to practical problems? Another of those damned, mysterious cyclic depressions had hit the state, and soon he would be facing a rash of strikes, lockouts, pleas from both labor and capital; there would be the question of the unemployed; the state institutions were in miserable condition; and the state schools were something to weep at. Also, with a certain grim satisfaction, he faced the prospect of cleaning out the rest of his political enemies, as well as the opponents of his party. It was a man-sized job and more, and yet like a small, malignant cancer, this Haymarket affair kept inserting itself—as if he had been elected Governor in relation to that and nothing else.

Wistfully, he recalled the first after-flush of the election victory. The Democrats were back in, and it was like tilting a thousand-gallon bucket of champagne and sending it flowing. Black bowler hats were transformed to shining silk, and night after night the lights shone on a sea of gleaming shirtfronts. Civil War vets, Democratic stalwarts, beginning to age considerably, pledged toasts to the "Solid South," and millionaire pork and beef kings, millionaire lumbermen, and millionaire railroaders, toasted the people's party. The Judge, soon to be the Governor, loved it, and though night after night it was the same, fatuous speeches describing his town-to-town buckboard campaign, his astuteness, his brilliance, he did not tire. Emma tired first, pleading that his health would not stand it, recognizing the signs of those constantly recurrent malarial attacks; but this was a reward he would taste fully. Not even the legend

of the Ugly Duckling did justice to this, and if he drank
too much, ate too much, slept too little, danced too much,
well, a man lived once and died completely.

In that mood, recalling such recent pleasantness, he was
found by his wife as twilight crept into his large, ma-
hogany-fitted office. He looked up to meet her inquiring
gaze.

"Do you want the lights on?" she asked him.

Smiling, he shook his head; he still had such pride in
Emma, she was such a well-turned, well-dressed woman,
whether a lawyer's wife, or a judge's, or the hostess in the
executive mansion! Her hair, graying a little, was as it
should be, and so was her face and her figure. If he did not
gain from marriage what others set such store by, he did
have certain values he appreciated completely.

"I'll go with you, my dear," he said. "Can we have an
early dinner?"

"For any special reason?"

"I'm going to Chicago tonight," the Governor said.

IV

THE trip from Springfield to Chicago, covering that
same unnatural separation of capital from center of com-
merce that exists in so many states, was a long and tire-
some one; and generally the Governor would conquer bore-
dom through work, or sleep, or companionship—cigars,
whisky, and a private room lightening and shortening the
two hundred-odd miles. Not that he cared much for
liquor, but his friends did, and he enjoyed slouching into
one of the big leather chairs the railroad put at his disposal, and listening to the stories told and the comments
passed. He never actually broke down his reserve, a wall of

protection he had long ago created; and that feeling of apartness gave him almost a spectator's position. Thus he could be together and comfortable with men he despised as well as with men he liked, nor did the talk of the cheap politicians, the ward-heelers, the county men, the old party hacks, and the rising speculators bite deep enough to move him to disgust. He could watch them, listen to them, hear their onerously repetitious dirty stories, listen to discussion of extramatrimonial affairs, and yet remain aloof. And if he tired of the whole thing, he could pick up a book and read, and his friends would look at each other and then lower their voices, so as not to disturb the Governor.

But, tonight, he brought no work with him and he went alone, without even a secretary. The porter had made up his bed, but though it was late, he had no great desire for sleep. He was on one of those journeys which are made as much to get away from one place as to go to another; and the fact that he had laid out a program for Chicago, a program that was in some ways a direct response to Darrow's insolence, gave him no peace of mind. He recognized that he had to take action and put this Haymarket specter in its grave. He would go to his office in the Unity Block, and he would operate from there for a day; that would be soothing. He would call on his friends and demand their instant appearance. Joe Martin would come; so would Schilling and Tree and Mayor Cregier and King Mike McDonald, who bossed the city, and half a dozen more; and some would give advice, some would plead, some would shout at him. Yet he knew that nothing of what they said would matter particularly; the upshot of it was already decided in his own mind. He would get the records, review the case, stretch out the review while he felt the temper of the public, and then crawl through the only loophole. Instead of writing any decision on the fairness or unfairness of the trial, the impartiality of judge or jury or appeal courts, he would extend to the three men the mercy of the sovereign state, saying, in so many words: "You have been punished enough; go and sin no more." Thereby, he would be merciful; he would be magnanimous; he would put the beast to rest, nor would he incur the enmity of certain forces. It was a weasel move put into weasel words, but almost no one would so term it. Only he, John Peter Altgeld, taking that course would realize the full implications of it.

He undressed and got into bed, but still he could not sleep, even though the jolting of a Pullman car usually acted like a bromide. Instead, his thoughts raced here and there with restless, pounding annoyance. He sought for an ethic, but there was no ethic; he recalled what Lucy Parsons had said, and in his mind he composed arguments against her. In his mind, he arranged his investments; he totaled his wealth, recalled how he had run ten thousand into a hundred thousand, and a hundred thousand into a million. He was the *millionaire governor!* What was he fighting? Why should he nail himself onto a cross of three miserable labor agitators? What earthly sense did it make? When he could free them so easily, with the same harmless bit of equivocation that a hundred other governors had used, why should he resist that thought? Why should he lie awake and fight a conclusion he had already come to?

If he took the other path, if he decided that the three men were innocent, had always been innocent—

He put that thought out of his mind. "To hell with it," he said. "To hell and be damned! Leave it alone! Let them rot in jail!" Life was short. At the age of forty-five, it comes on a man that perhaps only fifteen years are left. He wanted more. He wanted to sit in the Senate, and he could.

He remembered Phil Armour, and he remembered Schilling saying bitterly, in reference to a sellout on the part of a certain labor leader, "Some men die for freedom, but a German writes a book about it."

He drove the thought from his mind. He was no more German than Abe Lincoln was English. He was an American. What if he had, by a freak of chance, been born on the other side? A few months later, and he would have been born here. He was an American; didn't his friends say that he was more American than any native son they knew?

He sought for an ethic, and there was no ethic to be found. Not even the ethic of power, for as a businessman he was nothing alongside Field or McCormick or Armour or Pullman, and he knew, if no one else did, precisely how a man came to be Governor of Illinois.

V

IN HIS office in the great Unity Building, which was his, which he had built and created, he felt much better. Daylight eases a problem, and by now he had become so thoroughly a part of Chicago that the city was, in a sense, an answer to problems. For wasn't Chicago like him, more American than any city on the continent, yet with a larger proportion of foreign-born than any city on the continent; ugly in its youth, but becoming less so, crude and vigorous and violent? In the downtown section, massive skyscrapers were rising, buildings unlike any other in the land, huge, blocked-out, frightening, giving a feeling of being flung and landing here and there or anywhere, like the toys of a capricious giant. Also, after the great inter-city labor wars

of the late seventies and eighties, the wealthy citizens of
the town led a movement against narrow streets. Narrow
streets, turning and twisting, could be too easily barri-
caded and held. In narrow streets a few rifles were as good
as artillery, and from the upper floors a handful might
defend such streets against a thousand. So the city-planners
laid out the new avenues broad and wide, with streets intersecting them at exact right angles; thereby, a Gatling
gun could sweep unobstructed for a thousand yards, a
howitzer could be precisely trained, and a field piece could
drive point-blank for a mile or more. Cavalry could charge
on an avenue as well as across an open field, and troops
could advance ten abreast.

And while sober, thoughtful citizens, such as Altgeld,
considered that there was something disgraceful as well as
hysterical in this sort of thing, they admitted that the city
benefited; from the pork- and beef-butchery beginnings,
they could make a dream of a continental metropolis,
noble and beautiful, central to half the world, and giving
wheat and beef and abundance to many millions.

His Unity Block was part of this dream. A long time
ago—how long ago, he hardly knew, but perhaps back in
those half-forgotten days when he ran like a small wild
beast through the virgin forest of the middle border—he
had conceived the dream of rearing towers. Since then it
had changed; the fancies of a child became the sketches of
a lonely man. When Emma discovered him at his desk,
shading in rectangular blocks, he would be half apologetic,
half ashamed; and then she would explain to someone else
that Pete wanted to build the biggest house in the world.
But that was hardly the truth; he wanted to build towers;
when he sought for verity in his world, the world charging
out of the middle west like a steam locomotive, he found

it only in material things. Other men died and they left a child, a family, a commercial empire; if he died, for a few weeks his friends would talk about Pete Altgeld, and then it would be done. In the dark hours of the night, when the fear of death was strongest, he understood full well why the ancient Egyptian kings reared such mighty piles of stone.

Partly out of that, he built the Unity Block; partly because he despised his own trade of politics. He wrote books; he built houses; he sought to imprint himself on life. Each time it was a larger piece of property, a taller building. It did not occur to him to ask why, with so much space available, Americans should frenetically urge their buildings toward the sky. If he translated it to himself at all, it was in terms of a monument rearing out of the soot and dirt of this wild and windy town, so that people could point and say, "Altgeld built that." He put four hundred thousand dollars of his money into the Unity Building, and he borrowed as much more, and then from day to day, he could not wait to see it in completion, planning in sleepless nights how he could hurry the construction. When the steel framework reared up, the building's nakedness became his own until he could cover it over with bricks. He made mistakes; stone caught between his framework and the McCormick building, which it hugged, threw the skeleton out of line, and it was not the hundred-thousand-dollar repair bill that made him sick, desperate, terror-stricken, but rather the thought that his building, his baby and darling might be lost forever. He saw it through the repair as a mother might see a child through sickness; and of nights, stealthily, he would slip out of his house, go and stand in the darkness across the street from the giant he was nursing, stand for hours on end staring up at the monstrous bulk, darker against the dark Chicago sky. And when the masonry enfolded the frame, finally, he felt like weeping with gratitude; and out of this came certain childish things, like what he said to Pastor Schloss of the Lutheran Church he now and then gave money to:

"You see, pastor, this is the kind of immortality that counts. It will stand forever."

To which the pastor answered, quite obviously, "Nothing stands forever."

This was the place to which he went now, home in Chicago, and sitting in his office there, he felt comforted, rested and assured, so much so that Joe Martin, coming in, smiled with surprise and said:

"Pete, you look good."

"I feel good."

"Well, I heard you were sick. But you don't look sick. You look like old times. But maybe I go too much by old times. I should call you Governor now."

"All right—if you want to."

"What can I do for the Governor?" Martin asked. There was a half-hostile note in his voice, mixed with the real pleasure he felt at seeing Altgeld.

"Send Emma some flowers, for one thing. You did that in Chicago. It wouldn't cost a hell of a lot more now."

"How is Emma?"

"Worried about me. Otherwise, fine."

"Has she something to worry about?"

"Only that I'm wearing out, running down. I say I've got twenty good years left, maybe thirty. But the smart boys don't count on me to live out my term. What do you think?"

"I don't play long shots."

"Why don't you ask me what I really want?"

"Why should I? You're the Governor. You call and I come. You call and big Mike comes too. I'm just a two-bit gambler."

"All right," Altgeld said. "Get it out of your system."

"No."

"Where did you want me to count you in? Superintendent of Hospitals, Secretary of State, Factory Inspector—?"

"Maybe it's your kind of honesty I don't figure," Joe Martin said. "I don't claim to be an honest man, but I never welshed on a bet; I never ratted on a friend. I bought votes and sold them, because that's my business, the same as running a roulette wheel."

"And you think I'm pulling reform on my friends?"

"I don't know what to think. A man becomes governor—"

"And what?"

"He plays both ends against the middle. I guess the next step is the White House."

"I wasn't born in this country," Altgeld reminded him.

"Jesus God, and the way you figure, that's the only thing that stands in your way."

"Maybe. Why don't you stop tearing at me, Joe? Maybe I don't know what to do. I'm sick of politics."

"You're not sick of it, Governor. You love it."

"And I hate it. Suppose I busted loose?"

"How?"

"Not something that concerned the party directly. Would the party stick by me?"

"Ask the party, Governor."

"I'm asking you."

"All right. I don't know; you're for labor, you're against it. You're against big business, but you're big business

134

yourself. You hate Big Mike and you hate Phil Armour too. Where do you stand?"

Quietly, honestly, Altgeld answered, "I don't know."

"When you know where you stand, then go to the party."

VI

SCHILLING, however, knew precisely why he had been summoned, and after an exchange of greetings, he sat waiting for Altgeld to break the ice; but Altgeld, watching the former carpenter, the friend of Parsons, considered how almost every man has his price, has an end to his ideal, a time when he tires. Schilling had served him well in the gubernatorial race; under the Judge's guidance, he had formed the Altgeld Labor Legion, and the Democratic Party had come forth as the party of the workingman, Jefferson's party. One hundred thousand dollars of Altgeld's own money had furnished the backing for this movement, and the workingman was told that here was Pete Altgeld, a worker himself, who would fight for him right down the line. He spoke in union halls; he paraded his recollections of railroad construction; he wrapped the denims tight around him. When he spoke to workers and said, "Old Abe Lincoln would be the first one to take up the banner of new democracy, the banner of the working class," they roared with satisfaction, the deep-toned roar which came from this kind of an audience. And when he spoke to a group of German workers, telling them, *"Ich arbeite mit meinen Händen! Und du arbeitest mit deinen Händen, und wo gibt es Hände, stark genug, um uns zu nehmen, was wir erarbeitet haben?"* the same, deep-toned roar greeted him.

Afterwards, the reward for Schilling was the post of secretary in the State Board of Labor Statistics, so that he no longer had to go hungry most of the time, as he did when he was business manager for the socialist paper in Chicago; and therefore it was hard for Schilling to demand from the Governor. His old comrades knew the tune he had played in the election, and now, looking at him, Altgeld wondered just how thin and rotten and incredible the whole political fabric of the great republic was, how much more it could be stretched, and whether it was not essentially the same all the way through, top to bottom, House, Senate, and White House, only the price changing, only the method of corruption becoming a great deal larger and more complex.

Yet he liked Schilling, liked him tremendously; at the bottom, Schilling was his own kind; he was declassed wholly, Schilling was not. Emma could make a great thing of both the stone house on Frederick Street and the State Mansion, but there was a point beyond which he couldn't travel. Those he could live with were not the masters, but the political servants, wisecracking, loud-mouthed, foul of speech, corrupt, graft-ridden, but still with a memory that they lived in the gold palaces only by sufferance; and a million-dollar tag didn't change it any.

So when he spoke, the Governor asked Schilling, straightforwardly, "Do they all expect me to pardon the anarchists?"

"All?"

"Not all. You know what I mean."

"Sometimes, my friend," Schilling said, "I think that you don't understand your own game. Whatever you think, the people elected you. More of them voted for you than for your opponent. There must have been a reason."

"I never put in a platform that I would pardon the anarchists."

"No, of course not. A thousand vote for this reason, a thousand for that. But there are many, many thousands who hope you will pardon Fielden and Schwab and Neebe —no, they believe you will. Pete, what I have heard! They look at you and their hearts go out, so they trust you."

"And they're fools."

"No," Schilling said tiredly. "They are not entirely fools."

"If I pardon them, then I'm through."

"Unless you believe in the people."

"What could the people do for me? What could I do for them?"

"I think that if you were born in this country, they could make you president. And this way, they would follow you to hell."

Altgeld shook his head.

"And the pardon?"

With a sudden rush of irritation, Altgeld snapped, "If they're guilty, they can rot there! If they're innocent, they'll get out! God damn it, talk about something else! And if you want to talk about the anarchists, bring me facts, not tears, not this stupid talk about the people!"

VII

BUT Judge Lambert Tree said, pointing to methodology, pure and simple, "There are two ways to go about this. If you extend mercy to these men, no one will dare to protest. Haymarket was a witchburning, a bloodfest, and the heat has passed. Do you think that at this point Marshall

Field or Cyrus McCormick give two damns as to whether those three men rot inside a jail or outside one?"

"I've thought of that," Altgeld agreed.

"On the other hand, if you imply that Parsons and Spies were innocent, as you must if you are to pardon Fielden on legalistic grounds, or even if you imply that the original trial was unfair, then I, personally, would not give twenty cents for your political future."

"I see."

"So the three courses are open. Ignore the whole thing— and you'll never get the labor vote again in this state. Extend mercy, and both labor and business will stand behind you—I would say, if you want another term as Governor, yes, and the Senate too. But if you take the third course—"

"I'm through?"

"I think so."

"You would not take the third course?"

"I don't think any man in his right mind would, Peter."

"Do you think that if I had sat on that bench instead of Gary and tried the case, the result would have been different?"

"I don't know what you would have done. I don't even know what I would have done. But I think there is a limit to what any one man can do."

"And where is the limit?" Altgeld asked.

"The point where he destroys himself."

"Then you would have to consider that Parsons destroyed himself," Altgeld murmured.

VIII

WHEN Altgeld came back to Springfield, he called in young Brand Whitlock, who was in charge of the archives, the chaotic piles of musty documents which had accumulated in cellars and vaults ever since Illinois became a state. Whitlock had been a reporter, and meeting him during the campaign, Altgeld became fascinated by the believing directness of the boy; there was something clean and winning about him, and Altgeld had wanted him for a secretary. But when Whitlock dogmatically refused to be secretary to anyone, the Governor persuaded him to take a job with the Secretary of State. That he worshiped the ground Altgeld walked on was obvious, and talking to him, trying to get at the reason for this without embarrassing the young man, trying to get some of the so necessary food for his own ego without tearing down any of the belief, Altgeld drew out of him a curious concept.

For Whitlock, America was young, and whereas the heroes of other lands were long-dead ancients, the heroes of this land were only of yesterday. His own grandfather was one such, and out of his childhood, curtained with the lovely translucence of childhood, came others, tall Abe Lincoln and Douglass and old Frémont of the middle border and John Brown, some of whom he had known and some whom he remembered from tales told, and many, many more, and as he said to Altgeld:

"They did what I would want to do, and you're doing it, too, sir."

"And what am I doing?" Altgeld asked.

"Well, if I'm out on a story and I talk to a plain man, and we talk about how rotten things are, everywhere, he will usually say, If only there were a few more like Pete Altgeld."

"What does that add up to?"

And somewhat ashamed of his own words, Whitlock said, in his almost formal manner of speech, "I think you're trying to serve the people, sir, because you're one of us."

And now Brand Whitlock stood in front of the Governor, eager and waiting, and Altgeld asked him:

"Do you know where everything is on the Haymarket case?"

"Everything?"

"I mean everything there is to be had. The verbatim testimony, accounts read into the trial, briefs filed with the Supreme Court, newspaper files compiled by the state—in other words, everything."

"There's a mountain of it," Whitlock said. "I know where it is, but my God, sir, it would fill your office."

"Then fill my office with it," Altgeld told him. "Do it today." And then, seeing that the boy hesitated, "Well?"

"Are you going to pardon them, sir?"

"What would you do, if you were in my place?"

The boy said, "I think I would pardon them, sir, the whole world be damned."

IX

AT A dinner which Emma Altgeld gave a few days later—such dinners as she was expected to give now, being the mistress of the executive mansion, there was a banker, a Methodist bishop from downstate, Professor Haley of the university, who was an economist and hoped for a place in the administration, and Joe Martin, who was only a tin-horn gambler, even now, but a friend of the Governor's. The banker's wife, a thin, frightened woman, fluttered about Emma pleadingly, but the wife of the Methodist bishop was large and handsome; and the party was rounded off by another man and woman. The woman was Lizbeth Cordwood, the sociologist, and the man was Samuel Gompers, the trade-union leader, who was making a tour, and who had been invited to meet the new Governor and dine with him. All in all, it was a varied and interesting gathering, and in the reception room Emma was pleased to note how well Gompers wore his evening clothes—not like Schilling, who was a shabby man and would always be one —and how nicely he chatted with the banker and the bishop's wife.

At the dinner, for the most part, things went nicely too. Being Governor had not changed Altgeld's regard for substantial food, the kind that sticks to a man's ribs and recalls to him the good memory of having eaten, and that and the wine mellowed conversation. Lizbeth Cordwood found common ground with the professor, who was a bachelor, and Gompers, with Mrs. Altgeld on one side of him and the wife of the bishop on the other, appeared to be enjoying himself enormously well—although whenever he spoke to the Governor, his voice changed just a little, assuming a note of deference and compliance that annoyed Altgeld considerably more than it humored him.

The conversation was not brilliant, but at least it had none of those ominous gaps which can be so embarrassing to a hostess, a fact Emma was grateful for, since the Governor was tired and hardly said more than a word or two. The talk ranged from economics, the depression in particular, to religion and the current squabble between the lay and clerical authorities in regard to schooling, with half a dozen other subjects in between. It was after the last course, while waiting for the dessert, that Emma, seeing her husband rub his eyes for at least the sixth time, explained, "You must forgive the Governor, he's been deep in the Haymarket thing," ignoring his angry look; but then it was done, and the banker said:

"If we hanged some of the agitators who are stirring this thing up, we might all have a little peace."

"That's not a very charitable way to look at it," Miss Cordwood said.

"I leave charity to those who are expert at it. They are expert enough to claim more money than my stockholders."

There was general laughter at this sally, even Mr. Gompers smiling, and Professor Haley said to the Banker, "Apparently, sir, you have little sympathy for the anarchists?"

"None at all, none at all, with apologies to the Governor."

"Why—with apologies to me?" Altgeld asked.

"Common knowledge you intend to pardon the wretches."

"Is it?" Emma knew the danger signs, but it was too late.

"Political, sir, so don't misunderstand me. A move which will placate labor, and that has a place. Four were hanged and they were shown what's what. So if three go free—well, politics."

"And what do you think, Mr. Gompers?" Altgeld asked.

"The labor movement," Gompers said, "has no sympathy for either socialism or murder."

"And you approve of linking the two?"

The banker laughed heartily. "Score for you, Governor. They have not accused you of murder yet."

"Not yet." And turning to Gompers, "If the labor movement has no sympathy, Mr. Gompers, how do you account for Chicago labor, as well as labor groups all over the country, badgering me for these men's release?"

"We have all sorts of elements—" Gompers began, searching Altgeld's face for some clue as to where his sympathies lay.

"But you are very quick to say murder."

"It was the decision of the court," the bishop said. "Surely, the individual citizen can do no better than to rely on the time-tested justice of the republic—"

"Is it very warm downstate?" Emma asked the bishop's wife, desperately trying to turn the conversation, and hearing her highpitched request, the Governor glanced at her and smiled a little, as if to say, it will be all right, my dear. But Joe Martin said, bluntly, "Wouldn't mercy be down your line, bishop?"

"Mercy? Mercy is a large word. Should there be mercy for those who would destroy the works of God?"

"Yet Christ forgave—" the banker's wife began, speaking for the first time that evening, and then, under her husband's glance, allowing the rest of her phrase to trail away.

"We temper a parable with our experience," the bishop said. "There are those whom even Christ would not forgive."

"Mr. Gompers," the Governor said, his voice more amiable than before, "perhaps you could clarify me on one matter. These men who were hanged—well, Parsons, for example—they were labor leaders after a fashion, or were they not? In every action they took, they fought for labor, or so it seems to me. In fact, one of the counts used against them was that they wished labor to take over this country. To me, naturally, they are enemies of a sort; I don't wish labor to take over this country. I employ labor, and I don't look at myself as a devil. But you, on the other hand, are a labor leader. Are the interests of these men so different from yours?"

"Very different. They use labor for their own ends, as every socialist and communist does, for their own selfish advancement. To put themselves into power, they would nail labor onto a cross!"

"And yet they died like heroes."

"As has many an evil man," the bishop said.

"I suppose so," the Governor agreed. "You have no sympathy for the anarchists, Mr. Gompers?"

"Personally, I have very little. However, there are unions in the American Federation of Labor which have cast doubt on the complete impartiality of judge and jurors in the case, and I would not place myself as standing in the way of a pardon."

"You would not," the Governor smiled, and then shifted the conversation abruptly, turning to the bishop's wife and asking, more pointedly than his wife, just how the weather was downstate.

Later, when all of the guests except Joe Martin had gone, and the Governor was sitting with him and his wife in the library, Emma begged his forgiveness. "It's all right," the Governor said. "I suppose I have what I deserve, Emma. I go to church now. The bishop was impressed with that."

"You ought to go away, like Emma's been telling you to," Martin said. "You ought to go to Europe."

"I've been reading the Haymarket briefs. It's an experience, Joe."

"I keep begging him to go away for a while."

"I like living," Altgeld said. "I even like having fools to dinner."

"What are you going to do about this?"

"When I do it, you'll see."

X

THERE were so many things to be done as Governor, so many routine things that often it was late at night before he found time for a few hours with the books, the records, the finely written transcripts of the Haymarket affair. By now he no longer attempted to deny, even to himself, that this strange business of the explosion of a mysterious bomb on a Chicago street had become one of the central and important factors in his life. Bit by bit, it had moved in upon him, until now he was living with those eight incredible men whom he had never even known—Albert Parsons, August Spies, Louis Lingg, Samuel Fielden, George Engel, Adolph Fischer, Oscar Neebe, and Michael Schwab. He studied their faces and features in the drawings of them by the newspaper artists, particularly the sketches Art Young of the *Daily News* had done two days before the execution. He read their statements to the court before they were sentenced:

SPIES: ". . . Before this court, and before the public, which is supposed to be the State, I charge the State's Attorney and Bonfield [Chicago police captain] with the heinous conspiracy to commit murder. . . ."

PARSONS: ". . . I have violated no law of this country. Neither I nor my colleagues have violated any legal right of American citizens. We stand upon the right of free speech, of free press, of public assembly, unmolested, and undisturbed. We stand upon the Constitutional right of self-defense, and we defy the prosecution to rob the people of America of these dearly bought rights. But the prosecution imagines that they have triumphed because they propose to put to death seven men. . . ."

SCHWAB: ". . . I know that our ideal will not be accomplished this or next year, but I know that it will be accomplished as near as possible, some day in the future. . . ."

FISCHER: ". . . I protest against my being sentenced to death, because I have committed no crime. However, if I am to die on account of being an Anarchist, I will not remonstrate!"

LINGG: ". . . I despise you! I despise your order, your laws, your force-propped authority! Hang me for it!"

FIELDEN: ". . . There is a part of me you cannot kill. . . ."

ENGEL: ". . . Can anyone feel respect for a government that accords rights only to the privileged classes and none to the workers? For such a government, I can feel no respect. . . ."

But it was the statement of Oscar Neebe that had the deepest effect on Altgeld. He alone was not sentenced to death, but only to fifteen years in jail; but he had been selected by the police at random, simply because he was a militant worker, and never was any pretense made that he had any connection with what happened at Haymarket. When it came time for him to speak, he rose and said:

"Well, these are the crimes I have committed. They found a revolver in my house and a red flag there. I organized trade unions. I was for reduction of the hours of labor, and the education of the laboring man, and the re-establishment of the workingman's newspaper. There is no evidence to show that I was connected with the bomb-throwing, or that I was near it, or anything of that kind. So I am only sorry, your honor—that is, if you can stop it or help it—I will ask you to do it—that is, to hang me, too; for I think it is more honorable to die suddenly than to be killed by inches. I have a family and children; and if they know their father is dead, they will bury him. They can go to the grave and kneel down by the side of it; but they can't go to the penitentiary and see their father, who was convicted of a crime that he hasn't anything to do with. That is all I have got to say. Your honor, I am sorry I am not to be hung with the rest of the men."

There were times when, reading something like this, in the early hours of the morning, Altgeld would simply stop, cease to act and react, and find himself and his thoughts suspended in a limbo—out of which he would painfully crawl—tired, beaten. Sometimes, Emma would come in and find him that way, and say to him, "Come to bed, Pete, it's so late." "This business, my God, Emma, Schilling came and pleaded with me, and I didn't listen." "But now you'll make it right, Pete," thinking, anything, so the dead would lie dead. "I can't bring them back," he would say. "I can't make Parsons alive." "You didn't hang Parsons." "I hanged him. We all did." "Well, that's because you're tired. You're talking that way because you're tired." "Emma, I'm going to fight them, I'm going to fight them to hell and be damned." "Don't swear, please, Pete—come to bed." "But it was rotten, from top to bottom, right from the beginning when that son of a bitch, Melville Stone, the stinking editor of a lousy daily wrote the verdict of the coronor's jury and boasted then, before the trial ever began, that it was fixed and they would die. And then a dirty little bailiff, Ryce, you remember him, he took bets they would die because he had instructions and money to fix the jury—" "Stop talking that way, Pete." "But I've seen dirty things—it's not Sunday School, being a politician —but I've never seen anything like this." "You'll make yourself sick over it." "I am. Emma, this is going to break like a bat out of hell." "What are you afraid of?" *"You're* not afraid?" She said, "What have I been afraid of, with you in it? I don't understand these things, but I haven't

147

tried to stop you. You do what's right, that's all." "How do I know what's right?" "You know." "Well, they want me to pardon these men because they're afraid, all of them, Stone is afraid, and Ryce and Gary, because they're none of them sure their religion is a lie and there isn't a hell for them to roast in, but just to pardon these poor bastards and say that they're guilty and write a clean slate for the men who murdered Parsons and Spies, by God, I won't do that. I won't do it. I swear to God I'll do what I please!" "You will, Pete." "I'm all right, don't look at me like that, only I'm mad."

His anger became meticulous. He read every word, every line. He saw that the jury was framed, but he had to prove it for himself, and he itemized the proof. He made for himself a brief that would stand up in a court of the gods. He came to the conclusion that Judge Gary, who had tried the case, was the most deliberate judicial murderer in all civilized history, but that too he had to prove, and he worked down to the essence of fact, so far as it was given to any man to know the facts. That, in relation to all this, a qualitative change was occurring within him, he knew, nor did he resist any longer that change taking place. Here were the facts and here was the case, and now he was sitting as judge, by the sovereign right and decision of the people of Illinois. The forged testimony, the perjury, the inventions of a hundred hired spies, the statements of thugs and degenerates, the confused blubberings of the human wrecks who came out of the police torture cells—all of this happening in his own beloved city, in his own Chicago, and he hadn't known.

Now he knew. He told himself, if this was his last case, he would judge it as a judge should. And then he wouldn't take what came quietly—he'd fight. There were long hours when he thought of democracy, what it meant, what it might be. There was a theory that no one had ever tried, except perhaps Tom Jefferson, long, long ago, and sometimes it seemed to him that another could try it, take democracy and make a fight of it—

He sometimes thought that if he could come out of this with his head on his shoulders, he could make a fight of it.

XI

IT CAN'T be said entirely how a man changes, why he changes, what ferments in him, what juices run together and come to a slow boil; for there are a hundred thousand factors unaccountable, not to be listed in any set of books. The child is the father of the man, and the child has his father too, and even the beating rain and the shining sun go to temper a man; sometimes change ferments slowly, sometimes quickly; sometimes change boils in rage; and sometimes there is an iron rod in a man that resists change, or a soggy clay core that soaks it up and never shows a difference.

The change in Altgeld, seeping through him now, inside and outside, doing quiet things inside, etching lines on his face outside—this change was not a thing entirely, not altogether, not accountable and not to be graphed. He was sailing, suddenly, a sea he had never really charted; nor was he too familiar with the charts of others. He was looking at persons newly and freshly; for example, his wife, the wonderful, calm Emma, had become a rock, closer to him than ever before, but, on the other hand, Schilling was understandable and pitiful; Whitlock was a boy such as he might have had, yet the emptiness of his childlessness was not the way it had been. A processional was filing in, and out of his memory form took shape, the wanderers on the many roads of the land, the men who had swung pick and shovel, the hard-handed, brown-faced farmers of Kansas, Nebraska, Iowa, Ohio, Missouri, scraping at the soil in epic hopelessness, for they had had nothing commensurate with their labors, nor would they, the evil-faced criminals who had stood before his bench, whipped and broken and turned into devils, the thousands of stolid workers, so bitterly silent, walking behind the coffins of Spies and Parsons and the others, the bereaved and the tear-stained, the homeless and hopeless and cold and hungry, and the shadow upon them of the towers that were reared over the land, such towers as his own great Unity Building—they filed in, processional-like, and they filled a space.

Yet the change was slow, stumbling, uncertain; where he sought for markers on the many roads, there were none, and those whom he tried to remember for sustenance, the Lincolns, the Jacksons, the Jeffersons and Paines—they had no certainty of direction to give him. He put out his hands and he felt his way, and most of the time his hands met so little that his reaction was more of fear than of hope.

XII

WHEN he did a thing, he simply felt that he must do it, Downstate, at Decatur, a black man was dragged from a jail and lynched. A year ago, two years ago, three years ago this would have been a natural and accepted part of the landscape. In this landscape you built your house and earned your bread, a million dollars of it. If men hungered, starved, sinned, or were lynched, the world was so, and you accepted it. Now he accepted nothing. Burning with rage, he talked to newspapermen.

"This," he said, "is not civilization, not decency, but barbarism. You and I were down there participating in that lynching—so was every good citizen of this state. Don't think any different. And the shame is ours."

Still he was not satisfied. He sat down and wrote a proclamation to the people of Illinois:

"Being authoritatively advised that at two o'clock this morning a mob broke down the doors of the jail at Decatur, overpowered the officers of the law, took from his cell a Negro confined there, dragged him out and killed him by hanging him to a post nearby, I hereby denounce this cowardly and diabolical act as not only murder under our laws, but as a disgrace to our civilization and a blot upon the fair name of our State. . . ."

It set him to thinking of civilization, of all that the very word implied. Joe Martin had a code of ethics based on gambling, on graft and the buying and selling of votes, yet it was civilized compared to the code of Phil Armour or Cyrus McCormick; yet what was Altgeld's own code in this state where a man was dragged from a jail and murdered by a mob?

He was emerging from the nightmare word-welter of Haymarket. The dead would sleep in peace, even if there was no peace for him. He said to Emma:

"My darling, we're going to see something no one in America ever saw before."

XIII

A WEEK after the lynching, he sat down to write. He began late one evening, a pile of white paper clean and virgin on his desk, a single sheet upon which he had written:

"Reasons for Pardoning Fielden, Neebe and Schwab, by John P. Altgeld—"

He wrote without much hesitation. He knew what he wanted to say, and the words flowed from his pen:

"On the night of May 4, 1886, a public meeting was held on Haymarket Square in Chicago; there were from 800 to 1000 people present, nearly all being laboring men. There had been trouble, growing out of the effort to introduce the eight-hour day, resulting in some collisions with the police, in one of which several laboring people were killed, and this meeting was called as a protest against alleged police brutality.

"The meeting was orderly and was attended by the mayor, who remained until the crowd began to disperse and then went away. As soon as Capt. John Bonfield, of the police department, learned that the mayor had gone, he took a detachment of police and hurried to the meeting for the purpose of dispersing the few who remained, and as the police approached the place of meeting a bomb was thrown by some unknown person, which exploded and wounded many and killed several policemen, among the latter being one Mathias Degan. A number of people were arrested and after a time August Spies, Albert R. Parsons, Louis Lingg, Michael Schwab, Samuel Fielden, George Engel, Adolph Fischer and Oscar Neebe were indicted for the murder of Mathias Degan. The prosecution could not discover who had thrown the bomb and could not bring the really guilty men to justice, and, as some of the men indicted were not at the Haymarket meeting and had nothing to do with it, the prosecution was forced to proceed on the theory that the men indicted were guilty of murder because it was claimed they had at various times in the past uttered and printed incendiary and seditious language, practically advising the killing of policemen, of Pinkerton men and others acting in that capacity, and that they were therefore responsible for the murder of Mathias Degan. The public was greatly excited and after a prolonged trial all of the defendants were found guilty; Oscar Neebe was sentenced to fifteen years' imprisonment and all of the other defendants were sentenced to be hanged. The case was carried to the supreme court and was there affirmed in the fall of 1887. Soon thereafter Lingg committed suicide. The sentence of Fielden and Schwab was commuted to imprisonment for life, and Parsons, Fischer, Engel and Spies were hanged, and the petitioners now ask to have Neebe, Fielden and Schwab set at liberty.

"The several thousand merchants, bankers, judges, lawyers and other prominent citizens of Chicago who have by petition, by letter and in other ways urged executive clemency, mostly base their appeal on the ground that, assuming the prisoners to be guilty, they have been punished enough, but a number of them who have examined the case more carefully, and are more familiar with the record and with the facts disclosed by the papers on file, base their appeal on entirely different grounds. They assert:

"First—That the jury which tried the case was a packed jury selected to convict.

"Second—That according to the law as laid down by the supreme court, both prior to and again since the trial of this case, the jurors, according to their own answers, were not competent jurors and the trial was therefore not a legal trial.

"Third—That the defendants were not proven to be guilty of the crime charged in the indictment.

"Fourth—That as to the defendant Neebe, the state's attorney had declared at the close of the evidence that there was no case against him, and yet he has been kept in prison all these years.

"Fifth—That the trial judge was either so prejudiced against the defendants, or else so determined to win the applause of a certain class in the community that he could not and did not grant a fair trial.

"Upon the question of having been punished enough I will simply say that if the defendants had a fair trial, and nothing has developed since to show that they are not guilty of the crime charged in the indictment, then there ought to be no executive interference, for no punishment under our laws could then have been too severe. Government must defend itself; life and property must be protected and law and order must be maintained; murder must be punished, and if the defendants are guilty of murder, either committed with their own hands or by someone else acting on their advice, then, if they have had a fair trial, there should be in this case no executive interfence. The soil of America is not adopted for the growth of anarchy. While our institutions are not free from injustice, they are still the best that have yet been devised, and therefore must be maintained."

So he began this paper, feeling not too different from a man who writes his own death warrant, yet feeling also an excitement and wonder at his own actions; for, as his friend Judge Tree pointed out, he was taking a course not too different from Parsons', a course which almost all men avoid because inherent in it are seeds of destruction. But with the course laid down, for all that it was poorly charted, he could not turn aside; excitement won out over fear; and for the first time in all his life he felt some of that curious peace which can only come from a solution, partial or otherwise, of the terrible contradictions which begin to destroy a thoughtful man, almost from the moment he applies his thoughts to justice or injustice.

Emma saw it; he was more gentle with her; things so small as passing a dish at dinner became an extension of what went on within him. If they had not started with love, she had no doubts as to what she felt for him now. She went away from his room one evening choked up with emotion, her eyes wet, yet at the same time with a buoyancy she had never known before. She didn't try to understand his actions; he was doing a brave thing, and though her own reaction surprised her, she was somehow not sad that things would not ever be the way they were. She had hitched her star to something when she married the awkward bumpkin of a country schoolteacher, but what was impossible to him when here he was, Governor of the state, and doing something which every sober friend of hers had assured her would ruin him? But she had stopped listening to her sober friends, and when coming from his room, she met the Governor's secretary and was asked, "Is he working on the pardon now, Mrs. Altgeld?" she said, "Yes." "It will be a blow, I'm afraid." "It will be all right," she said.

After a time, Pete Altgeld felt it would be all right too. There was enough potency in the cold facts he put down on paper. He proved that the jury was fixed. Piling up thousands of words of sworn evidence, he summarized it thus in his pardon message:

"It is shown that he [Ryce, the special bailiff] *boasted while selecting jurors that he was managing this case; that these fellows would hang certain as death; that he was calling such men as the defendants would have to challenge peremptorily and waste their challenges on, and that when their challenges were exhausted they would have to take such men as the prosecution wanted.*"

He inserted affidavits; he reproduced verbatim testimony of examination of the jurors who finally sat on the case, as for example that of H. T. Sanford:

"Q. Have you an opinion as to the guilt or innocence of the defendants of the murder of Mathias J. Degan?

"A. I have.

"Q. From all that you have heard and that you have read, have you an opinion as to the guilt or innocence of the defendants of throwing the bomb?

"A. Yes, sir; I have.

"Q. Have you a prejudice against socialists and communists?

"A. Yes, sir; a decided prejudice.

"Q. Do you believe that prejudice would influence your verdict in this case?

"A. Well, as I know so little about it, it is a pretty hard question to answer. *I have an opinion in my own mind that the defendants encouraged the throwing of that bomb.*"

Case after case of this sort, Altgeld quoted, concluding finally:

"No matter what the defendants were charged with, they were entitled to a fair trial, and no greater danger could possibly threaten our institutions than to have the courts of justice run wild or give way to popular clamor, and when the trial judge in this case ruled that a relative of one of the men who was killed was a competent juror, and this after the man had candidly stated that he was deeply prejudiced and that his relationship caused him to feel more strongly than he otherwise might, and when in scores of instances he ruled that men who candidly declared that they believed the defendants to be guilty; that this was a deep conviction and would influence their verdict, and that it would require strong evidence to convince them that the defendants were innocent, when in all these instances the trial judge ruled that these men were competent jurors, simply because they had, under his adroit manipulation, been led to say that they *believed* they could try the case fairly on the evidence, then the proceedings lost all semblance of a fair trial."

Then he went on to give his opinion of the judge. He felt no mercy, no charity toward Gary; he had sat on a bench himself—he knew well enough the extent of any judge's power. Recently, in a magazine article, Judge Gary had reviewed the Haymarket case, and now Altgeld quoted from Gary's article:

" '*The conviction,' Gary wrote, 'has not gone on the ground that they did have actually any personal participation in the particular act which caused the death of Degan, but the conviction proceeds upon the ground that they had generally, by speech and print, advised large classes of the people, not particular individuals, but large classes, to commit murder, and had left the commission, the time and place and when, to the indivdual will and whim, or caprice, or whatever it may be, of each individual man who listened to their advice, and that in consequence of that advice, and influenced by that advice, somebody not known did throw the bomb that caused Degan's death. Now, if this is not a correct principle of the law, then the defendants of course are entitled to a new trial. The case is without precedent; there is no example in the law books of a case of this sort.'* "

To which Altgeld wrote, in answer:

"The judge certainly told the truth when he stated that the case was without a precedent, and that no example could be found in the law books to sustain the law as above laid down. For, in all the centuries during which government has been maintained among men, and crime has been punished, no judge in a civilized country has ever laid down such a rule before. . . ."

Then Altgeld went on to block out a broad picture. Something strange and ominous and significant was happening in the land. Just in the time of his own life, the people had been disinherited, divided, confused. Between those who labored and those who profited, a wide gap was making, and over that gap a bloody, murderous war had been raging for a dozen years. From underground had come organizations like the Knights of Labor and the Molly Maguires, painfully trying to weld labor together, to make a united force out of it—and counter to them, from the jails, the sewers, the gambling towns of the west, the city slums, from the pest-holes and horror spots of America, had come crawling the dregs of the land, bums and gangsters, thieves, gunmen, professional murderers, the rejected of society and the enemies of society, and they had been given a badge of pardon and immunity and welded together into the strangest army of mercenaries the world had yet known, the Pinkertons. They were a private army, privately armed and equipped, privately trained in the technique of violence—with only one purpose in mind, to battle and crush the rising organization of labor.

Reminding the people how quickly, how efficiently the so-called Haymarket murderers had been railroaded to the scaffold, Altgeld in contrast pointed to case after case of Pinkerton murder that had gone unpublicized, unavenged by society. Coldly and deliberately he wrote:

"Now it is shown . . . that in 1885 there was a strike at the McCormick Reaper factory on account of a reduction in wages and some Pinkerton men, while on their way there, were hooted at by some people on the street, when they fired into the crowd and fatally wounded several people who had taken no part in any disturbance; that four of the Pinkerton men were indicted for murder by the grand jury, but that the prosecuting officers apparently took no interest in the case and allowed it to be continued a number of times, until the witnesses were sworn out, and in the end the murderers went free; that after this there was a strike on the West Division Street Railway and that some of the police under the leadership of Capt. John Bonfield, indulged in a brutality never equaled before; that even small merchants standing on their own doorsteps and having no interest in the strike were clubbed, then hustled into patrol wagons and thrown into prison on no charge and not even booked. . . ."

So it went in the pardon he wrote, affidavits, case after case, facts and details coming alive under the slow and methodical manipulation of his pen, and when it would occur to him that he was the first Governor of an American state to write of such matters, he would pause and again try to grasp what might come of this. But that was impossible, for there were no precedents; as there had been no precedents for the conduct of Judge Gary in deliberate judicial murder, so were there no precedents for what he did.

Yet it was not a matter of courage that was concerned; the motivation was chiefly neither courage nor an obligation to others. If he had an obligation, it was to himself, and it was only for himself, for his need to make reason and justice out of the world he inhabited, that he wrote the bitter finish to his act:

"It is further charged with much bitterness by those who speak for the prisoners that the record of the case shows that the judge conducted the trial with malicious ferocity and forced eight men to be tried together; that in cross-examining the state's witnesses he confined counsel for the defense to the specific points touched on by the state, while in the cross-examination of the defendants' witnesses he permitted the state's attorney to go into all manner of subjects entirely foreign to the matters on which the witnesses were examined in chief; also that every ruling throughout the long trial on any contested point was in favor of the state, and further, that page after page of the record contains insinuating remarks of the judge, made in the hearing of the jury, and with the evident intent of bringing the jury to his way of thinking; that these speeches, coming from the court, were much more damaging than any speeches from the state's attorney could possibly have been; that the state's attorney often took his cue from the judge's remarks; that the judge's magazine article recently published, although written nearly six years after the trial, is yet full of venom; that, pretending to simply review the case, he had to drag into his article a letter written by an excited woman to a newspaper after the trial was over, and which therefore had nothing whatever to do with the case and was put into the article simply to create a prejudice against the woman, as well as against the dead and the living, and that, not content with this, he in the same article makes an insinuating attack on one of the lawyers for the defense, not for anything done at the trial, but because more than a year after the trial when some of the defendants had been hung, he ventured to express a few kind, if erroneous, sentiments over the graves of his dead clients, whom he at least believed to be innocent. It is urged that such ferocity or subserviency is without a parallel in all history; that even Jeffries in England contented himself with hanging his victims, and did not stop to berate them after they were dead.

"These charges are of a personal character, and while they seem to be sustained by the record of the trial and the papers before me and tend to show that the trial was not fair, I do not care to discuss this feature of the case any further, because it is not necessary. I am convinced that it is clearly my duty to act in this case for the reasons already given, and I, therefore, grant an absolute pardon to Samuel Fielden, Oscar Neebe and Michael Schwab this 26th day of June, 1893."

And then, underneath, he signed his name, John P. Altgeld, Governor of Illinois, and then it was finished, and he went to bed that night and slept quietly and easily.

XIV

EMMA had two ladies from the United Charities in to tea when the subject of the anarchists came up, and one of them, a Mrs. Byce, said, "We hear the Governor is going to pardon them?"

"Perhaps," Emma smiled. "The Governor does a great many things without consulting me."

"How strange," the other, Mrs. Benson, remarked. "I mean you would think—"

"Then he is going to pardon them?" Mrs. Byce said.

"I couldn't say."

"But won't that encourage them?" Mrs. Byce said. "I mean, they could just come out of the penitentiary and go on throwing bombs."

"Dynamite," Mrs. Benson nodded.

Mrs. Byce said, "Do you know, I read just enough of it to go into a teacup could blow us all sky-high."

"But surely, Mrs. Altgeld," said Mrs. Benson, "you don't approve of this sort of thing?"

"Of dynamite?"

"Of anarchists and communists."

"No, no, indeed."

"But you said, the Governor—"

"I said nothing about the Governor," Emma smiled.

"It would encourage them."

"There's no denying that it would encourage them," Mrs. Byce said. "I mean, to let them out of jail the way you would let a wild beast out of a cage."

"I'm sure the Governor has taken that into consideration," Emma said. She excused herself for a moment, and as she stepped out of the room, Mrs. Byce, lowering her voice, said, "Poor thing, I'm sure she knows as little as she says."

"You are?"

"She's a lady. They say he's no better than an anarchist. Has a spittoon in his room. Eats with his fingers. She doesn't invite people to dinner. He doesn't talk very well."

"You don't say."

"He is a foreigner, you know. Of course, he's Governor. But you can't forget that he's not an American."

"No, I don't suppose you can."

"They don't—I mean they haven't—well—"

"I've heard."

"Separate rooms. That's why they have no children."

"You don't say."

"They say he has a harelip. They say if you look at him very closely, under his mustache, you can see it."

"Really."

"You know Mrs. Henly Smith?"

"I've met her."

"They had a son with a harelip. They put him in an institution."

"No!"

"Yes. If we meet him, look carefully, under his mustache."

XV

WHEN Emma had read the pardon message, she said to her husband, "Why do you hate Gary so?"

"I hate what Gary stands for."

"But a lot of other people stand for the same thing. You don't hate them all."

"I hate pimps. I don't like murderers, even on the bench. As bad as the master is, I like his tool less."

"I see."

He asked her bluntly, "What do you think will happen, Emma?"

"I think some people will be with you and others won't, that's all. If they don't want you to be Governor again, we can go away, we can take a trip somewhere, can't we?"

"We could take a trip I suppose—"

Yet the next day, when Mike McDonald called from Chicago, she knew what a dream it was to think of a trip, of pleasant sunny afternoons when there would be nothing for them to do but rest, but be together; she knew because she stood by Altgeld when he answered the telephone and heard him say:

"Yes . . . yes, that's right. . . . You don't? . . . I say I've made up my mind, that's all . . . that's all. . . . You can talk as much as you please, I'm listening. . . . No! . . . I told you before that my mind was made up; in case you've forgotten, I'm the Governor. . . . He can go to hell and be damned. . . . The party?—the party wasn't here when the world was created, the party's changed, and it's going to change a hell of a lot more!"

He put down the phone and sat at his desk. He said to his wife, "Emma, it's going to be hard, it's going to be different. You were right, I hate Gary, I hate a lot of men. I love men too. They're going to line up. We're not all on the same side. I hate Gary. In that article Gary wrote for the *Century* he poured out his venom on Captain Black and his wife. I've got venom too. You remember, Black defended them. I was a lawyer, Emma, it doesn't matter that I differ from them, that I don't believe in what they fight for; I'm supposed to believe in justice, and I could have defended them and I didn't. I sat back, I sat it out, and they hanged Parsons by the neck until he was dead. Black defended them and went to their grave, and there he said something for which Gary never forgave him. Do you know what he said, what blasphemy, this—'I loved these men,' Black said. 'I knew them not until I came to know them in the time of their sore travail and anguish. As months went by and I found in the lives of those with whom I talked the witness of their love for the people, of their patience, gentleness and courage, my heart was taken captive in their cause.' That was Black's blasphemy, for which Gary never forgave him, and do you know what his wife did, Emma? She wrote, in a letter to the *Daily News,* these devilish words—'Often, as I took up one or the other of the daily papers, I would recall reverently those words of my Divine Master: *For which of my good works do you stone me?*' That way, Emma, she too earned Gary's hatred. Now it's my turn. Let him know that I despise him, and all that he stands for."

XVI

MR. E. S. DREYER was a banker, a citizen of Chicago, and in many other ways a pillar of the community, and if he had been able to go to bed at night and sleep, history would have forgotten him and his round cheeks and his mustache, and the deals he made, the profits he garnered and laid away, the club he belonged to, the cigars he smoked; but he could not sleep much of the time, and when he did sleep he dreamed of four men standing on a scaffold, and they all said to him, calmly and logically, "You, Mr. E. S. Dreyer, murdered us."

His doctor gave him bromides and said, "Nonsense! And as for Parsons and the rest of them, I say good riddance to bad rubbish."

"I acted as I saw my duty, and why should I have anything on my conscience?"

"No reason at all," the doctor said.

"But I don't sleep and I don't rest."

"Worry."

"If I sleep, I don't rest. I dream."

"Keep your bowels flushed," the doctor said. "That's important. Keep your bowels flushed."

But the keeping of Mr. E. S. Dreyer's bowels flushed proved singularly ineffective. Actually, no one in his own circle would have condemned Mr. Dreyer. For years he had never spent an evening at his club, at the dinner table, or indeed anywhere else where there was conversation without the conversation shifting, sooner or later, to labor; and when it did, how could Mr. Dreyer be blamed for joining in the chorus of vituperation and hatred? Hatred for labor, fear of labor, antagonism toward labor were as much Mr.

Dreyer's second nature as any of the habitual functions he performed daily, dressing, undressing, eating with his right hand, and putting on a hat when he went outside. So it is not surprising that when Mr. Dreyer was made foreman of the grand jury in the Haymarket case, he should have raised a whisky and soda at his club and cheerfully pledged the death of the whole lot. Nor is it surprising that he confided to many of his good friends that the anarchists would hang, or he'd see himself damned. Nor is it surprising that he fought for the murder indictments and drove them through, so that finally all over town people who knew him said:

"If anyone gets the credit, Dreyer should."

What was surprising was that after the hanging of four of the defendants, Mr. Dreyer's peace of mind departed. Insidiously, the most natural reaction in the world, his own, became distorted until he began to think of himself as a murderer. And no matter how he hated socialism, no matter how much he piled up for himself proof of the abiding evil of communists, he could not tell himself, successfully, that he had not participated in the murder of Parsons and the others.

He worked out his own atonement; he gave money to the cause of amnesty for the three who still lived. He signed petitions, he got others to sign petitions. He had bitter fights with his wife and his cronies, but he knew that his own peace and sanity depended upon the release of the three men. And he kept calling the Governor until Altgeld, annoyed by his insistence, asked Schilling about him. Schilling told him, and indicated that Dreyer wished to deliver the pardons to the jail. Altgeld's first reaction was of disgust. "He can go to the devil," he said.

"You'll need support in this. Let him do it," Schilling

insisted, and finally Altgeld agreed, and when Dreyer called again, Dose, the Governor's secretary, made an appointment for him.

"I want the pardons made out now," Altgeld said. "But I want it done quietly. Get Whitlock to write them out, and tell him to keep his mouth shut." Then, after a moment, Altgeld said, "Send Hinrichsen over here."

Big Buck Hinrichsen was head of the Democratic State Committee, and his own political plum was the job of Secretary of State. When he swaggered into the office of Altgeld, whom he did not care for particularly, he was rather curtly told to sit down, while the Governor went on writing. Then Altgeld said:

"Buck, I'm pardoning the anarchists."

"What?"

"You heard me. I've already ordered the pardons written, and my pardon message is at the printer's. I've put my reasons down there, and when you get a copy you'll be able to read the why and wherefor."

"And you think that's a smart move?"

"It's not a question of whether it's smart or not. I'm doing it." Watching Hinrichsen, he added, "Do you want to sign the pardons in person, or do you want to leave it for the clerk?"

"I don't know. This whole business strikes me as one hell of a move. I don't like it."

"I didn't call you in to ask you if you liked it," Altgeld said quietly.

"Did you speak to Mike?"

"I'm Governor," Altgeld smiled. "Do you understand that, Buck, for the time being I'm Governor."

XVII

IT DID Altgeld good to see Brand Whitlock's face as he came in with the pardons. The boy was looking at him in a way no one had ever looked at Altgeld before. Altgeld was sitting behind his desk, and at one side of the room, in front of a bookcase and under a portrait of Abe Lincoln, the Chicago banker stood, nervous and eager at the same time, his plump face expectant.

"Here are the pardons, sir," Whitlock said.

"How do you feel about it?" Altgeld asked him.

"I feel good. I feel terribly good, sir."

"It's what you would have done if you were in my place, is that right?"

"I think it's what I would do, sir. I hope it's what I would do."

"This is Mr. Dreyer," Altgeld said. "This is Brand Whitlock, Mr. Dreyer, one of our men in the State Department. Brand, Mr. Dreyer is going to take the pardons to Joliet and see the men out of jail."

Whitlock stood there, wondering what he was expected to say to this, and able to say only, "I'm glad."

"Well, it's time."

"I wonder if I could ask you a question, sir?"

Altgeld was signing the pardons, one by one, carefully, and blotting each just as carefully. "Go on," he nodded, without looking up.

"Did you know Albert Parsons?"

"I never knew him," Altgeld said flatly.

"Oh—"

The Governor folded the stiff sheets and offered them to Dreyer. At first Dreyer didn't move; then he shuffled over to the desk and took them, his face working all the time, like a man about to be ill. Then he started to say, "Well, Governor, well, Governor—I hardly know—" Suddenly, he began to cry. His face worked convulsively, and the tears rolled down his fat cheeks. He walked over to the window to hide his face from them, from Whitlock who was staring at the floor in great embarrassment.

"Go along, Brand," the Governor said.

"Thank you, sir. For everything."

The boy went out. Altgeld looked at his watch, said, somewhat harshly, "You'll miss your train, Mr. Dreyer."

"I'm sorry. I'm terribly sorry."

"All right."

"I want to explain. The grand jury—"

"I know. You don't have to apologize. You don't have to explain."

"Foolish of me to act this way. It's a little bit of atonement."

"You'll miss your train if you don't go along, Mr. Dreyer."

He was glad when finally Dreyer had gone. It was most unpleasant to see a man cry, and the more unpleasant when he himself felt no sympathy for the banker, none at all. He called in his secretary and told him:

"Dose, I'll have to give out a statement, I suppose."

"It's gotten out, sir, and the veranda's full of reporters."

"What do they say?"

"They say it's the biggest story since Lee surrendered."

"Is it? What in hell are you so nervous about? They're not going to hang us."

"Yes, sir."

"Tell them I'll see them in half an hour."

"Yes, sir."

"What the devil is wrong with you? Are you frightened?"

"I guess I've got too much imagination."

"Well, sit on it. Go and tell them what I told you to!"

He found Emma in her dressing room, sewing a lace collar on a blouse. She turned to him with a smile, her fine head tilted and alert. He kissed her, and then he sat down on a stool, looking up at her, watching her.

"Then you've done it?" she said, continuing to sew.

"That's right."

"Are you sorry?"

"Are you sorry?" he asked her.

"I guess I'm a little sorry, Pete. I'm ambitious, Pete. I always was that way, I guess you know. I wanted you to be the greatest man in the country. You are, you know?"

He laughed at her.

"Well, I know. A woman knows a lot about her husband. But I'm not much of a wife, Pete. I'm frightened, I always have been. You used to frighten me."

"Me?"

"Sure, Pete. Well, I'm still frightened. But I'm not sorry you did it. I would want to do something like signing those pardons. I never will—"

"I think we're making a mountain out of a molehill, and that nothing much of anything will happen."

"Pete, if the worst kind of thing happens, could you go away with me and be happy with me?"

"Run away?"

"If they force you, Pete?"

He grinned and kissed her. Then he went back to his office. The reporters came in and crowded around expectantly.

"Go ahead," he said.

"Will you be quoted?"

"No quotes."

"Then you've pardoned the anarchists?"

"Right."

"Clemency, sir?"

"An absolute pardon," Altgeld said slowly. "The men were never guilty. You can have my pardon reasons later. They can be quoted."

Whistles from several parts of the room. Men scribbling furiously.

"Will you imply in your reasons that Parsons and Spies and the others were innocent too?"

"I do."

The reporters edged toward the desk. Altgeld put his elbows on the desk, his face in his palms, his blue eyes bright and expectant.

XVIII

THAT night, while he slept, the news went through the land that the Governor of Illinois had pardoned the anarchists. All night long, as the stories were filed, telegraph keys clicked, and the details coming in, extracts from the pardon message, comments of the Governor, built up to an effect that scrapped the prepared editions in places so far apart as San Francisco, California, and Savannah, Georgia. Editorial conferences were hurriedly summoned, and newspaper owners were roused out of bed to render a decision. The news came to President Grover Cleveland as he was preparing for bed, and in his bathrobe he stamped back and forth across his chamber, swearing softly and then ordering a cabinet meeting for the next day. For King Mike McDonald of Chicago, there was no sleep at all that night, for a steady stream of raging bosses, heelers, and

other large and small fry flooded upon him, and finally
Marshall Field came to talk in no uncertain terms. Business at the Pinkerton Detective Agency, which had slowed
somewhat, became suddenly most brisk, and three very
important industrialists had a private meeting with Pinkerton himself. Congressmen were turned out of bed by
telegraph messengers, and four United States Senators sat
over their cigars all that night. Brand Whitlock lay awake
making drama out of the slow movement of incident, for
it seemed to him that nothing he had ever known was just
like this, a man high in the governing circles of the nation
making a choice between justice and all else that life might
offer; and Emma Altgeld lay awake, thinking of the crude,
uncouth farm boy who wanted to know all there was between the covers of books and who spoke the weird half-
German, half-English of the backlands. But the Governor
himself slept, quietly and easily.

XIX

AND the next day it broke!

He rose in the morning and he trimmed his mustache
and beard and he looked at himself in the mirror, and then
ate breakfast and took a horse around the grounds before
the papers came. He was feeling fit and eager and a load
was gone from his chest, and Parsons and Spies could lie
more easily in their graves. Then he came into his office,
and his secretary had the papers for him.

That was the beginning.

In a sense, the *Chicago Tribune* was restrained, for
though it reported the story bitterly and one-sidedly, the
worst it said editorially was: "*The Anarchists believed that
he* [Altgeld] *was not merely an alien by birth, but an alien*

by temperament and sympathies, and they were right. He has apparently not a drop of true American blood in his veins. He does not reason like an American, not feel like one, and consequently does not behave like one." But it set a keynote, and every Chicago paper of importance followed suit, the *News,* the *Inter-Ocean,* and the rest.

The theme was plain, outlined and underlined, not only anger, but a growling rage such as had never appeared in American newspapers before. As John Peter Altgeld read the stories, smiling thinly as more and more newspapers came in, from downstate, from Cleveland, from west and east and south, one matter after another shaped itself into focus. Nervous, his secretary asked, "Do you want all the papers, Governor?" "All of them." "I think this is hasty anger," the secretary reasoned, trying to make it better. "Not hasty at all, not at all." It amazed him that the Governor seemed to be in such fine spirits. But at lunch that day, Altgeld told his wife:

"The hardest thing in the world is to see what's in front of a man's nose. I could have pardoned the most depraved murderer, the worst sexual pervert, the most successful forger, the most skillful bank-robber, and they would have slobbered with approval. There's only one thing that hits them in the belly, and that's any threat to their rule. I shook the oligarchy, Emma, and I'm going to shake them more. I'm going to ride this. It's just beginning, but I'm going to ride it all the way through. I told them their justice was no justice, but a fraud, and so are their courts, and so is the whole dirty rotten fabric of their state. And they're going to take it, because the people will be with me."

A new pile of papers were put down alongside him, the first one from the east coast with the headline: "ANARCHIST

GOVERNOR SLAYS JUSTICE." And another: "RUIN AND REVOLUTION DECREED BY GOVERNOR ALTGELD."

"This isn't the people," he said. "Emma, let me see you smile."

"I can't smile. I can't smile at that."

"Why? Because fat-bellied owners issue directives and tell them what to write?"

"Because the whole world is reading that. My God, Pete, every one of them, every paper, every writer, every single one—"

"What did you expect?"

"I don't know. You were right. You didn't do anything wrong."

"My God, Emma, right and wrong—you keep harping on that. There is no right and there is no wrong. We live by pig ethics and a pig code. I live by it! You do! That's this precious damned world of ours!"

"But I thought—"

"That some would be with me? Well, some will. The socialist papers will be with me, the labor papers—what is left of the old Abolitionist sheets, they'll be with me, and maybe here and there will be a man with guts, maybe one in a hundred. But I told them that their justice was not justice. I told them that they are capitalists, building a country for capitalists, and that means war to the death."

"And for you—"

"Let them shout! Let them wake up the country! I am sick to my stomach of the cheap little rats, the McDonalds, the Mark Hannas, the Armours—all the dirty little buyers and sellers of votes. There are seventy-five million people in this country, and they're strong—My God, Emma, they're strong! I'm talking to them, and they'll hear me. They haven't any voice now—this trash, these rags—it's not their voice. But they can be given a voice. They can be given a party. They can be made to understand that their votes are like a sledgehammer, ready to drive these rats back."

So he sat in his office and did his work as Governor and read the papers and the mail and the telegrams. As he said, there was a voice here and there raised to support him, but the rest, by and large, all of it, not slackening, day by day, was hate, filth, condemnation, threats in the mail. It became a phenomenon, a thing that had never been seen before, not even when Booth slew Lincoln, not even when the guns fired on Fort Sumter; and no part of the nation was laggard. They called him an alien; they questioned his citizenship; they denied that he had ever fought in the war; they denied his legitimate parentage; they demanded his impeachment; they demanded that Federal troops march against the Capitol of Illinois; they called him a socialist, an anarchist, a communist; they inferred that he had personally directed the throwing of the bomb; they wrote ugly, dirty stories of his relationship with his wife; they accused him of being a Jew and part of an international Jewish plot; they called him a dictator, a Nero, a Pontius Pilate; they said that he had both murder and lesser crime in his dark past; in almost every church in America, sermon after sermon was preached against him; and the newspapers that came onto his desk, raging with filth and venom, were like a geographical index: *The Los Angeles Times, The New York Times, The Atlanta Journal, Harper's Weekly, The Nation, The New York Sun, The Chicago Journal, The Washington Post, The Boston Herald, The New York World, The Philadelphia Press, the New York Herald, The New York Tribune, The Louisville Courier-Journal, The Pittsburgh Commercial-Adver-*

tiser—those and a thousand more, all racing for a goal in venom. He was cartooned wild-haired, with pistols in each hand, with daggers in his teeth, with bombs, with sticks of dynamite; he was pictured strangling liberty, crushing liberty under his feet, snarling at the full-blown female figure of liberty, knifing her, shooting her, even raping her.

And sometimes, there were statements of support. Almost without exception, the socialist and labor papers supported his stand. And here and there, small papers, small-town papers, little western sheets, hand-set, run by one or two men—these came out to back him, to praise him, to say that there were men who admired and loved him.

Yet the other could not but have its effect. Emma saw the change in him, the widening streaks in his hair, a redness about the eyes; his carriage was not so erect. She came on him once as he sat at his desk, reading and re-reading a foul little verse from *The New York Sun:*

> *O, Wild Chicago, When the Time*
> *Is Ripe for Ruin's deeds,*
> *When constitutions, courts and laws*
> *Go down midst crashing creeds,*
> *Lift up your weak and guilty hands*
> *From out the wreck of states,*
> *And as the crumbling towers fall down*
> *Write ALTGELD on your gates!*

He turned to her and said, "It's not nice, is it, my dear Emma?"

"How can you stand all this?"

"All of it and a lot more."

"Won't it ever stop?"

"This is only the beginning, Emma. We go on from here. It's only the beginning for them—and for me too."

Part Four

THE SECOND VARIATION

On a march evening of 1895, he finished a quiet, intimate, yet triumphant dinner, just himself, Altgeld, Governor of Illinois, Emma, his wife, and Hinrichsen, the Secretary of State, the three of them under the big crystal chandelier, intimate, confidence resolved, Emma watching her husband with affection and admiration, Hinrichsen noticing how she looked at the Governor and thinking that a woman had never looked at him that way, and Altgeld smiling, pouring out a glass of clear yellow wine for each of them, and proposing the toast to his wife.

She said the toast should be otherwise. "After two years, Pete—"

Hinrichsen proposed that they drink to the Governor. "Not to myself, Buck." "This is your night, this is what you worked for." "Only a beginning, a plan—the work still comes." "Then we drink to that," Hinrichsen said. "Then to success, to the plan." The Governor said, all right, he would drink to that. He stood up with his second glass of wine and had to grasp the edge of the table to keep himself from reeling, and smiled again to quiet the look of alarm that came into his wife's eyes.

"A people's party," he said simply.

His wife rose and walked around the table to offer him her arm, but there was something of annoyance in the manner of his refusal, as he said, "Go into the parlor with Buck, my dear. They'll be coming soon." And as she still looked at him, "I have a little work to get out of the way."

"Yes. But you won't keep them waiting?"

"Suppose you call me when they're all here."

"All right."

He turned away, and when Hinrichsen looked at her questioningly, she shook her head. Hinrichsen offered her his arm, but she didn't move until the Governor had left the room, and then she sighed and her whole body seemed to loosen, wilt.

"He'll be all right, Emma," Hinrichsen said.

"Yes—"

"The man's tired. My god, when you think of what he's done—when you think of any man coming out from under the past two years, and coming out with half the country afraid of him, hating him, and half the country worshiping the ground he walks on—well, that's something to consider."

They were walking into the parlor, and she stopped suddenly, pulling her arm loose, facing the big man. "Is it for me, Buck? Is that what I should consider? Do you know that he's dying?"

"No." And then added, very slowly, "I knew he was sick—"

"The way he walks—you've seen that?"

"Yes."

"He's forty-eight years old, and he's dying, and all he's ever known is struggle, no rest, no peace. I'm tired of it. It had to be this kind of a finish for him, out of his childhood, out of all the rotten terror of it. Well, I don't want him to have this. I want him to go away, to have a little peace."

Hinrichsen nodded.

She smiled, relaxed, became the hostess again. "He doesn't know what peace is or what a man is supposed to do with it. There are cigars in the cabinet, Buck. Please help yourself. Do you want some brandy?"

"I'll wait, thank you, Emma."

She sat down on a small, plush-covered lady's chair, the wooden rosebuds of the back making a frame for her, hands crossed demurely, a gentle lady with graying hair, but still good to look at, still alive and attractive. She asked the big, red-faced politician:

"Will he carry it off?"

"What do you think?"

"I think he could do almost anything. I remember how he was a boy with a German accent, and he read a book with a dirty finger marking out the words. That was when he fell in love with me, do you know?"

"I know."

"And he doesn't want to die. My God, Buck, none of us want to die. They tried to destroy him because he pardoned three men who were innocent, but he came out like a giant, and the people want him—"

"Emma, stop it!"

"Yes. You like him, don't you?"

"Yes."

"At first you hated him. People hate him at first."

"I like him."

"All right. I won't be hysterical, Buck. Schilling will be here, and Joe Martin and Darrow and Sam McConnell, and it will be like old times, won't it?"

"That's right."

"And then he'll want me to go, Pete will—it's no woman's world yet, is it, though it will be some day—but afterwards he sits down and tells me, word for word; it comes clearer and better, I suppose."

Hinrichsen said, "You're a remarkable woman, Emma." He took a cigar from a gold case, snipped the end neatly with a cutter that hung on a gold chain on his vest, and, as he lit it, said, "Would it be violating any confidence to tell me why he hates Grover Cleveland the way he does?"

"You know."

"I know what anyone does, Emma. I know that during the big Pullman strike, the president pushed Federal troops in. I know that Pete stood up to him. I know what the Federal marshals were. But there's more than that. You don't have to tell me."

"I'll tell you. Do you know how someone is bought, bought body and soul and hand and foot? Do you know you can buy a president? You want to know why Pete hates him—well, because he's a frightened man, a stupid man, a man who sold himself. When he came into this state with his troops, his guns, those thugs whom he swore in as Federal employees, Pete was ready to fight him. Yes. And what would that have meant? State militia ranged against Federal troops. Pete knew what it would have meant, and it was too big, so the men out at Pullman lost. Little men whose wives and children had nothing to eat, and they put themselves together to ask for something more. The Army came in, and they lost. Do you still want to know why Pete hates Grover Cleveland? It's not a confidence."

II

GOVERNOR PETE ALTGELD walked to his office with a slow, shuffling step. Sometimes, it was this way, sometimes less, sometimes more. Inside, a process was at work, the nerves were going, the fine connections were breaking down. He was like a man in a house going bad, the roof leaking, walls splitting, floors rotting; and like a man in such a house and unable to repair the damage done, he would sometimes vent his fury on himself. This was not the night-time fear, the fear that spread over his body so strangely, as if he were all a sponge and the fear water soaking through, creeping over his heart, paralyzing it almost with a signifi-cance of death and uselessness and finality, the utter ending of an ending; but this was impatience and anger in which he could curse God for giving him the body he had, ma-laria-wracked, disease-ridden; not fall into superstition and black magic, thinking of sin and payment of sin, but demand life and strength, harshly and imperiously—yet uselessly.

Sitting down at his desk, he put his face in his hands, and then lowered the whole of himself in the dark, until he lay with his shoulders and face and hands hunched upon the desk, inert and lost and angered and terrified, searching for himself and for something strong to put his two hands on, to hang onto and to hold himself up with.

The thought of Parsons held out sustenance in the fact of Parsons' lack of fear; Parsons had stood on the edge of death and had not been afraid, but Parsons was young and strong and smiling, and Parsons had faith, more faith than he, more direction and singleness of purpose. Parsons had starved and gone hungry and ridden the rods of freights from town to town, talking to ragged mobs of workers, and never known what it was to have a hundred dollars of cold cash in his pockets, and never known the taste of yellow wine after a fine, rich dinner—so why did he look to him for strength?

Thoughts of Parsons revived him from his despair, and substituted anger for misery. He had enemies; they hated him; he hated them. Parsons was quiet in his grave, and he, Pete Altgeld, had nothing to be ashamed of. He had fought Pullman, the way he knew, going over his tax accounts, making the city bite into him, the way he had fought the *Tribune*—the way it sometimes seemed to him he was fighting the whole nation. He had fought the president too. They could do nothing to him that he wasn't strong enough to take, say nothing about him. In New York, they said of him that he was a Burr without Burr's brains, a Johann Most without Most's decency, a Eugene Debs without Debs' courage—without Debs' courage. He turned that over and over; Debs had courage, no doubt of that—the same kind of courage Parsons had; they were cut out of the same cloth, and that was why he had waited so anxiously during the big strike to meet Debs. They had an appointment, carefully arranged by Schilling, and then Debs never showed up. What sort of wild ideas lay in back of his head as he waited to meet Debs? The President of the United States was sending troops into the sovereign State of Illinois. He was defying the president. If his militia had turned their guns on the Federal troops, what would have happened? Could history hang on such thin threads, or was it part and parcel of the sudden, impossible world he created as he waited for Debs to come? It had seemed to him then, only months ago, that a whole era of history was coming to an end, and that out of chaos would come something new and possible; but Debs never came; the Federal police took him, and the half-formed dream dissolved without ever being. Now he had another way, a better way. He was not a Debs, a Parsons. He was a democratic politician, and, as some said, the best America had ever produced. . . .

His wife's voice broke through the darkness into his thoughts. "Pete?"

"Yes."

"Sitting here in the dark?"

"I must have dozed off."

"You're feeling all right?"

"Fine. Fine."

"Are you—"

"As a matter of fact, I never felt better."

"They're here. They're all inside, waiting for you."

"Yes?"

"I put out brandy and cigars. You're sure you're all right?"

"Fine. Don't wait up for me, Emma."

He always said that and she always waited, sitting and performing careful needlework on some useless piece of linen, sometimes until the gray light of dawn dissolved the shadows around her lamp.

III

By MIDNIGHT, in the parlor, the cigar smoke lay like a blanket of dirty gauze, and the faces of the older men had that gray look which comes with weariness and age. Darrow was lost in some inner contemplation; Joe Martin sprawled low on the couch, his legs thrust out; Schilling was hunched up; and Hinrichsen enveloped the lady's chair. McConnell, talking as he sipped brandy, was saying to the Governor:

"Populism is a lost cause. No matter how I look at it, it's a lost cause. The people's party is going down, down, down, and in ten years it won't exist."

"For the tenth time, I tell you this is not populism."

"It amounts to the same," Joe Martin said.

"Like hell it does! I'm not a socialist—you ought to know that if no one else in this fool country does. I'm the Democratic Governor of one of the biggest industrial states in the union. I'm no populist—I'm a Democrat! Do I have to drill that into your skulls?"

"Pete—Pete, wait a minute," Hinrichsen said. "You're tired. We're all tired. Let's not get to calling names." And to McConnell, "Sam, let me put it this way. The party is rotten. All right, I grant you, that's a point of view. It's Pete's point of view, it's mine. It's rotten to a point where it doesn't matter a damn whether you vote Democrat or Republican. Suppose the Republicans put up McKinley, as they're very likely to do; suppose the Democrats put up Cleveland again? What's the difference—you tell me?"

"Don't be an idiot!"

"Yes, one's a Democrat, one's a Republican, but to the Morgans, the Vanderbilts, the Rockefellers, the Armours, the McCormicks, the Goulds—to them it's no damn difference at all. They'd as soon have Grover as William or any other horse's neck that suits them. There's no more two-party system, there's a one-party system. Just in the past twenty years we've seen monopoly grow until it's like a fat, over-stuffed hog, embalmed in gold—gold—gold!"

"And I say that's socialism!"

Altgeld snapped, "Schilling, for Christ's sake, will you tell him what socialism is!"

Schilling bestirred himself; Darrow began to grin, and Joe Martin flipped a coin back and forth, from hand to hand. "The hell with it," Hinrichsen sighed, spreading his hands wide, and Schilling said gently, "It's not socialism, Sam, not at all, not at all. It isn't socialism. No matter how you look at it, socialism does away with the private ownership of the means of production. We don't propose that. So it's not socialism."

"Don't give me any damned schoolbook lectures," McConnell growled.

"Look, look," Altgeld said pacifyingly. "Let's understand each other. Our party, it's the party of the little man, always was, always, ever since Tom Jefferson made it. Read him. He made a party for the little man. Now it belongs to monopoly, body and soul. Grover belongs to monopoly, the party does, body and soul. And the password is gold. Ask the little man, the farmer—all over the state they're losing their farms—ask the small businessman how he's going to pay his debts, and he pays or goes bankrupt. Ask the workingman; every month he gets a dollar less in his pay envelope. I mean, we got something in common, something to fight for, to give them. Give them silver, sixteen dollars of silver to a dollar of gold. Free silver coinage; that's a beginning. Gives us the farmers, the worker, small business—and the silver states. Gives us something to stand on. Then we fight; then out goes Grover onto his fat behind. Sure I hate him; I hate his guts; I want to see him down and nothing and less than nothing, but I want to see the party back where it belongs, back with us, back with the people and not with monopoly. And if you think we're alone, talk to anyone who's been kicked out because he tried to buck the millionaires."

"And when you throw out the millionaires," Joe Martin said, "where do we find our money, Pete? I don't have to itemize a campaign for you."

"From the people."

"A dollar Democrat to a thousand dollars Republican?"

"At its worst, yes. But we won't be alone. You and I aren't paupers, Joe, but we're sitting here and talking about this."

"We can't do it," from McConnell.

"I tell you we can. We can win Illinois. We can bring a solid delegation to the convention. We can line up the silver states, the farm states, even most of the south. The hell we can't do it!"

"And a candidate?"

"Dick Bland of Missouri."

"No!"

"Why not?" Altgeld demanded.

"Because he's a roach! Because they're all roaches! You've talked to me three hours, Pete. Sure this can be done. You're right. It's been done before, it can be done again. I like it. I like to think of myself down there in Washington, pulling reins. I like to think of Cleveland out on his ass. But there's only one man in this country who could run on that sixteen-to-one nonsense and make it."

"And who's that?"

"Yourself."

There was a sudden quiet in the room. They looked at Sam McConnell, the Chicago judge who had suddenly became such a power in the city, as much perhaps as Mike McDonald, and then they looked at the Governor to see whether he was smiling or not.

"You're serious?" Altgeld asked.

"I'm serious as hell."

"I won't argue with you, Sam. I was born in Germany. I was three months old when they brought me here."

"No."

"That's right. I'd like to be president. I'd like to roll that on my tongue. But let's talk sense."

"I'm sorry, Pete."

"Never mind. Let's get down to business, it's late enough. I say it can be done, I swear it can be done. Will you come along with me?" He looked from face to face. "Sam?" A brief nod. "Buck?" "Sure as hell." "Clarence?" A nod again. "George?" A slow smile. "Joe?" "Right to hell, Pete."

"Any doubts?"

"I got doubts," McConnell said. "I don't think Bland can do it. I think we'll split the party at best. I hate that thought like hell."

"We won't split the party."

"What about your own health?" Darrow said. "You're going to have to carry this."

"I feel good. I could say I never felt better."

"Have you any money promised?"

"That's a long way off. We'll get the money. We start small, we start gently. We work in the state committee, slowly, gently, first a word here, then a word there. Talk to people alone, and don't hit them over the head. Let it come from them. Get them thinking on how it would be to call a special party convention on silver. Don't lay it down the line. Just talk silver. And don't worry about the votes I control. Maybe there are enough of them to swing it, but I want it overwhelming. Every step of the way I want it overwhelming. We're not going to split the party—we're going to steer it, away from the east, away from Wall Street. Joe, I want you to work on Coughlin. Bathhouse John's been an alderman so long he's prepared to die that way. Well, start him thinking. Talk his own language. Maybe he can even be mayor some day. He'd like to think about that. Let him get out the torchlight parades and beer parties—that'll be along about June. Clarence, feed publicity; never mind my name, I want to be out of this, but I want the country to start watching Illinois. And George, we're going to need labor. My god, silver's no utopia, but it can't be worse, can it?"

"I think it might be worse," Schilling said slowly, more tired than the others, looking now, at this late hour, as if he had sold his soul. "But labor will support you, Pete. Who else has labor got to look to now?"

"How's that?"

"I'm tired, Pete. Labor will support you."

"At least one big meeting on silver, George."

"I'll promise ten thousand at a meeting."

"Fine. The convention should be called next month, for June, I think. We'll be a year ahead of any other state."

But they went on talking, and it was three in the morning before they finally left.

IV

Emma sewed a pattern onto a piece of yellowed Irish linen. The needle went round and round, scooping and searching; when she heard her husband come in, she didn't look up, but went on with her embroidery, isolated in the pool of lamplight. Watching her, Altgeld wondered what her reaction would have been had she remained downstairs with the cigars and the brandy and the talk, and he was suddenly sick and ashamed of himself, and knowing he had spoken too much, was puzzled to find sense in anything he had said. It was all muddled and disjointed now, and the grandiose concept of taking the government of a great nation away from those who owned it, seemed not only far-fetched but completely pathetic. His guilt magnified itself in relation to his wife, and the excitement with which he had finished the session evaporated. Watching Emma, he sat down in a chair. Finally, she put away her work and said, "It's very late, Pete, and hadn't we better go to bed?"

"It was very successful, Emma."

"Yes, I'm sure."

"I mean, they listened to me. They didn't think it was impossible. They didn't think it was just a wild dream."

"I'm sure they didn't, Pete."

"And I feel fine." He accentuated that; he came into the light. "I feel fine—I never felt better, Emma."

"Yes."

"You're angry with me, aren't you?"

"I'm not angry, Pete. I'm tired, that's all. Two o'clock one night, three the next. How long can you keep that up, Pete?"

"I feel good, I told you."

"Yes." She rose and put her hands on his face. "Pete, Pete, why do you hate the way you do? Why must everything be twice as violent for you? Why can't we be like other people?"

"I'm not like anyone else. No one is like anyone else."

"I'm sure, I'm sure."

"And Sam McConnell is in it with us, Emma, I'm going to elect the next president. I'm going to sit in there as secretary of state. I'm going to say what and how and why—"

"Pete!"

"Emma, Emma, let me dream, it's going to be so god damned hard."

"Pete, sometimes you frighten me." She took his arm. "Come to bed."

V

As TIRED as he was, Schilling could not sleep. Blind paths hemmed him in; gates were closed. How many years now had he followed Altgeld, blindly, trustingly? When he put his finger here and there, to add up the figures, he was not without justification and confirmation The day after the three Haymarket prisoners were pardoned, he, Schilling, went out to the cemetery. At Waldheim, in Chicago, a monument had been erected over the graves of the five dead men. Parsons, Spies, Fischer, Engel, and Lingg lay quietly, and now men spoke words over their graves. By the hundreds, they shook Schilling's hand, and there was one tall, knifelike man who was introduced to him as Eugene Debs. Debs—Debs—Schilling had heard the name. Yes, Gene Debs. He took Schilling's hand in both of his, and his words didn't come like the words of other men, but fell on each other, like a hammer driving home a spike. "When a new kind of history is written, a people's history, they will not be forgotten, and not you, Schilling." People wiped the tears out of their eyes. "Well, what I did was nothing," Schilling said, "and who can make the dead alive?"

There was standing next to Debs a little, withered Irishman, Brian Donahue, who had seen with his own eyes what had been done to workingmen called the Molly Maguires; he crossed himself now and shook his head, but Debs put a hand on his shoulder and said, "Sometimes the dead aren't dead. When workingmen go on strike, then Parsons is with them and so is Spies, and who can kill

them now? Ask Brian if the Molly Maguires are dead."
Donahue said, "There are those walking and living and
breathing and buying and selling, and sure as God was
Jesus Christ whom they nailed to a cross with His hands
outstretched because He wanted men to be free, then the
five blessed martyrs who lie here are as alive as you are
and I am. We will sing songs about them and make stories,
and my grandchildren and yours will not be quickly for-
getful." "So it's no small service," Debs said. "No small
service, Schilling." "We all did what we could." "But what
you did—all right, but some time I want to meet this
Governor of yours." "Altgeld?" "Would he sit down and
talk with me?" "We could meet again and go into it,"
Schilling said.

But it was more than a year before they met again, and
then Debs was waging war, with the Pullman Company and
Pullman's warm ally, the government of Grover Cleveland,
and Federal troops with fixed bayonets were bivouacked
in the empty lots of Chicago, and three thousand thugs and
desperadoes, wearing the badges of Federal marshals, were
ranging the streets of Chicago, beating and killing work-
men, and their wives and children, too, and many an innocent citizen who happened in their path.

Schilling met Debs in his strike headquarters, a gloomy
basement lit by one lantern; now the strikers were be-
leaguered; warrants were out for the leaders. They moved
from place to place, like hunted men, and a handful were
doing the work of a hundred. But for all of that, Debs was
delighted to see him, shook his hand warmly, and said,
almost pleadingly, "Will he act, Schilling? Will he act?"

"What can he do? Range his own state troops against
the Federal police?"

"He's the Governor of the state."

"And you'd ask him for civil war? My god, Debs—"

"What have we now, if not civil war? Does the Governor want photographs and affidavits of the dead workers who lie on the streets of Chicago?"

"He's doing all that's in his power. He's standing up to Cleveland. He's fighting him in the only sane way, with the law and within the Constitution. The Federal troops will be withdrawn. The people are with him, but every newspaper in the country is against him—worse than with the anarchists."

"But we'll break first."

"He can't take sides. Debs, don't you see that if he takes sides, then he's finished. All he can demand is the law, the letter of the law—"

"The law that murdered Parsons. The law that beats us, starves us, murders us, turns us into beasts."

"I tell you—"

"All right!" Debs stood up, towering over the little carpenter, drawn, haggard, and unforgettable too. At forty, he was coming out of one stage, into another, a man in flux and transformation and search, a man who reminded Schilling of Altgeld, yet so different that a real comparison could hardly be made. "All right!" he repeated. "Go back to the Governor! Go back and tell him that a worker dies or starves or rots as easily in his administration as in any other!" But when Schilling turned to go, Debs called him, his voice muted, contrite, "I would want to meet Altgeld. If I could meet him—"

Schilling went back to the Governor, but Altgeld and Debs did not meet. But afterward, when the strike was broken, Debs arrested, Altgeld took the lead in a public subscription to feed the Pullman workers. At least that.

A man does what he can do. But Pullman became another enemy of his, another of those he swore to war on, hunt down, get his claws into, and when Schilling reasoned that it was not Pullman the man, but the system, what Pullman represented, Altgeld angrily exclaimed, "It's the man, I tell you! Is there any law in this land that forces a man to be an unspeakable swine?"

Again Schilling met Debs. Now he could almost see the process of thought behind Debs' face; in defeat, Debs was calmer, in a sense more determined and more confident than he had been at the height of the great strike. His face told about jail; the pallor confronted Schilling like an accusation. But he spoke gently and warmly. When asked if it was hard, "Not very hard. I had a chance to read, to study, to learn. I think that something new will have to come."

"You mean socialism?"

"A strike is won or lost, that's not a decision. We'll lose more strikes, we'll win, too. But even when we win them, we get the crumbs that fall off the plate."

"I was a socialist," Schilling said. "This isn't a country for socialism. Even the workers don't want socialism."

"They don't know. They live in a pit. Do you want sunshine, if you've never felt it on your skin?"

"Socialism is a theory, an idea. Sometimes I think it's a crazy idea, put forward by people out of their minds. It never worked anywhere."

"It was never tried."

"They tried in Paris."

"Paris! My God, Schilling—you're going to sit there and tell me that in the French commune, socialism failed? It was never tried. The French and the Prussian monopolists made sure it was never tried. They murdered thirty thou-sand French workers in Paris alone. Do you forget so quickly?"

"But here in America, the people won't have it. What's the use of dreams—the people won't have it!"

"Some day—"

"But today! What about today? Today, at least, there's a leader. There's this man Altgeld."

"Altgeld." Debs said it very quietly.

"You don't believe in him?"

"He's one of their men. The state he serves is their state. He's a politician, no better, no worse."

"And the anarchists?"

"I admit that he has a sense of justice. But the bullets in the guns of his militia are no softer than the bullets in the Pinkertons' rifles."

"You have to believe in him. I know him. I know him for years and years. I tell you he's for the people, for the workingman. He believes in the people."

"Maybe he believes in them—"

"You could say that Lincoln was one of them too. But Lincoln was different. Lincoln fought for us, for the peo-ple."

"There were four million black slaves then. There are twenty million wage slaves today."

"If the workingman supports Altgeld, I tell you, things will change. There will be no more shooting and clubbing of workers. The courts will be ours as well as the million-aires'."

"I wish I believed that. Schilling, I wish I believed it."

And now, trying to sleep, Schilling sought for his own belief, and found it in no sustained line, no horizon, but only in bits, in fragments that were not enough to make a whole, but only enough to bedevil a man and keep him from sleep.

VI

ALTGELD took the first step the next month. For three weeks he worked frantically, setting every block in place, calling people, writing to them, lining them up, laying the foundation, so that when at last the Democratic State Committee met, he could sit back and let the motion for a special party convention on currency come from the floor, from the rank and file. The date set was June 5, 1895. It was done quickly, quietly, expertly, and when it had been done, the section of the party headed by Cleveland woke up to the fact that they had been duped; at first, that was their only reaction; they had been duped, and Pete Altgeld was making a bid for state party leadership on the incredible issue of free coinage of silver, the old homily that was the tool of every rabble-rouser in the west. It was John R. Walsh, a Chicago banker, an old enemy of Altgeld's via certain loans on the Unity Building, who first realized the full significance of what was happening.

For years now, a gap had been widening in the ranks of the Democratic Party. Populism, the movement among the western and middle-western farmers for a people's party, the natural outgrowth of the people's party of Thomas Jefferson, had grown to great strength in the seventies and eighties; actually, the rise of industry had given it a death blow, and now part of it was going into the new socialist movement, part—the great part and impulse—into the free-silver wing of the Democratic Party. The grange associations, the other farm associations, the small businessman, and the worker who saw his wages decreasing steadily, all sought desperately for some solution to the ruin that faced them. Money was scarce, and when the Federal government, under Grover Cleveland, stopped buying silver, money became scarcer. Debts piled up; farm after farm was put on the auction block; wages continued to drop. There was a wonderful and beautiful simplicity in the very simple answer that there was not enough money. Free silver coinage would solve all problems. Sixteen silver dollars to one gold dollar meant that the blood of the nation would begin to circulate again. The farmers could pay their debts. Prices would go up, but wages would go up even more quickly. It was hard to pick holes in this theory. You could talk your head off to a farmer or worker about cyclical depression, about capitalism and monopoly, but when you said that there wasn't enough money, that was something he understood, and when you offered silver money, to which there was practically no limit, as the cure-all, why he understood that too, and likely enough from there on was your man. Certain labor leaders tried to point out that money was no more or less than a relationship between the social factors of production and consumption, but their only tool of proof was the strike, and from San Francisco to Portland, the strike had been drowned in a sea of blood. In a country so desperate, Free Silver became an almost religious frenzy; even Altgeld saw in free coinage prosperity, an end to depression, and perhaps the break-down of the monopolies.

And in Altgeld's call for a silver convention in Illinois, John Walsh, the banker, saw something almost as frightening as the labor movement. He got on the phone to the president, and for a half hour hammered home his point. He liked the word *revolution*. He said, over and over, "I tell you it's revolution, Grover. I tell you if it isn't stopped, it's revolution." "They won't listen to him—they won't listen to that damned anarchist!"·"They're listening." "As for the state, maybe. As for the country, it's out of the question." "My god, are you blind, blind?" "Then what do you suggest?" "Write something, act, issue a call to the party." "That blows it up." "Well, you can't blow it up any bigger than it is."

Walsh held a private meeting in his office. Marshall Field came, and half a dozen other Chicago bankers and politicians. They talked heatedly and at great length, Walsh hammering home the point:

"You're fools if you think it's going to split the party. I know Altgeld a little better than the rest of you. He's not trying to destroy the party—I wish to God I thought he was —he's trying to take it away from us, take it whole, and take the country along with it."

"Nonsense!" someone said.

"Nonsense—when you meet something head-on that's bigger than anything you could dream up yourself, then it's nonsense. I assure you, Pete Altgeld is the most dangerous man in America—not that anarchist tripe—he's dangerous at our own game, politics, votes. And unless he's stopped—"

"He'll be stopped," Marshall Field said.

"How?"

"There'll be a communication from the president to the Honest Money League. This dirty little upstart will be washed back to where he came from, the sewers. And meanwhile, Walsh, you hold a loan of his, don't you?"

"I do," Walsh said thoughtfully. . . .

The letter from the president came to Chicago, and Altgeld met it better than halfway. He called the press into his office; he had a way with them that was something of his own; he talked to them quietly and intimately, and there was sandwiched between his words a host of implications which reporters understood, for all that they were unable to reproduce them in their papers. He framed his interviews in an attitude. This time his attitude was one of suppressed mirth.

"What do you think of the president's letter, sir?"

"Bad."

"How do you mean—bad? Bad for the silver cause?"

"My word, gentlemen. I say bad, I mean bad. Badly written. Trash. If anyone else's name was signed to that amazing flow of meaningless words, it would have been the laughing stock of the country."

"Mr. Governor, isn't that putting it a little strongly?"

"Strongly, oh my sacred aunt! Suppose I had signed it?"

The reporters looked at him, at each other. They grinned. He grinned back.

"You gentlemen are writers. I talk within the limits of the craft."

They grinned more broadly.

"What is your opinion of the president, Mr. Governor?"

"Aside from the fact that he has sold America to the monopolies and his soul to Wall Street?"

They were still grinning.

"That's off the record. Aside from that, well—unprintable."

They roared; they came closer to his desk. Casually, he eased forward a humidor of cigars. "Help yourselves—" Some of those in front did; it was fine Havana. "Tell you something, gentlemen, speaking of the president. Who elected him? The people. Who pays him? The people. So maybe the people are beginning to be uneasy about this habit of his of sending Federal troops into sovereign states to shoot down strikers. You know, sometimes farmers don't like to lose their farms just because they can't meet their debts. Hard-headed people, farmers; it ain't easy to reason with them. I know. My own father was one of them. You tell them—just be patient and soon you'll die of starvation and go off to heaven and get your just reward, well, it just doesn't seem to sink in, they're so damned thick-skinned. So maybe they're beginning to wonder why their Democratic president is married the way he is to Wall Street and so dead-set against silver money, which might let them pay off a debt or two, and they might be wondering where all the U.S. marshals come from, the way you see them flooding our west, like cockroaches over old cheese. Tell you something else, gentlemen, I was talking to a workingman. I said to him, Joe, how do you like being without a job ten months? He said, Governor, I don't like it one damn bit. I said, Joe, you think you got a right to stand there and tell me you don't like unemployment? He said, I sure as hell have, Governor. So I reminded him, Joe, your president, down there in Washington, thinks it's a Federal crime for you to talk like that. So Joe said, The hell he does! Then maybe it's time, Governor, that we had a new president down there in Washington. These are good cigars, gentlemen. No strings attached to them."

More of the reporters lit up. An *Inter-Ocean* man, unmoved and hostile, said, "Any comment on the fact that the president is gunning for you, Mr. Governor?"

Altgeld leaned back and sighed. He took a cigar and picked at the end of it. "Gunning for me. . . . You know, they tell a story about old Davy Crockett. Davy, he's out taking a walk in the woods, and he sees a neighbor taking a sight on something. Davy never did like this neighbor. Too close, too crafty, too mean. So Davy just stands and watches him. Full ten minutes he stands there and watches this neighbor taking a sight with a sixty-inch squirrel gun, and for the life of him, Davy can't see what this gent is aiming at. Finally, his curiosity gets the better of dislike, and Davy saunters over. Out hunting, neighbor Jones? he asks. Neighbor says, shhh—shhh. Davy stretches his neck, but can't see a thing. What in hell's name are you shooting at, neighbor Jones? he asks. Neighbor Jones says, Crockett, sure as hell you're going to scare away the best dinner I seen in a fortnight. I got a sight on that big black bear up there in that tree crotch, and I'm taking a long sight because I don't intend to miss. So Davy looks up at the crotch, and to save his life he can't see a blessed thing. Then he looks at neighbor Jones. Then he busts out laughing. Damn you, Crockett, neighbor Jones yells, you sure as the devil scared away my game. But Davy's just standing there, holding his sides and laughing, until at last he gets up enough wind to say, Never was no game in that tree, neighbor Jones. You been standing there all this time taking a sight on a louse on your own eyelash."

VII

On June 5th, the silver convention met at Springfield. Bathhouse John Coughlin, who had staged more torchlight parades and beer picnics than he cared to remember, planned the convention from beginning to end, and it went off without a hitch.

On the evening before it began, there was a torchlight procession through the streets of Springfield to the executive mansion. The delegates walked arm in arm, eight abreast, chanting, "Altgeld! Altgeld! The son of Illinois! Altgeld! Altgeld! The son of Illinois!" Almost every citizen turned out to watch, and hundreds of children scampered in and out of the column, shouting and laughing and hooting. Bathhouse John had planted thirty kegs of beer under ice at the fire-house, and since he let the word get around, it was practically certain that none of the citizens would go to bed before the demonstration had run its course. It was a part of Bathhouse John's unique genius as a politician that he sincerely loved people, and that made him see a demonstration not as a shouting, noisy mob, but as a rounded whole of the people. He handed out passes to the state grounds to every boy who would bring a date, and now as the parade came onto the lawn in front of the mansion, it was surrounded by boys in their best suits and girls in crisp white organdy; and as they all gathered there, the Cook County band began to play a wonderful new song that was taking the country by storm:

> *Oh beautiful for spacious skies,*
> *For amber waves of grain,*
> *For purple mountain majesties*
> *Above the fruited plain.*
> *America! America!*
> *God shed his Grace on thee,*
> *And crown thy good with brotherhood*
> *From sea to shining sea.*

All this time, Altgeld was standing behind the doors, Emma next to him, Brand Whitlock on the other side, and through a space in the curtains he watched them come up and onto the lawn. It was the first time he had ever heard the song played and sung by many young voices, and it moved him curiously. He watched the faces in the flickering torchlight, thinking all the while of the hours he had spent with Bathhouse John, planning this, of how fixed and precise and manipulated every detail of it was, from the first beginnings to this to wherever it would take them —then meeting Emma's eyes, and knowing almost as well as she what was behind them, what thoughts, what fears, what endless, inescapable confusion.

Then he felt the pressure of young Whitlock's hand and realized that out there they were chanting his name and calling for him. He couldn't go; he was rooted where he stood, and he felt that no force on earth could impel him out there onto the veranda. He looked at Emma with real terror in his eyes. Whitlock was urging him:

"Please, sir, you must go out."

He shook his head. All the hundreds of times he had spoken from platforms were nothing now; stark, craven fear took hold of all of him, head and foot and body and soul and brain; and then Bathhouse John, red-faced and triumphant, burst in crying, "What an ovation! What an ovation! Greet them, Governor!"

The mood snapped. He went outside, and bowed, and the cheers rose up over the old cottonwoods. Afterwards, he hardly recalled what he said, something about no compromises, a straight path—

"Sixteen to one!" the crowd roared, and Bathhouse John sent his plug hat sailing, up and over the treetops.

And the next day, John Peter Altgeld stood for five full minutes in front of a cheering, half-hysterical convention. When he said, "The time has come for us, the democrats, the Democratic Party, to stand once more for democracy and no longer for plutocracy," a roar went up such as he had never heard before. It was no longer a question of opposition. It was a question of how far, and in what direction he, Pete Altgeld, wanted to go. He was the leader, acknowledged, and the party in Illinois would follow.

When he declared for silver, they screamed approval. "Free money and free people!" They stood up as one man, shouting, "Altgeld! Altgeld! Altgeld!"

"We point the way," Altgeld said. "We have declared for democracy. It only remains for America to follow."

VIII

His reaction was one of lethargy and despair. He would work himself into a state of hypertension, and there would be a long, dreadful, sleepless night, during which pain crept through the stillness into every bone and muscle of his body—and he would lie in the dark with the awful realization that he was dying, that his miserable, short, ugly body was beyond repair or rejuvenation. Seeing what was happening, Emma was drawn to him more than ever before. The shadow of a great man was rising over the land, such a man as Jackson was, or Abe Lincoln, a people's hero, the sort of man they spoke about in the shops, on the farms, and in the work gangs; and it seemed a peculiarly bitter piece of mockery that living with such a man, sleeping with him and eating with him, she should find an infinite pity overshadowing every other emotion. In some ways, he was almost childlike; he gave vent to fits of temper before her; he did petty things; he retreated into self-pity—yet even for her and through all of this, his stature increased, and for the first time she found in the substance of her own life that incredible dignity of mankind that is like nothing else. The mixed, blurred, faulty wonder of her husband extended itself to all people, and she found herself, after so many years of married life, beginning to be in love again.

For the first time, his triumphs became personal and

intimate to her. When the Illinois silver convention rang a bell through the land and the other states fell in line, Missouri, Texas, Mississippi, she was more pleased than he.

When Grover Cleveland went south to rally, if possible, a whole area of the land against Altgeld, she drove her husband to head a delegation to the Exposition of the Cotton States, which was being held at Atlanta, and his triumphal tour of the south excited her as nothing ever had before Now they would sit for hours and talk, in a way that they hadn't before and about things that they had never spoken of, breaking down the strange shame and reluctance that can exist for a lifetime between a man and his wife. His dreams and ideas somehow became more real, more solid for both, when he made word-pictures of them for her. He placed things before her almost naïvely; he let his thoughts run and leap, and then bound them in with doubt. They were sharing something they had never shared before.

Buck Hinrichsen, meeting her on the lawn one summer day, said, "My word, Emma, you look as if you inherited a million dollars."

"I feel that way."

But best was that through this man, her husband, her own native land was coming into a focus it had never had before. She understood why so many people had remarked that he was the most American product they had ever known. His love for the land was no ordinary thing, no simple thing; not patriotism as she had understood patriotism, but an amazing identity with motley millions of people drawn from every land on the globe, a fullness that could not be content with this nation or that nation, but only with a nation of nations; that saw in the boiling, many-layered society of states the only complete hope of men.

There was one evening when she had Brand Whitlock and Bill Dose in for dinner—he liked small dinners and young people—and the talk turned to Tolstoy. Altgeld read everything of Tolstoy's that came to the country, finding in him something he found in no American or English writer of this time. Yet tonight he was drawing an analogy between Tolstoy and Clemens, to the protests of both Whitlock and Emma. Whitlock went further than Emma, who would see Clemens only as a clown; but even Whitlock demanded, "How can you draw any comparison between *Tom Sawyer*, or even *Huckleberry Finn* and a work like *War and Peace*, sir? I don't see it, for the life of me."

Emma said, "Dickens, yes. I could see a comparison with Dickens. But Clemens—"

"Never Dickens!" Altgeld snorted. "Never, never Dickens! Not in the same breath, not in the same sentence. What is asked of a writer? You want to write, Brand—you sit at night, scribbling away. What do you demand?"

"Of myself, sir?"

"Of anyone. Of anything you read."

"I don't know—I never thought of it that way. I suppose, to be entertained."

"And only that?"

Emma said, "Wouldn't it depend on whether you were reading for entertainment or for learning?"

"We've made such a curse of learning, Emma, that you'd put it a world away from entertainment."

"I mean, would I read your lawbooks for entertainment?"

"Even there, Emma, you're ridden with a concept. There's drama in my lawbooks none of your garden novelists could dream of, the whole stuff of life and death, the best and the basest in men, crime and grand villainy and petty purse-snatching, the whole astonishing record of what man will do to his fellow man. But that's off the path. I asked Brand what he wants in a writer, and he says entertainment, which, in a way, is true—"

"And more than that, sir. I don't know quite how to put it."

"Would it be in this? When I put Clemens and Tolstoy together, it's because the one has found the soul of America and the other knows the soul of Russia, but Dickens never went deeper than the soul of a shopkeeper. I've never been to England, but, my god, I find no smell of it in Dickens, no taste of it, no love of it, no real hope for it either, and I want a writer to give me that, and to give me people who love and hate and suffer and dream sometimes, like the poor devils in my lawbooks, or like the men and women in Tolstoy and in Mark Twain, not paper cutouts pasted over with so much fancy trimming that never an inch of the flesh shows through, if there is any flesh. So when you write, Brand, turn your stories into something more real than life itself. You only know what's outside a man in life, but sometimes a writer can show the inside and the outside at the same time."

"You ask a good deal," Whitlock smiled.

"Do I? Do you know what is most important, Brand, the be-all and end-all—simply good and bad, truth and untruth, and there's no one to lay down a yardstick. Ask Dose. He's watched me long enough. Do you think I believe in democracy, Brand?"

"I think so."

"You're kind. I wish I had a dollar for everyone who thinks otherwise. But I'm not asking too much when I ask for the real thing, for some of the flesh of life. You believe in democracy, but it doesn't happen by itself. If you don't get out the vote, someone else will. Maybe there isn't any democracy here, maybe there never was. You believe in democracy, but if you leave it to happen you go down under and there's nothing. So you become a cheap ward politician, blown up, only you do it better. You beat them at their own game. But you can't look in the mirror and face yourself. That's the reality—"

Whitlock listened, embarrassed, and was grateful when Emma turned the talk back to books; she did so deftly and easily, but she shared too much of her husband's moods not to be affected. She thought to herself, "It will be better when the thing is under way. He can't stop now. If he stops, it will be the end of him."

IX

HE DIDN'T stop. He drove onto the state Democratic convention with a fury and intensity the country had not seen before. For the next several months, it seemed that there was hardly a day's press where the name of Altgeld didn't break into the headlines. Instead of withering under the abuse that was showered upon him, he gained stature and appeared to draw sustenance from it. The more the silver theory was attacked, the more he leaped to its defense, and by now he believed that it was the only issue upon which the American masses could be united. He used the language of his enemies; he attacked them; he gave them no peace. He had Bill Dose line up a staff of researchers, and they dug into the lives of his enemies, of the Democrats who supported Cleveland, of the gold people. They wanted it hard and dirty and low—well, he would give it back to them in the same coin. When Carlisle, Secretary of the Treasury, attacked him, he flung back proof that some years ago Carlisle himself had spoken for silver. He did the same with Bishop Woodry; when the bishop accused him of godlessness, he gave the number of those who had died of starvation in Woodry's parish, and his researchers gave him the facts of the bishop's forty-thousand-dollar-a-year income and what was done with it.

His mood changed. He drove himself, but he was happy, more lighthearted than he had been in years. He engaged in a war to the death with the *Chicago Tribune;* he sent his blows in twenty different directions. For years he had studied law, practiced it, judged it from the bench; now he forged his knowledge into a two-edged sword and let his enemies know that he was ready to use it. He dug up every technical violation of a state law, of statutes that went back to the time when the state was created, and he served out a steady stream of subpoenas, dragged his enemies into court, had their books examined.

And he pardoned. Pardoning John, they called him, and he grinned back and continued to pardon. Wherever there was reasonable doubt, wherever a man had been framed, a poor damned woman railroaded, a worker condemned with only a mockery of a trial, a homeless, unemployed wretch dragged into court and tried and convicted to clear an embarrassing blotter, a labor organizer beaten up and jailed for assault, he used the power of executive pardon. He did it because it made those who hated him scream with rage and anger and demand his impeachment, but he also did it because he could not live without groping for the essence of right and wrong, and because a long time ago certain men, whom he never mentioned now, had died upon a gallows.

When the reporters asked him, "Governor, what do you make of the threats in the eastern papers?" he smiled and told them, "This is the sovereign State of Illinois. When the people of Illinois tire of me—the people, mind you, not the newspapers—they can throw me out. Until then, I'm Governor."

So when, the following June, the state Democratic convention assembled at Peoria, the eyes of a whole nation were turned there, and a hundred newspapers screamed, in one variation or another: "Is this the beginning of Altgeld's reign of terror?"

He had worked hard; he had planned well. Forty-eight delegates to the Democratic national convention, the whole number for the state, declared for silver, voted John Peter Altgeld state chairman, and pledged to support him.

Once more he listened to the bands, the shouting, the torchlight parades. He sat in a hotel room with his old friends, smiling just a little, and when someone asked him, "What do you make of it, Pete?" he said, "It could be a beginning for something. It could, you know."

X

BACK at Springfield, Sam McConnell called him, and said, "Pete, you'll have to see Bryan."

"Who?"

"Bryan. You heard me. William Jennings B-r-y-a-n, the nightingale, the boy orator of the plains."

"Sam, Sam, look—I don't have to cover up for you. I'm sick, I'm sick as hell. And I've got a big job to do. I want to get it done. I want to do one decent act before I make up my bed, and that's to put a president in the White House who isn't an errand boy for Rockefeller or a book-keeper for Morgan. We decided that Richard Bland might carry it off. All right, there's enough to do, isn't there?"

"Take it slowly. I said see him. Shut him up."

"My God, Sam, do you know what he wants? Do you know what that fool with the pap still wet on his lips wants? He wants to be president. That's all he wants."

"I know. That's why I say, see him. Shut him up."

"Suppose you shut him up. Do I have to talk to every hare-brained idiot who decides he wants to be president? Bland's no knight in armor—I know that. But he's been in congress, he's been in the Senate. He's as honest as any of us, and he's with us. He's made a hell of a name for himself in Missouri, and he's stood steady on this silver thing for a long, long time, and the people will look at him and say, this isn't a revolution, this is an honest man and it's time we had one like that in Washington. Do I have to make political speeches to you?"

"You don't have to, Pete. For God's sake, talk sense."

"I'm talking sense. But when every minute counts from now to the convention, you want me to waste hours with idiots."

"Have you ever heard Bryan talk?"

"You know I've heard him. I heard him at the silver convention. I've heard auctioneers and street hawkers and Indian medicine men, too."

"Pete, see him. Please. Do it for me. You can whittle him down. I don't know who else can. I've insulted him, laughed in his face, and done everything but pull his long, lovely hair—and he still wants to be president. And, so help me God, Pete, I'm afraid of him, the way you're afraid of a little boy who's a lot stronger than most men."

"I'll see him."

"Pete—thanks. You know, I'm getting no younger; neither of us is. You get old and you get afraid. You have bad dreams. Well, this is our last chance, Pete. God help me, I don't know my country any more."

So he saw Bryan. In his thirties, tall, handsome, the long dark hair like something out of another century, Bryan first strutted, then orated, then wheedled. Altgeld watched him, chin in palms, and answered shortly and dryly.

"You don't trust me," Bryan finally said.

"Look, son, it's not whether I trust you or not. But it's funny about this job of running the country, and what it means to our people. Not that you can't fool them—"

"Then I'm a fraud!"

"Not that you can't fool them—they've been fooled so many times that it makes you ache to think about it. They've been fooled into thinking that their two parties are different, when right now they're as alike as peas in a pod. They've been fooled into voting for the wrong man; they've been fooled into voting themselves into serfdom and chains. They've been fooled into voting themselves into starvation and misery and heartache. And still when it comes to a president, they think it's a job for the best man the country can produce."

"But *I'm* not the best man," Bryan said. "Why? Why can't I convince you?"

"Maybe you wouldn't be able to convince the voters for the same reason. You're a young feller."

"I've been in government. I've been tried—"

"Sure. Sure you have. And maybe someday you'll be five times the man Dick Bland is. Maybe now. But it isn't just a job of making one man president—you know that as well as I do. It's a job of throwing a pack of scoundrels out of Washington and giving the country back to the people who made it. It's bigger than any one man. It's too big to jeopardize. I'd like to be president too, son. I'd like it a hell of a lot. Well, I can't. Neither can Sam McConnell. Neither can Daniel. Neither can Hinrichsen. You see, we can't fool the people. We don't have the forces, the money, the ballyhoo, the machine."

"But the people would follow me. I tell you—"

"Bill, you're a good speaker. You got a good tongue there. You got a head on your shoulders, too. But I think you're a little young to be president. Don't break down this thing. We've worked too hard on it. We've built too long and too carefully."

"All right. If that's the way you feel about it, there's nothing else I can do. Unless they want me—"

Altgeld rose and put his arm around Bryan's shoulder. He walked with him to the door, talking, repeating words and more words. And afterward he felt sick and angry and disgusted. To have to plead like that with a fool, with a strutting peacock who wanted to be president! Afterward, he wanted to wash his hands of the whole thing, be rid of it and done with it, with politics, with this whole business, never to argue or plead or bully or cozen again as long as he lived.

XI

BEFORE the national convention began, Emma took a suite of rooms at the Sherman House. She was glad to be back in Chicago; in some ways, after so long a time at the executive mansion, it was like a homecoming, like a return to an upset normalcy that was not comfortable but certainly natural. It was good to shop again, to stand on the lakefront, to walk on the dirty streets, to watch the crowds that were like crowds in no other city in the world, to see the haze of smoke hanging over the factories, to feel the strong smell and to hear the violent sound of Chicago.

She thought it might be good for Pete's health, but it wasn't; it couldn't have been. He took over the parlor of the suite, and no matter how she aired it, the smell of cigar smoke and stale alcohol never departed. Instead of getting better, the gray pallor of his face increased, and the shuffle in his walk became more pronounced than ever.

All day long a steady stream of men went in and out of that room; all day long the rising, falling sound of voices came from there. A core was being made there, a unit of forces from every state in the union. From the very beginning, Emma had followed the steps of insurgence, the first wildcat state committee meeting, the silver convention, the vicious, all-out attack on Grover Cleveland and the other big business forces who controlled the party, and finally the state convention—yet with all that in mind, she still found it difficult to comprehend how in the short space of one year, her husband had become the undisputed leader of the National Democratic Party. Yet it was a fact. From Texas, from Missouri, Arkansas, Virginia and Pennsylvania and Colorado, from state after state came the delegations, and in almost every case their first point of contact was the suite of rooms in the Sherman House.

She became conscious of two Americas: the surface, vocal America, the America of the Newspapers, the pulpits, the courts, the banquets, and the after-dinner speakers —that America hated and castigated Altgeld; to that America, he was the enemy of his land, the first villain, a horned devil who had espoused socialism, communism, and every other ism that had ever existed—except, of course, capitalism and patriotism—and whose sole purpose was to bring down the republic in ruins. But there was another America, almost voiceless, the America of the farmer, the workingman, the small businessman; and to them, for all the screaming of the newspapers, Altgeld was something rare and new, the kind of a leader they had been waiting for. By an accident of birth, he had been denied the presidency, but no accident denied him leadership of the party.

So they came from every corner of the land, eager to see him, to put eyes on him and shake his hand, to be able to say to him the words most of them had planned so carefully: "We cried down there when we heard about Haymarket and what you had done." "You got friends in California, Governor." "I remember old Abe—he used to say, trust a man whom the rich hate." "Down our way, they tell it, everyone hates Altgeld but the people."

They found a small, tired, bearded man. They heard a low voice that had a file-like quality. When he moved, they realized that he was weak and sick, but that was an impression that didn't last, and after a day or two they could no longer think of him as a sick man. The most lasting impression was that of the blue eyes, alert, sparkling, two spots of youth in an aging body.

They came with no united purpose, no formed plan, only the confidence that this was an opportunity for revolt that had not existed before. They met Buck Hinrichsen at the door, and he brought them in and introduced them to the Governor. Those who had been politicians and nothing more than politicians had a new feeling; the job-seekers, for a while at least, thought of other things than their possible spoil; the plain citizens thought about how some day, telling this, they would remember how it had been to meet Pete Altgeld. Altgeld talked to them; he told stories; he dug up mutual acquaintances from their states. Sometimes, he mentioned Dick Bland of Missouri, and hoped they would see their way to supporting him. They all came with local favorite sons, and there was a real danger, which Altgeld recognized, in starting a boom too early. He laid the emphasis on issues they held in common, an anguished need for security, a hatred of monopoly, a dread fear of this new thing that had arisen, government by injunction, or an extension of the power of the court to a point where it could quell revolt by declaring action illegal even before the action had occurred, and the faith in free silver coinage as a cure-all for every kind of evil.

Emma tried to hoard his failing strength, but from the beginning, it was a losing battle. This was his great moment, the time he had worked for and hoped for; now he was not going to hold back, and nothing on earth could make him hold back. When a delegate asked him, "Have you got a slogan for this convention, Governor?" he answered, sharply and shortly, "No compromise—that's our only slogan!"

XII

A BIG man came to the hotel suite and told Buck Hinrichsen that he wanted to see the Governor, but he wasn't a delegate—still he wanted to see the Governor, he thought it was important that he should see the Governor. His name was Mark Woodbridge, six feet and three inches, with the coal dust deep in his pores and in the lines of his hands, saying plainly enough that he was a miner and never would be anything else. He was dressed in a black Sunday suit of clothes that clung to his ankles and his thick wrists, and he kept turning his hat nervously, over and over.

"What about?"

"About Peoria. About the strike in the mines down along Peoria way."

Well, didn't he know that the Governor was up to his ears with the delegates and with the business of the campaign, and that this was in the nature of a caucus? And the Governor couldn't see just anyone, although the Governor would. All this patiently, for Buck Hinrichsen was old-timer enough to know that at convention time you don't insult anyone, ten voters or one voter.

"Well, suppose you tell the Governor I'm the brother-in-law of one of the four men he pardoned, up on murder and convicted for killing during the strike. At the Peter Little mines, you remember?"

"I remember," Hinrichsen nodded. He did. He had argued the matter with Altgeld, pointing out that this on top of the Haymarket pardon would be insane. "Then I'm insane, because these men are as innocent as you are, Buck, and maybe more so," Altgeld said, and then had gone ahead and pardoned them.

Hinrichsen said, "Wait a minute," and then went in and told the Governor. "I want to see him," Altgeld said.

Woodbridge came into the room, and stood there, looking at the little bearded man who was Governor. Two southern delegates were in the parlor, and Bill Dose, who had been taking dictation, and Sam McConnell, standing by the window and smoking a cigar.

"Glad to meet you, Woodbridge," Altgeld said.

Woodbridge nodded, still turning the hat, appearing to fill all the space left in the room. His Adam's apple moved convulsively, and Altgeld guessed that he was embarrassed and not a little awed.

"You must have had a good reason to come all the way up here to see me," Altgeld said, trying to make things easier. "If you came up just for that?"

"I did."

"All right. Don't worry about these folks here."

"Well—"

"Go ahead and talk, son."

Sam McConnell turned to look at the miner, and now the two southern delegates were watching him.

"Well—we had a meeting down our way. Maybe I ought to start back. My sister would have been left with three kids, if you'd have let them hang him."

"Him?"

"At the Peter Little. I swear to God, Mr. Governor—I saw it happen. They were innocent, all right. Never came near the place where the men were murdered. My God, our own men were murdered, and by the scabs they brought in from upstate. But then they arrested the union leaders—"

"I pardoned them, didn't I?" Altgeld said shortly.

"Yes, sir. I want you to know you didn't make no mistake. So we held a meeting and took up a collection to send me up here, to tell you that you and whatever man you're standing for got three thousand votes down there, just as solid as anything could be. That's all."

"You came up here for that?"

"Yes—we didn't know what else to do. They thought they ought to send me."

"Thank them for me," Altgeld said.

"Yes, sir."

"I hope you get a good man to vote for, a good man for president."

"Yes, sir. The way we feel—well, they told me to say it ought to be you. We don't know how you do it, but we feel it ought to be you."

"Thanks."

"I couldn't go back and say to them that it'll be you?"

"No—it won't be me. It'll be a good man."

"All right. I'll tell them that. Thank you." He started for the door, but Altgeld stopped him.

"Wait a minute. What did it cost you to come up here?"

"Twenty—" Altgeld was digging into his pocket; the miner stopped short, shaking his head to the rhythm of his turning hat. "No, sir," he said.

"Expenses, that's all. You ought to get it back."

"No, sir," the miner said evenly. Then he left. Then Altgeld turned to Judge McConnell and murmured, "Jesus Christ! Oh, Jesus God."

"So it's three thousand votes if he isn't lying. That doesn't make anyone anything."

"You couldn't see if something was painted on the wall. Underlined, too."

"Maybe."

"All right. Then let's get down to work."

XIII

THEY drafted a platform, a rough draft scribbled down in pencil, in a smoke-filled, whisky-sodden room, Altgeld, McConnell, Jones the Arkansas Senator, and Tillman of North Carolina, and Bathhouse John of Chicago, and Schilling for part of it, and Darrow called in to lend his acrimonious voice, and Boies, the Governor of Iowa, and a half dozen more, coming in and out, summoned hurriedly, in the middle of the day or the middle of the night —and always it was Altgeld's flat, probing voice that took the lead, that pulled them out of the morass of generalities back to the fact:

"I tell you, gentlemen, that you either open your eyes or go back to the tall woods. We're not living in Jefferson's day. In Jefferson's day there wasn't a factory in this land

that employed more than a hundred men, and now how
many are there that employ ten thousand or fifty thousand? That's the fact, the core of it. Are you for the workingman or against him?"

"Of course, we're for him! For Christ's sake, Pete, stop
harping on that."

"Then if you're for him, put it down in black and
white. Put it down specific, where he can read it."

"Generally—"

"Oh, my aunt! I am so goddam sick of that!"

"What are you asking for, Pete? Come out with it? Do
you want socialism?"

"Socialism! Now what in hell is socialism? Suppose you
tell me! If we're against government by injunction, is that
socialism? If we're for arbitration of labor disputes, is that
socialism? If we're for a square deal for labor, is that socialism? Would it be socialism if a workingman could
come into a court and know that the damfool on the bench
wasn't a hired hand of Pullman or John D. Rockefeller?
If that's socialism, then you're a monkey's uncle!"

"Now wait a minute, Pete. Now just take it easy. We've
all agreed that we're for a general plank on the rights of
labor. Nobody's disputing that with you."

"Sure. You're aware that you've kicked over the bucket
and the milk's out. You can't put it back, you can't lick
Grover's ass any more, and you either get the farm and
labor vote, or this is the biggest defeat the party ever suffered."

"If you want to put it that way."

"And I tell you you're not going to get labor's vote without putting down in black and white just why a workingman should vote for us. We got good intentions and a
little gravy to splash around, and the Republicans got

twenty million dollars to spend. That's what a general plank needs—it needs twenty million dollars to make the lies stick."

"Governor, be reasonable!"

Be reasonable, be reasonable—it was a refrain that they threw at him, hour after hour and day after day; and day after day, he fought back, snarling sometimes, spitting, wheedling, pleading, and then snarling again. And sometimes it would appear to him, with a clearness and lucidity he had never experienced before, that all of this was hopeless, that though he had fought Grover Cleveland and the trusts he represented, and defeated Cleveland—through some amazing process the trusts had won, and these too were the trusts' men; and even his own actions were checked and frustrated on every hand, so that he was as little a master of himself as these men with him, and their evasions, for which he despised them, were not too different from his own evasions.

As when they brought him to bay and demanded, "Then what are you against, capitalism?"

He laughed that away. "Go look at the Unity Building," he told them, and that too was an evasion.

"Yes or no?"

"I'm for democracy," he said. "I'm for justice, that's plain enough." But inside, the question lingered, and the answer he gave them was as meaningless as his silver formulations sometimes seemed, and there was less and less sense and reason in the world. But he fought because only by the equation of justice and democracy could he draw strength from his failing body to go on, and the incredible strength of him, the rasping voice out of the huddled body, the sparkling, intense blue eyes, the fury of his attack forced them back, and point by point they yielded.

One by one, they wrote in his demands, specifically, ". . . we especially object to government by injunction as a new and highly dangerous form of oppression . . . we denounce interference by Federal authorities in local affairs as a violation of the Constitution of the United States . . . labor creates the wealth of the country . . . we demand the passage of such laws as may be necessary to protect it in all its rights . . . we demand a Federal income tax, to be graduated . . ." They argued about form, but Altgeld said, "Put it down. Put it down in black and white, and we'll shape the form later."

They put it down. The platform became his platform. But an undercurrent of rebellion was kindling. When he had finished and won and lay back in his chair in a state of semi-exhaustion, a condition so common of late, Judge McConnell said to him, "Don't drive them too far, Pete."

"I have to."

"We lose this chance—"

"Then we lose all," Altgeld said flatly.

XIV

ALTGELD was glad to see Joe Martin. He had been in and out with others, but Emma had begged him into one of the very few quiet dinners she was able to manage. "Joe, make him get hold of himself," she had said. Martin asked, "Is he bad?" "I don't know. He lives on nerve. I don't know, Joe. It would be terrifying if one man thought he could remake a country, a man whom they spat on and ground underfoot and thought they had destroyed—but he's doing it, do you see, Joe?" "I know he's doing it."

"But he's afraid—if one little prop is pulled out. Do you know how shaky it is?" "I know, Emma. I think I know how shaky it is, if I don't know anything else. I think I know that." "Well, he can't get hold of himself—"

So Joe Martin came, and they talked of old times. Martin drew him into memories bucolic and slow, the corn growing for the harvest, sleepy brown rivers, like the Wabash, how it was for so many of them who had come out of the bottom lands when the first growth of giant timber still stood in some places. And then Martin told his own tales, the way only he could:

"I never told you that time, Pete, going out to the coast on the old Union, and they had the card tables in the parlor car. There I was comfortable with a newspaper and a cigar, and perfectly willing to let it go that way, but three Texas badmen, real frontier tinhorn gamblers, they couldn't let it rest, oh no. They had to make their Chicago bunco pay off, and then I had no peace until I got up and sat in their game. Just quiet five-card draw, you understand. Just a simple city game for a simple city boy like myself. Oh, my goodness, Emma, I do not like tinhorn frontier gamblers who like to act like badmen, but very polite after they saw me take out a roll of bills like my fist to pay the waiter. Jack-high at a dollar to open and a dollar to raise, and they were dealing the deck, but polite-like, and just taking ten or fifteen dollars from me now and then. So by the time I was losing a hundred, they knew all about me, that my name was Steve Hennessy, that I was married, two kids, that I just played a little cards, now and then, that I had sold all my Chicago property, my wife's inheritance, six thousand dollars, and was off to the coast to buy a little piece of land and see if we could go it again. Well, I'm small and I look the part, gentle and quiet, and I figured if they had some decency about a character like I described myself to be, I'd leave them alone and call it quits and figure an evening at the price of a hundred. But no sooner do I open up than they graciously give me the opportunity to recoup and push it to five to open, five to raise, all the time dealing the deck in a way to make a South Side amateur blush with shame. So I drop another hundred and tell myself, like in the Bible, I'll give them another chance. So I tell them that a loss like this—well I never lost so much before, my wife will never forgive me, how can I explain?"

By now, the Governor was leaning back, chuckling to himself. He had heard the story before, many years ago, but like all good tales, it grew better and more mellow with time. It was right for him now, as right as anything could be. Emma protested, "Joe, how could you—like the Bible? That's blasphemous. You mean Lot?"

"Maybe I do, Emma. I'm not a church-going man, but I think even a bad man should be tried three times, don't you, Pete?"

"I do," the Governor grinned.

"But to lie that way—wife, children."

"My dear Emma, I was creating a character for their sympathy. They were bad men. They had no sympathy, no love for their own kind. I don't like men like that. I don't like men who take from children, and the way I played poker I was like a child. So when they refused to let a little man escape, but assured me that they would double the stakes again, I agreed. Tears in my eyes, but what could I do? Anyway, I had nothing but contempt for them now. I played a half hour more and lost two hundred more, and then I let them suggest a double. I sighed. I remember how I sighed. I said, this is my last chance, gentlemen. Why not a hundred to open, a hundred to raise? Emma, don't you think that if they had one little bit of conscience, one bit of human kindness, they would have let me be? No. I win the first hand on two pair, six hundred dollars. I have almost all my losings, but I am greedy; what little man wouldn't be greedy? I lose three hundred in the next hand, then win it all back. I've lost my head now, and they deal to fit. Tinhorn dealing. They deal me four kings pat, the oldest, cheapest dodge known. You see, the feller on my left, he has two aces. First card on the deck is nothing, second and third are aces. Suppose I stand pat, well, this tinhorn draws three with two aces. If I draw one, well he still draws aces on three to four of a kind. And see how safe it is—suppose I lose my head and draw two. Well, he still draws three aces to beat three kings. Well, I play the part, and before the draw I push that pot to where it holds twelve thousand dollars. Twelve thousand dollars, and I'm running sweat and trembling the way a little man should. Everyone in the car is watching now, and that suits me, because even cheap tinhorns can be bad men. But still no sympathy on their part. All right, I say to myself—up. And there's three thousand more in the pot. And then I ask, not for one, not for two cards—but for three. Three."

At that point, Altgeld said, half-choking, "Joe, you're lying." Six years ago, when he first heard the story, he had said the same thing.

"So help me! You see, Emma—now I'm due to draw the aces, both of them. I have aces high. Gent on my left, he just has aces. Well, you could have heard a pin drop when I ask for three cards. Three cards, gentlemen, I say. And very happy that we're surrounded with rubbernecks. No one moves. Three cards, gentlemen, I repeat."

"That was wicked, Joe," Emma said.

"Was it wicked? They were bad men, Emma. They had no mercy and no sympathy; like coyotes, they were wild and mean and on their own. If you don't fight that kind their own way, they destroy you, Emma. Ask the Judge."

He, like others from long back still called him Judge now and then. Judge Altgeld, it had a nice sound. "Joe's right," he said.

"Only that kind"—Joe Martin mused—"that kind doesn't think twice about force. That kind pulls a gun and knows he's going to kill. We don't think that way. That's why they always have the advantage."

"Not always," Altgeld said. "You took the pot, didn't you, Joe? Well, not always. That's all I say. Not always."

XV

THE convention had opened when Buck Hinrichsen came to him and said, "Governor, I think you're making a mistake."

"I've made a lot of them, Buck. I wish I had a dollar for every one."

"I'm talking about Richard Bland. Maybe he's the man for the job. Maybe if he was up here, he could convince everyone that he is. But he won't come to Chicago, and I think that's a hell of a note."

"Do you, Buck?" the Governor said, coolly.

"Don't blow up at me," Hinrichsen said. "Why won't Bland come here?"

"Because he has some queer notions about democracy. I don't say he's right, Buck, and I don't say he's wrong, but he thinks that the people, through their delegates, should

225

choose the man they want to run for president. It's just as simple or complicated as that."

Hinrichsen grinned.

"Yes? It sounds like a lot of hogwash, doesn't it?"

"It does," Hinrichsen said.

"Buck, did you ever read the Constitution of the United States?"

"I read it."

"It's hogwash, isn't it?"

"In some ways it is. You want me to talk straight, don't you? Well, presidents are made; they're made from little men. Sometimes, they're made from dirty little men who aren't fit to wipe your shoes. I don't have to tell you that. My God, Governor, you made this convention, you took the party away from Cleveland, you rigged it and engineered every move, all the way through. Do we have to have wool over our own eyes?"

"You believe that, don't you, Buck?"

"Sure I believe it. I know it."

"You're just crazy as hell, Buck, that's all. If you had eyes in your tail, you couldn't see less. I didn't do it. Get it into your head that I didn't do it. Just so long as you think I did it, alone, you're going to be a cheap, two-bit politician, like the rest of them. Just a cheap ward-heeler, like the rest of them."

"That's nice. That's nice as hell, Governor."

"Wait a minute," Altgeld said. "We don't want to fight, Buck. I got to fight enough of them without having to fight you. Boy, don't you understand—there are currents. You feel them, you sense them, you listen to them, and then if you ride on the current you can move this way or that way. But you can't hold the current back, and no man is strong enough to make a current all by himself."

Hinrichsen was half satisfied, no more than half satisfied. Altgeld told Emma, "Talk to him, won't you. He'll listen to you." "Why must it be Bland?" Emma argued. He said, "Because at this point, if it's not Bland, it'll be Bryan. Oh, my god, Emma, we're making a revolution— we're taking up the country the way Tom Jefferson took it up, only now it's a hundred times bigger and stronger than then, and what in hell were his enemies compared to a Rockefeller or a McCormick? And for that Bryan!— do you know what he is, Emma, a fool, you understand, a god-damned fool!"

The next day, Illinois caucused in Altgeld's suite. The delegation had come to a deadlock on Bland, and Altgeld himself had called for the caucus. The Governor was a few minutes late; when he arrived, most of the delegation was present, and looming among them, grinning, back-slapping, pressing moist palms between his two large hands, was young William Jennings Bryan, shaking his great head of black hair, sounding off with his bell-like voice, passing cigars, and talking, talking. Altgeld stood at the door, his blue eyes burning with anger. Like a file being drawn over metal, his voice cut across Bryan's.

"Buck," he said, and Hinrichsen came to him. Bryan stopped. The silence was empty. Overtones of Bryan's voice rocked back and forth. "Out here," Altgeld said. They stepped into the passageway, but the flat tone of the Governor's voice penetrated the room.

"What is he doing here?" Altgeld demanded.

"He came."

"Who invited him?"

"No one. He came. There's no need to be hard on him."

"Suppose you let me decide that. This is an Illinois caucus. Get him out."

Judge McConnell joined them. "Take it easy, Pete. I know how you feel, but take it easy." His voice was a whisper.

"Buck, get him out. This is an Illinois caucus. Get that damned fool out of here. Tell him he has no more chance of being president than I have, and I wasn't even born in this country."

An hour later, Altgeld put it to the Illinois delegation. "Either," he said, "you follow me, or I climb down and let anyone else who wants to step in. One way or another. I'm not playing for pennies. This is life and death. I told you before there wouldn't be any second chances. You want to dance around a maypole with Bryan—all right. You want to win an election, all right. But from my point of view the two don't mix."

They told him they were with him. They shook his hand and assured him that they were with him. But after they went and only Sam McConnell was left, he dropped into a chair, white and trembling.

"I'm sick," he told the judge. "I want to crawl away. I want to crawl into bed and forget there ever was such a thing as a Democrat."

"You're not that sick, Pete."

"You mean I'm not dying?"

"Who'll hold them in line? Hinrichsen is biting at the traces. My word, you don't need brains, you don't need ability; a golden voice is enough."

"Yes—"

"You're not that sick, Pete."

"Don't worry. I'll be around. You'd see me in hell, wouldn't you, before you'd let me out of this? Well, I'll be around."

228

XVI

THE convention was in full swing, and Chicago reacted properly to this very essential business of American democracy. A preacher roared that there were more prostitutes in the middle-western metropolis than in all the rest of the country put together, and perhaps that was so. The beer wagons clattered day and night, and freightloads of Old Granddad and Golden Wedding poured in. The police had instructions not to arrest delegates unless they actually tore up a piece of the town, and there was hardly a night without a torchlight parade or a street meeting with free beer. The feeling penetrated, for it was more than an ordinary convention, and a sense of revolt and pending drama reached even as far as packing-house town and Pullman city. The thousands and thousands of workingmen picked up their heads and listened. Things were stirring in the land, a noise, a ripple; the worst part of the depression was gone, and labor had the strength to do a little more than exist. A man called Debs spoke about socialism and a man called Altgeld spoke about democracy. Coming out of the plants, shoulder to shoulder in the packed thousands, labor had a new feeling of solidarity. At meetings, they listened to their leaders asking them to trust the little Governor. Among themselves, they still shook their heads; but there was the easing of tension that comes with an armed truce, or perhaps with the calm before the storm. Old union men could not remember when it had been so quiet and good as it was now, and they were bending their ears to the hope that Altgeld had found the way—a way within the framework of their land and yet without violence and Gatling guns and death and Pinkertons. The peculiar American persuasiveness was taking hold again, for here all things were possible. And even in the mansions of the rich by the lake, a part of this was shared; for though they hated the very guts of the Governor, whom they referred to as "that damned man," they felt that another crisis had passed, that a great new era of prosperity was in the offing, that the mores of their lives, their over-plushed homes, their many-faceted ethics, their double and triple standards, their gilt and glitter and sense of kingliness were insured and strengthened; and they could afford to talk about the people now and ask, was not their party more surely and certainly the people's party? Had they not brought such prosperity here as the world had never known? They could unbend. The Democrats had shown their true colors, and one could display responsive virtue by writing a check for ten or twenty or fifty thousands dollars, or twice as much for Mark Hanna, who controlled Republican destinies in the east.

There is no one spirit for a great city, but sometimes there is a commanding overtone, and it was like that in Chicago when the convention opened. The saloons were as full as the shops, and at the huge beer halls, twelve-piece bands ground out the new hit tune, "Casey would waltz with a strawberry blonde, And the band played on; He'd glide 'cross the floor with the girl he adored, And the band played on." The new theatre was packed every night, and the curious motor cars which had so recently made their appearance acted as a prod to the imagination and let it roam wildly in the brave new world that was coming. If Lucy Parsons still roamed the streets, still set up her little stand to sell her husband's book—well, that was a sort of civil fixture by now, and even the police were beginning to leave her alone, instead of hauling her off into jail again and again. And if at nightfall, the vagabonds, the homeless, the unemployed—who, somehow, were still numbered in the hundreds of thousands—crept here and there, seeking a bowl of soup or a place to sleep, well, that too was a part of life that one accepted and became conditioned to.

XVII

RICHARD BLAND of Missouri was not a colorful man. At this time he was just past his sixtieth year, and those who knew him only casually, in deference to his long term of service in congress, conceded that he was a reliable man, but were not ready to say very much more about him. Part of him was the standard congressional cliché, the string tie, the frock coat, and the resonant voice; but there was more to him than that, a hatred of the great industrial combines that had taken over the government, a sympathy for the farmer, the forgotten man of the frontier, which expressed itself in a tireless battle for free silver coinage, and a readiness to believe that this was a new age for America and for all the world, an age of monopoly capitalism, an age which required a new party, new men, new ideas, and new consideration of the millions who worked with their hands but owned no tools. Early in the battle to oust Cleveland and turn the Democratic Party into a people's party, he had joined Altgeld; he had gone down the line with Altgeld, with the courage not of an old man but a young man, and quietly he had made Missouri one of the pivot-forces in the struggle. When they approached him about the presidency, he said, "You've been talking a lot about the people. Suppose you let them decide whether they want me." Would he come to Chicago? "No!" The *no* was very definite. He didn't believe a candidate belonged at the convention. Altgeld pleaded, "Richard, look at the practical side of the matter. If you want to speak about democracy, then talk of the forces. You're one of the forces. You have to come to the convention." He said, emphatically, "No. That's all, my mind is made up." "But you'll run," they asked him. He said, "I'll run, all right. If you want me."

To Altgeld, it was incredible that after all the work had been done the situation should now be so underestimated. The convention whooped it up, flung their hats in the air, and talked about patronage as if they were already in the White House. It turned Altgeld's stomach. They were casual about the fight he had led for sixteen months. Grover was out; they were in. They performed snake dances. They cheered, Rah, rah, rah, sixteen to one, silver, silver, rah, rah, rah. He remarked to McConnell, "And they want to run the country." "Have you ever seen the Republicans?" McConnell asked him. He shook his head. "Well, just the same." But it didn't help that the other party was as infantile, as shallow as his own. The other party had twenty million dollars; his own party had been maneuvered into a revolt they did not even comprehend. Taking over a government, or holding a Fourth of July celebration—it was all one and the same thing. He wished fervently that Bland had come up to the city, the more so when Bryan cornered him and pleaded:

"Let me talk, Governor."

He wanted to remark that he had rarely seen Bryan do anything else, but he held onto his temper and answered, pleasantly enough, "We got a pretty full agenda, Bill."

"A short speech."

"I don't know."

"My god, Governor, what have you got against me?"

He answered truthfully, "You want to be president too hard, Bill. I want to win this election."

"But let me talk, please. I would ask you on my knees."

"You don't have to."

"Will you deny Nebraska the right to raise her voice? Is it for nothing that we hacked a nation out of the prairies, fought the Indians, and pledged our lives to the cause of democracy?"

He looked at Bryan as if he had never seen him before. "Oh, my aunt," he whispered.

"You'll let me talk, please, Governor?"

"If there's time, I'll let you talk," Altgeld sighed.

"I've been working on an address."

"If there's time." He remembered that Hinrichsen had remarked upon going up to Bryan's room and finding him there, in front of the bureau mirror, one hand thrust into his waistcoat, declaiming. "He can speak," Hinrichsen said. Now Altgeld repeated, "If there's time, Bill, you can speak." And he told McConnell afterward that the thought of all Nebraska standing impotent on her prairies had been too much for him. "Let him speak. I don't want it said, Sam, that I shut anyone up."

"I suppose you're right."

"Do you know that Buck is impressed with him. People listen to him talk and a sort of glaze comes over their eyes. Something happens to them."

"I know "

Nominations began. Speakers went on for hours, and some of the delegates listened and others didn't. Some smoked cigars and others caucused in the anterooms. Every so often there would be a calculated roar of cheers and then a screaming frenzy that ended in a snake-dance, as a group of natives attempted to stampede the house and start a boom for their favorite son. But other groups of native sons would regard this with bored disinterest. Few listened; some of the speakers spoke to some of the audience; some spoke to the thin air.

Altgeld sat in the Illinois corner, watching this the way a man from Mars might; he appeared bloodless and shriveled. He kept trying to swallow the astonishing fact that this same crowd might make up a government and operate this great union of states.

XVIII

FINALLY, William Jennings Bryan spoke. Altgeld watched him rise to his feet, walk to the platform, and mount it. He faced the crowd, thrust his fingers into his waistcoat, and moved his head, ever so slightly. The ebony hair rippled. The light caught his ruddy skin, and it glowed. After the procession of the middle-aged and the old, the whiskered and the bearded and the mustached, the pot-bellied politician and the doddering congressional veteran, this appeared to be the apostle of youth itself. For a long minute, he stood silent on the platform, allowing his personality to impress itself, giving those who still did not know him a chance to whisper to their neighbors and to be answered, "Bryan—Nebraska." His dark brows knit and then relaxed. His mouth was stern and then gentle. He began to speak with deference and humility, his magnificent voice, even on a muted note, penetrating every corner of the hall. As he started with the usual, "Mr. Chairman and gentlemen of the convention," the noise and chatter among the delegates went on uninterrupted, and hardly more than a third of them actually listened. But his next sentence caught them, and face after face turned to him. The voice throbbed and impinged and penetrated:

"I would be presumptuous, indeed, to present myself against the distinguished gentlemen to whom you have listened, if this were a mere measuring of abilities; but this is not a contest between persons. The humblest in all the land, when clad in the armor of a righteous cause, is stronger than all the hosts of error. I come to speak to you in defense of a cause as holy as the cause of liberty— the cause of humanity!"

The chatter had stopped. They were watching him now, and Altgeld had the impression that at least several hundred delegates had known the content of the speech in advance, planned for it, and were ready to act on it. Yet, in spite of himself, that magic voice had caught him up: inside, his heart sank, as he laid against this mounting effect his quiet hope that by speaking sanely and directly about Bland and for him, with the aid of a few dozen who understood what was at stake, he might turn this shaky rebellion into a victory. He was pulled from the rising crescendo of Bryan's voice by Sam McConnell who whispered hoarsely, "Well, you asked for it."

"He can speak."

"Nobody denies that. And nobody listens to what he says."

"They're listening," Altgeld said. "That's the amazing thing, they're listening. Do you hear?" He doubted his own ears. A roar of applause went up. Bryan was saying:

"The man who is employed for wages is as much a businessman as his employer. . . . The farmer who goes forth in the morning and toils all day—who begins in the spring and toils all summer—is as much a businessman as the man who goes upon the board of trade and bets upon the price of grain. . . . The miners who go down a thousand feet into the earth, or climb two thousand feet upon the cliffs, and bring forth from the hiding places the precious metals to be poured into the channels of trade, are as much businessmen as the few financial magnates who, in a back room, corner the money of the world."

Altgeld growled, "He's an idiot, do you hear him? And they're swallowing it—they're swallowing that incredible nonsense. Everyone is a businessman, and therefore we're for business and for everyone."

Darrow had joined them now, spreading his hands and shaking his head mutely. Bryan's voice thundered through the hall. He had garnered his speech from everywhere, books on oration, Patrick Henry, Cicero, Daniel Webster, and now he spilled it forth in pounding waves of sound:

"We do not come as aggressors. Our war is not a war of conquest; we are fighting in the defense of our homes, our families, and posterity. We have petitioned, and our petitions have been scorned; we have entreated, and our entreaties have been disregarded; we have begged, and they have mocked when our calamity came. We beg no longer; we entreat no longer; we petition no more. We defy them."

Darrow was listening open-mouthed. When he turned to Altgeld, the Governor smiled slightly, and shrugged. "It doesn't matter what he says. This is a lesson, Clarence."

The audience was won; they rode on the waves of sound. They shouted applause at the proper intervals; they hissed when they were supposed to hiss. They swayed to his rhythm. It was like nothing Altgeld had ever seen, and yet it was—it was a camp meeting, a revival, the subconsciously awaited and hoped-for climax to the hotel room, the bawdy houses, the packed saloons and beer halls, the drunken rolling in the gutters, the whole astonishing apparatus with which democratic America nominated her democratically elected presidents. The emotion of the hall could have been graphed like the steep side of a mountain; it rose with the speaker. It burst when he flung wide his arms and screamed:

"Having behind us the producing masses of this nation and the world, supported by the commercial interests, the laboring interests, and the toilers everywhere, we will answer their demand for a gold standard by saying to them: You shall not press down upon the brow of labor this crown of thorns, you shall not crucify mankind upon a cross of gold!"

The hall went wild. Men sprang on their chairs, yelling, whistling, clapping. Men danced on the floor, jigged, let go with Indian warwhoops. Hats sailed everywhere. Arms waved. One or two of the women present fainted, and others wept. Men embraced each other and pounded each other. The place had become a madhouse, and in it all and over it, Bryan stood, calm and smiling.

Clarence Darrow turned to look at Altgeld. The Governor sat as he had been before, his pale face without any particular expression.

XIX

EMMA noticed that after Bryan's speech, her husband seemed less worried, less perturbed; he found time even to go for a walk with her along the lakefront. He said, "You know, dear, you get to think that something depends on you wholly—it doesn't."

"No."

This was a holiday. They sat on an old pier; they tossed

stones into the water. The sun and the wind brought some color into his face. Emma, in a simple black skirt and a white blouse, dangling a big straw hat, looked like a girl. She had the poise and walk of a girl. She took his arm, and they were not too different from the hundreds of other couples strolling along the lake. They watched the boats on the horizon and speculated on what they were and where they were bound.

"If a few hours are like this," Emma said, "what would a month be, or two months—or a year?"

He told her that when this was over, they would go to Europe.

"And if you win, you'll not only be Governor again, but with one arm in the White House. Pete, we'll never go anywhere. That's all right. I would have been the wife of the town grocer, more likely than not. Now I'm Pete Altgeld's wife. I'm not complaining."

"You should complain."

"No. But I've done all right, haven't I, Pete? I've learned."

"We both learned."

"I'm really a happy woman, Pete, a very happy woman. Happier than you are. Because I have what I want."

"What do you think I want, Emma?"

"I don't know. Do you remember Parsons, Pete?"

"I remember."

"I think—I think you want to believe in something as directly and as fully as he did. But you don't, do you, Pete?"

"No, I don't," he said.

It was a fine, rich few hours. He had brought a book of Elizabeth Browning with him, and they sat down on a bench, and he read her the sonnets, a little embarrassed but not too much embarrassed to lose the pleasure of still being able to read love poems.

XX

WHEN the balloting began, Altgeld was uncertain but not too uncertain, perturbed but not too perturbed; and sitting in his corner of the hall, checking off in his notebook the support he had reason to expect, the votes he had been promised, he thought it not wholly unreasonable that Richard Bland should come in on the first ballot. He wanted to think that; he was very tired by now, and he felt the approaching symptoms of another malarial attack. He was tired of the convention; he was sick to his stomach of it. The enthusiasm, which had carried him through a year and a half of struggle for mastery of the party, had waned very considerably. Drawn together like this, the political supporters of his party were far from impressive and not inspiring—the paunched southern Senators who could not talk for five minutes without launching a tirade against the *damn niggers,* the congressmen who, drunk or sober, unwound with the same patriotic tirades, the pinched-faced office-seekers, the few money men who, realizing their exclusiveness in this people's convention, tried to edge in and boss the show, the cynical politicians who played it in votes, dollars and cents and patronage, and gave Altgeld credit for no more than being one of them, but somehow sharper, and the smirking newspapermen, who managed to unmask the entire thing with just a smile and a whisper—not inspiring was any of this; he wanted it to be through and done.

The first ballot went off fairly smoothly. As Altgeld had suspected, Bland ran first with 223 votes, not enough to nominate, but certainly an impressive showing. What surprised him was that Bryan had shown second. He had expected something for Bryan, fourth or fifth, one or two states at the most to follow Nebraska. No sooner had the vote appeared, than Buck Hinrichsen ran up to him and said:

"Governor—we're going to split."

"What in hell do you mean, Buck?"

"I tell you, the delegation won't hold for Bland. They want Bryan."

"That's nonsense."

"Is it? We're calling for a caucus."

"We?"

"That's right. I feel Bryan's the man."

"Buck, have you lost your head? You know what I've put into this, if the others don't."

"I'm sorry, Governor. I feel Bryan's the man."

"Sure you do. What in hell has he promised you? Has he promised to make you Secretary of State, of War, of the Treasury? Well, why don't you count how many cabinet posts there are and how many promises he's handed out before you sell him your liver?"

"I didn't think you'd look at it that way."

"How did you think I'd look at it? All right—if they want a caucus, they can have it."

But at the caucus, his lethargy departed and he became the old Altgeld, slashing, cutting, parrying. He was brilliant, quick, mocking. Did they want to be tight-rope walkers—well, he'd stretch a rope across Lake Michigan, and they could walk it to their heart's content. Did they think Bryan could be elected; well, what had he said? He defied them to repeat one sentence from the Cross of Gold speech. "Bryan—" very slowly, "My God, we're Democrats, do you understand! We have a party, a tradition, we've produced some of the greatest men this land has known, Jefferson, Jackson—and you tell me Bryan, Bryan. Well, we're here to vote for Bland! We're pledged to Bland! We don't break our pledges! We sold the people a bill of goods —we don't change our merchandise. We don't toss the election to William McKinley because we were spellbound by a silver voice."

He won them. With the second ballot, he could stand up and say, evenly and decisively, "Illinois casts forty-eight votes for Richard Parks Bland of Missouri."

Some of the hall cheered, but more were silent, staring at the small, bearded man who had mysteriously wrested leadership of the party from Cleveland. But then his own delegation was at him again; Bryan was gaining. They demanded a caucus once more.

He granted it. And once more he drove them back, cowed them, and retained the right to say, "Illinois casts forty-eight votes for Bland of Missouri."

Now they were at him. It reached a hysterical, feverish pitch. From all over the hall, Bryan's supporters crowded toward Altgeld, screaming, "No cross of gold! No cross of gold!" The place took on all the elements of riot; the pounding of the speaker's gavel could no longer be heard. Bryan supporters surged over the Governor, tearing at his clothes, and were literally thrown back by Altgeld men. Big Buck Hinrichsen found himself forcibly defending the little Governor.

But Altgeld sat calmly; he never moved, neither smiled nor frowned, but watched the incredible chaos with the interested eyes of a scientist who has observed, for the first time, a totally new and unexpected phenomenon. When they called for caucus again, he shrugged and nodded, and the action of filing from the hall acted as a check. At least part of the tumult died, enough for them to take the next ballot. Silence came as Altgeld led his delegation back to its place. He walked slowly; his shuffle was accentuated; yet a faint smile showed as he said, "Illinois casts forty-eight votes for Bland of Missouri."

But now, for the first time, the Bryan thing took on appearances of a landslide. His vote topped Bland's. His supporters, screaming with joy, tumbled out of their chairs and fell into a snake dance. Round and round the hall it twisted, shattering chairs, signs, stands, men roaring with laughter as they embraced those in front, men sliding on their behinds and giggling hysterically. All control was going. Whisky bottles arched through the air and smashed against the ceiling, raining fragments of broken glass. Like a weird chant, "Cross of gold, cross of gold, cross of gold . . ."

The Bryan supporters had momentarily forgotten Altgeld, but his own men, men from half a dozen states who had worked with him these past eighteen months, crowded up to him, pleading, "For god's sake, stand firm! Stand by us!" "If Illinois holds, we can break this!" "For the love of God, hold!" Schilling had appeared from somewhere, almost magically, pleading, "Hold them, Pete, please." And Sam McConnell, voiceless, but his eyes pleading. Yet already they were screaming for the caucus.

This time, as he faced them in the caucus room, Altgeld knew that he was beaten. He knew that far ahead he was beaten, and far behind too. It was not merely the fact of Bryan; it was more than Bryan and beyond Bryan, the whole structure in which he played the roll of his life, the structure that made a mad circus of a national nominating convention. He did not need Buck Hinrichsen's whisper: "For God's sake, Governor, you're still running the party. But hold off now and you're not running anything, not anything." He did not need the set faces to tell him that he was beaten; he knew. He knew better than any of them how well he was beaten, how completely.

He nodded. "All right," he said.

They filed back. For the first time since it began, there was a degree of quiet in the convention hall. State after state was called and reported. Illinois was called. The Governor of Illinois rose and said, "Illinois casts forty-eight votes for William Jennings Bryan of Nebraska."

He sat down, felt a hand grip his shoulder, saw Sam McConnell, and beside him Schilling and Martin. He was able to smile at them, and then he turned away to see the convention go finally and completely mad as William Jennings Bryan was nominated for **President of the United States by the Democratic Party.**

Part Five

THE THIRD VARIATION

THE FIRST TUESDAY AFTER THE first Monday in November is a curious day. Some things are American, others imported, others a blend. It is a country of that sort. Seek for a thing deep in the twisted roots of some old first-growth oak, and you will find that a part of Spain crept in long, long ago, or a part of Bohemia, or a part of Poland, or Germany, or Sweden, for sometimes that kind of thing rooted as deeply and securely in the soil here as the ancient oak itself. But some things are American; not just an election day, or any election day, but a traditional and sacrosanct raising of the ego, an incredible bow to the individual in a world that has stamped on the individual and ground him down into the earth, and proved to him that, aside from the fact that he might be president or a millionaire, he should not think for himself, act for himself, defy either custom or prejudice or stupidity, or assert himself in any fashion as a singular product of God's handiwork. But on election day all this sloughs away, and nakedly and unashamedly he comes forth as a man. He holds destiny in the subtle joints of his fingers, and though year after year he is faced, on his ballot, with Tweedledum and Tweedledee, back of his mind, back in that unused space that only hopes and yearns, there is the thought that this time it will be different. Perhaps the hope is backed by a little more than faith, for the citizens sees his land, sometimes, through the patriotic mud that is so constantly flung in his eyes; he knows, somehow, what is the flesh and the blood of the land, even though the words to express it have been stolen from him and perverted; and on election day, to at least some of him, comes the thought that he— by himself—has the power in his worn fingers to change everything, to throw out the barons, the thieves, bandits, the cheap politicians, the mealy-mouthed double-talkers. That he doesn't is a weary disappointment. He isn't sure, but few men are sure when they are alone, and in the voting booth he stands alone. He weighs truth and false-hood, and it is like trying to untangle a ball of yarn after a cat has had a day with it; he tries to find his way through the millions that have been poured down the drain of campaign—and in the end he votes without conviction. Conviction is only in the day itself, the first Tuesday after the first Monday, that it might be, sometime.

II

For Tuesday, and a while before and a while after, Emma engaged a suite of rooms at the Palmer House. She would have preferred Springfield; she wanted the sense of security that Springfield could give her, for the past several months had been like a lifetime, and when she looked at her husband now she felt that perhaps it was more than that, the ending of a life. But when she broached it to him, he shrugged and said:

"I would want it as much as you, Emma, but the best we can do is to go there as soon as it is over. I have to be in

Chicago; they'll want to see me, and all of them can't see me if I'm in Springfield."

"Haven't they seen you enough, Pete?"

"Apparently not." It was like that. With Bryan nominated, sitting in his chair in that insane convention hall, it had occurred to him that perhaps he had lost as much as Bryan had won. But a moment later, Jones, the new national committee head, pushed his way through the mob up to his chair and asked, bewilderedly, "Governor, what do we do?" "Do? You have Bryan." "For god's sake, Governor, you're not going to walk out on us?" Altgeld began to laugh; he reached out and grabbed Jones' arm, laughing hugely. "When in hell have I walked out on anything?" he managed to say. Jones asked, "You'll see Bryan?" "I'll see him. Don't be a fool." It was like that.

"Apparently not," Altgeld said again. "A little more, another few days, Emma."

"All right." She gave in. One learned, in time, that there was no purpose in arguing with him. At one of his meetings, in the audience, she had sat next to two women who discussed him aloofly and with objective curiosity. Overhearing, she could not bring herself to stop them or to move away. One said, "Look at him." "He's dying, you know," the other said. "You know what he's dying from?" "I've heard—" "Well, you can tell from the way he walks, there's no doubt. Just think what his wife feels." "I feel sorry for her. I don't feel sorry for him."

Emma wasn't sorry for herself. Today, on election morning, she considered that she would not change places with any woman in the world. She was Pete Altgeld's wife, and she had been with Pete Altgeld these four months past now, watched him, worked with him. It was to her that he said, late one night, "Emma, I'm beginning to learn something. I'm beginning to learn that a person grows with struggle—maybe no other way." Now she had only to think of the Emma Ford that she had been once to realize the fullest implications of that.

Today, she was here in the suite in the Palmer House, and it was her day as well as her husband's; she was more afraid than he, and yet more certain than he. When he was out voting and Hinrichsen called, she could say:

"Come up, Buck. Of course."

"He's not angry?"

"Why? Why should he be angry? You don't know Pete."

"I thought he might have figured it as a double cross."

"Buck!"

"All right."

"Buck, did anyone work harder than he trying to elect Bryan? If he doesn't get elected—Pete, I mean—it will only be because he used all he had for Bryan."

"I know. I don't know why."

"You should. Don't be a fool. Come up and talk to him."

It began as that kind of a day. Some reporters came, and she told them to return later. She wanted to be sedate and calm today, which was important, if ever it was important for her to have been that way. Waiting for her husband, she looked over the day's papers, the screaming, last-minute attacks on her husband, the somber editorials, informing the public that if Bryan were elected, a silent dictator would enter the White House, John Peter Altgeld, and the republic would come to an end. An end and a finish; anarchy, socialism, and ruin.

She thought of two times since the convention, when her husband had seen Bryan.

III

SHE had not been there the first time. It had been after the convention, directly after, and Pete had told her of it, how Bryan came up, a little afraid, a good deal abashed, but still glowing and walking on clouds:

"Governor—"

"Hullo, Bill," Altgeld had said. "Congratulations."

"Well—well, it came out that way. I guess that's all, it just came out that way."

"It just happened," Altgeld grinned, telling Emma how Bryan had stood there, more like a boy than ever, more like an overgrown, handsome farm boy, realizing only by slow degrees what had happened, that he was the party candidate for president of the United States, and wanting desperately to ask Altgeld a question he couldn't frame, "Are you going to be with me? For me or against me? Because I did this; I never believed I could do it, but I did it."

"What do you think, Governor?" he managed to say.

"I think it's going to be hard. Bill, I think it's going to be hard as hell."

And Bryan nodded, smiling a little foolishly. That was the way her husband had told it to her. He had a way of leaving things out. He came back from the convention with the blood drained from him, but he could nevertheless laugh and say, "Do you know, I'm learning, Emma. And in the process, the edges are rubbed off. There are a lot of edges to be rubbed off, Emma, and I suppose that eventually, I'll smooth out."

She was with him the second time he saw Bryan. The simple disobedience of his body, which refused any longer to obey him, allowed for a few weeks' rest before the final phase of the campaign set in. Emma suggested Colorado Springs, and he agreed with the proposal, albeit somewhat reluctantly. But once on the train and in their compartment, he collapsed; it was as if the springs and the hinges and the wires had melted away, and there was no strength left to do anything but lie in a chair. Emma read to him, tended him, and sat and talked with him. They talked for hours. All of his groping for a perspective was being channeled now, and after the nomination of Bryan and his own physical letdown, the pieces, peculiarly, fitted better. He was able to arrange himself in the scheme of things. Quite confidently, he said to his wife:

"When this campaign is over, I think I'll know what to do. I think it will be very clear."

He didn't talk about victory or defeat. The campaign was a stage; it would be over, and then there would be another stage. It was there that he told her, for the first time, of going to the funeral so long ago, back in '87, and how he had stood there in the cold winter morning, watching the endless column of workingmen go by. He said:

"If I had spoken to any one of them, Emma, it would have dissolved; but to see them like that, all together, one expression on ten thousand faces, well, it meant something. I mean, in their relation to me, in mine to them. But when I want to put my hand on what it meant—well, I stop short. I always stop short. But after this campaign—"

At Lincoln, Nebraska, the train laid over for two hours. Bryan was waiting there, and hardly had the train stopped when he was knocking at the door of the compartment.

"Governor, how are you feeling?" he demanded, speaking words that were rehearsed, swallowing over them, and striding in with both his hands extended to Altgeld. The

Governor sat in a chair, his legs wrapped in a robe, and Bryan was not unfamiliar with the thin smile that greeted him.

"I'm fine, Bill. How are you?"

"Like an ox," Bryan answered, grinning at Emma. "The last thing in the world to trouble me is my health. But I heard you were sick; I worried."

"Bill, sit down and stop panting. You knew damn well a year ago that I was sick. Emma, get him something to drink—get him a lemonade, we're in Nebraska." Emma called the porter; Bryan eased his big bulk into a chair, rose again with Emma. "Sit down, sit down," Altgeld said. Bryan smiled sheepishly. The rehearsed lines were finished, and he sat there with his hands on his knees, staring at the Governor. Altgeld said, "Well, how does it feel to be the candidate?"

Bryan shook his head. "I don't know—it's a feeling I can't get used to." The bars were down; he started to speak, swallowed, and then said, "Governor, I swear—I never thought—"

"You didn't. You sure as hell never thought so! But you couldn't stop. You rode it like a kid riding a washtub down a snow slide. Wait a minute—I'm not angry. Just forget that. You're the candidate and only one thing matters, that next year you should move into the White House. That's all that matters, Bill. Understand that."

Bryan moved between anger and withdrawal; he hung there for one long moment, and then Altgeld thrust out his hand and said, "This is for what's gone, Bill."

They shook hands, and Bryan was smiling again. The lemonade came, and he sat there sipping it. Altgeld watched him, studying him at this close range, as he told Emma afterwards, wondering how he could relax him and turn out what was inside, considering that there was something inside. Emma began to talk to him, asking about his family, about the life here in Nebraska. Young as he was, he showed Washington conditioning; it was difficult for him to state a thing as a matter of fact rather than as a proclamation. And he wanted Altgeld to speak. Able to contain himself no longer, he asked bluntly:

"Governor, what are our chances?"

"When? Now, tomorrow, or on election day?"

"On election day, of course."

"Well, I don't know," Altgeld said. "It's a long time to election day, isn't it?"

"But you could guess, estimate."

"I don't guess," Altgeld smiled. "I don't guess, Bill. When you know certain things, you can add them up. Sometimes you know some things and there are other things that you don't know. Is that what you mean by guessing? You never know all the things, not even after the votes are counted. Right now, how much do we know?"

"We know that McKinley's a bag of clothes, and that Mark Hanna's got him dancing on strings. We know that the people are pretty well fed up with the way Wall Street runs the country."

"Do we?"

"We know that the people want free silver coinage."

Altgeld's voice dropped; his voice had a tendency to grind and rasp and hammer; when he spoke softly, he could eliminate this. He wanted to eliminate it now; he wanted nothing to stand between him and William Jennings Bryan. In the normal course of things, it was difficult enough to talk to Bryan, but now Bryan was in the saddle; he came to Altgeld because Altgeld still led the party, but he couldn't forget that he was in the saddle in spite of the

Governor of Illinois and not because of him. Now Altgeld said:

"Bill, we talk a lot about the people—I do, you do, and if I had a dollar for every time they mention the people in that esteemed congress of ours, I'd be a very rich man. But what are the people? Do they have leaders? Can they talk in one voice? Can they even go into the polls and vote? Some can, but enough of them can't to let us worry about it. This isn't the first presidential election, and every president, even such incredible buffoons as Rutherford B. Hayes, have been elected by a part of the people. We're going to tell the people something, but Mark Hanna and the Republican Party are going to tell them something else. How are the people going to know what's right?"

"Because we stand for what's right."

"My word, Bill, that's not enough. Maybe we do, maybe we don't. But how do we get across to the people what we stand for? For every newspaper that's for us, there are twenty against us. We've got four hundred thousand in the campaign chest—maybe we stand to get a few hundred thousand more. The Republicans have six million already —some say ten million—and stand to get millions more. That never happened before. That much money was never collected before in the history of this country to be spent on a presidential campaign. Ten million dollars—why, there was a time when that would run our government for a year, and now it's being poured down the drain to elect William McKinley president. Well, there's a reason for that; things go together; they're connected, Bill, and we have to understand just how they're connected, so we can know how to fight them."

"What things?" Bryan asked. "The Republicans have always had money. We knew that—we're a people's party, not a Wall Street party."

"That's right, we are—sure. But still, there are some things. Take this agitation for war with Spain—"

"I'm for Cuban independence!"

"And I am too. But there's more to it than that. On the one hand, we throttle the independence movement in Cuba; we cut off supplies, arms. We let them starve. On the other hand, we move toward war with Spain. That's an indication of something else. Monopoly capitalism in America has become a giant, a bloody, ruthless giant. That's where the ten million dollars comes from. And they're going to start spreading, that's what this Cuban thing amounts to. America isn't big enough any more— the world is the next step. You have to see that coming, Bill, and then you'll see what we're up against in this campaign. It's not only free silver, government by injunction, the rights of farmers and workers and small businessmen; it's that, but it's something else. It's the first real bid by our side to stem this thing that has grown up in our own lifetimes, this thing that's like nothing else the world ever knew. And they know that—and because they know it, they're going to fight us with no holds barred. Inside of that frame, you've got to talk to the people, Bill, and there's only one way we can talk to them."

"I don't wholly agree," Bryan said. He was not a constant listener, and Altgeld wondered whether he had heard all he said. "It's going to be a hard fight, but the people are with us. No one likes monopoly, no one likes the trusts. We'll take our case to the people."

"Sure, we'll take it to them. But with integrity. That's an old-fashioned word, but it works. We can't equivocate, we can't compromise—"

They were words Bryan liked. He nodded savagely. Altgeld sighed and said, "We must stand on our platform, Bill. My god, we must stand there firm as all hell, just firm as all hell." But afterward, he told Emma, "How much of it meant anything, and how much of it went in and out? He's all right, but this is too big for him. Maybe it's too big for anyone."

IV

EMMA was alone when Buck Hinrichsen came up, somewhat sheepishly, but Emma said, "Anyway, you felt that you had to see him today, and that's good, isn't it?"

"I think so."

"Shall I order some breakfast for you, coffee anyway?"

"Nothing, nothing, thanks. How is he feeling, Emma?" Hinrichsen was dapperly dressed, fawn gloves, fawn spats, a large single-pearl tiepin, tight-fitting black coat, and a black bowler hat which he mechanically dusted with the edge of his gloves. He looked and acted the part of a routine middle-western politician, unimaginative, shrewd, calculating, a little better than average scavenger in the offal-heap of spoil; but with him, as with so many others, a relationship with Altgeld had induced a qualitative change. He became something more than he was; he had found a direction and he groped along it. His switch from Bland to Bryan had not altered his belief that there was nothing in America like Altgeld.

Emma replied, "I don't know."

That could be; he understood that.

"You think you know Pete, but then you don't know him. I'm married to him, and I don't know him. But I learned about strength and I learned about struggle, Buck.

You know, they crucified him; they nailed him up, and they put nails into every part of him. But it wasn't enough."

"I know."

"Why did they have to do it? Every paper in the country—until there isn't a little child anywhere who won't dream of that evil face, the popping eyes, the leer; that's the way they've painted him. No man ever was treated that way before. Buck, what's happening to this land of ours?"

"That's politics, Emma."

"It's more than politics, and you know it. What did he do that they hate him so? Because he pardoned three men who were innocent? Because he spoke up for labor?"

Hinrichsen nodded.

"Did you see the cartoon in *Harper's Weekly?*"

Hinrichsen nodded again. He had seen the cartoon, Altgeld cloaked like a devil, the face contorted diabolically, the flames of hell rising from a smoking capital, and in his hands a shredded Constitution. Over his shoulder leered the insane face of Guiteau, Garfield's assassin, drawn to parody Altgeld, and a skeleton hand reached forward, holding a revolver. The caption beneath had read, "Guiteau was a power in Washington for one day. Shall Altgeld be a power there for four years?" No one who had seen it would ever forget it.

"Is that politics?" Emma asked. "Is it politics when you see those pictures every time you open a paper? I won't ask you if you think we can win, Buck; I won't insult your intelligence that way. They own this free country of ours. They own the press; they own the pulpit; they even own the food that comes from the earth. Do you see how much I've learned? Only, sometimes I wish I never knew any of it. Sometimes I wish I had been Emma Ford, quietly, stupidly, but maybe more happily. You ask how Pete is—

when we went across the state and he spoke from the train, well, each time after he spoke he had only enough strength to crawl back into bed, and each time I thought he was dying. Do you know how pleasant that can be, Buck?"

Again, Hinrichsen nodded, and now Emma was overcome with remorse. "But you don't have to listen to all this. I'm insufferable. Can't I tell you something nice? I think that this time, when this is over, we'll tour the Continent. That's something I've always wanted—to get away from this and see all those wonderful civilizations, Italy and Paris and England. Do you know, we'd be presented to Queen Victoria—Pete says so and calls her an evil old bitch in the same breath. You see, my language has improved too; it would in such circumstances. . . ."

They talked on, and Emma relaxed. Hinrichsen told a story very well. His own anger could be biting and contemptuous, as when he told about hearing what he described as ". . . a dirty, miserable character called Theodore Roosevelt . . ." speak at the Coliseum just a few weeks before. Then, speaking to the Republican College League, Roosevelt had screamed: "Mr. Altgeld is a much more dangerous man than Bryan. He is much slyer, much more intelligent, much less silly, much more free from all the restraints of public morality. The one is unscrupulous from vanity, the other from calculation, and would connive at wholesale murder and would justify it by elaborate and cunning sophistry for reasons known only to his own tortuous soul. For America to put men like this in control of her destiny would be such a dishonor as it is scarcely bearable to think of. Mr. Altgeld condones and encourages the most infamous of murders and denounces the Federal government and the Supreme Court for interfering to put a stop to the bloody lawlessness which results in worse than murder. Both of them would substitute for the government of Washington and Lincoln, for the system of orderly liberty which we inherit from our forefathers and which we desire to bequeath to our sons, a red welter of lawlessness as vicious as the Paris commune itself. . . ." And so forth and so on. "Well," Hinrichsen said, "I got to Mr. Roosevelt afterward and I asked him, Have you ever met Altgeld? Oh, no, he said, oh, no, never. Of course, that was after he had satisfied himself about my credentials. They were Teddying him to death, our Chicago big boys, Teddy this and Teddy that, and there was something about young Theodore very much like a fat little teddy bear, believe me, Emma. A very estimable young gentleman, a damn highbrow snob—forgive the language, Emma—snotnose, I don't know of any other way to describe him, but estimable, distinctly estimable, and didn't want to talk to me or answer any questions until he had really ascertained that I was Secretary of State and not just some poor old bum who had pushed my way into his august presence. Then—oh, no, he had never met Mr. Altgeld, and wouldn't, of course. By god, he said, I should have to fight him if I did. How can I meet a man socially whom I may have to face with bared sword on the barricades?—So help me god, Emma, those were his very words! Can you imagine? But this young fellow is a card, Emma, someone we're going to hear from. It's not just that he's an idiot or a political climber; he's some weird combination of a moron and a Jeff Davis, and I'll be damned if I can figure it out."

Hinrichsen paused, then spread his hands wide. "But I learned something. It made me see where I was wrong with Bryan, so dead-wrong. Bryan is like setting up pins in an alley, setting them up for no other reason than that they should be knocked down. That's why I'm here. I want to apologize to the Governor. I want to shake his hand."

"You don't have to apologize, Buck."

"Let me be the judge of that, Emma. When I make a mistake, I make them. That's an old story. You hear him, and then you go away, and you say, what a wonderful speaker he is, and then you vote for McKinley. And Mark Hanna just lets Bryan talk. But tell me, were you in New York with Pete?"

"Yes. It was one of the good things. He walked into their own stronghold, and he was better than they were, better than any of them. Even their newspapers had to admit that Cooper Union was packed, and there were ten thousand more in the streets who couldn't get in, and workingmen—wherever Pete spoke, it was the workingmen who came to hear him. I never saw that before at political meetings. And they listen to what he has to say—"

Hinrichsen watched her and listened to her. He had been part of the same process; he had reacted to Altgeld; he had become something else, and so had she. He was listening to her when the Governor returned. Hinrichsen held out his hand and the Governor took it. There didn't have to be any explanations. But it seemed to Hinrichsen that he had never known what a small man Altgeld was, how frail; of the solid, earthlike strength of four years past, there was left now only the bright, searching eyes and a slow smile that let you into him, that invited you.

"Hello, Buck," he said. "Have you come to bring me felicitations or condolences?"

Hinrichsen answered, seriously, "I came to see you."

"Thanks." Then, after a moment, "A good line at the polls."

"How does it look?"

"Why, I don't know, Buck. What do you think? You've got a politician's nose. What kind of a smell is in the air today?"

"I think that even if Bryan loses, you'll still be Governor of Illinois."

"If Bryan loses, I lose too. Let's face it, Buck, the ticket isn't going to win here and lose the rest of the country. Well, that suits me. Emma will tell you—it suits me just fine. I've had enough, Buck. If I'm licked today, I'm licked. My ears are pinned back, and I'll leave them right there. This is a dirty, rotten game we're in, and no matter how you fight it, it's still dirty. I want to wash my hands of it. I want to pay off my debts and go away. My word, Buck, I've never been out of this country, if you don't count the few months when I was on my way here. I want to see things; I want to relax."

"We've still got a chance."

"What kind of a chance, Buck? I saw Bathhouse John. He knows. He's got a scent like a hound dog. You know what he said, he said this is just what comes of trying to mix politics and good government. And, by God, he's not so wrong."

"I still think we got a chance."

"So do I. But not a hell of a big one."

V

For a short while after Hinrichsen left, they were alone, and Altgeld went into the bedroom to lie down. Emma had drawn the shades; it was dark and warm and comfortable, and stretched out there, he was able to let his thoughts wander without any special attempt at cohesion. Vagrant thoughts, old ones and new ones. In his own mind, he felt that the election was lost, and as one does, he thought of the mistakes they had made, how they could have done things differently. If only Bryan had stood fast! If only he had answered charges with counter-charges! If only he had fought! But he didn't know how to fight; accused of socialism, he had denied it; accused of being pro-labor, he had denied it; accused of being against the reactionary supreme court, he had denied that too; he denied being anti-trust, anti-business, anti-labor, and in the end he was nothing but a golden voice that talked on and on of free silver. Well, that was the way, and now it was over. His own gubernatorial campaign had lagged a bad second, and he found himself accepting, very calmly, the fact of his personal defeat. He had come into that frame of mind slowly, and he wondered how he would react to the one chance in ten of victory—to go back to Springfield for four more long and trying years. He had pleaded with Sam McConnell to accept the gubernatorial nomination, but McConnell knew better. But McConnell wouldn't have been any more successful. If he, Pete Altgeld, only knew why—why would the people not rally to a concept of decency and honesty—if it was that? If there were men of good will and firm purpose, the system had to work; it had worked in the past; there were other changes, and somehow the country went on and became firmer and stronger. It had to happen now. Certain men today were richer, more powerful than any who had lived in the past, and it was only natural that they should buy their way into the government. But was it their government—was it their country, body and soul? He had a quick, frightened vision of Rockefeller, Morgan, Pullman and the rest of them—laughing, laughing uproariously at the antics of the middle-country bumpkins, of the naïve followers of Abe Lin-

coln and Andrew Jackson, a pell-mell rabble that pre-
sumed to take over this union of states. Ten million
dollars sloshing in the middle of a barrel, and a memory
of Banker Walsh, who held some notes of his, saying to
him, "This party of yours is a phase, Altgeld. When you're
ready to talk sense, let us know. You don't run a political
campaign on a few hundred thousand, and there's enough
money for all, I assure you. Make things easy for yourself;
don't worry about those notes. The Republican Party is
only too glad to see money go to the Democrats, in reasonable amounts, of course, but they have to be assured that
you stand for the same things we do. You're laboring under a misconception of democracy, Altgeld; a democratic
election is a contest between individuals, but for the health
of this country, both parties must have certain understandings with business. . . ."

He heard voices outside and sat up, kneading his eyes
with his fists. It was better not to think too much today.
He heard small voices, and when he went outside, Emma's
friend, May Wilson, was there, with her two little girls,
one five, one seven.

May Wilson said, "I thought that here it would be like
a madhouse today."

"It will be, it's still too early."

"The reporters were here this morning, and we got rid
of them," Emma said. "But they'll be back. How do you
feel, Pete?"

"I feel good," he smiled.

In a little while, he was sitting on the floor with the two
small girls. They were fascinated by his beard. "Daddy has
a mustache but no beard. You got a nice beard. You got a
beautiful beard." "I never thought of it as being very
beautiful, but I suppose it is a nice beard." "Very nice,

very, very nice." That was the younger one; the older one didn't think it was polite to discuss personalities, and told her sister so. She said, "Do you know stories. Could you tell us a story?" So he told them the tale of the princess who lived on a glass hill, and how many horses and brave young men tried to ride up that slope. But it was the end of peace for that day.

VI

JOE MARTIN came after the two children had gone; he came up straight from the South Side, burning. "Strongarm methods," he said. "They got Pinkertons covering the polls. It isn't enough that they had a rumor going around about a blacklist, they're out there writing down names, or pretending to. They're intimidating anyone whose looks they don't like; anyone in old clothes, off the line."

"John said Hennessy would be there."

"I spoke to John. He says, do you want a riot?"

"I want a riot! You're god-damned right I want a riot! You get Hennessy there and instruct him to vote everyone, everyone. And if he needs men, tell John to put a hundred or two hundred on the spot. They're testing it early, and it's not going to work."

"The Pinkertons are armed."

"Tell him to arm our men—wait a minute!" Martin was on his way to the phone. "Get hold of Buck Hinrichsen— he may be at the Sherman House. I'm going to call out the militia if necessary—I'll put this whole damn state under martial law."

In a little while, he was on the phone to Hinrichsen. Two reporters from the *Inter-Ocean* and one from the *Tribune* came in. Emma pressed cigars and drinks on them. An artist from the *News* appeared and pleaded, could he draw the Governor? Just a single sketch? "All right," Altgeld said, "all right." Sam McConnell sauntered through the door and stood there, grinning. Altgeld dropped into a chair. The reporters began to hammer away, joined now by a telegraph correspondent of the *New York Herald.*

"Would you say that you are confident, Governor?"

"Of course, I'm confident."

"They say that in New York Mark Hanna is taking all money, six to one, on a McKinley landslide. What do you think of that?"

"What do I think of that? Why, gentlemen, if I had a ten-million-dollar slush fund, I'd be in the betting business too. And since it's Morgan's money, why, gentlemen, what does Hanna stand to lose?"

"Will you comment on the bad feeling between you and Mark Hanna, Governor?"

"Bad feeling? I wouldn't call it that. You know, gentlemen, I've worked with a lot of political bosses and I've fought some of them too. They're like other folks. Sometimes, they're very decent. Sometimes, they're thorough going scoundrels. I'll leave it to you to decide where Mark Hanna belongs."

A late arrival, the correspondent of *Harper's Weekly,* asked caustically, "Do you believe that Mark Hanna would be as much of a power in the White House if McKinley wins as you will be if Bryan wins?"

"If Bryan wins, young man, I intend to be the Governor of Illinois, no more, no less."

"Governor, Hanna is charging you directly with being an anarchist and a socialist. Will you comment?"

"Well, being neither, I'm not too well learned on the

subject. I'm not sure one could be both of them at the same time—you know, they charge me with being a communist too—and maybe I'm all three, if you consider that a man who put up some of the finest office buildings in Chicago is that."

"Do you approve of socialism, Governor?"

"I disapprove of government by the trusts, by injunction, by terror and murder. Only my enemies raise the question of socialism in this election. Read through our party's platform, gentlemen, and see whether you find the word socialism there."

"Governor, is it true that there are differences between you and Bryan?"

"Young man, are you married?"

The reporter nodded.

"And are there no differences between you and your wife? Well, a party's like a family."

He took them like that, parrying, stroking, cajoling, and sometimes attacking savagely, for the next half hour. More reporters came in and out. The artist from the *News* finished his sketch. Schilling entered and whispered to McConnell, who glanced at Altgeld. The Governor nodded.

"All right, gentlemen," McConnell said. "This is election day, you know."

They filed out. Martin was still inside, hanging over the telephone. Clarence Darrow entered, followed by a waiter who pushed a table of cold meats, hot soup and beer. No one spoke until the waiter had gone, except Emma, who, filling plates, ladling soup into cups, said, "Please eat. This is going to be one of those days. So you might as well eat."

Schilling shook his head sadly, so sadly that Altgeld laughed to see his face. McConnell said, "I'm glad someone can laugh. George has a beauty, oh, a genuine beauty."

"What is it?" Altgeld demanded. "It gets to a point where it can't be worse. What is it now?"

"Tell him, George."

Schilling sipped at his soup and watched Altgeld. He began apologetically. "I got a message from Debs that he wanted to see me. Gene Debs, you remember?"

"I remember."

"It's a very simple thing, and they did it very quietly. Debs began to get word of it last night, and I've been checking this morning. I checked New York, Cleveland, San Francisco, and St. Louis. Debs had word from Pittsburgh and from Philadelphia and from Portland. Then three cities in upstate New York. Now, today, Newark in New Jersey. So that makes it almost all over, doesn't it? From that you would—"

"What the devil are you talking about, George?" Altgeld demanded.

"They closed the factories early. I thought you heard. Sometimes an hour early, sometimes two hours, in some places they only worked half a day. I'm not exaggerating. Hundreds of shops were closed down. In some places, they were frank, just as open about it as they could be. They put up signs—"If Bryan is elected, this plant will remain closed." In other places, they were more quiet. So they did it by passing around the word 'Bryan is elected and you don't have to come back. The shop stays closed.' Maybe not those exact words, but always the implication was the same."

"It's a bluff," Darrow said. "It's just a damn bluff."

"It's a beauty," McConnell sighed. "In all my life, I never heard of one like that. It's a beauty, all right."

"Of course, it's a bluff," Altgeld agreed. "Suppose you

try to explain to a million workers that it's just a bluff. George, do you think it was coordinated?"

"Can there be any doubt? It's not only coordinated, it is Mark Hanna. Pete, that's a smart fellow, that's maybe the most dangerous man in America."

"I suppose it is coordinated. What were those cities, New York, Pittsburgh, San Francisco—?"

Schilling went through the rest, numbering them off carefully on his fingers. McConnell pushed away his plate. "I've got no appetite," he said.

"Is it legal?" Darrow asked.

"If McKinley wins, it's damn well going to be legal. I don't know. If we could prove conspiracy—no, no, we'd never be able to prove it. If a man closes down his plant, he's within the law, isn't he? That's what we recognize, isn't it? The right of one man to dictate the fate of a plant that produces more than the whole country did a hundred years ago. If he closes it down and fifty thousand men are out of work, well, that's his business. Who's going to challenge it?"

"But it's the dirtiest trick that's ever been pulled in any campaign."

"The smartest, too," McConnell nodded.

"What did Debs say?" Altgeld asked.

"He's been up all night, telegraphing, sending out men, trying to work through the unions. But it's an impossible job. It's too late. Debs thought also that it was impossible. Debs—" His voice trailed away. Debs had said to him, "Schilling, this is the cleanest lesson in economics that I ever had. This makes me a socialist; other things, yes, but until the day I die, I won't forget this. Quietly, they took over the government; quietly, they made it plain to the people that they are the government. Tell Altgeld I'll fight, but it's no use, not one god-damned bit of use. His way is no good. Tell him that. Tell him that he's chasing a rainbow. Or leave him alone, and he'll wake up tomorrow and have the answer."

VII

TELEGRAMS, messengers, more reporters, ward-workers, long-distance calls, more telegrams, consultations when it was too late for consultation, frantic appeals at a time when some precincts had already closed their boxes and proceeded to count. If any man was removed from innocence in politics, it was John Peter Altgeld; he knew that ballot boxes were stuffed; he knew the workings as well as the principles of election-day resurrection, where a thousand cemeteries gave up their dead of five generations past; he knew of the countless infant fatalities who somehow grew to sufficient maturity to become loyal party voters; he knew of the birth certificates forged for numberless ghosts who had no existence outside of the ward-heeler's file; he even knew the mechanics of such mundane and plug-ugly methods as Bathhouse John practiced, those of loading brewery wagons with bums and thugs, and voting them all day long, round and round the city; he even knew how much laudanum was necessary to load a watcher's coffee, so that he would watch no more, and he was not ignorant of that fact that while votes, by and large, cost five dollars apiece, among certain sections of the population votes could be bought for two dollars, and the contents of a municipal jail could be voted at fifty cents a head. He had seen elections where, out of a total electorate of one hundred thousand, each party had voted twice that number, and he also knew that a conservative politician marked off at least one seventh of the national vote as being fraudulent. This was a part of American democracy, and it was practiced by both parties with equal efficiency although not with equal funds; and it was taken for granted by everyone except very small children and a few maiden ladies.

But in this election there were new refinements that made the fumbling and tradition-bound efforts of Bathhouse John seem completely adolescent. It was a step forward when Pinkertons were hired to promote riots in Bryan meetings with stinkbombs and smokebombs and wild screams and when the newspapers created daily false stories of anarchist assassinations; but even that was unorganized in terms of the insurance and bank scheme. Rumors of this trickled in for weeks before election day; but the farm population was widespread; communications were bad; and while the farmers were almost wholly for Bryan they could not be either reached or organized either by their granges or populist committees in the same terms in which the workers were organized and reached through the trade unions. So, at first, when one farmer told the story of having his fire insurance canceled because of the possibility of Bryan's election, it was shrugged off; but when farmer after farmer reported the same thing, the shape of a national campaign became apparent; but the full shape of it was not realized until a few hours after Altgeld had heard of the closed-shop technique: then Dreyer, the same who had delivered the pardon message, called and said he had to see him. Dose said the Governor was busy; busy was a small word; actually, the suite had become a madhouse by that time. But Altgeld said, "Let him come up. One more won't matter." But he mattered; he pulled Altgeld into a corner and told him about the banks. More than four hundred banks were involved, and they were demanding all call loans and overdue mortgages. They had timed their demands for today and tomorrow and along with the demands had gone the information that both loans and mortgages would be extended if McKinley were elected president. The majority of the banks involved—and there might be hundreds more, for all Dreyer knew—stretched right across the corn and hog belt and into the south, like a girdle over the grange and populist territory, where Bryan was strongest. "I wanted you to know," Dreyer said, wiping the sweat from his face, nervous, possessed of a shame that seemed as much of him as his skin. "I'm not for your man, but I'm not for this. What in God's name is a free vote, if you tell a man that when his candidate comes in, he's going to lose his farm and everything else he owns?" "I don't know what a free vote is," Altgeld said, "but thank you for telling me." "Well, I'm glad I told you. It's in confidence, you understand, Governor?" "In confidence, of course."

VIII

Toward evening, it began to quiet down. Only Darrow, Schilling, Martin, and McConnell were left. An hour before, Altgeld had told his secretary, "Bill, it's washed out. We haven't a chance in a million. So you might as well get down to Springfield and catch up on my work. Emma wants to go right back there; I don't blame her."

A *Tribune* reporter had asked him if he intended to stay up all night for the returns. "I have no doubt about the returns," he smiled. "I intend to sleep." He said as much to McConnell, and that old friend of his nodded. "You're right, Pete. We've got nothing to celebrate." "Except that we've learned something." "Maybe we have and perhaps we haven't. This isn't the last election, Pete. Every four years, something like this will happen. Perhaps they'll take the simple way and run Jack and Jill; but if they try to buck it, do you think they'll do better than we did?" "If I knew what we were bucking."

But Darrow didn't think it was lost. "You underrate the people," he insisted. "That's the trouble with all of you. All of you underrate the people. Barnum was clever when he said a sucker is born every minute, but sometimes the people learn."

Altgeld had relaxed into a chair. The strain was leaving his face, and he was smiling at Emma who stood watching him. "I'm all right, my dear. No, Clarence; Mr. Barnum is a superficial and foolish man. Yes, I've met him, I know. A bad man—anyone is who thinks of people in such terms. We're not dealing with suckers; we're dealing with men and women who think and who react, and who are frightened and unorganized, and, God knows, I don't blame them for that. Unless we try to understand what happened during the past few months, everything we put into this is going to be thrown out, worthless, lost."

"We can still win," Darrow insisted, and Altgeld replied, somewhat sharply:

"We can't win. That's what I'm trying to get into your head, Clarence—we can't win. From the very start of this thing, we were beaten, but we didn't know. Because we didn't know what we were fighting and how to fight it— and, God help us, we still don't!"

Schilling said goodby. There were tears in his eyes. Emma kissed him and said, "Go to bed, George. This is a fine thing. You have bags under your eyes." Clarence Dar-row went with him. Night had come, and this was election night in Chicago, with great bonfires lighting up the sky.

They went to the window and watched. Joe Martin had said very little; now he said, "Meatpacker and whore to the world," softly, so that Emma didn't hear but only McConnell who stood next to him. The judge put his arm around Altgeld and whispered goodnight. Emma walked with him to the door, leaving the two men at the window. They stood there in silence until Emma returned, and then Joe Martin murmured:

"Some men, Pete, get pleasure from different things, cards, women, and I've known some of our American aristocrats whose hobby was putting diamond fillings in their teeth, but I think, with you, it's hitting your head against a stone wall—" The tone of his voice robbed it of all offense; they stood in the shadow, and Emma couldn't see his face, but the intonation was more bitter than regretful.

"You thought there was no chance, right from the beginning?"

"None," Martin said.

"And you don't know why I did it?"

"I know," Martin said tiredly. "I know, Pete. All right, so I know. It always was this way; it's always going to be this way. The strong are going to take from the weak, and men are going to go hungry, and they're going to die, and I wouldn't give you twenty cents for the power of an ideal or a Christian sentiment. Because if there are worse liars than the swine who operate our free press, it's the sacred pastors who stand in their pulpits and methodically cut your throat. Your trade unions don't cut any ice with me, Pete; it's the men who own the guns and the schools and the churches and the factories who pay off, and you've let them crucify you. . . ."

A short while after that, he took up his hat and coat and

272

left. Emma ordered dinner sent up. She was amazed at how well her husband ate. A great load seemed to have been lifted from him. From the time Martin left, he didn't mention the election again, and when Emma suggested that they might have the phone switched off and messages held, he agreed eagerly. They ate a good dinner, and then Altgeld stretched out on a chair, his feet up on a stool.

"I wish you would read something--I don't know what," he said.

She had a copy of *Huckleberry Finn* in the bedroom; she brought it in, opened it, and read at random from here and there. They both knew the book well. He asked for the part about the duke and the king and then the part about the vendetta. He was half awake and half asleep after an hour of this. She helped him into the bedroom, and as soon as he was in bed, he was sleeping.

Emma couldn't sleep; she sat at the window, in the dark, watching the lights of the city, thinking about this and that, and about many things and about nothing at all. The election seemed a long time ago, and it seemed more than a lifetime ago that she had read each day in the papers of a labor leader called Albert Parsons, who was going to be hanged by the neck until dead. And when had she read of a party a New York millionaire gave where a racehorse was the guest of honor, eating a champagne mash of oats out of a golden trough, and where each of the guests was given a diamond horseshoe worth several thousand dollars as a souvenir? Her thoughts were not of condemnation, not relative; she thought of one thing and another, watching the sprawling, windy, incredible city that had come out of the prairie and the woods, as her husband had, confused as he was, uncertain as he was, and as incredibly strong and inevitable. . . .

The next morning, they learned that William McKinley was president-elect of the United States and that John Tanner was governor-elect of the sovereign State of Illinois. Even though in the state, Altgeld had run more than ten thousand votes ahead of Bryan, the two had gone down together. But, to this, Altgeld reacted with almost no emotion at all. He ate a good breakfast of wheatcakes, bacon, eggs, and hot rolls. "I must have slept like a log last night," he told Emma. "I feel good."

When Schilling called on the phone, Altgeld was able to laugh at his hollow voice. "Get some sleep," he said. "My god, George, you've been up all night. How do you expect things to look?" "But we've lost—don't you understand?" "We've lost. That's right. Go to sleep, and then think about it."

And he asked Emma, "You have the tickets?"

She nodded. He suggested a walk along the lakefront before they left. "You know, we'll be coming back here soon to live. You're not disappointed?" She said, "Pete, I would have given five years of my life for you to have won that election." He took her in his arms as he hadn't for a long time.

IX

IN MANY ways, many men reacted, for something was taking shape, and in one fashion or another, some more clearly, some less clearly, they saw it. To Schilling, who came to see him still sleepless, Gene Debs said, "So it came out as I said." "That's right. Do you want to gloat?" "No, Schilling, I don't want to gloat. You made your bed with them because it was soft to lay in, and Parsons' been dead a long time." "What the devil does that have to do with it?" "Because you walked out on us, but whenever you came back, we were here. All right, we said, this is an honest man, we'll support him. Now we're going to hoe our own row. They showed us their strength; now we'll show them the good right arm of the workers. We're strong, too, Schilling, and we're learning how to fight." "So you'd crucify him with the rest?" "I don't crucify him. God damn it, Schilling, what kind of a fool are you?" Schilling was tired and without words to hit back; he stared at the tall, lean organizer, and he nodded, and he walked out. And home, in bed at last, he was able to let his tears flow, weeping for the first time in as long as he could remember.

But Debs didn't weep, sitting behind the kitchen table of the little shack that was his home, hard chin in hands, the *Chicago Tribune* spread out in front of him, Altgeld spread-eagled, flayed and defined: ". . . his criminal sympathies, his anarchistic tendencies, his fostering of evil, his patronage and protection of Debsism, free riot . . ." and on and on: Debs didn't weep, but read with cold eyes.

Someone had said to Debs, not long ago, that whatever was done to Pete Altgeld in their own time, history would right it; history would wring the truth from it: but now and today, Debs reflected that history was a forlorn hope. Life was on his side, but let the abstract truth be for the scholars; he had a bitter impatience. Through the thin walls, he could hear from next door how a baby whimpered for food; the Monday before, he had gone to the burial of Johnny Ames, a stockyards organizer who had died from tuberculosis, contracted on top of too many beatings, too much exposure, too much starvation. Let others wait for history; he had seen a ditch on the edge of packing-town filled with the cold-blue dead of a Polish family, starved out. Let them tell him that this was a land where no one starved! His thoughts roamed to people too numerous to count, and there was one emotion, one drive, one plea—and that was hunger.

His long-fingered, work-hardened hands turned the pages of the *Tribune*. He read with serious and intent interest.

In the Union League Club, at the same time, the celebration was winding up or running down—as you would have it—as the earth turned and the sun rose and the new day came in. There had been a unique celebration, for the small gods of Chicago had forgotten their careful manners. They say that a reaction from fear will express itself in multiple ways, even to the extent of fat bankers lining up from a wall to play that old and venerated game of Johnny Ride the Pony. That was in the early part of the evening, when restraint still operated, and it was small and harmless pleasure that was gotten from pork-butchers, steelmen, bankers, rolling-stock operators, and many others joining hands and dancing ring-around-the-rosey and roaring out, "Well, I guess I'll have to telegraph my baby, I need the money bad, indeed I do." That was when a victory was only expected, not yet conceded; when actual confirmation of the fact that William McKinley was president was received, champagne was flowing like Niagara Falls, and a late supper was served, beefsteak, venison steak, pheasant, grouse, rib roasts, stuffed turkeys, and with it appropriate trimmings, sweets, nuts. It was after that the real entertainment began, something to remember. However, this was reaction to a danger that was gone, and no one can be condemned for relaxing.

The people of the city and of the country relaxed too. The brief excitement had worn off; an election had come and gone, but the republic was maintained, and what was all this talk of an end to freedom, not to mention the substantial good things of life? The citizens woke up, and it was the same, the shadows in the same places, the smell of coffee the same, the voices the same.

X

FOR Altgeld, there was the need of making an estimate. They looked to him now, as they had when Bryan won the nomination, and Bryan himself had called and asked, hopelessly:

"Governor, what are we going to do?"

"Wait for the next time. Make some use of what we've learned." But he himself was unsure of what they had learned. When he wrote down his statement, the words came hard and they sounded flat, for all their bumptiousness: "Consider that only six months ago our great party lay prostrate. It had been betrayed into the hands of the thieves and monopolists by President Cleveland—" He read it to Emma. She asked him, "Thieves?" He felt he was overemphasizing it and changed the word to "jobbers." He was writing without certainty, ". . . It arose with new energy, it cut loose from the domination of trusts and syndicates . . ." "It's good," Emma reassured him. "Don't be afraid." That was a reversal, and he stared at her for a long while. When had she ever told him not to be afraid?

"You mean because I've lost everything, there's no more to lose?"

"I didn't mean that, Pete."

"Do you think I'm afraid?"

"I don't think you're afraid of anything on earth, Pete. That isn't what I meant."

"Then what?"

"I want you not to think that you're beaten, Pete."

But with each word he wrote, the vastness of the defeat sank in. When he put on paper, of his party, "It drove out the political vermin and with a new inspiration it again proclaimed democratic principles and espoused the cause of toiling humanity," he could only whisper, "My God, I sound like Bryan."

He felt more like himself when he wrote, "It was confronted by all the boodle that could be scraped together on two continents; it was confronted by all the banks, all the trusts, all the syndicates, all the corporations, all the great papers." That, at least, was the sober truth; and whatever his own future was, or the party's, let it be set down that this single time at least, the Democrats had fought bravely against great odds. He wrote bitterly, "It was confronted by everything that money could buy, that boodle could debauch or that fear of starvation could coerce. . . . "

But reading it to Emma, the condition became more plain. Everything had been with the opposition; they had won, very simply, because the force and the wealth of the nation were with them. He said to his wife, dully:

"All day now, I've been nursing myself on the belief that four years from now we could make the people understand. But four years from now they'll close down the factories again."

He finished writing what would afterward be called the manifesto of democracy. For him, it was a confession of defeat.

XI

Two months were left now. They had lived in the executive mansion for four years, and Emma, when she began to pack, shook her head hopelessly. Her husband was a type who practiced an almost automatic accumulation. Books piled up in high stacks, and it broke his heart to part with any of them. He saved newspapers and magazines, explaining that he would never know when he might want something. Brand Whitlock helped Emma sort out the stuff; the Governor himself was not too interested. He told them they might keep what they thought was worth keeping, throw the rest away. There was a certain absentmindedness in all of his actions now. Without saying anything to Emma, he would wrap himself up in coat and muffler, go out, and begin a slow shuffle across the lawn; it broke her heart to watch that, and now and again she would ask young Whitlock to join him. Apologetic, she would tell the boy, "He's very sick, you know," realizing how furious her husband would have been had he overheard. Brand Whitlock would take long strides to join Altgeld, thinking all the while, desperately, how he would open the conversation. But the Governor liked him, and his greeting would invariably be, "Hello, son, and what is it today?"

"I was reading in the papers that there's almost no doubt that there'll be war with Spain. What do you think, sir?"

"And you came galloping across the lawn to tell me the papers are promoting a war with Spain?"

"Well, sir, no—that is, not exactly—"

"All right, Brand. Yes, sure, there's going to be war with Spain—that's the beginning. That's going to be a lot of war, a different kind of violence. Just beginning. My god, there's going to be the kind of bloodletting that will make our thing between the states look like a skirmish."

"But why—why?"

"Why do we want Cuba? You tell me. Why do we want the Philippines? Why do we want Puerto Rico? You tell me why. And when are we going to be satisfied—oh, the devil with that! Tell me about yourself. If you come out to walk with me, don't sweat over some proper conversational subject."

"Yes, sir."

"And do you understand—come to see me in Chicago. I'll be a new man when I get out of here."

But that was bravado. Chicago was just another stop now, for it did not seem to him that he was going anywhere at all. Much like an automaton, he cleared up his work. His accountants came down from Chicago, and though he had known much of it, he was nevertheless astounded to discover how deeply in debt he was, how much of a poor man he was. Being Governor of Illinois, being nominal leader of the national party—none of that had swelled his wealth, but rather drained from him almost every penny he had. As the figures shaped up, he began to wonder how a poor man could function in an office, even considering that he should be elected to one, except by joining the systematic robbery of the people that was taken for granted by so many. That, he had never indulged in; not because his character morally prohibited it, but because he had such a deep-seated contempt for graft, because out of the years it had emerged, in his eyes, as a cheap and despicable practice.

He cleaned things up, put things away, washed his hands of them, and went off to tell Emma that they were poor. Yet he was half ashamed as he said it. "We won't starve," he explained. "I'm still a good lawyer, I think, and I think I have a few friends."

"I'm glad."

He realized what she meant. One thing after another had to be sloughed off; now it was the money.

"We're going to be free," she said. "We're going to do a lot of things that we wanted to do, aren't we, Pete?"

She didn't mean traveling this time; she didn't mean long afternoons in the sunlight; she actually meant, in the essence of it, that they would be free—to speak their own minds, starve, go to jail, or walk as much as they wanted to along the lakefront of Chicago. They would be free to find the direction for which he had been searching.

He put his arm around her; he said to her, "I'm an old man, Emma, and if I were a religious man, I'd say I am dying of my sins. We don't speak about that, do we, but you know I've been looking at the wives of other men. It's reassuring; it's rewarding too. I'm very lucky."

He said that to Hinrichsen when the Secretary of State offered condolences. "To hell with all that," he said. "My heart isn't breaking, Buck. Don't act like it is."

"I only wish you had been born in this damned country."

"Would that make me an American, Buck?"

"It would make you president."

"You're lying in your teeth. I told you, to hell with that. I told you I don't want any sympathy. I'm beginning to open my eyes. Do you know what it is to feel free, Buck? Hell—of course you don't. Well, the only real freedom is to recognize what you have to do, and I'm beginning to get there."

He was in a better mood as he prepared his farewell message for Tanner's inauguration; he put down the things he wanted to say, the things he wanted noted, marked, and remembered. Among other finalities, death is the aching knowledge that you will leave things half finished, unsaid, open to misinterpretation, lies and slander. Doc Arbady of Chicago, who was his good friend, had said to him, not so long ago, "You ask me a straight question, Pete, and this answer is straight. Locomotor Ataxia means that you are dying. That's broad, but not so broad as it might be. Consider that every man begins to die at a certain point, thirty, thirty-five—from then on, it's downhill, but slowly, and some of us live to be a hundred. With you, the process is quickened. The way you walk is a sign of that. Those pains are another sign, the dizziness, weakness, vomiting—all of those are symptoms. Maybe you'll live for ten years; that's possible, but I don't say it's likely. If I were in your place, I would do everything I have to do soon. Early each day." He had thanked Doc Arbady and he had acted on his advice. And once he had overcome— at least partially—the heart-paralyzing fear, the urgency of death was not altogether unacceptable. At least, there was a ready satisfaction in each act completed, such as he felt when he had written this farewell message, when he had read it aloud to Emma, slowly and emphatically.

"I'm glad you can say those things, Pete," she nodded.

But he didn't say them. He sat on the platform with Governor Tanner, and afterwards he reflected that this was merely cheap and childish. For the first time, a retiring governor of the state was kept voiceless, and the carefully prepared speech remained in his pocket. The new governor said, afterwards, "Sorry, Altgeld, but there was no time on the program. It's a shame that you couldn't talk, but I presume you understand."

"I understand," Altgeld smiled.

Then they went north to Chicago and home, hands washed clean. At the station, Joe Martin alone waited, and he put his arms around both Altgeld and Emma.

The wind came in from the lake, cold and fresh. It was a bright clear evening as they rode through the streets of the city.

XII

HE WAS not yet fifty years old, but he was old not young, an old man who puttered around at this and that. His friends came to Emma and wondered what they could do, and she shook her head hopelessly. The newspapers were after him again, but for once he didn't seem to have the energy or the desire to fight back. They had a new tag for him, said to have been coined by the bright young Teddy Roosevelt, "The Illinois Communist." A new and lurid quality had come into their stories; as the Governor of Illinois, he had been a dangerous man; he had shown a devastating tendency to strike back; as Altgeld, the private citizen, the red, he was fair game, and as fair game they went after him. When he told a reporter that private enterprise might be wrong—a lot of things had to be looked at differently, that particular paper flared forth with the headline: "ALTGELD CALLS FOR REVOLUTION!" When he argued his first case in court, the judge stared at him hostilely; he won the decision in spite of the bench, and his antagonism was hardly concealed. What assets he had left disappeared like snow under a hot sun; the brokers, bankers, and businessmen of Chicago were smilingly hard. "Pay your debts," they told him. That a fortune of his had gone down the drain of the party, and that many of them were Democrats as well as Republicans did not seem to matter. When Joe Martin came to his rescue with thirty-five thousand dollars and forced him to take it, he said, "You know, Joe, I won't live long enough to repay this. I've lost the knack of making money." "You repaid it a long time ago," Martin said. He took it, and he saw it go after the rest, good money after bad, as they said. His busi-

ness partner and cousin, John Lanehart, had died, leaving
more debts, and somehow he found the money to pay
them. It was no longer a case of becoming a rich man; it
was how to become a poor man gracefully.

He read a good deal in those days. Emma was making a
home again—the house in Chicago was practically all that
they had left—and in his study there he found himself
learning. He wanted to know all there was to know of what
had happened in the past two generations. The repetitious
phrases of the reformers, the lurid accounts of John D.
Rockefeller, Jim Fisk, Commodore Vanderbilt, Leland
Stanford, Phil Armour, J. P. Morgan, and all the rest were
not enough. He knew how it had happened; he had seen
it happen here in Chicago, and some of the spoil had even
been flung to him. He wanted to know why it had happened, why a great nation had been delivered over to
them, hand and foot and mouth, and why now, under their
pressure, this same nation was setting forth on an imperialist march to master the world. He was drawn into a may-
oralty campaign; the Democrats had put up young Carter
Harrison, whose father had been mayor of Chicago when
the Haymarket people were hanged, and they wanted Altgeld to lend his weight. He did so, but in place of his old
enthusiasm was a scientific curiosity. Here in Chicago the
two parties had become like one, and though the Democrats were victorious, all the fine-sounding ideals for which
he had battled nationally were thrown overboard and their
loss was hardly noticed except by a very few. His attitude
toward politics was not becoming one of cynicism, but
rather one of anger. The whole hysterical pageant was re-
lating itself to those cold-eyed, cool-headed men who ruled
their dozen industrial empires like no kings the world had

ever known. In order that they might have peace, in order that they might have numberless and willing servants, they observed an ancient ritual on the first Tuesday after the first Monday each November. And in order that the ritual might be well observed, they employed his kind, the politicians, the modern gladiators who coldbloodedly performed on specified occasions, but ate from the same bowl and lived in the same enclosure. It was overt and cheap and almost ridiculous when Mark Hanna dangled William McKinley on the several golden strings provided by the Morgans and the Rockefellers and the Carnegies, but was it less so, he wondered, when they allowed an opposition candidate to win, as they did sometimes, and then bought in on the new administration, bought out the cabinet, the congress, the large fry and the small fry. . . .

He wasn't shocked when the *Maine* went down and the war cries echoed from coast to coast. He was beginning to understand, not fully, but better than he had ever understood before, and he began to come out of his lethargy. He woke to life suddenly, and Emma found herself dragged out to meetings, to the theatre, to certain dinners. Once again the parade of people, strange people, all kinds of people to the home of Pete Altgeld began. He felt a renewed strength. And when Darrow and Schilling came with their proposal of a third party for the next local election, he was ready to listen.

"But don't go off half-cocked," he told Darrow coldly. "This is going to be hard and murderous, and I don't think we're going to win. You have to begin somewhere, and we begin here."

"But you'll be the candidate?"

"I'll run for mayor, that's right. But just remember that

we're operating on a shoestring. I'm broke." And to Schilling, he said, "I want to meet Debs, George. Will you arrange it?"

"Here?"

"Here or anywhere. I don't care."

XIII

THEY sat in the kitchen of Debs' house, a pitcher of beer on the table, two glasses, Altgeld's hat and coat on a chair at one side, a small black dog poking at Debs' hand, the smell of recently cooked cabbage, an open ten-cent copybook in which Debs had been writing, a bottle of ink and a pen, and a plate with two slices of dry bread on it. They had shaken hands and spoken a few words of greeting and now they sat and looked at each other.

"We should have met a long time ago," Altgeld said.

Debs was not impressed. He poured two glasses of beer, carefully, not spilling a drop. "I'm not sure," he said.

"I want to talk about some things, Debs, but I want you to trust me. You don't trust me, do you?"

"No."

"I suppose you have reasons."

"A lot of reasons."

"Would you mind—"

"I don't mind. Generally, I don't trust your kind. I don't trust lawyers; I don't trust rich men, I don't like them. I don't like the miserable little lackeys of the trusts, of Standard Oil and New York Central and Carnegie Steel and the rest. That's generally. Specifically, you were governor—well, what happened? Is it any better now then when you became governor?"

"No—it's worse."

"Beer?" Debs asked. Altgeld nodded. They both sipped at their glasses.

"Would it have been any better if you were governor?" Altgeld asked.

"Maybe."

"Why did you support me in the election?"

"You were the lesser of two evils. That's all. That's the whole reason."

"And you don't believe that if Bryan had won, if I had won, it would be any better?"

"That's right," Debs said quietly. "No better. We would be at war with Spain sooner or later. Maybe it would have been a little harder, a little more expensive for them to buy out the Democrats, but it wouldn't cost more than the ten million they spent on McKinley."

"You're a socialist, aren't you?"

"That's no secret," Debs said.

"And that's the only thing that represents any hope to you? You don't see any good coming out of capitalism?"

"You don't answer that question by saying yes." Debs smiled for the first time. "There's some progress under capitalism. You know that, Altgeld—I don't have to draw pictures for you. You remember when there were no railroads, and today the railroads are here. It's true that maybe a hundred thousand men died of disease building them; it's true that the capital came by giving the promoters a billion acres of public land; it's true that they were built by idiots more than by engineers, and almost all the lines had to be relaid; it's true that the iron rails wore like cheese, and that not so long ago there were seventy-six different track gauges, and that for a period of twenty years there was never a train that ran on schedule, and that God knows how many of the public were killed riding the rotten rolling stock, and that more than five thousand workers were murdered in rail labor battles—but we have the railroad, and that's progress, isn't it?"

"I don't mean that," Altgeld said, differently on the defensive than he had ever been, not knowing whether Debs was laughing at him, liking him or quietly contemptuous.

"Do I think we can ever legislate the evils away? Maybe we can. That's why I'm a socialist, not to make a revolution and a commune, as the *Tribune's* so glad to say. But maybe. If we had ten million votes for socialism, I still don't know if they'd hand over the government to us. It's their government. It was their government when you were Governor. That's why your militia shot us down when we struck, Altgeld. You want me to forget that?"

"I don't ask you to forget it. I know what I did when I was Governor. I took an oath. I enforced the law."

"Their law."

"The law of the state. I'm not proud. I'm not ashamed. I did what I had to do. I'd do it again. If the law is no good, then it has to be changed. The Governor enforces what law there is."

"That's an evasion."

"The hell it is!" Altgeld snapped. "I'm no socialist, Debs. You ought to know that, if no one else in America does."

"I know it." He hesitated a moment, drank down the rest of his beer, and said quietly, "Who's with you, Altgeld? You try to walk in the middle, and who's your friend? You try to make your peace with this rotten system —why? You're the first man since Lincoln who can speak to the people, who doesn't despise the people, and whom they love. That's right, they love you, they trust you. You

288

could have been a Fisk or a Gould or an Armour, but you didn't. But it's not the way it was when Abe Lincoln became president. When they marched off to the war and the paper uniforms melted in the rain and the rotten guns blew up in their faces, then it became different. My god, Altgeld, you can't be a Lincoln today; there'll be no more Lincolns in America—that's gone. We're not a democracy, we're an oligarchy. If you didn't realize that when they closed down the factories before election day, you never will. You were there—you saw McDonald sell out the street-car franchises for ninety-nine years; you saw what happened at Pullman. What in hell am I talking for—you pardoned the anarchists, didn't you?"

Altgeld nodded, his face like a mask, his blue eyes staring fixedly at Debs.

"Come with us," Debs pleaded. The barriers were down. He leaned across the table, his long, powerful hands gripping the edge. His face was an earnest of silent pleading. His tongue wet his lips, and in the live muscles of his cheeks, his chin, was all that he wanted to say and could not find the words for. "Come with us, Altgeld," he repeated. "The world found democracy through America— it's going to find socialism through America. It's going to find the life God made man to live. It's going to find the workers building the kind of palaces that will make your lakefront mansions look like shacks. There's going to be a republic of farmers and workers, where men are equal and free. A land without unemployment, a land where children grow up strong and clean and decent. It's going to be a beautiful, great land! God almighty, Altgeld, what's your stake with them?"

No expression on Altgeld's face, no reaction. "I'm not a socialist, Debs," he said quietly. "That's honest. I'm a dying man, Debs. I've got nothing to hide, nothing to fear. I just don't go along with you—I can't." He made no explanations; in his dry, rasping voice, there was a quality almost of anguish. Debs realized why men loved him; he was the end of something. Beyond him were the mighty forests cut down, the lashing wave of the frontier, the democracy of democracies, where all was possible and nothing impossible. Yet in that moment Debs pitied him and hated him, and the intimacy was gone, and they were just two men sitting at a kitchen table, and finally Altgeld said, "You know why I'm here."

"Schilling told me."

"What do you think of a third party, Debs?"

"I told you before. The third party for America is the party of socialism. It can't be different."

"Then that means you won't support me as an independent candidate for mayor?"

"We'll support you," Debs said wearily. "We supported you for Governor—we'll support you as long as you run, Altgeld. What I'm fighting for won't come tomorrow, and until then I want to live."

They shook hands, and Altgeld left him. Debs watched him walk away, a small, feeble man whose feet dragged as he walked.

XIV

ALTGELD was like a child; his excitement was like a running fever. As he told Emma, "If I was standing for president, it wouldn't be this way." For the first time, he was on his own; for the first time in his political life, he was a candidate with no strings attached. It was like breathing fresh air after living for a generation in a stuffy room. It was like coming out of a cell into freedom. When Bath-house John, now against him, told him, "It cannot be done, Governor—it cannot be done," he answered, "Damn it, I'll show you that it can be done!" He forgot his illness; he forgot Doc Arbady's black predictions. When the *Tribune* said, "The devil must be given his due, and there is no doubt but that John P. Altgeld is one of the most astute political minds in America," he responded with the first press conference in a long while. He was sick with nervousness as he waited for the reporters. He had seen to the cigars himself, fine black perfectos. He had invited men from the labor weeklies as well as the big dailies. Joe Martin served as doorkeeper and welcoming committee. Emma saw to the setups, cold lemonade as well as soda and water for the Scotch and rye whisky. While waiting, to hide his own nervousness, he lectured his wife and best friend on the importance of the press. "If the boss is against me and the reporter likes me, Joe, well that's a damn sight better than for the boss to be on my side and the reporter to hate my guts. Sure they're out to get me and they rake me over the coals. But look what they do to Teddy Roosevelt, the bosses' own little boy—I don't think there's a newspaperman in the country who doesn't know him for what he is, a puffed-up little ass, and, my word, but it comes through in their stories."

The press was taken up to his study, and there he was, behind his desk, the way they remembered him, chin on hands, the blue eyes sparkling.

"Going back in harness, Governor?"

"I've never been out of harness," he said, fetching a laugh with the first sally. "I've just been taking a few deep breaths."

"How does it feel to be out there alone, Governor?"

"Alone? Have a cigar, son," he said, holding them out and passing them around. "Tell you something, they used to say about old Dan Boone that he was never lost—not just because he was at home in the woods, but because he was pretty well content with where he happened to be. Changes a man's viewpoint. That's the way I feel."

"What about streetcar and gas franchises, Governor?"

"They've been used as political spoil. Our public services are a rock around the public's neck, and the men who promoted them are latter-day bandits. You may quote me, gentlemen. This business of fifty-five- and ninety-nine-year franchises is a disgrace. I would grant no franchise for more than ten years or some such limited period, and then the public service reverts to the public."

A labor reporter asked, "What about the right to strike and the right to assemble?"

"Inviolate, in so far as the power of the mayor would be concerned. There would be no limitation except that of conditions, by which I mean traffic, transportation, and so forth. The streets belong to the people of this city, and if they want to picket on them or hold meetings on them, they damn well may!"

"Does that go for communists and anarchists?"

"It goes for all citizens of Chicago, regardless of their race, color, or political persuasion."

"Does this mean that you've lost faith in the Democratic Party, Governor?"

"It does not. The bigger the independent vote, the more strength to the party."

"What about the war, Governor?"

"I'm for Cuban independence, and I'm in favor of using American arms to help Cuba gain that independence. But I think the annexation of the Philippines, the Hawaiian and Sandwich Islands is shameful, and one more step on the road toward American imperialism. . . ."

It went that way. For the first time, there were no strings attached, and he could speak his piece, talk out straightforwardly and forthrightly. He could say where he stood, what he was for and what he was against.

When he held his political councils, with Sam McConnell, with Clarence Darrow and George Schilling and Joe Martin, with Eugene Debs, they were open and to the point, unlike any he had ever participated in before. Clean air flowed. The little money they had was apportioned carefully but wisely. Harrison, the Democratic candidate, and Carter, the Republican, were both campaigning on a wild, communist-socialist witch hunt, pouring an almost insane flood of invective upon Altgeld. Rather than answer this, he decided to devote all his energy to getting his own platform across at a series of public and labor meetings.

He had always written his own speeches. But now he had twenty or thirty appearances in the same city, which meant at least a diversity of material—in addition to which he had to keep up his private law practice, both to pay his bills and to find whatever money he could for the campaign. He rose very early, and wrote before breakfast. At the table, Emma was his sounding board and critic. After that to court or his office; perhaps a street meeting before dinner, and then appointments and consultations during dinner. There was rarely a night without two meetings, and often enough there were three and four appearances to be made the same night. Emma was amazed at how well he stood it; she was personal attendant, secretary and adviser. She learned how to mix the guests of honor properly before a meeting, how to circulate among them, how to make the wives of small businessmen and workingmen feel at home with each other, how to arrange an agenda at the last moment, and how to jot down her husband's interpolated remarks, so that they would have a record later to check against the newspaper accounts.

The meetings were very heartening. In both the West Side and the South Side, he spoke to the largest political meetings those neighborhoods had ever known. Everywhere, halls were jam-packed. Men came from the shops in their work clothes; storekeepers, small tradesmen, women who took their children along because there was no one at home with whom to leave them, a new and alert cross-section for political meetings. In Chicago, as well as elsewhere in America, it was the time-honored practice to pack political meeings by scouring the flophouses, the vagrancy cells in the jails, the Salvation Army halls, the downtown alleys where the homeless curled up to sleep after poking sufficiently in the garbage cans. Very often, ward-heelers were sent to packing-town and to the McCormick and Pullman plants, where they distributed thousands of tokens. Each of these tokens, presented at the door of a political meeting, could be redeemed for ten cents, which not only assured a packed house for the newspapers to extol, but made a friend for the party. Of course, not everyone would come, but brisk trading went on for the tokens, and since only three per individual were acceptable at the door, the plan was near foolproof. Bathhouse John established and favored the practice of setting up a keg or two of beer adjacent to the hall, with the understanding that once the speeches were finished, everyone was welcome to see the bung punched and wet his whistle. However, even if he favored any of these methods, none was practical for Altgeld's thin wallet. The meetings were advertised at the union headquarters; volunteers gave out throwaways at the shops and in the neighborhoods; nevertheless, precedent was broken, and night after night, the halls were full.

He had learned a good deal about how to speak to people. He was fortunate in having an edged, clear voice, the kind that carries without effort. He could lean over the rostrum and talk to men at the rear of the hall, yet retain the intimate, toned-down quality of conversation. He answered questions simply and matter-of-factly, as, for example, when a man asked, "What do you intend to do about unemployment?" "See that no one in my city starves. That's all I can do, but I can do that." Generally half of every meeting was given over to questions and answers. He was establishing a new technique in Chicago politics. He minced no words. "I say a mayor is responsible for his police," he told one meeting. "I have in my possession the case histories of more than three hundred working people, clubbed and beaten by Chicago police in the past five years. I promise you that no worker will ever be clubbed in my administration. I say there's no justice for a poor man in Chicago today, at the judge's bench or at the police magistrate's rail. I'll fight to give you justice." He let go with venom, with hate, "This is a graft-ridden city—I know. I played ball with the local politicians. I talk from experience and I don't claim absolution from guilt. But I say that if I am elected mayor—I intend to clean up this city." "You're lying!" flung back at him and his own thrust, "Good. Never believe a politician! That's the one American axiom that sticks. So write down what I say, and present it for signature as I leave here." He could come out with those strokes, stabbing strokes that were something new; and once he said to Emma:

"The strange thing is that for once I'm speaking the God's honest truth."

Night after night, the faces spread before him. Night after night, their carriage took them from one part of town to another. For Altgeld, it was the long fight against odds that he loved so much; he was living again. He had taken the Democratic Party from Grover Cleveland. Now he would take Chicago from both parties, a gift from the people to their man.

XV

AT DINNER one night, with Darrow there and Schilling and Joe Martin, and their wives, and one fourteen-year-old boy who had been brought to meet the *Governor*, Altgeld basked in a warm family radiance; for this was the American home and the American family, with stout stone walls to keep out the cold and a good roof to ward off the rain, and here was what had been built and would endure for the very reasons that man loved peace and security, and in the eyes of the fourteen-year-old boy, watching him so intently, was the future and the promise. He spoke of his boyhood and he spoke of his Civil War experience, and he smiled as he recalled one march in the rain where their uniforms, a mixture of shoddy and paper, had literally washed off their backs.

"But that was in the bad old times," he told them, men and women and a boy, full of food and the after-dinner warmth. "The people were swindled because a new thing was happening, and the people still had to wake up to it. Now the people are awake."

The boy said he would want to go to war if he were old enough, and his mother looked at Altgeld. "Will it last that long?" the boy wanted to know.

"I hope not," Altgeld said.

"But it could?"

"Not if the people are awake," he smiled, thinking of how the crowds cheered when he condemned the attack on the Philippines.

"Are you a socialist, sir, because you're against war?" the boy asked. Darrow looked at Joe Martin, who was grinning broadly. The apologetic mother was eased by Emma's smile.

"No, I'm not a socialist. There are other people who hate war."

"That's not a very polite question," the mother said.

"Perfectly justified," Altgeld laughed. "After all, Eugene Debs believes that the only opposition to war is that of the socialists. In fact, he thinks I will lose the election." But the manner of his speaking left no doubts of his own opinion. Emma had never seen him so confident, so secure, so absolutely certain of the future. She watched him lean toward the boy and say:

"You're seeing something, young man, that is worth cataloguing and filing away. In my opinion, you are witnessing the last imperialist war. From here on, the people's voice will sound. The brief march of the oligarchs is over."

XVI

EMMA remembered that dinner when they sat in their home, sat up through the evening into the morning, charting the election results. It was different from that other time in the Palmer House. The hokey excitement of a presidential campaign was absent. There were just a few of them who sat past midnight, charting and studying the precinct results, getting reports from their independent watchers, keeping a tally, keeping that unique score that is the pulse of a democratic people.

By the early hours of the morning, when the shape of the election became apparent, Altgeld's face was deathly white. Darrow was somber, and Schilling was voiceless and hopeless. Only Joe Martin attempted to simulate cheer; only he kept pointing out that they had expected a stuffing of boxes, that they had expected every dirty move known to the game, that they had at their disposal only too few watchers, only too few tellers, and that they had fully intended to fight a fraud.

"But it's not a fraud," Altgeld said dully. "I know how large a fraud can be built. Three votes to our one on the Democratic side, two to our one for the Republicans—"

As the vote mounted, as the enormity of Altgeld's defeat was hammered home, harder and harder, Schilling moaned, "Where are the people?"

In the small hours of the morning, Altgeld's independent vote had passed forty thousand, with almost every precinct reported and told. For the Democrats, Harrison was close to the hundred and fifty thousand mark, and Carter, the Republican, had passed one hundred thousand. Altgeld went through the formality of conceding defeat. Crushed, Darrow said his goodbys and went home. Joe Martin cut a fresh cigar, and Schilling sat in a big chair, crumpled and beaten as an old bag of clothes. Emma brought them coffee, and they drank it in silence. No one mentioned sleep or home. They wrapped themselves in their own gloom.

Finally, Schilling managed to say, "The working people voted. You can't tell me they didn't vote. If someone tries to tell me that, I will not believe it."

"For Christ's sake, George, believe it!" Altgeld snapped.

And Martin asked, "What do you make of it, Pete?"

"Nothing but what's there. It's better to believe a dream than to believe the fact. I suppose those who followed Debs voted. But tell a man in packing-town that his six dollars a week will buy him more under me than under Carter or Harrison. They just got no reason to vote, no damned reason at all."

Part Six

THE RESTATEMENT

I N ITS EFFECT UPON THIS INDI-
vidual or that one, the news of Altgeld's defeat was most
varied. In the Union League Club, for example, his going
down produced hardly a ripple; for they were close enough
to the mechanism of things to have no doubts as to the
outcome, and they had never believed that this upstart rebellion would produce more than the handful of votes it
did. On the other hand, those old-line Chicago politicians
who had worked with Altgeld in the past and responded
to his masterly direction were somewhat saddened that he
had been fool enough to buck a machine, to the building
of which he himself had contributed. They felt that his
sickness had affected his mind, and they also felt he had
been badly swayed by his radical associations. There were
those, like Gene Debs, who understood very fully the
meaning of Altgeld's defeat, and there were also those who
wept when the news came.

Lucy Parsons wept, and she had not wept in a long, long
time. Lucy Parsons' struggle was a long one; it went on
into the future, and it had no ending. She had thought to
herself in the beginning, when the blinding shock of her
husband's death began to wear off somewhat, that no man

dies completely—that no man, no matter how small, no matter how unimportant, no matter how insignificant, dies so completely that something of him is not left to go into the lives of others, a word, a gesture, a smile, more or less, something that enters the stream of human life and adds to the continuity of all living, all struggle and all hope; and certainly what her husband had been was in the lives of many men, in her own life, in her children's lives. Out of that concept, it seemed to her only natural, obvious and direct, that she should attempt to take up her husband's work and carry it through. She recognized what a tall order it was, and how poorly she was equipped. She had her children to care for and to raise; a living, no matter how small, had to be earned for herself and for them; and she could not rest until her husband, who had died upon the gallows like a common murderer, stood forth before the world with his name cleared and his purpose plain. To add onto this an agitator's career was not a comfortable action, but comfort was something she neither looked for nor expected.

She was a stubborn woman, and when her purpose was laid down and made plain, she followed it through. As the years passed, she became one of the fixtures of Chicago streets. She was to be found here and there, first in one place and then in another, with her little stand set up, and the pile of books which contained her husband's thoughts and writings displayed. Visitors to Chicago, tourists, curiosity-seekers from one or another European city, were advised to be sure and see Lucy Parsons before they left, much as they were advised to see the stockyards. Those people who thought about it were amazed by the persistence of this small, dark woman, whose face still retained traces of beauty, but most of those who saw her did not think much about it, except to be as satisfied as one is to view the wife of a notorious man who came to his end on the gallows.

But this was only a part of Lucy Parsons' life. Another part was her children, whom she loved so passionately, and who represented the continuance of her husband's flesh and blood as they grew into maturity. And still another part was her organizational work, through which she attempted to carry on what her husband had done. She spoke at union meetings; she was to be found on almost every picket line in the Chicago area; she would stand for hours at night in the bitter cold, distributing leaflets; she would trudge the streets, selling copies of the socialist paper. She was stolid, tireless, and as strong as a piece of tempered steel; perhaps the part of her which was American Indian contributed toward this, and there is no doubt that as time went on she came to resemble more and more those forebears of hers who had pitched their teepees on the treeless plains from time immemorial. Her face became lined and the bones made strong ridges as the flesh fell away; sun and weather darkened her skin; her eyes reflected that inward peace with time which so many Indians make, and which gives them such enduring patience; and her voice reached back for the soft, drawling inflection which was as much a part of her people as anything else.

The men who worked with her came to accept the fact that Lucy Parsons was what she was, in so many ways stronger than they were. They used her strength because she offered it without ever asking for pity, and pity was one of the few things that made her deeply angry. Otherwise, she was calm, and apart from her family displayed little emotion. She studied constantly, reading during every spare moment she found, and even Debs admired and was amazed by her grasp of the labor situation in America.

II

FROM the day Altgeld pardoned the three Haymarket prisoners, Lucy Parsons watched him. She read all that he wrote; she read the stories the newspapers printed about him. She would give precious hours to go to some meeting where he was speaking. Step by step, she followed his battle against Grover Cleveland, and she had furious arguments with friends of hers who did not trust him, and who insisted that whatever the label, a politician was a politician. And finally, when he came forth on his independent ticket, she knew that her hopes and her dreams were justified. She remembered one night, about six months before the Haymarket incident, when her husband came back from a heartbreaking trip into Pennsylvania. For once, his mood was black; he seemed not so much beaten as worn thin, and he said to her:

"Where do we go, Lucy? Everywhere, the people plead and there's no one to tell them what to do—no one to lead them. I don't mean someone like me, I mean someone with power and dignity and office, to stand up and make cause with the worker. If there was even one man in congress, one man to say, follow me. . . ."

Albert Parsons had gone down to Coal Center on the Monongahela River, one person and alone, to see if there was any hope of organizing the miners. A thing was happening in Coal Center that had happened and would continue to happen in one part or another of America; but when it happened, those involved would isolate the area from the rest of America; it would burn out where it started.

Coal Center was a fairly new place; it had come into being on top of the railroads' insistent demand for fuel; and as more and more track was laid down, as the country grew, Coal Center mushroomed. America grew up on the black gold.

At first, in what later became Coal Center, there were only a few farms. This was an area up the river, about fifty miles from Pittsburgh, and it was the beautiful Appalachian hill country, where the mounds of earth lay like the upturned bellies of fat sows, where rippling brooks trickled down to the rich bottom meadows, where the cows found good grazing on the hillside, where a man could have, not too much, but enough, meat and drink out of the earth, and sometimes a deer to be killed in the pine woods.

Into this place, a hundred years before, had come the Scotch-Irish landless; they were tall, hard men who pushed into the Indian country and built themselves houses of logs and earth, and cleared the forest away for farms. They were men with a fierce sense of liberty and independence, and in the Revolution they, who were called *the woodsy folk,* took their long hunting guns, formed themselves into a brigade, and fought in the Pennsylvania line of the Continental Army for six uninterrupted years. They did not go back to their plowing and their planting, and during those war years, there was great suffering in the Monongahela Valley. But finally, the war was done; they went back to their farms, and the bucolic progression of their lives began once more. Generations passed, and they raised up their sons and daughters, and sons and daughters buried their parents in the good Pennsylvania earth. They remained basically the same Scotch-Irish stock, for the many succeeding waves of immigration passed over the Appalachians, looking for the richer and easier western prairies, and as their numbers increased, they cleared more of the land. Some of them went away to the cities, but many remained. They lived simple lives; in their churches they followed the same stern Protestant faith that their forefathers had brought to America, and in their churchyards the stones were marked with recurring names, Stuart, MacGregor, Cameron, Lynn, MacKee, Williamson, Angusson, McDonald, Bruce—those and a dozen more names, over and over, from generation to generation. Sometimes, flood interrupted their lives; sometimes war, sometimes a plague of disease; but they were a sturdy stock and they endured and increased.

And then, in the late sixties, it was discovered that there was coal under the green buttocks of their hills. That wasn't merely a local manifestation; a similar process went on in Ohio, in Illinois, in Wales, in Belgium, and in Germany. But to these Pennsylvania farmers, it was local and unique. Men came into their valley and bought land. Overnight there was more hard money present than the valley had known in a century, and good money was paid to those who would work in the shafts—more cash for a week's work than a farmer saw in a whole year. And with that money, a man could buy incredible things, slick-action guns to replace their old squirrel rifles—and who could live without such a gun, once having seen it?—bright goods for dresses, sweet candy, canned goods with a different taste, upholstered chairs, such as no one in the valley had ever owned, high-heeled shoes for the women, ready-made dresses, and so many other things that it would be impossible to list them all. Not only that, but one did not have to make a difficult trip to Pittsburgh to buy; no sooner had the company begun to sink the shafts than they opened stores right there in the valley, and the stores had stocked shelves six feet high. The first farmers who had sold out to the coal company walked around with pockets that bulged with cash and silver, and after they had bought everything they could see that they wanted, they still had money left, so the company opened a bank for them, and men from the company spoke to each farmer, convincing him why he should deposit his money in the bank.

The farmers in the hills and up and down the valley heard the news and flocked in to see; when they saw what their neighbors had bought, they turned green with envy, and all the way back to their farms their wives nagged about what the others had and they didn't have. Days went by and they resisted their wives' nagging, but even so they were remembering the fine new Winchesters, the beautiful hunting boots, the silver spurs, the checked shirts, the Stetson hats, the cases of rings and brooches and necklaces —because a man wants to give things to a woman he cares for, and when his neighbor gives and he can't, it eats into him.

Then men from the company made their way into the hills. They had a proposition for the farmers, a proposition that was beautiful to hear and simple to understand. There were days when a farmer had a little time on his hands; suppose they signed up to work in the shafts on those free days? They would be well paid, and the company was willing to give any farmer who signed a contract an advance bonus of fifty dollars. Of course, it was not really a bonus; it would be deducted from their pay, but slowly, just a few dollars a week, and look how high the wages were! What farmer could resist such an offer as this; not only did they sign, but their sons signed, and every company agent rode out of the hills with pockets bulging with contracts. So the hill farmers came in and bought as well as the valley farmers, and, soon after, they came in to work in the shafts. And what the company men had said was true; they were well paid for their work in the shafts; only a dollar or two was deducted to repay the original debt. Not only that, but when a farmer had to go back for plowing, the company man in the store opened a big ledger and said, "Sign here, and you can have anything you want on long-term credit."

Never had the valley dreamed of such prosperity. Indeed, some of the farmers decided not to go back to their farms for the plowing, but to work the year round in the shafts where they could make twice what anyone could on a farm. And to make it easy for them, so that they would not have to kill themselves trudging to their farms and back, the company put up a line of wooden houses next to the store. It's true that these houses were each attached to the next, that they were built out of green wood, almost paper-thin, and that each contained only three rooms; but they were painted bright green and red, and they rented for a ridiculously small sum, on the average of three dollars a month per house. It more than made sense to live in them, and after the first batch of houses were rented, the company just kept on building, for more and more farmers saw the practicality of living in town.

Nobody was surprised when the company built the saloon. There had been a tavern in the valley where you could buy hard cider, and certain individuals dealt in corn, but this was the first saloon. In the past, drinking had been a thing for parties, or infares as they called them locally, or something before dinner to whet one's taste. The faith of these folk did not hold with drunkenness, and liquor did not go well with work in the fields. But men found that after ten or twelve hours in the shafts, there was a hunger that only hard liquor could ease, and there was not much protest when the company brought in the first saloon, or the second, or the third. It is true that old Pastor Mac-Nulley raged about the wages of sin, but the wages of coal mining were something you could put your hand on—and, for some reason, the farmers felt they were not to blame. MacNulley blamed them; but they had seen this thing happen in such a way that no human being could resist, and as MacNulley continued to preach, church attendance fell off.

But no one could blame the company either. During those first two or three years, the company was very, very good about everything. Take the saloons; the men found it hard to tell their wives that they had spent a dollar or two in one evening drinking, so they were grateful when the company opened ledgers in the saloons, and all one had to do to get a drink was sign his name. For that reason, even the God-fearing men did not protest too hard when the company began to bring in girls and make a brothel a subsidiary of each saloon. By now, several thousand families were living in lines of wooden shacks in the valley, and in spite of the high wages, most of the families found that they somehow could not quite make ends meet. On the farms, a shortage in terms of food was unknown, but, naturally, they had all sorts of things here that they did not have on the farms. Rather than give this up, they mortgaged their farms. In this too, the company cooperated, and the representative of the company bank handed out mortgage money right and left. A new wave of prosperity hit the town, which was now called Coal Center, but hard on it the people discovered that somehow they were losing their farms. Short-term, high-interest mortgages turned them into workers overnight, for by the time a thousand dollars of mortgage money had been used to pay store and saloon debts, very little was left.

After those first few years, a change began to take place in the manner of the company representatives. Now, in everything they said, they made vague reference to the owners back east; the owners ordered this and that done. Bad times had hit the country. The rent in the houses went up to five dollars a month; the owners did that because of bad times. Week by week, wages were lowered; the farmers, who were no longer farmers, were given to understand that now there was more than enough coal, and the only reason the company remained in the valley and continued to sink shafts was to keep the people from starvation. But this must not be a one-sided thing. The people of the valley must cooperate too. They must not grumble because wages dropped. They must not spread these ridiculous rumors that in Pittsburgh prices were very much cheaper. Didn't they know that it cost money to haul the stuff in from Pittsburgh?

But even if the people did grumble, there was not much more that they could do. In the time of a decade, their world had changed marvelously, and they were a part of the change, and because their farms were like a dream now, they accepted the change more or less passively. The town was a large community now; it had three newspapers and stores and there were new saloons the company didn't own. It had habits of its own now. Morning began with a shrieking steam blast; out of the shacks came the men and children, down to boys of eight and nine, lunchpails in hand. A torrent of humanity flowed toward the mine. The very landscape they passed through had changed. There were new hills, black and ugly; the old earth was scarred and subdued. The torrent flowed down into the earth, and in the bowels of the earth they remained until darkness. Then the whistle shrieked again, and the earth gave up the old men, the young men, the children, now dirty, soot-covered, soul-weary in a dragging line that returned to the shacks.

That was how coal came to the beautiful Monongahela Valley, and along with it came hunger. Wages continued to drop; each year there was a period of partial layoff, and every six or seven years, the mine closed down and there was no work or wages at all. These intervals were called, vaguely, bad times, and during these bad times the people became more fleshless than ever, babies wailed with hunger, and the mouths of the women grew thin and bitter. In the first period of bad times, the company bank failed; nobody understood how the bank could fail even though the company continued, but the bank failed and that was all there was to it. It was then that an agitator, as he was called, a heavy-set man with a foreign accent, came into Coal Center and began to talk about something called a union. But the people there had known few foreigners and resented them, and therefore nobody made much of a fuss when the heavy-set man was found down by the riverbank with a bullet in his head.

It was always said that things couldn't become worse, but as the years went by, they did become worse and worse. Semi-starvation became a constant factor; the new generation of valley folk had grown up small and disease-ridden; and along with everything else, hope was disappearing.

It was in this situation, about a generation after the mine had been opened, that the miners came together and decided not to work the mine until wages were raised. They didn't know that what they were doing was striking because they didn't know the word then, although they learned it soon enough. And in retaliation, the company closed the mine.

Word came through to the outside, and it was into this dying town that Albert Parsons came in 1886.

III

IT MUST be understood that Lucy Parsons was not alone, a woman bereaved eternally, one person weeping for the defeat of a midwest politician, Altgeld by name; it must be understood in the context and fullness of things that if she wept, many wept, that if she made connection with the past and saw the future darkly, others did. Her actions, however, were in relation to a man hanged so long ago, and going through those things of his she had saved and treasured, she found a letter, one of those letters which he would write always, a letter in which he talked to her simply, reaching out for her strength and love, and which he began, always:

My Dear Wife:

. . . I reached the place about 2 o'clock P.M., and found myself a total stranger in a country town, which is a quaint, singular looking place, located in the narrow valley along the banks of the Mononga-hela and overshadowed by the towering hills of this region. The streets are dotted with groups of three and four men, coarsely-clad, grim-visaged, sturdy and solid; the weather cold and shivering; the prospect all but inviting. Not knowing which way to turn, I naturally inquired for the office of the *Messenger*. Once there, I inquired for the proprietor,

Mr. Winehart, and at once introduced myself to him. I found him to be a young man of 35, a genuine type of the modern American—lank, thin-visaged, keen-eyed, quick-witted and resolute. After a few words, I inquired if he had received my note. He replied that he had, and had published it; upon request, I was handed a copy of the paper.

The day was cold and depressing, the town un-inviting, and the man who stood before me chilly as an iceberg. Imagine, then, my situation when I read the comment on the announcement [of a mass meeting to be held by Parsons], which advised the workingmen of Coal Center to receive Agitator Parsons with—rotten eggs, and throw him into the river! I said to myself: "Steady, steady—there is hard work ahead!"

"Well," said I, looking up and addressing the editor who stood nearby, "how is this?"

"That's our opinion of agitators in this region," he replied.

"I should expect such treatment from the coal syndicate," said I, "but not from those whom it oppresses."

I remembered that the *Messenger* was the only paper in the valley which stood by the miners in their long strike, and while wondering at its hostility toward me the editor said:

"Well, sir, these are our sentiments. These infernal agitators are a curse to us. They have ruined this valley. They have kept the miners idle, and they ought to be drowned."

While he spoke his jaws were firmly set and his countenance determined and pale.

"Well, sir," said I, keeping perfectly cool, "I have seen the papers of this valley abusing you because you stood for the struggling miners, and I judged from it you were something of an agitator yourself," and I eyed him closely and I perceived I had fired a shot that struck him.

"Our valley is ruined and these agitators have done the work."

I paid no attention to this latter remark and began to read his paper. After five or ten minutes, I said to him:

"I am a stranger here and, of course, don't know whether I can get a hall or not. Do you know of any hall?"

"Yes," said he, "there are two, but I think Guiske's is the best."

A smile of satisfaction ran over my face as I reflected and said to myself: "I have melted this man; he need not have given me this information," and on principle that "he who hesitates is lost," I said: "Do you know Mr. Guiske and would you spare the time to walk down that way?"

"I don't care if I do," said he, and putting on his coat we strolled leisurely down-town together. Meantime, I was engaged in conquering my antagonist. I said nothing about Socialism, but asked questions about truck stores, coal bosses, miners, etc., etc. Walking three blocks, we did not find the proprietor of the hall in, and upon the invitation of the editor we strolled around the town to find him. This took another half hour.

Well, then we returned to Guiske's store. An hour or more passed in casual conversation when the hallman appeared. Winehart engaged the hall, which is upstairs over two brick stores owned by the same man. He accompanied us to the hotel. Winehart said: "This is Mr. Parsons from Chicago; give him the best you have in the house, and send the bill to me." He remained with me until 1 o'clock that night, and on bidding me goodnight said: "Parsons, I made a mistake," and, holding my hand, he continued: "Count me your friend; put down my name for the *Alarm*. We must have you here again right away, and we will endeavor to raise the money and send for you from Pittsburgh before you come back to Chicago, when we will have over a thousand men to hear you."

The impression created upon the audience that night was tremendous. It seemed to stun them. They acted as a man who has been travelling a whole day and felicitating himself that he is near his journey's end when it suddenly dawns upon him he has travelled the wrong direction, and must retrace his steps. He stops, sits down to rest, and ponders.

Things are in a bad way in this region. There are no leaders among the wage slaves here.

Oh, that I had the means! I would batter down the ramparts of wrong and oppression and plant the flag of humanity on the ruins. Truly the harvest is great, but it takes time and means, and no great means either, but more than we have. But patience, patience.

Your loving husband,

January 26, 1886   Albert R. Parsons

It was not this old letter that made Lucy Parsons weep. Her memories of the past were in the past, and along with them was the cutting edge of her sorrow. She wept because Altgeld had gone down, and because so much of hope had gone down with him.

Part Seven

THE CODA

Watching the small, thin man who argued the case for the union, Judge Kohlsaat indulged in philosophical reflection. The mighty are fallen and they become of low degree—or words to that effect occurred to him; and today, on the eleventh of March in 1902, the world was neither interested in nor concerned with a Chicago labor lawyer, John Peter Altgeld by name, who was engaged in pleading the case of the local cabmen's union. Idly, Judge Kohlsaat wondered what the half-organized, struggling union could have paid Altgeld to make it worth his while to prepare long and scholarly briefs, and to stand in court for two long days arguing them. Certainly not half as much as a random corporation fee ten years ago, certainly not a quarter as much—perhaps nothing at all, for although labor leaders were accused of having vast sums of money with which to promote their activities, Judge Kohlsaat could never quite decide where all this money came from.

Judge Kohlsaat was bored; invariably, injunction proceedings bored him, for such a parade was made of rights, justice, constitutionality, precedent, custom, freedom, liberty, offense against liberty, and so forth and so on that the words lost all meaning; and in time it seemed that the very words were laughing at each other. And today, several times, Judge Kohlsaat had to restrain the impulse to say to the two lawyers, "Now look here, both of you. A dirty little combine of immigrant Irish and Central European hack drivers have set themselves up against the Pennsylvania Railroad. I repeat, the Pennsylvania Railroad. Such things can't be. Let us be reasonable, gentlemen. Let us stop all this wearisome nonsense. This is twentieth-century America." The impulse, however, was restrained; the long hours passed. The judge occupied himself variously. Sometimes he glanced at the briefs, which rested before him. Technically, they were to have been read and digested before this session opened, but after years of reading lengthy briefs, they turned into bitter medicine, and the judge was content to glance at them now and then and check some of the statements therein contained against the arguments of the attorneys. The judge would follow the progress of a fly across his stand. He would straighten creases in his robe. He would hum to himself. He would doodle with his pencil. He had a long history of investigation of means and methods of passing time, and in the course of a day he would inquire into all of them.

Sometimes, he listened to what the lawyers were saying. Altgeld interested him; Altgeld had been a judge too; Altgeld had been governor of the state; Altgeld had smashed Cleveland—the judge blinked and stared at the dry little man with the rasping voice. That man! Life is something or other, the judge reflected. That man pardoned the anarchists. The judge wondered why. A miscalculation, perhaps, one of those brutal miscalculations that change the whole course of a man's life. How he must have regretted it! Why, without that pardon he could have been anything, anything at all—lived in the governor's mansion all the rest of his days. Well, one man did this and another did that, and there was no understanding why. But run with the dogs and you become a dog yourself—and here was Altgeld.

The judge's attention drifted once more. He found himself staring into the sunlight that streamed through the windows. He remembered an appointment he had made and had not kept. He noticed that one of the spectators in the court, an old man who had wandered in off the street, was intermittently dozing; the gray head would travel forward and then snap back to the erect position. Let him sleep, the judge thought, that's his privilege.

Altgeld was on his feet—"Your Honor!"

The judge recognized him and set himself to listen, at least briefly. There was much about Altgeld that disturbed him; he found it hard to face those biting blue eyes.

"Mr. Altgeld," the judge said. The attorney for the Pennsylvania yawned. The judge took out his watch and laid it in front of him.

"I take exception," Altgeld said, "to a definition by my worthy opponent here"—nodding at the company's lawyer —"of my clients as a disreputable foreign element. I do not think it pertains to the case in question or to the facts so far presented. But since the matter has been brought up, and since it cannot be denied that so many members of this union were born in Ireland and Germany and Lithuania, and since they are engaged in a struggle which for them is a life-and-death struggle, and since I have referred to them consistently as American, I would like to say a few words on this precise subject."

The judge nodded. That was the difficulty with an injunction proceeding; it provided no real limitations, and if one attempted to prevent either lawyer from straying, one could too readily be accused of prejudice. In such cases, the decision rests with the judge, not with the jury, since no jury is involved, and the godlike position of the judge obliges him to listen to the debate, whatever direction it takes. Then, according to the briefs and the subsequent arguments, he either sustains the existing injunction —which the Pennsylvania Railroad had obtained so readily, and which made it a Federal offense for the union to picket or carry on any agitation whatsoever—or he reverses it, or he indulges both the railroad and the shadow of justice by allowing the matter to go to appeal, a matter of many weeks, during which time the injunction is in force and the strike is broken automatically.

"I've called myself an American," Altgeld went on, thoughtfully, "for a good many years—" He rested one stiff arm on the table, watching the judge, leaning forward a little, giving the judge an impression of great tiredness, an impression that he might fall, were not the table there for him to lean on. "—but perhaps without justice, since I was brought to this country in 1848, and I was born elsewhere. No, this isn't the first time I've considered the matter, nor is it entirely at the prompting of the Pennsylvania Railroad's representative that I speak of it. I've asked myself, again and again, am I an American? Your Honor, I've even asked myself, what is an American? What do we mean by the term? What is its sacred import? Of course, that sort of an inquiry becomes puzzling and complex, and is apt to lead one up blind alleys, as, for example, when I hear a hack driver termed a disreputable element, since he was born in County Mayo, Ireland. But I cannot recall anyone stigmatizing Andrew Carnegie as a disreputable element simply because he was born in Scotland. Naturally, there is a qualitative element, but one wonders where it resides, in the man, the man's profession, or in the land of origin? One could argue the virtues of Scotland and Ireland—"

The judge interrupted: "I must beg you, Mr. Altgeld, to keep to the point. I have no desire to throttle discussion, but there are some limits we must impose on ourselves."

"I'm sorry, Your Honor. A circular route is one of the many burdens age imposes. I beg the pardon of the court, and I will attempt to hold more closely to the point. I was speaking of Americans—I can't help but mention some of my own feelings. I am in the habit of calling this my land, my own native land. That is not entirely correct, but almost so. Perhaps in no other country would a foreigner be justified in referring to himself as a native, but that has always seemed to me to be one of the unique distinctions of America. This is my land; it has been so for as long as I can remember, and I think it will be so for whatever time is left to me. It is my land because it made me, it shaped me, it nourished me. The thoughts I think came from this land, and the dreams I dream came from this land. . . ."

The judge was listening now; so was the lawyer for the Pennsylvania Railroad; so was Joe Martin who had just entered and slipped into a seat at the back of the court; so were the sergeants-at-arms; so were the few spectators, even the old man who had come in off the street to find a warm place to sit.

" . . . Yet those men I represent in this court are accused of being foreigners. Their actions are called foreign actions. Their struggle, which is a very basic struggle, Your Honor, a struggle for bread and warmth, for life itself, is called an un-American struggle, and treason toward a country which welcomed them with open arms.

"Well, Your Honor, I would not insult your intelligence

or my own by reiterating the old saw about no white man being native to these states. We know only too well that the wealth and the goodness of this land came about through successive waves of immigration. Is there a land on earth that did not give us its blood, its people, its culture, its legends, yes, and its food, its way of work and play, and its knowledge of how to earn liberty and keep it? How can I define America except to say that it is a place where these things jelled, where the many techniques of liberty were put to good use.

"But, Your Honor, is there a point where the struggle for freedom stops? I ask that in all seriousness, Your Honor —I ask it in relation to the fact that our Federal Government, through its appointed court, has decreed that this trade union I represent cannot carry on the fight for its people's existence.

"I ask you to consider the question of what is American, Your Honor, and what is not. Is there any struggle where men fight for freedom, black men or white men, here or in the Philippines or in South Africa, that is not America's struggle? Can freedom lose anywhere without lessening us, without weakening us and sowing the seeds for our own destruction? Can we throttle the voice of freedom in our own land yet continue as a democracy? What, then, is American? It was here in America, Your Honor, that the first trade unions this world ever knew were formed, as long ago as the 1820's. I hear them call May Day, the workers' day, a foreign importation; but you and I, Your Honor, remember when the first May Day was created, here in Chicago in 1886. What insanity has brought us to a condition where all men who work with their hands are suddenly un-American if they should even think, much less act? I have already argued, at great length, Your Honor, perhaps at too great length, the case of the men I represent, the reasons why they must combine and fight—or else cease to live. I take this time only to answer the attorney for the Pennsylvania when he charges that the hack union is a disreputable and foreign element. I only wish to remind him that disreputable and foreign elements, as he calls them, fought in our Revolution, and I, myself, was a member of a brigade, many of whose members were foreign-born, which marched off to preserve this Union. But if there is a point in our history where the struggle for freedom, for progress must stop, if we are to freeze still while the world goes on—then I agree that the word American is misused. I think American is a word for life, but if we must talk only in terms of death, then it might as well go overboard and be consigned to the past."

He sat down and began to shuffle through his papers. The opposition attorney made notes quickly and then prepared to rise. The judge looked at the sunlight, at his watch, at the rear of the courtroom, and then said:

"Court will adjourn until tomorrow." The judge felt listless and uncomfortable, and he felt that what Altgeld had said would spoil the rest of his day and his dinner too. The attorney for the Pennsylvania, a brisk young man, already wedded to success, dumped his papers into his briefcase, shook hands with Altgeld, saying, "Fine show, Altgeld. I learned a point or two," and went out, just as briskly, head up, whistling as he left the court. The spectators filed out. Only Altgeld and a sergeant-at-arms and Joe Martin were left, Altgeld sitting in the band of sunlight which had crept across the room now and enveloped him, turning his graying hair gold, and boxing him with whirling, dancing specks of dust, and Joe Martin standing at the rear of the court, lips pursed thoughtfully.

II

As Joe Martin walked down the aisle, Altgeld sighed, stretched out his hands in front of him on the table, and leaned his head back. Martin came up quietly, but Altgeld must have seen him before, for now he said, "Hello, Joe. I didn't know it was your turn today," weariness in his voice and a trace of annoyance too.

"That was an awful damn fine talk," Joe Martin said, ignoring Altgeld's remark. Some time ago, he and Darrow and Schilling and a few other close friends of Altgeld had decided among themselves that one of them would always go with him whenever he left town, knowing how sick he was and how liable to collapse. This pact was a secret among them and Emma, but by now Altgeld knew what was going on, and he resented being coddled, resented the implication that he was no longer physically responsible. Tonight, he had a speaking date at Joliet, and Joe Martin had been appointed to go along with him and see him through it.

"Was it?" Altgeld said. "I guess I'm tired of hearing my own voice. I'm tired of courtrooms. I'm tired of being respectful to the bench—"

Joe Martin sat down at the table and watched him.

"Just tired," Altgeld said.

"Do you want to go?"

"In a minute—just—let—me—ease—out." His face was gray. Martin poured a glass of water from the pitcher on the table, and Altgeld gulped it down.

"Better?"

"I'll be all right in a moment."

"Emma said I should try to get you home for dinner—

call off this Joliet thing tonight. What do you say, Pete, just a quiet dinner, the three of us, and then I'll give you a lesson in poker?"

Altgeld shook his head.

"Why not, Pete? You're all worn out. What in hell's difference will one speech make?"

"No. I got to go, Joe. You don't have to come with me—I know what those meetings do to you. I'll be all right."

"I'll be damned if I can see it."

"Look, Joe. They called the meeting for me. They called it because I promised to come. It's a protest in support of the Boers in South Africa. All right, it's a long way off. The Boers never hear that we're supporting them. They just go on fighting and dying. But it's important—it's important for men to talk up, even if only one person hears."

"It's just as important for you to rest," Martin said stubbornly.

"Look, Joe—don't argue with me, please. I've had enough argument for one day. Do you have the tickets?"

"I have them," Martin said.

III

On the train, going down to Joliet, Altgeld wrapped himself in his own thoughts. He still seemed to hold it against Martin that he was chaperoning him, and he answered the few words put to him gruffly and shortly. Then, until dinner, Joe Martin left him alone. In Altgeld's mind, the events and words of the day were leaping around, hammering each other, disturbing each other, making chaos where there should have been order. His head ached, and even now, weariness ran through his body, like sand through an hourglass that is continually tilted, head to foot, foot to head. He tried to inject himself into the personality of Judge Kohlsaat, and when he did that the words spoken in the court sounded like the bleating of lost sheep. What were all the brave words he had spoken about America, about himself? A picture superimposed itself of Judge Kohlsaat trying to pluck a little hair from the inside of his nose, feeling so delicately and quietly and all the while attempting to look intelligent and interested; and all the while the words went in one of his ears and out the other. Why didn't he pull the hairs from his ears? Why didn't he put both his hands up to his ears and try to pluck out little, curly black hairs simultaneously? . . . The bench, the judge, the court, the power and the justice and the reason and the dignity and the motto: Let the truth come into its own, let the truth come into its own, let the truth come into its own; and to the clacking of the wheels it went, its own, its own, its own. He remembered how long ago it was that he had last told that favorite anecdote of his, about the blind men who had gone to know the elephant and what they had found. What had they found, he asked himself now? What had he found?—that a judge and a bench and a courtroom built in something of the Greek style could all be purchased by the Pennsylvania Railroad, or by Standard Oil or by Carnegie Steel, or by anyone who had enough money and was so inclined to purchase a court or a bench or a black robe or a congressman or a woman or a bottle of whisky, or a handful of cigars, or this or that or anything, or the truth, or what appeared to be the truth, a reasonable facsimile, a likely image, a reproduction made so like the original as to defy imitation although it was an imitation, identification although it was an imitation, and imitation of an imitation, and imitation of the truth, and to the rhythm of the wheels, the truth, the truth, the whole truth and nothing but the truth. . . .

IV

HE APPEARED to be dozing when Joe Martin said, very gently, "Dinner, Pete."

He got to his feet, grinning. "I must have fallen asleep. Do you know, I guess I forgot to eat lunch."

"Hungry?"

"I could eat a cow," he said. "Nothing ever seems to interfere with my appetite."

They walked into the dining car and sat down. When the waiter, a tall, thin colored man, came over to take their order, he stared at Altgeld a long moment and then said, "Pardon me, sir, but you're Governor Altgeld."

Joe Martin smiled and nodded. Altgeld, unfolding a napkin, held it in front of him and stared at it, without speaking.

"I thought you was, sir. I served you four years ago. It's a real pleasure to see you again, sir."

"Thank you." An old habit, a good habit for a politician, made him ask the man's name.

"Sidney Jackson."

"Well, thank you for remembering me, Mr. Jackson. Thank you."

"Why you don't forget, sir. My God, you just don't forget, that's all."

That or the little nap he had made him feel better. He ordered a steak for the main course, and followed it with apple pie and cheese. Cigars and coffee finished it, and he leaned back in his chair, looking at Joe Martin, smiling comfortably.

"Feel better?"

"Much better. Joe, we're getting old. The body slows down. But you rest it a little, and then you feel fine. I feel fine. I could almost say I never felt better than I do right now." He considered a moment, then brought his hand down on the table with a crack that stiffened every person in the car. "I've got it—Joe, I took the wrong tack there in court, wrong as hell, pleading. I'm not going to plead tomorrow. I'm going to demand. What the hell, the case is gone anyway."

"Demand an injunction on the Pennsylvania?"

"You're right in principle."

"Pete, how do you do it? How do you go on, year after year? Don't you get tired? Doesn't it beat you down?"

"It beats me down. It's just a little harder to get up, that's all."

V

THEY got off the train at Joliet, Altgeld leaning on Joe Martin's arm. Glancing sidewise at him, Martin saw that the gray pallor had returned. They got a cab and drove to the Munroe House. Martin had reserved a room for them, but when they registered at the desk, the clerk shook his head and said that if the gentlemen would only wait a little while, the room would be ready.

"But I wired for a room hours ago," Martin insisted.

"Yes, yes, but not any room. I can't put Governor Altgeld into any room. The room I have for you, our very best room, will be ready in a little while."

Altgeld shook his head, whispering, "Any room, Joe, for God's sake, tell them to give us any room. I can't stand here. I have to lie down somewhere."

Joe Martin pleaded, but the clerk would not give in on his point, that Altgeld must have the best room in the hotel. Finally, Joe Martin roared, "Damn it, give us a room!"

Then, bewildered and hurt, the clerk gave in, and had them taken upstairs. Once in the room, Altgeld stumbled over to the bed and stretched out on it. He lay motionless, his hands flat on the bedspread, his blue eyes fixed on the ceiling.

"How do you feel, Pete?"

"All right. I was just tired and I got a dizzy feeling. I guess I ate too much."

Joe Martin pulled off his shoes. "You don't have to go through with it," he said. "You're sick—you're sick enough to be in bed. Why don't you tell them that you're sick?"

"I got here, didn't I?"

"Sure you got here. That's smart as hell. That's awful damn smart."

"What are you afraid of, Joe?" Altgeld asked gently. "Are you afraid I'm going to die?"

"Other men have."

"I've been holding its hand, Joe. For years now—it's day to day. I've felt tired like this before. What difference does it make?" Then he was quiet. Martin sat there, staring at nothing at all. An old-fashioned clock on the mantelpiece ticked out the hours, hard and sharp, clack, clack, clack.

About ten minutes later, someone knocked at the door. Joe Martin opened it, keeping his body between the crack and the room.

"Mr. Altgeld can't be disturbed."

A dry-faced man with glasses said, "I'm the editor of the local sheet. It would be a good thing for us to have an interview with the Governor."

"He can't be disturbed," but from inside the room, "Joe! Who's there? Will you stop being such a damned old woman!"

"A newspaperman."

"All right, send him in. Stop that damned whispering."

The editor came in, and Altgeld sat up, leaning on one elbow. "Make yourself comfortable," he said, "and fire away. It's got to be short. I'm due at the theatre in half an hour. Why don't you come there and listen, and when it's over, we can have a chat."

"Just one or two questions. You condemn England's action in South Africa?"

"As I condemn ours in the Philippines. As I condemn imperialism, whether it be British or American or German wherever it shows its ugly head."

"And you believe the Boers are fighting a just fight?"

"The man who fights for his native soil, for his home and for his family against a foreign invader—he fights a just fight. You don't have to look any deeper than that."

"And you're going to speak about the Boer War tonight?"

"That's right."

"You'll be outspoken, I suppose?"

Smiling, Altgeld said, "I haven't minced words since the last time I ran on the Democratic ticket."

VI

THEY stood in the wings, peering out at the house. The hall was jammed, and there was a line of people standing in the rear. In the wings behind them, the men and women of the Choral Society were clearing their throats and softly going, ah, ah, ah. Ex-Mayor Haley, officiating, bustled back to Altgeld and said:

"I think we'll sit on the stage. I think that's better, don't you? Then the Choral Society can line up in front of us, and we can slip out behind them, if you want to."

"Any way you say."

The director of the Choral Society, standing behind Altgeld, said, "But, mayor, we were to sing first."

"Let me get it over with," Altgeld whispered.

"Only it seems funny, the main speaker starting a program instead of finishing it."

"Just let me get it over with," Altgeld said.

"It doesn't matter," Haley shrugged. "Of course, it's customary for the main speaker to finish a program instead of beginning it. But if you want to speak first, I don't suppose it matters."

Altgeld followed Haley out onto the stage. The audience, impassive at first, broke into applause when they recognized him. A few in front rose, then a few more, then a wave until the whole hall was on its feet, clapping in tribute. Joe Martin stood in the wings, smiling with pleasure. A man could have a brother, or he could have a friend like Pete Altgeld; or a man could have half of the world and not know Pete Altgeld. The audience stood there, clapping, for almost a full five minutes.

Haley said, "Here, I think, is a man I don't have to introduce to you. You know him. Illinois knows him. America knows him. I give you John Peter Altgeld."

He began to speak softly. He put both his arms on the rostrum, leaning forward, talking to them, sometimes from the script he had in front of him, sometimes without looking at the script. For about half an hour he spoke to them, simply and straightforwardly, about imperialism, what it meant in human terms, what it meant when you stripped away the cheap glitter of Rudyard Kipling, and left the broken bodies of men and women and children. He told them of the concentration camps the British had built in South Africa.

He paused, beads of sweat running down his brow. Reaching for his handkerchief, he almost fell. He gripped the rostrum again and mopped his brow. Then, the handkerchief still in his hand, he sought for words:

"I told you about concentration camps. They solve nothing. Put a thousand or ten thousand men into them; they solve nothing. You don't break men by torturing them. You don't break man's spirit—"

He hesitated and stared at his script, as if he were seeing it for the first time. By now the audience was aware that something was wrong, and he could hear the murmur passing from person to person. He made an effort, smiled, and said:

"It's all right, all right. Sometimes, we get tired. That's natural, that's only natural. We are filled with despair. We ask ourselves, what is the good of such meetings as these? But there is some good out of them." He spoke slowly and forcefully, not looking at his script at all. "There is always good when men gather together for liberty—good when any man puts his shoulder alongside his neighbor's—"

His voice trailed away. He continued to smile for a moment, then shook his head, as if he were puzzled. He turned back to his script and read, his tone low and labored:

"I am not discouraged. Things will right themselves. The pendulum swings one way and then another. But the steady pull of gravitation is toward the center of the earth. Any structure must be plumb if it is to endure, or the building will fall. So it is with nations. Wrong may seem to triumph. Right may seem to be defeated—"

His voice trailed off and the last few words came out in a whisper that was barely or not at all heard. He smiled again and picked up his papers. He turned, walked back to his chair, and dropped into it. Haley rose and waited for the applause to finish. But hardly had he begun to speak when the audience saw Altgeld stagger to his feet and shuffle painfully toward the wings. Two members of the chorus caught him as he almost fell, and Joe Martin came running out to help him off the stage. Haley followed. Altgeld put his arm around Joe Martin and Haley supported him on the other side.

"Where can he lie down?" Joe Martin cried.

Altgeld shook his head. Then he began to vomit. The two men supported him as long spasms racked him, through and through.

Some blankets were found, and Joe Martin persuaded him to lie down. He lay there on the blankets, his eyes closed. Joe Martin took off his shoes, loosened his clothes, and then covered him with another blanket.

Meanwhile, the meeting had broken up. People were gathered in knots, through the theatre and on the street outside. Haley was trying frantically to find a doctor, but it so happened that there was none in the audience. Then Haley realized that the state medical society was holding its banquet here, and that all the doctors would be there. He sent a messenger over there, and three doctors came back to the theatre. One of them was Cushing, an old friend of Altgeld's. He knelt down beside him, taking his wrist and feeling his pulse.

Altgeld had lost consciousness now. Mutely, Joe Martin stood over him, watching for a reaction on the doctor's face. But Cushing shook his head, shrugged as he rose.

"What is it?" Martin asked.

"I don't know. It looks like a stroke."

The other doctors agreed. They wrapped Altgeld in the blankets and carried him back to the hotel. There, the doctors worked over him, rubbing his wrists and ankles, using smelling salts. He opened his eyes very suddenly, like a man waked out of sleep. For a moment, he appeared puzzled, then said, "Hello, Cushing," just as if nothing at all had happened.

"How do you feel?"

"Fine. Just tired. Did I get through the talk?"

"You got through it," Joe Martin said. "It was a good talk."

"I must have fainted."

"You're going to get into bed and rest," Cushing said. He and Joe Martin helped him off with his clothes. Martin fumbled around in back of him until he demanded, "Joe, what in the name of Heaven do you want?"

"Shirt buttons."

"Well, mine button in front. And stop trembling. I told you I was all right."

"Sure, sure, I know, Pete."

Suddenly, Altgeld sat up, glaring at his friend accusingly.

"Joe—Joe, you didn't think I was dying and wire Emma? Joe, you didn't do any damn fool thing like that!"

"No, no, of course not."

"Well, don't. You hear me? I have to be careful of her. It would be insane, frightening her out of her wits."

"You'd better get some sleep," Cushing said. "Mr. Martin, I'll stay with him for a while. Do you have a room?"

Martin shook his head.

"Well, see about getting one—or are you going back to the city? He can't be moved tonight."

Joe Martin walked over to Altgeld's bed, smiled at him, and then bent over and took his hand.

"Goodnight, Pete."

"Goodnight."

He went downstairs to the lobby then. At the desk, he bought a handful of cigars, lit one, and sat in a big leather chair, puffing it silently. Some reporters came in and spoke to the desk clerk. He nodded at Joe Martin, and they walked over and began to question him. He answered the questions, and finally they went away.

It was quite late now, and still neither Cushing nor the two other doctors appeared. Sometime after one, the room clerk said, "Will you want a place to sleep, sir?"

Joe Martin shook his head.

The room clerk locked up his ledger and his cigar cases. He put out all the lights except two. Outside, two drunks staggered by, singing. The night porter, a colored man, stopped by Joe Martin and asked:

"How's the Governor?"

"I don't know—"

"Mister, you tell him he's got the prayers of good people."

"I'll tell him," Joe Martin said.

The clock in the lobby said half past two. The little gambler lit another cigar. There was a long ash on it when one of the doctors came downstairs. Joe Martin stared at him.

"As well as can be expected," the doctor said.

"Will he live?"

"I don't think so. You'd better notify his wife."

"He doesn't want me to notify his wife unless I'm sure."

"Then a friend of the family—"

Joe Martin walked down the street until he found a

335

Western Union office. He wrote out a telegram and sent it to Clarence Darrow. Then he walked back to the hotel. The other doctor, James Herrick, was waiting in the lobby. He and Martin stared at each other. Then Cushing appeared.

"He's dead," Cushing said.

Joe Martin nodded. He stood there for a little while. Then he walked over to the chair where he had been sitting. He dropped down, his hands hanging limply, and he began to cry. He just sat there crying, and after a moment, the doctors became embarrassed, turned, and went back upstairs.

VII

His body lay in the Public Library building, and all day, from morning until late at night, the doors were open. Only once before in the history of Chicago had there been such a thing as this, and that was when the working people walked after the coffins of Parsons and Spies and Fischer and Engel and Lingg.

Today, it rained. The cold March rain poured down, but they stood there in the rain. It was fifteen years since Albert Parsons had gone to his death, but someone who remembered would have thought that the same people were here, stern-faced, ageless, some in their Sunday best, some in their workclothes, the men coming off the shifts in the factories, the heavy-armed workers from packing-town, the farmers who had driven in, women, children too, who were brought that they might look at Altgeld's face before he was laid away in the cold earth, shopkeepers, clerks, girls who worked on the looms from morning until night to keep alive, but who could give up a day to look at the face of this man, the striking cab drivers, whose case he had pleaded, well-dressed men and men in rags, the people as broad as the people can be, coming out in their wholeness for one who belonged to them.

Joe Martin was there. Emma Altgeld was there, and there, too, standing in the rain with the others were Bryan and Schilling and Darrow and Debs and Lucy Parsons, too, and many others.

Two by two, all day long, they filed into the building to look at Altgeld. And then they went out into the rain.